DRIFTWOOD AND STONE

Pamela Gordon Hoad

Pamela Gordon Hoad

First published 2021 by Silver Quill Publishing

www.silverquillpublishing.com

A CIP catalogue entry of this publication is available from the British Library

Cover photograph copyright © Pamela Gordon;

Artwork copyright © Fiona Ruiz

Typeset in Georgia

ISBN: 978-1-912513-64-2

Silver Quill Publishing

Other books by Pamela Gordon Hoad

The Harry Somers series of historical thrillers set in the
Fifteenth Century:

The Devil's Stain
The Angel's Wing
'The Cherub's Smile
The Martyr's Scorn
The Prophet's Grief
The Seraph's Coal

Acknowledgements

I should like to record thanks to the friends who have supported me during the long process of writing and preparing *Driftwood and Stone* for publication. As with my previous books, I owe a particular debt of gratitude to my son, James, who raised many useful points on the draft, both as proof-reader and historian, and to Oliver Eade, who advised on innumerable matters, technical and literary.

I have benefitted from a wide range of literature on the history of Sheffield in the mid-Nineteenth Century. Further details are given in the Historical Note at the end of this book.

Any errors are of course my own.

In recognition of the part played by the indomitable people of Sheffield in the vibrant story of their town and (later) city

Chapter 1: June - August 1860

Out in the yard the cats were at it again. Let the whole street know about it with their noise, they did. Aunt Ada would be out after them with her broom any minute now. Except that she wouldn't be able to see them. Beyond the faint gleam from the oil lamp in the kitchen it was black – like the cats. Chrissie Mallon turned from the window, folded a worn skirt and put it in her second-hand carpetbag. She heard the back-door open and her aunt's snort of disgust as the cats scampered away. That was one coupling she was too late to prevent.

Hours later, in the fitful morning sunlight, Chrissie stepped out of the cottage onto the stone step she had scrubbed three times a week for the past five years. She put down the carpetbag and turned to face her aunt whose bulk filled the narrow doorway. Chrissie lowered her head, demure as a novice in a nunnery.

'Goodbye, Aunt Ada. I'll give your love to Gran.'

'You look after her. You do your duty to that poor old soul. Remember the torments of Hell are waiting for sinners.'

Chrissie ignored the warning but gave a fleeting smile. She unfolded the bundle under her arm and extracted a bonnet trimmed with lace and dainty rosettes under its brim.

'Shameful hussy!'

Aunt Ada's shriek accompanied the slamming of the door but Chrissie was unperturbed by either sound. It was a small victory to be spared more Biblical bullying. She slipped the bonnet over the springy tussock of her auburn hair and tied the ribbons under her chin. After that she picked up the carpetbag and set off down the sloping track into the centre of the village.

It was over. She didn't doubt there would be drudgery to come but her situation would be different. She was no longer the confused twelve-year-old sent to Malin Bridge to skivvy for Ada and her husband, Uncle George. Then, she'd welcomed the move away from her grandmother's spiteful temper – and those other bitter memories: the childhood which taught her both to mistrust and beguile. Now, the old witch who'd betrayed her had grown frail. In future, Martha Bamforth would depend on her granddaughter for everything and it would take more than a sarcastic crone's malice to intimidate that self-assured young woman.

Chrissie grinned at the notion that she'd acquired experience at Malin Bridge which should serve her well in the town: precisely the experience her aunt so deplored. She'd learned how to handle the men who ogled her and the farm boys who offered a farthing to peep at her drawers: what to give and what to refuse, what to expect in return. It wasn't just Uncle George, she mused smugly, who'd put his hand up her skirt and given her keepsakes. She'd gone into the bushes by the riverside with one or two of the older lads who took her fancy but she'd been clear with them what she would and wouldn't do. She'd declined offers to be seen 'walking out' with any of them and she took it for granted they would accept her terms.

Chrissie had a fine sense of her worth and thought that the country lads accepted her decree because she was an assertive beauty. It didn't occur to her that, in the village, the reputation of her tedious relatives gave her protection. She'd have mocked the idea, but Uncle George was a skilled tradesman managing an anvil shop at the forge in the Rivelin Valley, where many of the local lads worked; and Aunt Ada's pious tongue-lashing was renowned. In any case none of this mattered any more. Her thoughts were dodging backwards and forwards. Town boys might be more obstreperous than those at Malin Bridge but this was a challenge she'd find exciting. She was ready to exploit the assets nature had given her. Otherwise they served no purpose. She had nothing else.

She'd expected to be sent away earlier, after Ada found them in the lean-to at the back of the scullery. It was a surprise nothing happened for a whole month, other than lectures on sinfulness and the bottomless pit awaiting the impure, although Chrissie realised her aunt would have difficulty getting other unpaid help in the house. That was the reason she'd come to the village in the first place. She'd begun to wonder whether Ada might have decided, while lambasting the sin, to turn a blind eye to its enactment. Perhaps it relieved her aunt of wifely duties which were distasteful. It certainly kept scandal in the house, away from the prying interest of neighbours and the self-satisfied sympathy of fellow chapelgoers. Meanwhile Uncle George rewarded Chrissie's tolerance of his fumbling hands not just with the bonnet but a pair of buttoned boots which showed her slender ankles to advantage. He could afford to be generous and Chrissie regarded the gifts as no more than her due.

Nevertheless, the respite was not going to last if put to the test. When the drayman came from Sheffield to deliver his message, she knew it could have only one outcome. Her grandmother was poorly and needed assistance, perhaps long-term in nature. It was obvious Ada, the old woman's only surviving daughter, had no intention of leaving her comfortable home – and George to his own devices. Conveniently she could resolve her conflicting duties by dispatching her wayward niece to care for the invalid. George could hardly object and the girl had no voice in the matter.

Round the corner and out of earshot from the cottage, Chrissie laughed aloud as she hooked back a coil of

3

tight curls escaping from her bonnet. But it was necessary to pay attention to the path. The track downhill was always tiresome for villagers concerned about the appearance of their footwear. In dry weather its potholes were choked with dust and threatened weak ankles with stumbling. After rain it was a quagmire. Chrissie picked her way delicately along the muddy verge, lifting her skirt clear of the puddles, revealing those smart buttoned boots, although there was no one of interest at hand to admire them. The menfolk were at their employment: the grinders and cutlers in the forges strung out along the banks of the two rivers where their machinery was fed by waterpower from the mills. Further away, farmworkers were busy in the fields below the moorland where the peewit called and the acrid tang of worked metal was moderated by the scent of hawthorn and new-mown hay.

It was different in the town. She remembered the insistent thud of the great hammer which powered heavy machinery, its throbbing far more intrusive than the rhythmic swish of waterwheels. Smoke rising from scores of chimneystacks hung in the air and blocked out the other side of the street on bad days. Everywhere you looked there was a higgledy-piggledy jumble of grime, noise and sweating humanity. The prospect did not trouble her. The village was populated by scandalmongers, narrow-minded killjoys always looking for something to forbid and someone to criticise. She longed to be away from them and she chuckled as she shifted her carpetbag from one arm to the other.

At the foot of the hill she reached the Stag Inn where the carrier would turn his cart for the return journey from Malin Bridge into town. Renowned for its hospitality, it was solidly built, four-square and sturdy, asserting its superiority over the adjacent row of file-cutters' rickety cottages. Mrs Armitage was standing outside, her sleeves rolled up, capable arms akimbo. The landlord's mother, mainstay of the hostelry and superlative brewer, was supervising a scrawny pot-boy as he manhandled a barrel towards the cellar steps. Without doubt, she could have undertaken the task more competently herself but she had status to maintain.

Chrissie was in no mood for conversation. She gave a perfunctory wave and crossed behind the inn to look at the swirling waters of the River Loxley, where they looped round to be joined by the Rivelin, similarly swollen from heavy rain. She liked to see the rivers in spate with spinning leaves and twigs in the brown foam. The turbulence reflected her restlessness. She noticed something caught against foliage by the side of the stream, something tattered but colourful: a rag doll, its skirt impaled by a fallen branch, its woollen hair streaming out in the current. Some child must have cried at its loss. Chrissie shrugged and walked back to the appointed meeting place. The carpetbag was getting heavier and she shifted it from hand to hand again. She did not want to put it on the damp ground and soil the material but there was no useful wall on which to rest it. She noticed her boots were spotted with mud and her irritation grew. How long until the carrier came?

'Chrissie, Chrissie, let me hold bag for 'ee.'

The excitable, unstable voice, shifting in a few words from treble to bass, caused her to turn. Of course, it was young Tom Webster, open-faced and beaming. She should have known he would come.

'It's a bit heavy," she said, handing him the bag graciously. "Why aren't you at the forge then?'

'I'm on an errand. Got a packet to give to carrier. Knives father wants to get to t'hafter in town today'. The lad drew a small parcel from his jacket. 'I helped shine 'em up.' The pride in his voice died away as he looked up at her intently. 'Are you really going for good, Chrissie?'

'Looks like it. When carrier comes.'

'Won't you come back?'

'Doubt it. Going to live in town again, like I did when I were little.'

'I'll come and find 'ee, Chrissie, when I'm a bit older. I will, you know.' Overcome by the confusing diffidence of adolescence and its no less perplexing assertiveness, the youth shuffled his feet.

She smiled despite herself. The boy was so good-natured and sincere, she hadn't the heart to give the glib reply which those words from another lad would have provoked. Good-natured and sincere like his sister. Damn! Why did she have to think of Sarah now?

'How's your sister?' she asked before she could stop the words coming.

Tom saw nothing odd in her enquiry for a girls' tiff was of no consequence. He knew they'd quarrelled but not that they'd stopped speaking to each other weeks before Sarah left Malin Bridge for the Hall.

'She's been with Mrs Ibbotson more'n six months now. Sent us a letter a fortnight back. She's to visit us come Michaelmas. She's learning all manner of fancy things. Not just to be a lady's maid but book-learning too' He paused then spoke with careful precision. 'There's a library up there and Mrs Ibbotson chooses things for her to read.'

'She always did like reading. Started to speak proper, too.' Chrissie paused, remembering their days together at the village school when she first came to Malin Bridge. It had always amused her to put on different voices, depending on who she was talking to, and she thought Tom's sister a refined model to copy. It became second nature to imitate Sarah's way of speaking, just like their teacher's. The younger girl had stayed at school long after Chrissie left and was a monitor helping to teach the smaller children. 'She'll do right well.'

'Aye, but she'll always need to earn her living.' Sarah's brother was unappreciative. 'She'll not get husband. She's too solemn and plain to take a lad's fancy. Not like you, Chrissie.'

She laughed at this cumbersome compliment, shaking free more of those entrancing curls, and deepened her voice. 'What dost tha know of such things, Tom Webster?'

His stammering reply was cut short by the appearance of a statuesque figure, rounding the corner by the Stag Inn. The woman, clad in black from sombre bonnet to shiny gaiters, was Aunt Ada's closest crony. She stiffened when she saw Chrissie, stepping out into the rutted roadway to avoid her.

'Good afternoon, Mrs Groomsley,' Chrissie called with exaggerated sweetness. 'Pleasant day, now rain's stopped, isn't it?'

The woman didn't answer but addressed Tom. 'Shame on you, lad! Why are you wasting time with this trollop? You should be at your father's forge.'

'I've a packet for carter.' The boy tapped his parcel and gave a triumphant grin. 'Father sent me.'

'Huh!' Mrs Groomsley swept off across the street and up the hill, her skirts spluttering through the discoloured spray.

Chrissie gritted her teeth. There was so much she'd like to say, such a rejoinder to make to that righteous pillar of the chapel and upbraider of the sinful, but she couldn't bring herself to do so in front of young Tom. Not after remembering Sarah.

'The boys call her the Black Crow,' he said, looking expectantly at Chrissie. 'What's a trollop?'

'No one you'll need to know.' She beamed with delight at the sight of the carrier approaching along the road from Hillsborough.

'Oh, but I will if you're one!' The lad's voice shot up an octave as he saw the cart trundling towards them. 'You're really going,' he squeaked.

'I told 'ee'.

As the carrier handed her up into the wagon the sun broke through the clouds, highlighting the swell of her bodice and the sheen of her curls. The man pressed her fingers unnecessarily but she slid them from his grasp.

'Give me my bag now, Tom. Thanks for holding it.' Without a thought she leaned forward from the cart, her unruly hair brushing his shoulder, and she planted a kiss on the boy's cheek. 'Goodbye then.'

He gulped and stared, before he remembered his packet, thrusting it into the carter's hands. 'I'll come and find 'ee, Chrissie,' he shouted as they drove off. 'I will come.'

She looked back at him and raised her hand slowly. A weedy girl of his own age emerged from a doorway opposite and ran across to join him: Lizzie Simmonite. Tom was pushing her away, angry that she had trespassed on his moment of supreme and disturbing emotion. Yet, Chrissie thought sourly as she watched, she could imagine a shared future for the pair. She could see them sitting either side of a Malin Bridge hearth in twenty years' time, staid and respectable, dull and dependable. Would something like that be her lot too? Not in a million years! She was done with the village, with Tom and Sarah Webster and Lizzie Simmonite, with the Black Crow and Aunt Ada and all the sanctimonious hypocrites like them. They were in the past, along with the childhood she'd left behind. Only the future mattered and the future would be different.

Squelching along the footpath on his way back to the forge, after escaping Lizzie's mewling, Tom didn't falter. His stride was sure-footed but his spirit was in turmoil. Concealed in his pocket, his fist was clenched around a single waving hair of extraordinary radiance which had

8

caught on the rough material of his jacket. It seemed to him a token, a promise.

*****

Despite her childhood recollections, Chrissie was disconcerted when the cart trundled into Sheffield. Only four miles from the countryside around Malin Bridge, the town was even busier and dirtier than she remembered. The nauseous smells turned her stomach and, tasting the stagnant smoke in the air, she lifted her forearm across nose and mouth. Progress along the congested streets was impeded by pedestrians as well as vehicles and Chrissie was thrown forward, bruising her elbow, when the driver jerked the reins. A man who had emerged unsteadily from a doorway on West Bar went sprawling in front of the horses, flailing in the gutter. The carter swore and manoeuvred round the obstacle, soon drawing to a halt at the top of Snig Hill, Chrissie's destination.

She climbed down and set off into the network of alleys and courtyards, known locally as the crofts, past narrow-fronted, decaying houses, cheek by jowl with grinders' dusty workshops, towards Tenter Croft where her grandmother had lived for forty years. The venomous old woman had come there, so she maintained, as a bonny young bride: the newly wed Mrs Martha Bamforth. That assertion was always hard to credit but no doubt the croft had been shabby then and it had worn no better than its baleful resident.

Entrance to the croft was through an archway, next to the privies, into a square yard. Low brick terraces faced each other across this bleak space, where the mud was churned by boots and encrusted with debris shaken from brooms or dragged into its confines by wandering dogs. Unspecified liquids collected in the shallow ditches, which

9

drained slops from the houses, and spilled over to form slimy puddles. The standpipe in the centre of the yard, which served all the occupants of the croft, dripped despondently and its brownish water was absorbed into the encompassing mire.

A younger Chrissie had splashed happily in the unsavoury pools with her companions, untroubled by fine sensibilities. Now, thinking of the muddy lane at Malin Bridge, she resolved to pick her way round the sludge without splashing her skirt. The smells of cooking, rotting garbage and excrement were more disturbing. They awoke unwelcome memories of her childhood. Unpleasantly evocative too was the miasma which hung in the yard, as in the roadway outside, thick and sulphurous. Her lungs had forgotten how to breathe in such rank air without retching.

She pushed at the front door opening into her grandmother's kitchen. It was much as she remembered: the dirty flagstones, coated with soot again so soon as you cleaned them; the plain wooden table nicked and scratched by generations of knives; the chipped basin, together with a bowl and pan soaking in grey water; Gran's treasured and hideous china dog on the mantelpiece; the huge pile of washing spilling out of the broken-handled basket. No!

She banged the carpetbag onto the table in irritation and heard a slight sound from the upper room. 'Gran,' she called, 'it's me, Chrissie.'

She climbed the stairs to the bedroom, the room where she had slept for twelve years, along with her grandmother and, at first, her mother and younger aunt. The room where her mother and aunt had died when the fever came, leaving her an orphan to her grandmother's care. She was in the bedroom before other thoughts crowded out the dim remembrance of her pretty young mother. The big iron bedstead now held only one figure, lying crookedly on top of the faded counterpane. Its thin grey hair straggled over bony shoulders and its face, a spider's web of wrinkles and broken veins, expressed distaste.

'So she sent thee.' The voice was surprisingly shrill, coming from such a slight frame. 'Always was a selfish bitch, Ada. Good-for-nothing. Tha's got that in common.'

'Glad to be welcome,' Chrissie said, as she sat on the sagging wickerwork of the single chair. 'What's the matter with 'ee, Gran?'

'Matter?' It came as a screech. 'Aches and pains all over. Can't keep food down, only gruel sometimes. Head's fair splitting. These three weeks I been suffering. Nobody cares. Nobody comes. Might as well be dead. Soon will be.'

Chrissie suspected this was said with too much relish to make the promised outcome probable. She took off her boots and stretched her legs while listening to a catalogue of symptoms, followed by a tirade against the uselessness of the doctor from the Public Dispensary and a medley of contradictory comments regarding Mrs Pyle next door. This neighbour, who was new since the girl had lived in the croft previously, seemed to be both an angel of mercy, providing the gruel which Gran's stomach could sometimes tolerate, and a nosy, ill-natured gossip, bad-mouthing all and sundry. Chrissie yawned and fidgeted until, at last, the old woman wearied herself and slept.

Chrissie went to the attic which she was resolved to make her own. She'd thought about that choice carefully. The attic had always been where Gran's sons slept, in later years just her youngest, Uncle Jack, whom Chrissie as a small child adored. The room, long deserted now, was dank and undusted. With no personal possessions on the shelves or in the battered tallboy, it felt anonymous. It held neither threats nor promises and it would be infinitely better than sharing the bed of a restless and malignant invalid.

She unpacked her bag and blew the dust from a drawer in which to stow her meagre possessions. Then she

11

went downstairs and took the kettle out to the standpipe. A fine drizzle had begun to fall, staining clothes and spotting faces with its sooty deposit. She didn't linger, but as she turned back to the house she saw a brawny, good-looking man at the adjacent front door: Mr Pyle presumably. He was staring at her. She was used to such attention and gave her customary response, lowering her head slightly and glancing up with her remarkable violet eyes, through her eyelashes, smiling shyly – modesty itself. They did not speak.

*****

Over the next two days Chrissie did what she could to clean the house. She scrubbed the stone flags until the original colour gleamed a little more warmly. She beat the fraying rug and tried to polish the range with blacking that had solidified in its box. She wiped the objectionable china dog, dislodging something sticky and disgusting from its speckled paw, and she moved the basket of laundry decisively into the corner of the room by the door. She needed to speak to her grandmother about that.

She went to the market, buying what she could afford from Gran's small purse of coins, and walked round the centre of the town noting things she remembered and those that were new. Her ears grew accustomed to the din of the steam engines which drove rolling mills, tilt wheels and furnaces, all jammed into crowded back-streets between cramped workshops and terraced houses. She marvelled at the distant cluster of immense chimneys, visible to the east along the valley of the River Don, Sheffield's principal river, into which the Loxley and other rivers flowed. Steel works had opened recently along that valley in cavernous buildings. Although not greatly interested, she ventured as far as the Bessemer Works where, she was told, some wonderful new process had been introduced to speed the conversion of iron into steel.

There were other workplaces too: breweries, a snuff manufactory, a shed where carpets were woven and, along Copper Street, a button factory. While she watched, a flurry of young women emerged from the factory door at the end of their shift with an excited burst of laughter. She guessed from furtive looks cast over shoulders that they were giggling about a superior-looking man with ginger hair who clapped his hands for them to disperse. He seemed to be some sort of overseer, concerned to preserve his dignity, and he ignored their merriment. She studied a handwritten notice on a board in front of the factory.

She looked at the billboards outside the music-hall on West Bar, intrigued by the entertainments offered – trapeze artists, jugglers, impressionists. She wondered what impressionists might do; she would like to see them. When men in the doorways of alehouses whistled and called out as she passed, she gave an enigmatic smile, tossing her curls free of the shawl which now replaced Uncle George's bonnet. She evaded muscular arms outstretched to detain her but lifted her skirts a little higher, above those delectable ankles, while she tripped away as daintily as a cat balancing out of reach on a garden wall. Sheffield might hold a multitude of delights but she was in no hurry.

When she was returning to Tenter Croft after one of her perambulations, she caught sight of a thin young woman with a child crossing the road in front of her. She was astonished. Surely it was Mary Brailsford! Mary was a year or two older than Chrissie and lived across the yard when they were children. She had a distinctive, crablike walk, due to a crooked foot, which Chrissie recognised. But could it really be her? Mary had disappeared suddenly a twelvemonth before her friend went to Malin Bridge. People said she'd gone to the fever hospital although that

13

explanation could carry a coded meaning. Chrissie never heard if the girl died but nobody mentioned Mary again so she supposed the grown-ups were keeping sad news from her: except it was not like Gran to show delicacy. Chrissie felt confused by the unexpected sighting and didn't call out to the receding figure.

A week after their reluctant reunion, to Chrissie's surprise and annoyance, Gran announced she would come down to the kitchen. She'd scarcely got out of bed since her granddaughter arrived and the exertion required to go downstairs seemed likely to defeat her but she would not be deterred. Chrissie acknowledged that the invalid was looking better, but silently she cursed the irony if Gran's health responded to care so grudgingly given. The old woman seated herself at the table with regal assurance and demanded that fresh tea be mashed. She looked round the room, ignoring the brightened range and refreshed flagstones, and gave a squawk of disgust. She pointed a distorted finger accusingly at the laundry basket.

'Tha's not done washing, good-for-nothing slut.'

Chrissie took a deep breath. 'I'm not doing other people's washing, Gran. It'll have to go back. Tell me where to take it. I came here to look after you, not skivvy for others.'

'And how'd tha think us'll live then? Where's money to come from? All my life I've taken in washing and none the worse for it. Not good enough for Lady Muck, eh? Tha'll learn! Put boiler on stove right now.'

Chrissie's temper flared. 'Listen to me, Gran. Let's get this clear. If you want me here to keep house and cook, it'll be on my terms. Otherwise I'm off and you can bloody manage on your own.'

'But what'll us do for money, tha ninny?' the old woman bleated.

'I'll get a job. You don't need me here all day. I'll earn enough to keep us.'

'In service? Tha'd not brook rules. Tha'd tumble master and cheek mistress and be out on thi ear afore a week's gone.'

'Not in service, Gran. In a factory. Lots of girls work there – a button factory. "Female hands wanted", it says on a board outside. I'll go there today. It'll bring in more than that filthy laundry ever could. So tha can keep a civil tongue in thi head.'

Carried along by her bravado, she flung on her shawl and went out, slamming the front door. She ignored Mr Pyle crossing to his doorway although she could sense he was leering and she didn't object.

*****

It was the best thing she'd done, she reflected afterwards: leaving Gran for a couple of hours while she went to see Mr Copley, the overseer of the women's button-shop, at the Copper Street factory. He smiled at her, stretching his gingery moustache to reveal spiky teeth, while he explained that they liked to employ women for cutting bone and pearl, manipulating the miniature dies for pierced designs and sorting the buttons into matched sets. Women's slender fingers were more agile for varnishing tiny faceted surfaces and working diminutive lathes; but a good eye and a steady grip were needed. He took hold of Chrissie's tapering fingers, spreading them wide on top of the papers piled on his desk. He nodded. She could have sworn he stroked her thumb as he closed his hand over hers.

'What's your name, young woman?' There was no mistaking his look.

'Chrissie Mallon, sir,' she simpered.

'Right, Mallon, I think you'll suit. You can have a week's trial starting Monday. You'll work for ten hours a day with two hours to get food.' The ginger moustache extended itself further, above smirking lips, while she purred her gratitude.

On her return home, triumphant, she found her grandmother still sitting where she'd left her in the kitchen: the old woman's unexpected burst of energy was quite spent. Chrissie helped her upstairs, saying only that she'd found work, and later she brought up some potato broth which was consumed in silence. The balance between them had shifted, the girl decided, and she was content.

As the weeks went by Martha Bamforth never acknowledged this change and reverted to foul-tongued abuse when the mood took her but Chrissie wasn't bothered. She had a life outside the croft now and she was making new friends. For the most part her workmates were sharp-witted, worldly girls ready with jocular rudeness and teasing obscenities, especially concerning 'old Copley of Copper Street' whose familiarities were notorious. She could hold her own with them and match their ribald gossip with her own anecdotes, whether true, embroidered or entirely imaginary. But she preferred the company of quieter girls who acted as foils to her own vivacity – one in particular, Annie Turner.

She didn't speak of the factory to her grandmother but her work made it easier to tolerate the old woman's temper and listen to her babble. She asked guardedly for news of Uncle Jack, Gran's youngest child, only a dozen years older than herself, who'd gone for a soldier after Chrissie left Sheffield.

'Broke me heart, that did, when he went.' Martha Bamforth scowled. 'Went out to that Crimeria place. Two of his mates he joined up with died there in front of him – Bert Brailsford and Ben Culley. Cut him up, that did.'

16

'I heard from Ada,' Chrissie said quickly. 'Where's Jack now?'

'India. Two year since he went.'

'Do he write?'

'Couldn't read it, could I?'

Chrissie grunted. Neither of them returned to the subject.

Another evening her grandmother lay in bed prattling about 'old Sheffield' of which, she declared proudly, she was part 'through and through', unlike the newcomers who infested the place nowadays and spoke different. Bored by this, Chrissie ventured to refer to her own parents hoping that Martha, who had never been one to share confidences with a child, might tell her more about them.

'How old was Ma when she met me father?'

Wizened lips twitched before composing themselves. 'No more'n about thee now, silly young chit.'

'And what was he like, me Da'?'

Blotched hands picked at the fringe of the counterpane. Milky eyes narrowed. 'Huh! Good enough to look at, I suppose – red hair like thee, more's the pity. Irish tinker, rotten top to toe.'

'Irish? No one told me that.'

'Mallon's Irish name,' her grandmother pronounced scornfully.

'They were married then? You can tell me, Gran. I've wondered.'

'Huh! Married right enough. Before God and man, and thi mother's belly swelling fit to bust. Off within the year he was, never would stick wi'a wife. Bad rubbish! Tha takes after him.'

Chrissie fell silent, thinking of the gentle face which had smiled down as she was lulled to sleep in infancy; of the ravaged, flushed face when she was hurried from the room

17

as her mother lay dying. As soon as Martha started to snore, she hurried downstairs, needing to occupy herself with some task to push away the memories. Nothing in the past was reassuring.

She remembered the rustling she'd heard earlier and the mouse droppings under the table in the kitchen, so she tore up an old cloth, straining to rip through its thick hem, and looked along the bottom of the wall for a hole. She found one beside the wobbly dresser so she scrunched up the rag to stuff into the gap and knelt down, peering at the broken plaster. Something glistened in the hole and she jumped back, thinking at first she could see the mouse's eye. Then cautiously she put her fingers into the dusty niche and drew out a tiny glass bead. The lump in her throat almost choked her and revulsion hammered inside her head. All that time it had lain there hidden, the last fragment of the child's necklace Uncle Jack had given her, which she had cherished and which she had later snapped in anguish. She threw the bead across the room as if it had lacerated her skin.

That night, lying on what had been Uncle Jack's bed, where his blond curls once festooned the bolster, she thought of him, of her mother and her own unknowable father, the handsome, unreliable Irish tinker. With uncharacteristic nostalgia she wept.

During the night Chrissie woke from a vivid dream of Aunt Ada advancing with her broom, just as if she was about to drive fornicating cats from the yard, her eyes round with disgust. 'Filthy Jezebel,' she spat in her best chapel-holy voice. 'I saw. Roast in Hell, you will.'

It wasn't so far from what happened, Chrissie remembered, and the outrageousness of it made her grin. Uncle George had retreated into the privy, metal-stained fingers fiddling with the buttons on his flies, while Chrissie straightened her crumpled apron, thinking what a waste of

18

time it'd been to starch it. She'd tossed her mane of curls. Silence seemed the best policy.

Her aunt scowled, stern and arid as the dry-stone walls on the hillsides above the village, and her voice subsided to a hiss. 'That I should harbour a viper in my house, my own sister's child! Unclean. Unchaste.'

Chrissie stroked the two shiny pennies in her pocket while Ada narrowed her eyes. 'Pray Heaven to subdue your evil, you wanton. Remember: *your adversary, the devil, as a roaring lion, walketh about, seeking whom he may devour.*'

'One Peter 5, verse 8,' Chrissie muttered with a hint of piety. She was familiar with that particular text, much favoured by Malin Bridge preachers.

Ada's eyebrows twitched with suspicion. 'I hope you don't mock Holy Scripture in your brazen sinfulness.' She brought the broom down heavily on her niece's foot. 'Go in and see to the dishes. They're standing in their grease.'

'And wash your filthy hands,' her aunt added with a scream.

Chrissie hadn't dared giggle at the time but the memory of it made her squirm with delicious amusement. No question: she was ready for a new adventure.

Chapter 2: September 1860

Could it really be only eight months since I left Malin Bridge? In so short a time, it seemed, I'd come to look on well-known sights with new eyes. Sitting in the carriage opposite my mistress, with neatly folded hands and tucked-in feet, I was astonished. As we drove down from the head of the valley, where the Hall stood impressively on a ledge several hundred feet above Dale Dyke, the hamlets, farms and water-mills became increasingly familiar. Yet they seemed shabbier, less prosperous than I remembered and, as the carriage neared Malin Bridge, I began to feel uncomfortable.

Mrs Ibbotson smiled and raised her eyebrows. 'Do you feel you no longer belong here, Sarah Webster?'

That made me blush. 'My family are here, ma'am, so I'll always belong. But I've learned so much at the Hall. It all seems different somehow.'

The old lady clasped her hands together as if applauding. Then she smoothed her lace gloves over her wrists. 'Quite right. You've moved on. You have a wider perspective. But your mother will be glad to see you and she'll welcome your help for a week now she's ailing.'

I knew we both regarded that sweet, fragile woman with affection. My mother had been my first mentor and model: wise, gentle and wholly devoted to her family, understanding, forgiving and never reproachful. Perhaps I had taken her for granted but I truly loved her.

Mrs Ibbotson's feelings for my mother would be different but I knew enough of the history to imagine them. Nellie Trotter had been a promising parlour-maid in her household after she and her late husband took up residence at the Hall, his family home. They kept a sizeable complement of servants in those days, far more than the elderly widow required by the time I joined her. Nellie had been bright, skilled with her needle, and her employer considered her the best seamstress in the district. Mrs Ibbotson probably regretted that my mother took up with the pious and utterly respectable Sam Webster from Malin Bridge. He was a knife grinder and a staunch Methodist, well thought of in the community, but Mrs Ibbotson had not cared to leave matters of the heart to chance. I'd often heard the story how she made it her business to meet her favourite maid's suitor. It would be impudent to imagine she judged him tedious and narrow-minded but I can't help wondering. At all events there were no grounds for discouraging the match.

So my parents had married and Nellie Webster left the Hall for Malin Bridge. She bore two healthy children, before a string of miscarriages. Over the years Mrs Ibbotson continued to send her needlework, where fine stitching was required, and occasionally she visited her former servant when passing through the village. That was how she'd encountered me as a child. I was more robust than my mother and Mrs Ibbotson told me she detected a grain of adventurousness beneath my serious demeanour. That alarmed me. Yet she deemed me worthy to be instructed and refined beyond my station and it was a great honour to be engaged to train as a lady's maid. Mrs Ibbotson had nurtured other local girls over the years and some now held positions in distinguished households. I knew she hoped I would not become the disappointment my mother had been, all that time ago, and for my part I wanted to do well and please her. I was rather prim.

When we arrived at my home, Mrs Ibbotson came in briefly, before travelling on to visit her nephew in Penistone. I'm sure she noted the neat parlour and the impeccable embroidery on the tablecloth and antimacassars but, as she climbed the spotless stairs to the main bedroom, she probably winced at a framed text on the landing: '*Vengeance is mine, saith the Lord, I will repay'*. There was a more conciliatory message beneath the picture of Christ with a posse of children, which hung beside it. I imagine the sight of my mother's wasted face worried her but she did not comment; my short stay was intended to speed the invalid's recovery.

Mother was certainly thinner than I remembered but I was anxious to believe the assurances she gave me. I felt awkward faced with the claims of a sickly parent and relieved that Mother was eager to hear about my life at the Hall. She pressed for details and I responded with enthusiasm, describing rooms, pictures and furniture, as well as my duties. Coached by my mistress and the housekeeper, I'd learned so much. I could lay out clothes suitable for visiting, entertaining or biding quiet at home and the beads and brooches which best accompanied each dress. After weeks of diligent practice I could launder and iron fine linen smoothly, free from creases or scorch marks. I understood where to sprinkle rosewater and how to insert bunches of lavender between folded underwear and stockings. I could help Mrs Ibbotson put on her crinoline and arrange her skirt over the great wired frame. I could dress her silver hair in loops or ringlets, as the fancy took her, and find the right cap for each occasion, primping the lace to hang in filigree cascades. Then there were the books Mrs Ibbotson encouraged me to read. They fell outside the normal requirements for a lady's maid but I'd come to see them as intrinsic to life at the Hall. I mentioned to Mother several worthy and instructive journals but not the more exciting novels which captured my guilty interest.

'Good lass, good lass,' Mother said quietly from time to time, proud to hear of my progress. She respected the superior status of a lady's maid, compared with the lowly position she once held, but she was anxious about so much reading. She scrutinised my serious face, under severely drawn-back hair, accepting that I was no beauty. Nevertheless, she would have valued the old-fashioned word, and judged it apt, when she dubbed me 'comely'. Mother sighed and closed her eyes.

'On Sunday we go to church at High Bradfield.' I said it softly, as if intended not to be heard.

Mother glanced up nervously, her reverie disturbed, and her hands fluttered above the bedspread. 'Oh, Sarah...' Her voice faded. 'Don't tell your father. Don't say a word about church-going. Let him think you still go to chapel – though don't tell a lie, mind. Him a pillar of the New Connection, he'll not take kindly to you backsliding.'

We were interrupted by the click of the latch on the front door and a rustle of bombazine skirts mounting the stairs. I was thankful for the diversion as Mrs Groomsley advanced ponderously with a covered dish in her mittened hands.

'Why, our Sarah's come,' she exclaimed. 'My, with lace on her collar too. Quite the little lady! Too grand for Malin Bridge folks, I'm sure.'

'It's not lace, it's scalloping, Mrs Groomsley.'

Our visitor did not pause for my protest. 'Brought you some stew, Nellie. Do for Mr Webster and Tom if it's too rich for you. Here, let me puff up that pillow.' She bustled about, rearranging the bedclothes, quoting Scripture on the worthiness of good works, ignoring me. She brushed aside Mother's thanks, insisting she preserve her strength by not trying to speak, and swept out while promising a rabbit pie for the next day. I felt overwhelmed.

'Mrs Groomsley's so good to me,' Mother sighed. 'I'm sure I don't know how I'd manage without her.'

'I'm glad.' It was a relief that she had a helpful neighbour and to be assured that Mrs Groomsley's domineering exterior shielded a compassionate heart. 'I'll make you some gruel, if you don't fancy the stew.'

'Thank you, dear.' Mother spoke abstractedly but she reached out for my hand and drew me closer. 'Sarah, listen. I'm not one for a lot of words but I need to say something. Something a bit deep.'

'Whatever is it? You said you were getting better.' Alarm caused my voice to tremble.

Mother stroked my hand. 'Aye, so I am, lass. I'll mend this time. But when it comes again...' She paused, her voice, in its turn, quavering. 'I'll not make old bones, Sarah, that's the truth of it. I know that and your father knows. It's proper you should too.'

'Surely the doctor...?'

Mother raised her hand to stop me. 'No good deluding ourselves. The fever'll come back and each time I'll get weaker. Now listen, lass. There's more I want to say. When it happens, when I go, your father and Tom'll be all right. They'll manage well enough, with friends to help. Whatever people say, you mustn't leave your position with Mrs Ibbotson. You can better yourself at the Hall and you must. Promise me you won't throw it all away.' She did not add 'as I did', but the unspoken thought hung between us.

Unwelcome considerations crowded into my mind: Mother dying; the expectation that I should return home to care for Father and my brother; duty; love; self-interest. I was not ready to confront such contradictions, still less resolve them. I nodded dumbly.

'Promise me, Sarah.' There was unaccustomed insistence in her voice.

'If you wish it, Mother, if you say so. I promise.'

She sank back, patting my hand. 'Good lass, good lass.'

*****

24

My brother, Tom, was unimpressed by my appearance; indeed he didn't notice my smart new clothes at all. Nonetheless he was pleased I was there because he'd missed having me to talk to. He was glad of a reason to stay at home and escape the persistent Lizzie Simmonite lying in wait to chatter whenever he left the house. After an early supper we sat together on the step outside the backdoor, in the mild September air, to watch the sunset giving regal splendour to the heather-covered hillside.

'Black Crow's stew were good,' he said, patting his stomach appreciatively.

'Don't call her that. She's a good neighbour.'

'Lets everyone know it too! Holier than thou isn't in it.' He paused and swivelled round to face me. 'D'you really like it at t'Hall, Sal?'

'My name's Sarah. Yes, I do like it. Mrs Ibbotson's very kind.'

'Don't meet many people though, I suppose. T'Hall's a bit out of way.'

'There's company sometimes. Mrs Ibbotson's nephew calls, from Penistone, and the local doctor and his wife and...' I swallowed my words. I had been going to refer to the rector from High Bradfield but realised that, if I mentioned him to Tom, Father might be the next to hear of the household's active Anglicanism. To mask my embarrassment I referred to something I would otherwise have left unsaid. 'There's a young relative of the late Mr Ibbotson calls too.'

'A young relative? That's unexpected. Is she grand?'

My confusion grew and I spoke quickly. 'He's a young gentleman. An apprentice engineer. He's working on the great dam they're building up the valley at Dale Dyke. He does some of the drawings. The dam will control the water to feed the forges in the valley, give them a regular supply.

You'll know about it, I expect. It's an enormous scheme. Mrs Ibbotson says it's very ambitious.'

Inevitably Tom was intrigued to hear this outpouring of technical knowledge and curious to see his sister blushing. 'What's his name, this engineer?'

I'm sure my flush grew deeper and I whispered. 'Arthur Rawdon.'

'Hey, Sal, you like him! I can tell. You take care. I've heard what gentlemen get up to with housemaids.'

'I'm a lady's maid, not a housemaid,' I protested rather too forcibly, 'and you don't know what you're talking about.'

'You look out though, Sal. I bet he's not even a Wesleyan either!'

To that I could make no rejoinder without acknowledging the truth of his assertion and we fell silent until my brother spoke again. I think he was uncertain why he did so, but perhaps he sensed that my embarrassment deserved some reciprocal concession on his part.

'I saw Chrissie Mallon before she left village. She's gone to live with her grandmother in town. She asked after you.'

I got to my feet, speaking crisply. 'Did she? I'm not interested. She's given to bad-mouthing, mischief-making. Good riddance to her. You're the one who needs to take care there.'

'That's all lies.' Tom also jumped up, his expression as dark as Mrs Groomsley's gravy. Then, looking along the back lane, he changed his tone. 'Father's come home from chapel meeting. We'd best go in for prayers.'

Black suited, stern faced, Father greeted me coldly. He'd never shown me affection and I'd heard him caution Mother against displays of fondness. A life of selfless service to the Lord, it seemed, was incompatible with expressing parental favour. I bowed my head meekly in

26

acknowledgement while Father fixed a disapproving eye on the trimmings to my cuffs and collar. He did not comment but later, in his earnest family prayers, he invoked God's aid against the temptation of fripperies and allurements of the flesh.

Chapter 3: Winter/Spring 1861

Martha Bamforth lapsed into stable but resented dependency on her granddaughter, saying little but, when she spoke, criticising much. Chrissie found this bearable. Throughout the winter her new workmates gave her companionship and with Annie Turner, somewhat to her surprise, she was developing real friendship. She was appreciated by other acquaintances too, in ways which were satisfying. Some of the men in the factory were attentive – one had even given her a posy at Christmas – but she had not chosen to encourage them with more than her usual flirtatious charm. Dapper Mr Copley, who praised Chrissie's smallest achievement, amused her. Other women on her shift were censorious when he bent over her shoulder and patted her hand but she presumed they were jealous. She was unconcerned by his attentions, playing on his interest with assumed modesty. She was careful not to encourage him too far but he was the grandest man she'd ever met, in a position of authority, and you never knew when his goodwill might prove useful. She realised there were unspoken rules about what was permissible in the confines of the factory but there was no harm in responding amiably to his pleasantries.

The neighbourly Mr Pyle was a different matter. She'd become familiar with his diffident wife, who kept an eye on Gran while Chrissie was at work, so it was only courteous to acknowledge the woman's husband, Ebenezer. She learned he was a saw grinder, a big man in his union, earning good money. They would have no cause to live in Tenter Croft, Gran said, if he spent less time in the alehouse and used his wages to rent somewhere better fitting his position. She described him as a bad lot, which made him all the more intriguing. He was tall and muscular, with a broad face and a direct look, which Chrissie brazenly returned. Yet he made no move towards closer acquaintance and she began to hanker for a more explicit response. Appreciatively, she contrasted his physique with Uncle George's and the immature youths who sought her favours at Malin Bridge. His dangerous masculinity fascinated her and she imagined his calloused hands moving along her thighs, his tongue exploring her mouth and his hard cock pressed against her. As her obsession grew, so did her frustration.

One evening in late February when moonlight gave a silver sheen to the frosty yard, she saw him go over to the privies and on impulse she decided she would empty her grandmother's chamber-pot before going to bed. She threw her shawl round her shoulders and picked her way across the frozen earth, wondering whether her appearance would spur any reaction. She was unprepared for its ferocity. As she reached the door to the closet he emerged and seized her arm. His bodily stench, metallic and beery, was overwhelming: gross and titillating. She had no time to think for he swept her into the shadow of the archway, grasping her breasts and thrusting her against the wall while the old woman's urine splashed them as the pot fell to the ground and shattered. She returned his probing kiss with enthusiasm but, when he sought to lift her skirt, she struggled to prevent him.

'Stop that. We'll be seen. That's enough.'

He tilted her head back, glowering. 'Why'd tha come then? I knows tha wants it.'

'Didn't know you were here. Let me go.'

'Liar!' He flicked her cheek lightly. 'Don't think tha can play games with me, Chrissie Mallon. Been leading me on since the day tha came here. I want 'ee right enough but I'll not be trifled with. Tha'rt no shrinking violet so don't come over coy. I know all about thee. Used to work with Ben Culley.'

29

'No!' She pushed him with all her strength. It would have had little effect if the ground hadn't been so slippery, but she caught him off balance as he lunged at her and he skidded, releasing his hold. She ran frantically for the house, slipping and sliding. He did not follow but she heard his expletive-laden growl.

She bolted the door, tearing her hand as she wrenched the rusty lever, and sank trembling beside the stove. It was not the thought of Mr Pyle's intentions which terrorised her for she relished the prospect of renewing their skirmish in more satisfactory surroundings. It was that name she had not heard for years until her grandmother spoke it months ago and now Ebenezer Pyle had repeated it – the name of Ben Culley. Dead and buried he might be, but the past had come back to haunt her. She steeled herself to defy it.

With testy insistence, her grandmother was calling for the chamber-pot. Damn her! Grimly, Chrissie lifted a cracked mixing bowl from the shelf and went upstairs.

'I slipped on th'ice and it broke,' she said, while pretending to extract a shard of china from the cut on her hand. 'Here, use this.'

*****

Even in the smoke-laden town the coming of spring was apparent. Small nondescript birds twittered on rooftops and buttercups forced their leaves between broken cobbles. The verdant hills which cradled Sheffield looked tantalizingly close and, as evenings became lighter, Chrissie and Annie Turner lingered on their way home from the factory, taking round-about routes away from congested, noisome thoroughfares. They filled their lungs with crisper air, bounced on the grass under their feet and admired the golden-tipped gorse bushes. They dipped their fingers in

30

sheltered dewponds, hoping the pure water would clean away some of the discolouration from the metals they handled in the button shop, then shook their heads with disappointment.

'Goes with the job, love,' Annie said. 'Like grinders' coughs.'

Annie lived with her family off Division Street, in a terraced cottage with three rooms upstairs and its own water tap in the scullery – a good deal more desirable than Tenter Croft's hovels. Her father had died the previous year and, as one of the oldest children, Annie needed to supplement the family's income while her mother cared for a brood of younger siblings. She was short, fair, inclined to plumpness, with an endearing turned-up nose and a gaiety which little could suppress.

Chrissie found her companion's unaffected good humour quaint but relaxing. Annie didn't irritate her as, in the past, those whose fortune seemed greater than her own had done. She thought of Sarah Webster, whom she had liked, but whose earnestness became irksome, provoking her to speak with careless cruelty. Reassuring herself, as if she needed to justify her new friendship, she decided the fatherless Turner family had little to rejoice about. Although they were unquestionably respectable in a way the Bamforths and Mallons never had been, Annie was not sanctimonious and didn't presume to judge others less upright than she was. She even grinned with guilty enjoyment at bawdy repartee, appreciating her workmate's saucy wit, so Chrissie could not fault her.

One evening they laughed and puffed their way up a steepening slope until they collapsed on the grass and kicked out their feet from beneath their dusty skirts. They were looking down on the tanneries at Upperthorpe and, further beyond that to the east, the blackened chimneys and

31

furnaces along the Don valley. Columns of smoke hung in the still air above the factories, like inverted jet earrings.

'All them new works in the valley,' Annie said. 'Town'll be twice as big in no time. Dozens of folk coming in from the country to work in 'em.'

'Like me?' Chrissie asked, with mock annoyance.

'No, daft 'appeth. You come from here, for all you went away a bit.'

'Town's grown right enough. Can't scarcely find me way round some places.'

'Some you wouldn't want to know, love. There's rough types moved into some parts.'

'Like Tenter Croft?'

'Don't tease!'

'Tenter Croft don't need no more rough types.' Chrissie grinned contentedly. 'It's got Ebenezer Pyle.'

Annie knew about her friend's neighbour and his unseemly advances. 'Why don't you send him packing?' she asked, then paused. 'Or would you really go with him?'

'I might – if he made it worth my while.' A toss of that bright auburn mane left no doubt that she meant it. 'But he won't get me for nothing, mind.'

'It's a dangerous game, love.'

'I can handle it.' Chrissie's confidence was real but she didn't seek to shock her wide-eyed companion. She took Annie's hand. 'Now tell me more about your young fellow.'

'He's not my fellow. There's nothing. It's just...'

'You'd like him to be.'

'Aye, I would that.' Annie looked down, blushing, her brass-blemished hands twisting in her lap. 'I like him fine. Dan's only a journeyman now but one day he'll have his own workshop. Will says he'll do well.'

'That your brother?'

'Aye, they've been mates since school, Will and Dan. Just as long as the troubles don't come between 'em.'

'What troubles?'

'Union troubles. Nowt we should fret about, love. They're both big for unions, say unions should be made lawful, but they argue. Don't agree how best to stick up for their trade without the law to back them.'

This was boring men's business, of no interest to Chrissie. She could think of a more intriguing subject. 'What's Will like?' she asked.

'He's a great lad. Head of family now, since me Da' died. He's right tall, with a mass of brown curls, not like my mousy rats-tails, more's the pity. Unfair, I call it.'

Chrissie smiled to herself. She'd be happy to meet Will with the brown curls, to see if he was as pleasing as his sister, but now was not the moment to pursue that possibility. The sun was setting and they had some way to retrace their steps so she got to her feet, knowing Annie would want to be home before dark. At the foot of the hill, when they entered the network of lanes and alleyways, they heard sounds of men running, hobnails clattering on cobbles, echoes rebounding off the stone walls. Immediately Annie drew her friend into a doorway and put her finger to her lips, her expression as solemn as an infant miscreant called to the front of the class to be reprimanded. Two men, one slight and the other burly, both well muffled despite the mildness of the air, thudded past. When they were out of sight the girls crept out from their refuge and Chrissie looked questioningly at her friend.

'Up to no good,' Annie said. 'Best not to be seen. Nowt to do with us.'

It was clear from her tone Annie would not explain further so Chrissie, although curious, simply laughed. They hurried on, holding hands, until they reached the plank bridge which crossed a runnel of sludgy water. Stepping onto it first, Chrissie stumbled on the uneven wood and turned her ankle. She swore loudly, stopping to wiggle her toes and rub her leg. Annie was full of concern.

'No harm done. Ankle does that sometimes. Me boot's all right, so's me foot.' Then, with a hand on the other girl's arm, she pointed beneath the low bridge. 'What's that?'

Annie feared another dead dog had been thrown into the watercourse to drift its way down to the fetid ponds by the River Sheaf. Reluctantly she peered into the mire under the planks and saw what had caught Chrissie's attention. 'Come away,' she said quickly. 'We shouldn't have seen it. Forget we ever did.'

'Looks like a bundle of bands from a grinder's wheel. Why's it tucked under the bridge like that, half in the mud? It can't have got there by accident.'

Annie had forgotten there were grinders at Malin Bridge and Chrissie might recognise the straps that drove their stone wheels, against which blades were sharpened.

'Forget it,' she said firmly. 'It's nowt to do with us. It's Mary Ann's business.'

'Mary Ann? Who's she?'

'No one. It's just a name. If a grinder breaks his union's rules or don't pay his natty money they take his bands so he can't work. Then if he comes in line or pays up, they'll tell him where bands are hidden. Sometimes they send letters threatening worse punishment signed 'Mary Ann' or 'the Man in the Moon', so nobody knows who really wrote 'em. It's how the unions control their members and make sure they keep rules of the trade. Taking bands and such like they call rattening.'

Annie had become unusually animated. 'It's fair enough if a grinder breaks the rules himself. But the other week Dan were rattened just because he didn't hold with heavy-handed action against another man. Tinpot bullies, they are, union bigwigs!' She clapped her hand to her mouth, wide-eyed with fright. 'Don't tell anyone what we've seen or about the men running. Best to know nowt about it.'

Chrissie was puzzled by Annie's outpouring. Union business sounded tedious and stealing a man's bands was plain childish, but she was sorry Dan had suffered because he disagreed with bullying. She bowed her head silently.

Shortly afterwards they came to the parting of their ways and Annie scurried off along Division Street. Chrissie turned towards Tenter Croft and her lingering thoughts of rattening were speedily dismissed when she recognised that familiar figure with the sideways walk. This time her shawl was thrown back, revealing thick black curls, and there could be no mistake: it was certainly Mary Brailsford. The young woman was shepherding a small lad in front of her and Chrissie saw her quickly pull up the boy's collar and draw down his cap. Was it really getting chilly?

'Mary! It is you. Don't you recognise me? I'm Chrissie Mallon.'

The dark-haired woman looked straight through her with steely blue eyes which gave no hint of recognition.

'Mary, you must remember. Us played together when...'

'I don't know you.' She seized the boy's arm and dragged him away, hurrying round the corner as if to escape some dire peril.

Chrissie stared after them; then she smiled and nodded to herself. The boy might be six or seven years old and if Mary was his mother she could have been no more than fourteen when she bore him. Reason enough for her disappearance years ago. But why refuse to acknowledge her old friend now? Babes born out of wedlock, even to girls so young, were not uncommon in the crofts. As children they'd known about these things and Mary had never been a prude. Was she overcome with shame years later? And why had she muffled the boy's face? Was there another explanation? The

35

boy must be disfigured or an idiot, fit only for the workhouse or a freak show. That would be cause for shame right enough. Poor Mary.

Chrissie shrugged and turned into the courtyard of Tenter Croft. Ebenezer Pyle was leaving his house, his wife watching him from the doorway. At least that circumstance should prevent any awkwardness. His powerful arms, bare below rolled up sleeves, gleamed in the flickering lamplight from the door as he crossed the yard. He felt no need for a muffler, Chrissie thought with satisfaction. He was no namby-pamby but a proper man.

'Evening,' she said pleasantly as they passed.

'When?' he asked quietly.

There was no mistaking his meaning and she knew her answer.

'When you buy me something nice,' she said as pleasantly as before.

He set his mouth thinly. 'For sale, are 'ee? Should have known. Us'll see about it.'

She moved to Gran's front door and greeted Mrs Pyle politely, without the least embarrassment. The crudeness of the potential transaction bothered her not at all.

Chapter 4: Spring 1861

I heard elation in the blackbird's song and the promise of unknown joys to come. I was filled with hope and didn't question the likelihood of nature reflecting my mood. Often, when clouds glowered above the hills and daylight itself was grey and murky, I felt miserable, my thoughts fastened on all that was dismal and sad, for no other reason than to harmonise with my surroundings. Now that I was so content it was only fair that the natural world should rejoice with me. Consequently, the wind from the moors had lost its bite, the bleakness of winter had been softened by the first green fronds on the hillside, the gentle sunlight drew open the curling buds to delight my eyes and, for me alone, the blackbird sang.

In the upper reaches of the valley, high above the bubbling stream known locally as Dale Dyke, the sound of the nearest water-mill was hardly perceptible. The wire-mills, forges and grinding wheels along the lower stretches of the River Loxley were out of sight and could have been a hundred miles away. Beyond Mrs Ibbotson's house the hills rose up to the dark crest of the moors and there were no settlements to be seen on the higher ground, except the little cottage where the former housekeeper at the Hall lived in retirement. As a child, I sought out quiet corners, above the waterfalls in the woods between the Loxley and Rivelin valleys, where I could indulge in the day-dreaming my father criticised. Now I had only to step outside the stately mansion to let my imagination soar like the buzzard.

There had been no worrying news from Malin Bridge and at Christmas, when I visited, Mother seemed cheerful, though pale and distressingly thin. There had been no more awkward confidences between mother and daughter and my father, sternly distant towards me as ever, seemed for once disinclined to censure my spiritual backslidings. In

37

consequence, I could relish my good fortune and permit myself more personal reveries, with only a scintilla of guilt.

My mistress's bell disturbed these reflections and I hurried indoors. The rector and the doctor from Bradfield, together with their wives, were to dine with Mrs Ibbotson that day and dinner was taken early at the Hall. It was time for me to help the old lady dress, in her second-best crinoline, and arrange her hair beneath a lace cap. Mrs Ibbotson was not at her dressing table, however, but standing in the window-recess looking out across the dale. She turned to me.

'I don't know if I wish to live to see it,' she said placidly. 'Mr Ibbotson's father had this house built above Dale Dyke, that he might study in peace and contemplate the seasons. My husband returned here after our journeying abroad with the same intention. He would not care for all these comings and goings in the valley, still less for the great water and the dam.'

I was as tall as the widow now, neither of us above middle height, and I had my own reasons for knowing about the dam. Nor was it the first time my mistress had mentioned the subject. 'It's awful difficult to imagine the valley full of water, ma'am,' I said, 'but it could still be beautiful perhaps, when trees have grown round it and the waterfowl swim across and make their nests there.'

'So it could. But it will not be as I have known it.' Mrs Ibbotson sat for me to brush her hair. 'So much water. A lake made by men.'

I was fully occupied for some while but later, when mistress and the guests were happily engaged together in the dining room, I was free to slip away into the kitchen garden. It was a warm evening and I smiled at the perky chaffinch on the gable of the outhouse although it flew away as I approached. I noted the tiny shoots peeping out from the pockets of earth between the stones of the wall and the tentacles of ivy which clung to its deepest recesses. They were at home here, I thought serenely, as I was.

By now I took for granted so much that seemed strange when I'd come to the Hall the year before and was overawed by its comfortable opulence. The heavy velvet drapes at the windows, embossed wallpaper in the reception rooms, the scatter of Persian rugs, upholstered sofas, polished whatnots and the display of china knick-knacks on side tables – there just as ornaments, not for use: all so different from the sturdy furniture in my childhood home. The big plain dresser, my mother's pride and joy, with the two large carving dishes standing on its top shelf and the best cups hanging from hooks, would scarcely pass muster in the scullery at the Hall. Then there was such a differentiation of tasks in the household: whether there were fires to be laid, puddings to be stirred or table linen to be folded, there were different people to perform each role – and all in the service of one elderly lady who, everyone said, lived very simply. I'd revised my ideas of simplicity.

I still felt ill at ease about other aspects of Mrs Ibbotson's way of life. The abomination of strong liquor had been so belaboured by my father and the other chapel preachers that I shivered with apprehension when the decanter of port-wine was set before mistress of an evening, or a bottle of Burgundy brought from the cellar when there were guests. Certainly these beverages lacked the fearful connotations of beer drunk in the alehouses. Yet my father had warned me that an Anglican lady, for all her good breeding, might display failings with respect to alcohol which no Methodist of the New Connection, or even a more liberal Wesleyan, could condone. I was duly horrified to see the demon drink on the respectable widow's table and not a little puzzled that, even after two glasses, Mrs Ibbotson showed not the least sign of reprehensible behaviour.

I looked down from the garden to the bowl of the valley, as my mistress had done from the window upstairs. It was difficult to imagine a lake there – a reservoir they called it. I'd made it my business to learn a good deal about the project. The dam which was being built would tower above the lowest part of Bradfield village. It was an ambitious undertaking: to hold back an unimaginable quantity of water, for the benefit of the mills in the valley and the town-dwellers in Sheffield. I knew those unfortunates lived in appalling dirtiness and squalor. I'd never been to the town, despite its proximity to Malin Bridge, but I'd learned of its narrow streets and dismal courtyards from Chrissie Mallon.

Chrissie! I hadn't thought of her for months. For a while after I came to the Hall a frightening dream recurred, in which Chrissie danced up the hillside before swirling round with a mocking laugh, her lovely face distorted with malice. More recently, recollections of her and the lies she told had faded but I still shuddered to be reminded of them.

Then I heard what I was hoping for – hooves thumping gently on the sun-dried track beyond the garden wall. Quickly I grasped some sprigs of freshly growing mint, as if my unlikely task was to gather supplies for the kitchen. The young horseman, returning from his work at the dam, came alongside, his head and shoulders visible above the wall. He rode at little more than a trot, although the bridleway was flat and straight beside the house, and his eyes were turned to the garden. The route past the Hall was not the most direct way to his lodgings. He touched his hat respectfully, at the same time brushing aside the strands of sandy hair which had fallen across his forehead.

'Nice evening, Miss Sarah,' he said, colouring slightly as he drew alongside. On all the evenings I'd contrived to be in the garden, since the weather grew balmy, he'd addressed me in this manner and I'd always concurred with his assessment of the climatic conditions, whatever it might be.

'It is so,' I answered earnestly as usual but then an unanticipated thing happened. He paused and held out, over the wall, a handful of slightly crushed primroses.

'I picked them by the wayside. I thought you might like them.'

I was quite overcome. 'Oh, indeed. Thank you Mr Rawdon.'

He tipped his hat and rode on.

On so slight an exchange, it seemed, much might be built. I know now that both protagonists felt it marked a new and joyful stage in our acquaintance, separate from the formalities of our positions when he paid polite visits to his aunt. We had given ourselves leave to speak more fully on some future occasion.

*****

Despite her reservations about the project, Mrs Ibbotson became unexpectedly enthusiastic to visit the site of the dam and she prevailed on her nephew to make the necessary arrangements. So, in early May, on a chilly, overcast morning with drizzle hanging in the air, my mistress and I picked our way carefully downhill on a track rutted by cartwheels and horses. We were escorted by a proud apprentice-engineer and two workmen ready to assist our progress until, where the ground flattened, high above the valley, we were greeted by the Consulting Engineer, Mr Leather from Leeds, to whom Arthur Rawdon was indentured. It was a mark of Mrs Ibbotson's rank and the esteem in which she was held locally, that the great man himself should come to meet us, when clearly our knowledge and understanding of technical matters were likely to be insignificant. We were standing at the level to which the new embankment would rise. Far below us, as nature intended, a

41

petty watercourse received its tributaries and grew in volume as it flowed onwards to become the River Loxley.

I decided that Mr Leather, although unctuous, was surprised and mildly pleased. These women, he probably thought, did not exclaim in ignorant amazement, as other female visitors had done, when he described the dimensions and capacity of the reservoir, the size of the pipeline to the city and the intended rate of flow. I'm sure he considered this information would be over my head, but I knew how to conduct myself well enough not to show signs of boredom or incomprehension while I concentrated on his lecture. Mrs Ibbotson, moreover, was sharp and intelligent, asking questions he had not expected from someone in her position. I suspect he found her directness disconcerting.

'All you can see in the valley bottom will be flooded,' he said magisterially, 'but it will be nigh three years before the work is completed. It's already more than two years since the first sod was turned, that New Year's Day. There's little enough to be seen yet, I grant you, to give a clear impression of what it will be like but the footings of the embankment are in place and the principal design is quite completed.' He gave a small complacent sigh to accompany this last statement. 'The building contracts are handled by various other firms, Mrs Ibbotson. You may have heard of the gentlemen concerned, Messrs. Craven, Cockayne and Fountain.'

Ignoring the curl of his lip as he condescended to mention the building contractors, Mrs Ibbotson acknowledged that she had met Mr Fountain, who owned a local business and had been an acquaintance of her husband. She looked sharply at Mr Leather. 'For so much water, the embankment will need to be enormous, will it not?' Then, without waiting for a reply, she added, 'I heard there had been a landslip some while back. Is that a worry for you?'

'A minor problem, long since overcome, madam,' Mr Leather responded. Then, recognising this was an interrogator unlikely to be satisfied without further explanation, he continued. 'Our earliest drilling showed a small area of instability, so the angle of the embankment was repositioned, moved upstream one hundred and fifty yards. The redesign occasioned some delay but it's still well within the field of deviation permitted by Act of Parliament.'

'You must assuredly hope there will be no more such alarms. The good folk who live in the valley rely on you and your workmen for a sound and solid structure.'

'The embankment will be one hundred feet high and five hundred feet wide,' Mr Leather intoned, ignoring mistress's last, uncalled-for, comment. 'To constrain 691,000,000 gallons it must of course be adequately robust. That's my responsibility. The design is thorough. No embankment could be stronger or more secure. At its summit it will be twelve feet wide. It'll be an engineering masterpiece, to stand alongside the finest of Mr Brunel's bridges and viaducts on the railways.'

We all felt there was no more to be said and Mrs Ibbotson indicated her approval. The engineer's self-confidence and his reference to the revered Mr Brunel were reassuring, so mistress conceded that the uncompromising demands of progress required the mastery of nature by ingenious feats of engineering. Then, amid mutual expressions of gratitude, a donkey cart was summoned and supplied with travelling rugs to cover the debris left by the cargos of stone it usually conveyed. Settled inside, Mrs Ibbotson and I juddered our way, not altogether comfortably, uphill to the Hall.

When I was sitting with mistress that evening the old lady laid down her embroidery and stared towards the darkened window. 'It's a bold undertaking to reorder what God in his wisdom has disposed. I trust that engineer knows

43

his business. He thinks he does, perhaps a mite more than he should.'

'Surely they wouldn't attempt such a venture without certainty.' I spoke hesitantly. 'They do most complicated calculations, to compute stress and volume, the engineers I mean. It's their training, to work out such things.' Then looking down quickly I added, 'so I've read.'

'You are become knowledgeable, Sarah. It's a credit to you that you seek to learn so much, even on so improbable a subject as construction works.'

I felt myself redden and blessed the shadows in the room which I hoped would mask my agitation but Mrs Ibbotson saw all.

'I'm not about to read you a sermon but it's right I should counsel you. Mr Rawdon is a worthy and engaging young man. He should have good prospects in his profession. But you must remember that he comes of a distinguished family, my late husband's nephew, kin to gentry. I don't judge he would trifle with you but I wouldn't have you delude yourself. Your stations are very different, albeit he is but an indentured apprentice now. No matter. I have confidence in you not to encourage his banter beyond what is proper.'

I bowed my head in acquiescence but my heart was racing. I should have guessed Mrs Ibbotson would know of our trysts over the wall of the kitchen garden. Mistress had said nothing I hadn't told myself already but if the old lady, with her insight and wisdom, deemed it necessary to speak in this way, surely it must mean that Arthur Rawdon's tentative interest in me was discernible to others. Discernible and therefore real!

Chapter 5: May 1861

He was waiting on the doorstep as Chrissie returned from the factory three days after she'd challenged his generosity. She was surprised to see him at a time when, if not at his workplace, he would normally be in the alehouse. Then she remembered it was the day of the week some called 'Saint Monday', when grinders felt at liberty to sleep off the excesses of their weekend drinking, so perhaps his indulgence had been greater than usual. She lowered her head as she neared her grandmother's door but Ebenezer Pyle came forward and drew her over his own threshold into his wife's tidy kitchen, careless whether prying eyes across the croft noted their rendezvous. She did not protest when he fastened the latch behind them.

'Wife's gone to sister's,' he said by way of explanation, thrusting a packet into her hands. 'I've got summat for 'ee.'

It surpassed her most extravagant hopes. The elegant short jacket, with braiding at the collar and cuffs, could only have come from Cockaynes, the stylish drapers in Angel Street. Never would she have expected him to patronise such an emporium or to afford so fine a gift.

'Put it on,' he said, taking her shawl.

She did so and they admired its close fit, peering together into Mrs Pyle's blemished mirror above the mantel. He ran his hands over its contours, lingering over her bosom. Then she took it off, folding it carefully and smoothing the material, awaiting his next move. A bargain was a bargain and he had fulfilled his side of it admirably.

'I don't want your brat,' she said coolly as he unbelted his trousers. She wished to appear worldly-wise.

'I weren't born yesterday, tha knows.' He pulled her to him. 'I don't want thee with a swollen belly, tha gorgeous bitch.'

His vulgarity excited her and she smiled to think how sophisticated she was, pressing herself against him, responding to his lust. She expected no finesse and he had none, taking her roughly while she stifled a gasp of pain.

'That coat's worth more'n once.' His fingers inside her bodice twisted her nipple.

She nodded. He would be a demanding lover but, she thought, a rewarding one. She would enjoy taming him.

He whirled her round by the shoulders and she did not care for what she saw fleetingly in his eyes. 'Don't try no monkey business, me lass. I don't want no rivals. Understand?'

Her instinct was defiance but she curbed it. She would bide her time. She did not answer him. He wrenched her wrist sharply. 'Understand?' he repeated.

She swallowed. Again, but less convincingly, she nodded.

*****

'Where's tha been?'

Her grandmother's querulous voice greeted her from the bedroom. 'Thought I heard thee coming a good while since.'

There was nothing wrong with the old woman's hearing. Chrissie put her parcel on the kitchen table and went upstairs.

'Don't care nothing for me. Be glad when I'm dead. Leaving me to starve, like as not. Leaving thi old Gran without a morsel to eat all day.'

This was tiresome but needed to be answered. 'What d'you mean? Mrs Pyle brings 'ee dinner, don't she?'

'Not today she don't. Looked in to say she couldn't. Poor soul. In a right mess. Husband beat her black and blue.

46

Pushed her out. Told her to go to her sister's and not come back while nightfall.'

The old woman was relishing her recital. 'He'll be up to his tricks again, mark my words. Got some new tart. S'happened before. She's told me.'

Martha Bamforth looked spitefully at Chrissie who was aware that her hair was more than usually dishevelled. 'Slut'll get what's coming to her, right enough. He's like a wild beast, that one. She'll wish she never opened her legs for him.'

'I'll get you some food, Gran.' Chrissie turned to the door.

A thin obscene cackle came from the bed. 'Got thi skirt tucked up at back, lass, showing drawers for all to see. Eb Pyle's been inside 'em, ain't he? Tha stupid cow! Bitten off more than tha can chew there. God knows what he'll do when he's had enough of thee.'

'Shut your mouth, you old witch, and mind your business.' Chrissie span round, pulling down her skirt quickly, despite her protestation.

'Old witch, am I? Fine way to speak to thi Gran. Bad lot, always have been. Even when tha was a mite. Making eyes at anything in trousers. Anyone could have thee if they gave 'ee a trinket.'

'Shut your filth!' Chrissie screamed in sudden fury. 'Don't you dare say that. You know what happened.'

'S'true though, shameless hussy, with thi big eyes and long curls. Learned soon enough what they'd give thee to stick their pricks in thi pretty little mouth.'

Chrissie could hold herself back no longer. 'Taught by a master, weren't I?'

The old woman howled as if her granddaughter had struck her. 'No! Not those lies again! Be quiet! Be quiet! Oh me heart! I'm dying. Kill me, tha will. Oh, I'm in pain. I'm dying.'

47

Chrissie fled from the room, her own heart thudding wildly. She wished fervently her grandmother's last words were true.

*****

Annie Turner duly admired her friend's stylish jacket while deeply appalled by the story of its acquisition. She normally shunned those loose-living young women who flaunted themselves and their ill-gotten furbelows. Yet Chrissie Mallon seemed to her somehow different: inclined to be coarse, immoral certainly, but open, amusing and, she thought, basically good-natured. 'Hate the sin but love the sinner'. Annie remembered her mother's favourite text and it seemed to validate her liking for her newest workmate. If Chrissie's accounts of her behaviour gave a smidgeon of titillation to her enthralled listener, Annie would not admit it but she concentrated on being an improving influence.

'Have you really never done it, love?' As they walked home, Chrissie was being mischievous again.

'Not till I'm wed. Make it more special.'

'Hope you're right but your fellow'll been with dozens. They all do.'

'Ma says it's different for men but I'm sure they don't all...'

'Wishful thinking, lass. Bet your Dan's had his pick.'

'He's not my Dan,' Annie countered feebly.

'He will be when he's had you,' Chrissie laughed.

The conversation was distressing Annie but she knew how she could deflect it. 'Whit Monday we thought of taking a walk round town and out to Norfolk Park. We could go to the Whit Sing there. Right grand that is. Everyone dressed up in best bonnets and Sunday suits. Congregations of chapels and churches all walking with their banners, singing hymns together. Started three or four years past. I went with Will last year. It were good.'

The spectacle might be worth seeing but the hymn singing did not appeal to Chrissie. 'You going with Dan this year? Things are looking up!'

'And Will too. Thought you might come to make a foursome. Would you like that?'

'Your brother'll have no time for the likes of me.'

'Nay, lass. I've told him nowt about you. Only that I like you.'

Chrissie loved Annie for her loyalty but she suspected some deviousness. 'So my job'd be to talk solemn with your brother and listen to hymns, while you and Dan sneak off into the bushes, eh?'

'No, no, don't say such things.' Annie was blushing and Chrissie loved her for that too. She put her arm round her friend's shoulder. 'Course I'll come. Heard so much about Dan and Will. Be good to meet 'em.'

Especially Will, she thought contentedly, the tall and dedicated union man with a mass of brown curls. She'd like to see if his thoughts ever strayed beyond the interests of his workmates – with a little encouragement maybe. She didn't doubt he'd be like all the others but she wasn't sure whether that was what she wanted.

*****

For some days Chrissie and her grandmother barely spoke. The old woman had not died but she became almost silent, which was at least a tolerable step towards her demise. Other developments were intriguing, although sometimes troublesome. Ebenezer Pyle did not lie in wait for her as he had on that first occasion but, later each evening when he returned from the alehouse, he called at Chrissie's house before going home. She had protested that Gran

49

would hear and Mrs Pyle would know where he was but she did not really care about them. When Eb gave her the delicate silver chain and embossed locket, which hung low between her breasts, she cared even less. Sometimes when he had drunk more heavily than usual, his roughness hurt her but she continued to believe she could handle him. She revelled in her hold over him and thought his possessiveness gratifying.

On the night of her conversation with Annie, she was still thinking about meeting Will Turner when Eb arrived, pushing the door open violently so that it crashed against the wall. The stink of sweat and sour beer wafted into the room. He was unusually flushed and seemed annoyed but she slid up to him, shimmying provocatively, and asked softly why he looked angry.

'Union business,' he said. 'Not thi concern. I want no prying, woman'

'Sorry I'm sure...,' she began, riled, but he gave her no chance to continue. Brusquely he pulled up her skirt and forced her to the ground, straddling her as he released his trousers.

'No! Not like this! You promised, Eb.'

'Shut thi noise. I makes the rules, me lass.'

He took her savagely, pinning her to the ground with his weight, drawing blood with his teeth. She struggled in vain, outraged to be used callously, furious at her helplessness.

'I told you I don't want your brat.'

'Tha'll have what I gives thee.'

'You don't own me, Eb Pyle.' An attempt at dignity which failed pathetically.

He laughed loudly, clamping her to the floor, and forced himself on her again.

*****

Unwilling to admit her foolhardiness, Chrissie said nothing about these events to Annie next day but when Mr Copley slipped his arm round her waist, while examining some defective buttons she'd drawn to his attention, she shivered. Mistaking her reaction for pleasure, he slid his hand higher, lightly pinching her breast. She sidestepped quickly.

'Good work, Mallon,' he said, leering so that his thin, inappropriate moustache stretched almost from ear to ear, glistening with moisture.

She dipped her head in acknowledgement, aware that her workmates had missed nothing of the exchange, but this was not the day to endure their sarcasm.

She pleaded a headache and left Annie after work, setting off for Tenter Croft by the most direct route, almost running in her anxiety to get home. She wanted no encounters, no exchange of greetings with acquaintances, no occasion to pretend politeness she did not feel. She was dismayed when, as she crossed West Bar in front of the music-hall, she heard a voice she did not recognise calling her urgently.

'Chrissie, Chrissie.'

She turned uncertainly to see a gangly youth bounding towards her, his light brown hair blowing across his cheeks. She stared as he drew near.

'Chrissie, I've found you! Twice afore I've come and looked but now I've found you.'

'Tom Webster,' she said doubtfully. 'You've grown, lad.'

'And you're as beautiful as ever, Chrissie.' His new voice was quite attractive.

'None of that blather! What are you doing in Sheffield?'

'Delivering knives for hafting. Do it quite regular now. All right are you, Chrissie?'

'Not so bad,' she lied, smiling at him against her better judgement.

'I told you I'd find you again. Now you must tell me where you live so I can call when I'm here again.'

'How's family?' she asked hurriedly, unwilling to answer his request.

'Ma's not so well. Me Da says she'll not last the year. We'll have to get Sarah home.'

'I'm sorry. But Sarah's well? Still at the Hall?'

'Aye, quite the lady now, I reckon, but she'll have to put paid to that and come home to look after Da and me if Ma goes.'

'She should do no such thing!' Chrissie was surprised at her own vehemence. 'She'll better herself as a lady's maid. You and your father'll manage fine.'

The youth gaped at her, astonished by her words, but Chrissie's attention had been caught by a slight figure turning the corner. 'I must go,' she said and lifted her skirts to hurry away.

'Chrissie! Please stay!' He started to follow but stopped when he saw the little woman crossing towards her. He thought they would pause to gossip. Then he stared in horror.

'Good God!' he gasped as the woman spat fully in Chrissie Mallon's face. He stepped forward to intervene but Chrissie ran on while her assailant gave him an ingratiating nod. She must be a lunatic, he thought, best left alone.

Chrissie was desperate to appear unconcerned but her mind was in a whirl. Surely this gesture of defiance by quiet, longsuffering Edie Pyle was unprecedented? What did it signify? Was she losing control of the situation she had contrived? That could not be allowed to happen. She must act decisively.

*****

As soon as she arrived home Chrissie bolted the door and went to sit with her grandmother. At first the uneasy truce of near silence between them held but then, reluctantly recognising that she might need old Martha's support, Chrissie offered conversation. 'Saw Mary Brailsford the other week,' she began. 'I thought she'd moved away years ago.'

'She had that.' Martha Bamforth smirked. 'Shame on her! Brought to bed of a bastard while her brother were getting killed overseas and her not more'n fourteen.'

'She had a child with her when I saw her, all muffled up he were, though it were warm. She pretended she didn't know me.'

Her grandmother looked at Chrissie with narrowed eyes. 'Don't live round here now but she comes to see her Ma now and then. Boy's a bit slow, they says. Heard she don't show his face.' She pursed her lips. 'Father were that Ben Culley, they says.'

The note of crafty triumph in Gran's voice was exasperating but Chrissie willed herself not to respond, her futile attempt at gossip defeated by the old woman's malice. At that moment, however, the expected hammering on the front door presented her with a choice of evils.

'Eb Pyle's early tonight,' Martha chortled. 'Can't hardly wait, can he?'

'I've bolted door.'

'Tha daft cow! He'll smash it down.'

'Needs to learn I'm not at his beck and call.'

'Don't know nothing, do 'ee? That sort don't learn lessons. Take 'ee by force if tha plays flighty, like as not.'

53

'He already has.' Chrissie paused while her grandmother's crumpled face quivered. 'Last night. Held me down when I said "No". Served me like I were a...'

'Open window,' the old woman ordered shrilly. Furious shouts now accompanied the hammering until he heard the creak of the window frame.

'Let me in, Chrissie Mallon! Let me in, tha fucking trollop. I'll give thee what for, tha slut.'

'Hold thi noise, Eb Pyle!' Gran's voice wavered but it was strong enough to carry to the indignant suitor. 'It's my house, this is. I'll have law on thee if tha don't go away. I'll lay charges! Disturbance of the peace!'

These final words were pronounced with such grandeur that both Eb Pyle and Chrissie were briefly dumbfounded. They became aware of a buzz of amusement from neighbours congregating at doors and windows in the croft.

'I'll see to thee, tha fucking bitch! See if I don't. Who you all staring at? Damn the lot of you!'

The thud of the adjoining door confirmed his departure and Chrissie quickly pulled the window shut. 'Thanks Gran.' Relief and surprise crept into her voice.

'Still some use, the old girl, eh? But tha'd best look out. He won't take kindly to being made a laughing stock. Edie Pyle'll suffer for it tonight but some dark night he'll do for thee, mark my words. Be a long knife up between thi legs then, not his cock.'

Martha Bamforth cackled contentedly.

Chrissie did not reply.

Chapter 6: Whit Monday 1861

The weather could not have been finer for a walk and open air hymn singing: warm sun, so there was no need for the girls to huddle in their shawls and conceal their shapeliness, and a slight breeze so that auburn curls could waft provocatively from underneath a lacy bonnet, against a pleasingly flushed cheek. They took a circuitous route round the edge of the town centre, crossing the turnpike road out to Ecclesall, where they saw carriages of gentlefolk driving out to the Botanical Gardens. Unlike Norfolk Park, opened to the public fourteen years earlier by the Duke for whom it was named, the Botanical Gardens were privately run for a strictly limited clientele.

Chrissie, who was wearing her Sunday best (courtesy of Uncle George and Eb Pyle), admired the rich silk dresses stretched over crinolines and the velvet tasselled mantles of the ladies in the carriages but their status was too far removed from hers to excite envy. She was more interested in the clothes of those nearer her station in life and, as they started to climb the hill towards Norfolk Park, there were many to engage her attention. She noted the flounces on skirts, the draping of bodices, the beading on jackets. She especially coveted the elegant low-crowned hats with feathers that some fashionable young women chose in preference to frilled bonnets.

Soon they joined the slow moving processions of chapel congregations and Sunday Schools, following their embroidered banners which colourfully proclaimed allegiance to Heeley, Crookesmoor, Darnall and districts of which Chrissie had never heard. The figures portrayed on the banners were crudely designed and, for the most part, looked minatory rather than cheerful, as they heralded the advance of their partisans. The great tide of Sheffielders rolled forward towards the park and filled the roadway. It was no longer possible to walk more than two abreast.

This suited Chrissie for the first sight of Will Turner had not disappointed her. He was well set up and good looking, if a trifle thin and stern in appearance. The brown fronds of hair curling over the bottom of his cap were entrancing and when he smiled, which he seldom did, the ends of his mouth turned up bewitchingly. He was certainly taciturn and she found it difficult to engage him in conversation because he responded with monosyllables to her questions and comments. She envied Annie and Dan walking together, chattering merrily, stopping often and falling further and further behind. By the time they joined the processions Chrissie and Will were far ahead.

Will's polite but distant behaviour began to irk her and she determined to secure a more meaningful reaction from him. She decided, despondently, to venture on a topic which might win his interest. 'Annie says you're big in grinders' union.'

He paused before answering. 'She shouldn't have said that. I'm not big in the union. Hold no office. It's not women's business, any rate.'

'Not Mary Ann's?' she asked archly, whispering instinctively.

'You'd best not make light of things you know little of, Miss Mallon.' His tone, while courteous, was severe. She felt abashed but not defeated. Around them the hubbub of the crowd threatened to drown their conversation so she drew closer, looking up at him.

'Sorry I'm sure. If I'm not supposed to know about things, I'm liable to speak out of turn. It don't come natural to hold me tongue.'

That small beguiling smile twitched the ends of his mouth. 'Beg pardon, Miss Mallon. Womenfolk don't generally want to know about unions and we keep things close. It's not a matter for public airing.'

'Annie said Dan's been rattened. She sounded upset about it.'

As if acknowledging Chrissie's interest in his sister's welfare, he seemed to relax. 'He were a foolish lad to provoke his union – fender grinder he is – all on account of his workmate who were breaking the rules. Friend's a jobbing grinder, not a proper member of the trade: undercutting union rates, paying no dues. Deserved what he got. Dan stood up for him, argued and refused to pay his own sub. Left union no choice but to ratten him. Can't break rules like that. Fair's fair, in defence of trade.'

This was not a subject Chrissie would ordinarily choose to pursue but Will had a delightfully deep voice and she wanted to encourage him to say more.

'All grinders belong to union, then?'

'Several unions for grinders, there are – saw grinders, scissor grinders, scythe grinders, fender grinders, sickle grinders, file grinders. Then there's unions for brick makers, nail makers, handle makers, fork makers...'

'What do masters think about the unions?' She cut short his recital, thinking how little Mr Copley would appreciate any attempt by workers at the button factory to organise into a union.

'Masters? We've no quarrel with them, unless they break rules by taking too many apprentices or let jobbing grinders undercut rates. Some masters belong to the union. Others bide quiet.'

Chrissie gave Will one of her most winning smiles. 'I'd say Annie were right to say you're big in the union.'

She was gratified that he seemed momentarily embarrassed but he quickly became grave once more. 'I said I hold no office. Don't always agree with them as do. But I'll back union in defence of trade. Have to stand up for ourselves as best we can. Law won't help us – law don't recognise unions - so we makes own rules. Taking bands from grinders' wheels is old established practice – as punishment or warning. Sometimes, if a man's stepped out of line, they takes the nuts what work his pulley-drums and hold everything together. Nuts cost twelve shilling a pair and must fit screws exact. That's a powerful consideration for those whose nuts are taken. But I don't hold with it when there's worse done.'

'Like what?' She urged herself to maintain interest, hoping he would smile again.

He did not. His face darkened as he cleared his throat. 'If bands or nuts be gone, anyone can see. At worst it's a cost to replace them. There's no danger. But there's been shots fired. Gunpowder used.'

'Gunpowder?'

'Years back Firth's boiler were blown up, but no one hurt – no thanks to them what did it. Two year ago James Linley were lodging in the Wicker. Whole family were in house when a can of gunpowder were thrown into the butcher's shop in front. They was lucky too but shop were damaged bad. Joseph Helliwell weren't so fortunate. Can of gunpowder were put in his trough at grinding wheel. Blinded him for a fortnight. Someone'll be killed afore long. Beyond all reason, that'd be. Destroy union too, it would. Police keep out of rattening, leave it to the unions, but if there's murder they'll be bound to investigate. Once they meddle with union's rules, defence of trade'll be finished. Us workmen'll be left helpless.'

'Eeh! You looks so serious, both of you! Talking so earnest.'

Annie, weaving through the crowd, had caught up with them. 'It's not much further to the park. Then singing'll start. Let's all walk together for a bit.'

Dan had joined them and he offered Annie his arm. 'They've made progress,' Chrissie thought wryly. She could not make the same assumption on her own behalf.

The hymn singing was ardent rather than tuneful. Chrissie was soon bored and, tall though she was, she could not see beyond the people clustered in front of her through the trellis of straw bonnets and waving plumes. It was also very warm and she began to fan herself before the first preacher took the rostrum to begin sermonising. She stifled a yawn ineffectually.

'This is not to your taste, Miss Mallon?' The resonant voice sounded unexpectedly at her ear. 'Shall we walk out to the shadow of the trees?'

She looked at Will with genuine gratitude and smiled. She was uncertain how to respond to this austere man but he was agreeably considerate They slipped through the audience to the edge of the crowd where unruly boys were scrambling and playing pitch-penny, while small groups of men stood smoking, less intent on their devotions than the womenfolk.

'There's a fair view over town from up here.'

Will, puffing slightly as they climbed further from the great congregation, stood still. Chrissie turned in the direction he pointed and took a step sideways to avoid the branches of a tree, stumbling on an exposed root and turning her weak ankle.

'Sod it!' She regretted the unfitting expression but Will seemed unconcerned by her language.

'Are you hurt?'

'Ankle does that sometimes. It'll be right enough in a bit. Need to hobble first.'

'Take my arm and we'll go down the hill slowly. Crowd'll be praying and singing some time yet. You'd maybe like a drink at the alehouse to refresh you. We could walk down to the Wicker, call at the Corner Pin.'

59

She looked at him appreciatively. She was tempted to tease him, as she might any other new male acquaintance, to suggest he wanted to lead her astray from the paths of virtue and abstinence, but she checked herself. 'You're not one for hymn singing and preachifying?' she asked instead.

'Let's say the Sunday School Band of Hope Union can't count on me joining.'

'One union you've no time for then?'

They both laughed and she found it necessary to lean a little harder on his arm. She felt an unfamiliar sensation of contentment.

While they walked back into the town, he told her more about his grinders' union and how it supported the families of men without work, 'on the box'. Chrissie was astonished to hear that, when they needed new labourers, masters were expected to choose from the union's list of workers, in order to keep idlers and ruffians out of the trade.

'They needs the skills we've got, you see,' Will explained. 'Best in world: Sheffield grinders. Worth every penny we earns. Hold our heads high. Beholden to no-one. Known all the world over for the quality of our work.'

She found herself carried along by his enthusiasm, almost interested in abstruse matters of demarcation between different grinders and mourning the unwelcome introduction of new grinding machines in bigger workshops. 'Don't even know what sort of grinder you are,' she ventured. 'Are you a fender grinder like Dan?'

'Nay, lass. Saw grinder. Finest of all. Strongest union. Highest paid.'

She scarcely heard him. Silently she cursed. Why, of all the assorted grinders, did he have to be a saw grinder? Ten to one he'd know Eb Pyle, also said to be big in the union. She had no wish to be the topic of scurrilous gossip between them. More than that, she had no wish that Will should learn what Annie in her delicacy had withheld from him,

60

concerning Chrissie's entanglement. She was puzzled by her unaccustomed fastidiousness.

As they approached the Corner Pin, along the street called the Wicker, her anxiety proved all too well founded. There, slouched against the door of the alehouse favoured by the saw grinders, was none other than her inebriated lover. His stained neckerchief hung loosely over his unbuttoned waistcoat and his expression, when he saw them, was venomous. Automatically she released her hand from Will's arm but it was too late. Eb Pyle blocked their path.

'By Christ,' he shouted. 'What a sight for sore eyes! My fucking floozy with a knobstick.'

Will stiffened and she could sense his fury, although at which epithet she couldn't tell.

'You're drunk, Eb, or I'd teach you some manners.' His voice was steady but his anger was obvious. 'I'm no knobstick and you know it. Neither scab nor blackleg would I ever be.'

'Keep company with those who are though, like Dan Crookes. Best watch your step, lad. Keep company with stinking trollops too, I see.'

'Enough of your filth!'

'Filth!' Eb snarled, lurching forward. He seized Chrissie by the arm and span her round to face Will, gripping her tightly. 'See this jacket, Will Turner, I bought it her. This chain round her neck – my hard-earned shillings paid for it. Then she throws me off and flaunts herself at any man like a bitch on heat. Scum! Bleeding whore!'

Spinning her round again, he slapped her viciously across the face and pushed her towards Will, but Annie's brother was already in motion. He swung out his fist, cracking it hard on Eb Pyle's jaw and sent him sprawling against the wall of the alehouse. The erstwhile aggressor subsided onto his bottom with a look of affronted surprise.

The effort caused Will to double over for a moment, coughing noisily, but he quickly recovered. 'Come now,' he said. 'I'll see you home, Miss Mallon.'

They walked swiftly, in silence, and Chrissie had never felt so mortified. Where usually she cared nothing for the strictures of others, she felt Will's unspoken reproaches tearing her apart. As they approached Tenter Croft she forced herself to speak. 'Thank you, Mr Turner. It were kind of you to see me back.'

He jiggled his head in acknowledgement.

'What he said about me...' she began lamely. 'What he called me...'

'None of my business,' Will replied sternly. Then, raising his cap, he turned and strode away.

*****

She dreaded her next encounter with Eb Pyle but knew it could not be avoided. Nothing would be gained by trying to shun him: she had no choice. So when, two days later, he pounded on the door early in the evening, she opened it immediately.

'Why the slut's at home!' He pushed past her. 'Wonder who else is lurking. No fancy man up thi skirts then?' He flung her against the table with his hands at her throat. 'How long've tha been going with Will Turner?'

'I've never gone with him. Only met him Monday.'

'That'd not stop thee dropping thi drawers.' He flung back his jacket and drew out a long shining blade, just as Gran had foretold. 'See this, tha fucking bint, this'll be for thi fanny one day but first it's for Will Turner's gizzard.'

'No, Eb, no! He's done nothing. He's never touched me. His sister's me friend, that's all. Don't harm him, for her sake.'

'How bloody cosy! So concerned for her friend's milksop brother who's never touched her. Fair breaks me heart to hear her. Wife saw thee talking in street to another likely lad the other day. Took delight in telling me. Looking to fuck him too, are 'ee?'

'That's right nonsense!'

'That's for me to decide. From now on I'll say what tha'll do. Understand? There'll be no more playing the tart with any man as takes thi fancy. No more can I, can't I? No more bolted doors. I'll have 'ee when I want and how I want. That clear enough?' He raised the knife so close to her throat that she hardly dared breathe.

'And you'll not harm Will Turner?'

He stepped back, sneering, as he replaced the knife in his jacket. 'Tha keeps thi bargain, I'll not hurt hair on his poncey head. Take off thi frock.'

She had known herself trapped since the fracas at the Corner Pin. She was now his creature to humiliate and abuse as he chose. Unbuttoning her dress, she slid it to the floor and stood before him naked, as she had never done before. He took off his belt.

When he had done with her, he chortled as she lay bruised and bloodied at his feet. 'Mustn't forget thi payment, love. Worth every penny.'

He spat as he flung a handful of paltry ribbons in her face.

Chapter 7: Autumn 1861

Despite Mrs Ibbotson's well-meaning advice, I continued to nurture romantic thoughts of Arthur Rawdon and he, consistently courteous and attentive, did nothing to discourage me. There was in truth very little in our behaviour to which the sternest and most unfeeling mistress could take exception and Mrs Ibbotson was neither stern nor unfeeling. I didn't know then my mistress had taken Arthur to task a week after our visit to the construction works at the dam, declaring that she would not allow him to trifle with her maid's affections or stand by to see a scion of her husband's family ruin a naïve girl's reputation. I learned later she had been impressed by his reaction. She had no doubt he was sincere in protesting his blameless honour, touched and amused by his boldness in saying he was ready to defy narrow conventions of class and status.

'I care nothing for such considerations. I wish to marry her, aunt,' Arthur had asserted. 'I cannot ask for her hand while I'm still indentured but in less than a year and a half, I intend to do so. I shall be of age then.'

The old lady had replied, she told me long afterwards, with wisdom and understanding although she had no great hopes that either virtue would be appreciated by the lovelorn apprentice-engineer. 'You're both young, Arthur, and she's of humble stock, though entirely respectable. When you're of age you must make your own judgement. She will also be more mature by then and in all probability will have a greater sense of decorum than you do. Give me your word you will in no way harass or molest her and I will not bar you from the house. In a year you may find much can change.'

His word was given and so, without comprehending why this should be, throughout the summer I was permitted to speak with him across the garden wall and sometimes to sit with Mrs Ibbotson when she received him on a familial visit. As Michaelmas approached, however, and darkness fell earlier, it would be more difficult to meet because it would be immodest of me to venture into the garden alone after nightfall. Despite my day-dreams, I wasn't rash enough to risk an accusation of unseemly behaviour and Arthur respected my position. His intentions were impeccable and he decided to set out his hopes for our future, before winter disrupted our regular meetings. Accordingly, as twilight fell one evening, he rode to the trysting point resolved, notwithstanding what he had said to Mrs Ibbotson, to make an irrevocable declaration.

For some weeks he had ceased to begin each conversation with comments about the weather but on this momentous occasion he took refuge in the well-tried approach, to hide his nervousness. 'Good evening, Miss Sarah. The skies threaten rain, I'm afraid.'

'It is so,' I repeated mechanically, disappointed by this regressive introduction.

'Miss Sarah, we'll not be able to meet here as the nights draw in.'

'Yes, Mr Rawdon, that's true.'

'Miss Sarah, may I speak to you?'

'Why, of course. Don't we always speak?' There was a hint of mischief in my words but I was puzzled by his formality.

'Miss Sarah, Mrs Ibbotson has said I should not declare myself until I'm of age and no longer indentured and, indeed, I cannot address you formally until some fifteen months hence when these things have happened.'

Now I was staring, transfixed, not daring to believe my ears.

'Yet it would be dishonourable to leave you in any doubt that my motives are honourable: that I will wish to speak in fifteen months' time; that I have no right to speak before then, nor any claim I can seek to put on either of us until that time. But, Miss Sarah, I do so want you to know, to be aware...'

'Mr Rawdon...' I began, perplexed by his syntax but rejoicing in what he seemed to be trying to say.

'Miss Sarah, may I speak to you in that way when I am of age? I don't ask you to wait if you feel it inappropriate but may I hope?'

'Oh yes, Mr Rawdon, you may speak and I will wait until we're both of age, as may indeed be necessary.' I didn't hide my eagerness but shuddered at the prospect of nearly four long years until I became of age and at my forwardness in answering so unconditionally. 'I must go in now, sir.'

'Sarah, believe me, I long to seek you as my wife.'

Mrs Ibbotson's bell rang out across the darkened, chilly garden. 'I will wait for you, Mr Rawdon,' I whispered as I turned away. 'I will wait.'

Later, as I read to mistress a tale of chaste love and suffering in ancient time, I rejoiced in the exhilaration of knowing Arthur Rawdon cared for me and found my homely features pleasing. To me it mattered not at all that he was a gentleman, nor did I ponder what alteration in my fortune such a marriage might bring, but I did experience qualms of uncertainty as to whether I might properly regard myself as betrothed, even if provisionally and in secret.

*****

It was a dismal morning in the last week of October when my gentle euphoria was shattered, a day to stay indoors. On the moor the vivid autumn colours of the bracken and heather had faded and few shrivelled leaves remained on the wind-blown trees growing high above the valley. The chill crept into the house even when the fires had been lit. I was folding Mrs Ibbotson's soft linen underwear,

66

smoothing the crochet-work at the hems and sprinkling it with lavender water, when I heard the knocker thump on the front door. I paused, surprised by the importunate hammering, while Susan, the parlour-maid, pattered across the entrance hall to answer it. Then I heard Tom's voice and knew instantly what his arrival portended. I moved to the landing, at the top of the stairs, and called down to him.

'Sal, I'm sent to fetch you home. You're to come at once.' He was breathless from running and sweat was trickling down his temples. 'Beg pardon, ma'am, should have come to side door.'

Mrs Ibbotson had appeared from the drawing room. 'Sit down, lad,' she said, beckoning Susan to bring him a chair, but he shook his head, breathing deeply.

I had come downstairs and was beside him. 'Mother?' I asked, knowing the answer.

'She's dying, Sal. You're to come at once.'

I looked at Mrs Ibbotson. 'Get your things,' mistress said. 'The carriage will take you both. Fetch the lad something to drink, Susan.'

She followed me upstairs to my attic room. 'Be brave, my dear. It's a painful time and they all have need of you. Stay as long as is necessary.' She paused. 'But I hope you may return before very long, Sarah. We have need of you here also.'

'Thank you, ma'am.' My eyes filled with tears. 'I will come back soon, when it's all over.'

*****

Father was at the door as the carriage drove up. He took my hand, more gently than was his custom and led me into the house.

'She's fading fast. She's not spoken these last few hours but she asked for you during the night and I told her Tom

67

was sent to fetch you. The minister's been with her and the doctor's called. Hephzibah Groomsley is taking care of her.'

We climbed the stairs to the bedroom and I was appalled to see mother's mottled and emaciated face. Her eyes, within great yellowy-brown circles, were open but unfocussed; the flesh over her sharp cheekbones was translucent.

'Mother, it's me, Sarah.' I took the fragile, withered hand. 'Can you hear me?' The distant eyes flickered for a moment and a tiny grunt signified she knew of her daughter's presence. 'I'll stay with her.' I looked at Mrs Groomsley. 'You've very kind. Please take some rest.'

For several hours I sat stroking mother's face and hands, talking to her constantly, expecting and receiving no response. Father came up from time to time, together with Tom who looked awkward in the sickroom, but mostly he stayed in the parlour downstairs, praying in a fierce continuum as if he was upbraiding God for his wife's affliction. Sometimes mother uttered heart-rending groans and, when the doctor called again, he poured a little liquid into her mouth to deaden the pain. He indicated that my vigil would not last much longer and, after he'd gone, I called my father and brother to tell them what he'd said.

Father fell to his knees by the bedside and resumed his voluble devotions, beating his breast and crying out for both mercy and repentance, increasingly incoherent. His fervour troubled me but it didn't intrude on the dying woman's new-found serenity. Then, just when Tom gave a loud sniff, mother's eyelids fluttered faintly and I gasped as I saw the clouded eyes focus. Father's stentorian tones stopped and he bent forward but his wife's feeble rally was directed towards me. We saw her lips move and strained to hear what she said but only one listener understood her message.

'Remember...,' she breathed hoarsely but, exhausted by the effort, she subsided onto the pillow and said no more.

Clutching her hand, I fancied that for a moment I felt a slight pressure. Minutes later the pattern of mother's breathing changed and the whistle in her throat intensified until it faded forever.

*****

In the days that followed I was busy with household duties, sewing mourning clothes, comforting my brother and seeking to make things easier for my morosely grieving father. The funeral took place with proper dignity and neighbours called with sorrowful condolences and small gifts of sweetmeats and pies. Mrs Groomsley was always at hand, tearful for the loss of her childhood friend and solicitous for the welfare of the bereaved family. Within two weeks, however, normal patterns of life were re-established for the Webster menfolk. When he was not at work, father was mostly out of the house on chapel business and Tom began to join the other lads again, in the evenings, for what he claimed were Bible-study meetings.

Only for me there was no normality to return to at Malin Bridge and, in my isolation, I lacked any stimulus or diversion to ease my sorrow. Reading matter at home was limited to the Good Book and my well-meaning contemporaries, who had remained in the village, were narrow in their conversation and interests. Above all I longed to see Arthur Rawdon. He had written a polite letter after mother's death and I acknowledged it in correct impersonal terms. This was entirely proper and all that could be expected, but it was not enough to sustain my flagging spirits. I tried to fight off a nagging horror that my life at the Hall was receding, as if it had been no more than a dream, and I made myself repeat out loud my determination to return there as soon as I could.

I was uncertain how to raise the question of my departure with father without incurring his wrath, for I sensed he had no notion of my wishes. Then, after a month, I received a note from Mrs Ibbotson conveying sincere regards and the gentlest of suggestions that I might soon find it appropriate to resume my employment. My heart leapt as I read it, recognising that this was the pretext I needed to broach the subject but, still in awe of my father, I decided to speak first to Tom. My opportunity arose next evening as I was washing the dishes, when my brother returned from his outing in a jovial mood. I thought wryly that his religious studies must have been unusually entertaining.

'Given that Lizzie Simmonite the slip,' he announced triumphantly, twirling me round, oblivious of flying soapsuds. 'Me mates told her I'd gone to Hillsborough Barracks to join th'army. She's run off there, blubbing, to try and stop me.' He sank onto a chair, rocking with laughter. I was shocked by his appearance and behaviour.

'Best get to bed before father comes; and turn your face to the wall. Your breath carries the fragrance of the alehouse.'

'How d'you know, Sal? Is it a scent you've smelled afore? Is that what life at t'Hall has taught you? You're well away from such a place!'

'You're wrong, Tom. I want to go back. Soon.'

'Eh? You mean to desert me and Da? I thought you'd stay to keep house. Tha'sh what lasses do!'

His diction was not clear-cut.

'That's not what mother wanted,' I answered pointedly. 'No more do I. You'll manage. Da's not short of a penny to pay for housekeeping.'

'Well, I'm blowed! Who'd'a thought it? Chrissie said you shouldn't stay here. Said you'd do better for yourself as a lady's maid.'

70

'Chrissie? Chrissie Mallon? You've seen her?' I was disgusted.

'Back in summer. Met her in Sheffield. I've looked for her since in town. I mean to find her again.'

I was irritated by Tom's continuing infatuation but still more furious with what I saw as Chrissie's interference, from afar, in my affairs.

'I don't want to hear anything about that meddlesome, bad-mouthing jade!' I slammed down the saucepan I was cleaning and Tom had the good sense to creep off to bed, more particularly because he heard his father's footsteps in the back lane.

After the exchange with Tom, it was perhaps inadvisable to raise the subject with father straightaway but he looked benignly at me as he entered. 'Still working, lass?'

'Almost done.' I drew myself up, head back. 'Da, I've had a letter from Mrs Ibbotson. She's asking when I'll be back at the Hall.'

Father frowned. 'Back at the Hall? Is she daft? Begging her pardon. How can she expect you back in her employ when you've got a motherless family to care for? Has she no concept of a daughter's duty?'

'I want to go, Da.'

He stared and I could sense his indignation rising, his attempt at kindness abandoned. 'Unfeeling, sinful girl! How can you say that? Down on your knees to beg forgiveness of the Lord. Your mother'll fair turn in her new-dug grave!'

'No! It's what she wanted. Mother told me to be sure to go back to the Hall after she'd gone.' I knew, as soon as I'd spoken, this was unwise.

Father's fury erupted. 'Wicked lies! She were a true wife. She'd never say such a thing!'

'She reminded me on her deathbed what she'd told me before. That's what she meant when...'

71

'Oh, the evil come upon this house!' He raised his hand and I thought for a moment he would strike me but the movement was only to invoke Heaven's assistance. 'Oh Lord, cast out ingratitude and falsehood from this sinful daughter! It is truly written: the devil, as a roaring lion, walketh about, seeking whom he may devour. Beware, Sarah, beware!' He checked his flow of invective, grasping his lapels and lowering his voice. 'I'll hear no more of this. You're overwrought. Pray God to teach you your duty and repentance for your transgressions.'

After he left me, exuding righteous disapproval, I sank onto a chair with my face in my hands. I should have realised I would never persuade him that his loving, obedient wife had urged me to escape from under his roof, to what he saw as the laxity of life at the Hall. Moreover, I doubted my right to destroy his belief in mother's absolute loyalty. Besides, wasn't he right to press claims of duty? Wasn't it my moral responsibility to care for my family? Wasn't I putting selfish thoughts before clear obligation? When a mother died, wasn't it always an unmarried daughter's lot to keep house? How could I have allowed myself to think otherwise? Only wayward, unscrupulous hussies would shirk the calls of duty – girls like Chrissie Mallon! How dare that filthy-minded liar presume to say what Sarah Webster should do!

As I wept fitfully, tossing and turning in my bed that night, I came to my resolution. Mother had meant well in extracting my promise, but perhaps her frailty had clouded her sense of what was appropriate, for she should not have tried to defy the decrees of convention. Since I was an infant, I'd learned the harsh virtues of sacrifice and self-denial and I knew those virtues required me to carry out my unquestionable duty. I prayed for forgiveness for presuming to think otherwise but, even more earnestly, I prayed that

Arthur Rawdon, in my absence, would continue to wait for me.

Chapter 8: Autumn 1861

During the months following the Whit Walk Chrissie learned to tolerate a life of bitter servitude, trapped by her grandmother's increasing demands and her lover's erratic moods. Only the mundane routine of the button factory gave her respite from Tenter Croft, where she was the butt of an ungrateful invalid and the chattel of an unpredictable, coercive tyrant. Yet Eb Pyle could still surprise her, for at times he was civil, even affectionate, and brought her small presents. Although there were no more jackets or silver lockets, trinkets and lace trimmings were useful. Unfortunately he was equally likely to be sullen and spiteful, scoffing at her reluctant submission, taunting her with renewed threats against Will Turner as a means to keep her compliant. Once or twice he hit her but he hadn't taken his belt to her again. She tried to persuade herself that Eb's occasional gifts compensated for his dominance over her; that her spirit was not broken, only biding its time to reassert itself; and that before long he would tire of her when some other easy-natured girl caught his eye. Yet, as the weeks went on, there was no sign of this happening and it became more difficult to sustain her pretence.

She tried to have as little as possible to do with neighbours whose prurience was all too evident from their scornful expressions and unambiguous gestures. The crofts may not have housed pious prigs, like those at Malin Bridge, but they had their own moral code – although it might not be recognised as such in other parts of the town – and she had offended against it. One day as she passed a crowd of gossiping women outside the pie shop, a lanky female pointed at her and yelled. 'See her! That's Eb Pyle's whore! Shame on her.'

Chrissie held her head high, pretending she hadn't heard, but she was stung by the woman's contempt.

At least she could be grateful she hadn't fallen pregnant and she clung to the hope that the childless Mrs Pyle was evidence of Eb's limitations. The thought that his aggressive manhood might be sterile was satisfying.

Chrissie's strength to endure her subservience was bolstered by one certainty, to which she clung fiercely, only regretting its long deferment. Never, she grumbled to herself, could a feeble, cantankerous old woman have clung to life with such pointless tenacity. Her loathing intensified each time her grandmother recovered from another 'turn'. Nevertheless, it stood to reason, nature must take its course soon and, when Martha Bamforth was in her grave, Chrissie was resolved to escape from Tenter Croft and her possessive lover. She would leave Sheffield and find work in another town where there were mills and factories looking for female labour. She would start anew, a shrewder woman, and Eb's hold over her would be null and void. What was more, she would have done all she could to protect Will Turner.

She'd never told Annie about the brawl outside the Corner Pin and she guessed that Will had been similarly reticent on the subject. In fact she'd spoken less often to her friend about Eb Pyle since Whitsun and it was doubly welcome to realise that Annie's waning interest in Chrissie's liaison was due to the emergence of Dan Crookes as her own serious suitor. By September it was acknowledged that they were 'walking out' and a month later they were planning to wed at Christmas. Chrissie could rejoice for her gentle workmate's happiness and also for Annie's preoccupation. Occasionally she enquired after Will, but each time she received the identical careless, sisterly reply: 'he's caught up with the union, same as ever'.

Chrissie's first thought was that something might have happened to Will when, one morning in early November, Annie arrived at her button-turning lathe in evident distress, her face blotched and puffy from crying.

They worked at opposite ends of the bench so Chrissie could not speak to her easily and leaving one's stool during working hours, without Mr Copley's permission, was forbidden. She endured three hours of worry on Will's account, until their short mid-morning break, before she could ask what had upset her friend.

'It's union business, turned right ugly. Will's got a face like thunder. You can tell there's fury boiling up inside him. And Dan...Dan...' Annie dissolved in tears.

Chrissie took her hand. 'Tell me what's happened. Is Dan hurt?'

'Not yet,' Annie sobbed, 'but he may be. There's four assaulted, one left for dead.' She composed herself determinedly. 'There's a foreman, John Sibray, works at Hoole's, makes fenders and grates. Hired non-union men, jobbers, because grinders were on strike. Been warned by the union. Threatened before. Will said they had to do something. But he never meant it'd turn to violence. At any rate, last night in fog, Sibray and three more were set on in street and thrashed. Bag o' stones used to smash 'em, drew blood.'

'But what's it got to do with Dan? You said he weren't hurt.'

'He weren't there. But one of the jobbing grinders who were with Sibray, George Wastnidge, he's friend of Dan's – the one were cause of Dan being rattened months back. Dan'll always stick up for him and then he'll be in more trouble himself. I know it. He's marked down for a knobstick already.'

Chrissie decided to risk a direct question. 'You said Will were against violence?'

'It's true. He's right grouchy union leaders have let it get out of hand. He stormed off to a meeting this morning to have it out with 'em.'

76

Chrissie patted her friend's hand. 'Will's word'll carry weight, won't it? They'll listen to him. He'll see Dan's all right. Don't fret.'

Annie's faint smile confirmed her wish to be reassured by the possibility of her brother's influence but Chrissie couldn't wholly reassure herself. She knew only too well there was another man with clout in the grinders' unions, one to whom violence came easily, who nurtured bitter grudges and who'd likely take any opportunity to settle what he thought of as an old humiliating score.

*****

During the next two weeks Annie's fears for Dan's welfare lessened, for he was neither rattened nor attacked, and Chrissie received no visits from Eb Pyle. Tentatively, she began to believe her hopes were to be realised and her situation might yet resolve itself without rancour. She was mistaken. Late one evening, just as she was about to go to bed, he stormed through the door, purple in the face, and hurled her against the wall, his belt already unleashed. She clung to his arm, trying to calm him, but he flung her aside and brought the leather strap whistling across her collarbone. Then, as she covered her chest with her arms, he aimed a kick at her stomach with his booted foot and dragged her to the ground. He wrenched her head back, twisting coils of her hair in his grasp, and smashed his fist into her face. She felt blood running from her lip and begged him to stop, keeping her voice low, desperate not to incense him further.

'Eb, I've done nowt to rile you.'

'Nowt! By Christ, tha's done enough, tha knows. What company dost tha keep? Thi friend's prissy brother went for me outside Corner Pin and now he's causing trouble in union. Come over all mealy-mouthed about how us runs things, been going on and on for weeks. Now he's called for a vote to change the committee members. Fucking bastard!'

'Eb, it's not my fault.'

'Liar! Why should he stick up for thee that day unless he were screwing 'ee?'

'Eb, I've told you...No! No!'

'I'll flay thee, tha lying bitch.'

Blows rained down on her and she could no longer hold back her screams so he clamped one hand over her mouth, continuing to punch with the other, until she lay motionless before him, almost insensible. Then, as before, he raped her.

*****

She stayed away from the factory next day, unwilling to show her bruised and swollen face to her workmates. Once, weeks earlier, when she'd gone to work with a black eye, Mr Copley had called her into his small office and, while expressing concern for her welfare, fondled her. Curling his upper lip to reveal his rats' teeth, he'd even expressed regret that he was not in a position to become her protector. The thought of his silky insinuations sickened her and she wanted no repetition of his intrusive sympathy.

She could not disguise her battering from her grandmother, who in any case must have heard everything. Of course it had been no more than prudence on the part of the helpless old woman to remain silent during the assault but her response, after the event, was characteristically cruel. 'Told you so,' she crowed, laughing mirthlessly. 'Tha asked for it. Do for thee proper one day, he will.'

After that, Chrissie stayed down in the kitchen, dabbing herself with dirty water to poultice her bruises, not daring to venture out to the standpipe. When, in the late afternoon, peremptory knocking shook the door, she started in terror fearing for a moment that Eb had returned – but he would have forced his way inside. If it was not Eb it must be some other unwelcome caller, so she decided to ignore the summons until she saw a face peering through the window at her, a face belonging to an official in uniform. She opened the door a crack.

'Mrs Martha Bamforth live here?' She nodded. 'Received telegram at the Barracks. Kindly pass it on to her.'

Chrissie shut the door and stood staring at the folded paper in her hand. She'd never seen a telegram before, had scarcely heard of such a thing, but she knew what it must mean. The implications were shattering. Every part of her body ached and her head throbbed as she sat down, summoning courage for what lay ahead. Then she climbed the stairs.

'Who were at door?' her grandmother asked from the bed.

'Telegram brought from the Barracks for you.' She spoke brusquely, for her own sake.

The old woman's eyes widened and she stared as if frozen. Then her cracked lips began to tremble. 'Read it me.'

Chrissie's voice was hard as she made out the words carefully, syllable by syllable. 'It's from the War Office in London, to inform whomsoever it may concern that John Bamforth were killed in action three months back, in an affray near Hyderabad.'

The atavistic keening seemed to come from deep in Martha's chest. Wordlessly she moaned and shuddered until convulsions gripped her whole body. Chrissie watched in silence, struggling to control her own conflicted emotions. Forcing herself to speak, she did so coldly. 'Don't take on so. It'll do no good. You'll do yourself an injury.'

Her unfeeling remark startled her grandmother into a furious response. 'Tha callous shrew! Much tha cares! Thi

79

uncle's dead, massacred by savages, my little lad, best of 'em all. John, they calls him. My Jack. Dead afore his old mother, left alone to the mercies of a thankless slut!' Grief for her son's slaughter and her own miserable lot erupted into hatred. 'Murderer! That's thee. Tha caused it. Tha drove him away. Never would have gone for a soldier if it hadn't been for thee. Tha killed my little lad!'

'Stop this nonsense, Gran! He went away because he had to. You know why.'

'Because of thi filthy wicked lies!'

Chrissie stood. 'They weren't no lies. Don't pretend. You knew everything. Now shut your mouth and say no more.'

'So tha tells thi old Gran to shut her mouth now, do 'ee? Hoity toity! Well, I'll not shut it, tha tart. Look at thee, all black and blue from thi fancy man, meat for any who'll take thee. I'll have my say. Tha drove Jack out because of what tha said, whining to me with thi lies, threatening to have the law on him.'

'Stop it! I warn you, Gran!'

'A fig for thi warning! A scheming trollop who gave herself to him over and over, then turned on him when her bleeding started and she were frit he'd give her a bun in oven.'

'That's a bloody lie! For more'n a year you turned a blind eye while he took me night after night. Me, ten year old and his own niece. I loved him when I were a little lass, loved him right and proper. Even when he started feeling me down below I thought it were a game, one on from tickling. I still loved him and he made a fuss of me, gave me presents. I were confused. Didn't know what to think. You knew and you never stopped him.'

Martha Bamforth screeched. 'I should'a horsewhipped thee. Brazen hussy! Had to send 'ee away, didn't I? Once tha started flaunting thiself to all and sundry.'

'I never did! You know what happened. Why I spoke out. I never told on Jack when it were just him and me, though I knew right enough you saw what were going on.'

'Wicked, wicked lies!'

Chrissie's abraded body cried out for relief, the relief of inflicting pain on one of her tormenters. She was not to be stopped now, whatever the consequences. 'I kept quiet because it were special. I knew it were wrong but it were special atween us. Until he sold me – that's what he did – sold me for half a guinea to that Ben Culley! Beer money! I said "no", what I did for Uncle Jack weren't for no one else, so he held me down while his bloody friend had me. That's what your precious little lad did!'

The old woman shrieked, rising on her pillow in desperate agitation, waving her hand in front of her face as if to brush away her granddaughter's words and the memories they evoked, which she had denied for so long. Then, with a deep inarticulate sound in her throat, she flopped back on the bed, staring but wordless.

*****

Chrissie sat silently in the kitchen long after darkness fell. From time to time she went to the foot of the stairs so she could hear her grandmother's breathing, noisy but regular. She didn't know if the old woman was asleep or unconscious but she had no intention of trying to rouse her. In the morning she would go for the doctor; then she would leave the house. Now those words between them had been spoken she couldn't tolerate living with Martha Bamforth any longer. The old witch could go to the workhouse for all she cared. Jack's death had shattered the façade they'd erected tacitly over the past eighteen months, which allowed them to bide together ignoring the truth they shared and jointly shunned. The hostility between them had been muted

81

to avoid acknowledging the one unforgivable, incontestable memory which poisoned their past and shaped their present lives. Now there was no pretence left to protect them. Chrissie's thoughts veered between desolation and rage. Self-justifying resilience was part of her nature but that night she came near despair as she confronted both the betrayal of her childhood trust by her own kin and her present degrading subjection to an abusive lout.

It must have been past midnight when she heard movement in the yard and low voices outside. Rousing herself from her mental turmoil, clutching at the straw this distraction offered, she lifted the curtain cautiously and peered through the window. Two men, both well muffled, were leaving the croft. The lantern they carried briefly illuminated them. One she knew well, from his bulk and his gait, was Eb Pyle; the other was slight and weasel-like, with quick stealthy movements. She realised she'd seen the pair before, their faces similarly concealed, when with Annie she'd identified the grinders' bands hidden in the gulley. After that she'd returned home and seen Eb outside his house. She'd admired his physique and hardiness, noting he had no need for a muffler. She'd been duped then by his crafty change of appearance, as she'd been duped later by his amorousness and the gifts he gave her.

'Ratteners,' she murmured to herself. She should have known Eb would engage in rattening, or worse violence come to that. The activities of the grinders' unions were still mysterious to her but it made sense ratteners would steal and hide bands at dead of night. She shrugged, listening again for her grandmother's unchanged breathing, and sank back on her chair to resume her sleepless wait for the dawn.

The sound was distant but Chrissie heard it clearly: a sudden thud, reverberating slightly, and once more she went to the window. There was far-off shouting and she saw the candlelight from a door across the courtyard as a neighbour in his nightshirt looked out to see what had happened. A slight glow in the sky flickered and intensified. Suddenly intrigued, she flung her grandmother's worn shawl over her head and set out in the direction of the shouts, in the direction, she soon gathered, of a burning house. Other people were hurrying out of doors, pulling day clothes over their nightwear, and she joined a stream of the curious and the concerned, making for the site of the incident. She alone perhaps was aware of the two figures slipping past in the opposite direction, returning to Tenter Croft, still well muffled. Mercifully, she could be confident that, enveloped in the unfamiliar shawl, she hadn't been recognised.

The sight, as she turned into Acorn Street, was alarming. Smoke billowed from a house where flames could be seen through a downstairs window, despite the bucketfuls of water thrown by neighbours, and there was a pervasive smell of sulphur. A ladder leaned precariously against the wall, too short to reach the casement in the garret, and a man was swinging down from the sill onto its uppermost rung. A child, wrapped in a blanket, whimpered at the foot of the ladder, calling up to his father. Four women were kneeling by someone on the ground screened from Chrissie's view.

She stood staring, trying to make out what had happened when one of the bucket carriers paused in front of her. 'Dan,' she exclaimed, relieved that the shadows hid her disfigured face, 'Dan Crookes! Do you remember me? Chrissie Mallon, Annie's friend. What's up here?'

Annie's betrothed wiped a grimy hand across his face. 'Murder,' he said. 'Murder intended. Devil take the buggers!' He hurried on with his bucket.

Chrissie approached the group of crouching women and one of them turned to thrust a bundle of soiled rags into her hands.

83

'Here, love, take these, will 'ee? We're wrapping her afresh.'

'What's happened?'

'Poor soul were on fire. Jumped from garret window, not a stitch on her. All scorched and her leg likely smashed. We've wiped her clean.'

The man from the ladder joined them, with the young boy sobbing in his arms.

'Harriet? Missus? Is she hurt bad?'

The prostrate woman, now wrapped in a dry blanket, stirred and reached out her hand. 'George, is it thee? I can't see. I'm blinded. What was it? I can't remember nowt.'

'Why, old lass, the parcel blew up in thi hands. Caught thi nightgown afire. Tha ran upstairs in a panic and I stripped it off thee. Then tha jumped out of window afore I could stop 'ee. Lad's safe though. I threw him down to neighbours. Harriet!'

The woman sank back, gasping for breath, and lost consciousness, while her husband knelt down vainly trying to revive her. There was movement in the crowd as a doctor pushed his way through.

'Stand back. We must get her to the Infirmary. I've a carriage at the end of the road. Here, good fellows, carry her gently. Why, man, you're burned too. Your legs are blackened. Come with your wife. Are any others injured?'

The woman's husband glanced round in startled recollection. 'Bridget O'Rourke!' he gasped. 'It were her picked up parcel first when it were thrown through parlour window. She slept in parlour. Wife went downstairs and took it from her to get rid of in street. Then it blew up. Mrs O'Rourke's chemise was right afire too. Where is she?'

The man was led away to the doctor's carriage while the dousing of the flames continued. In a short while Dan Crookes and two other men were able to enter the house and search the smoke-filled rooms. They emerged carrying an appallingly burned woman who was bundled in a blanket and taken away. Chrissie could see charred flesh peeling from her body as she was covered.

Dan came over to the woman at Chrissie's side, whom she'd spoken to earlier.

'Bridget's dreadful burned, Ma. I doubt she'll live.'

Mrs Crookes nodded sadly. 'Poor harmless Bridget. It weren't meant for her, I'll be bound. Nor yet for Harriet Wastnidge. It were George they had it in for.'

'George Wastnidge?' Chrissie repeated the name, remembering what Annie had told her about the earlier attack on him. She turned to Dan. 'He's your friend?'

'Aye, friend and neighbour. Workmate too. He's a right good lad, for all he defies the union. They've threatened him often enough. He were told to keep cellar grate fastened a fortnight back or they'd blow house up with a bomb dropped through it. But I never thought they'd do it – not to murder womenfolk.'

He covered his face with his hands and Chrissie guessed he was thinking of his own disagreements with the union and the safety of his bride-to-be. Will Turner had said there would be murder done before long and it seemed that moment had arrived. She thanked Mrs Crookes for her offer to mash some tea but excused herself, saying she must return to her grandmother. She did not want to reveal her black eye and cut lip and she had no wish to hear speculation as to the perpetrators of the bombing. She walked back along the dark streets, numbed by the certainty that it was her brutish lover who was responsible for this atrocity.

'For all it were meant for George Wastnidge,' she thought, 'Eb were ready to blow up two women and a little lad. He's a right monster. And he'd do the same for me if I crossed him bad enough.'

She crept back into the croft and closed the front door furtively, anxious not to be heard by anyone. Then she stood tensely, listening. All was silent. There was no sound from next door and, after a moment she realised, there was no sound from upstairs: no sound of Martha Bamforth's breathing. Disbelieving, Chrissie lit a lamp from an ember in the grate and climbed the staircase. The counterpane was awry, as if the old woman had sought to throw it off, but the wizened arms that lay across it were stock-still, the talon-like hands rigid and the rheumy eyes fixed in an angry, unseeing stare.

Chrissie held her breath as exultation and distaste contended within her. Then, with cool determination, she reached out and twisted the cheap wedding ring from her grandmother's stiff, gnarled finger.

Chapter 9: December 1861

She'd been sorely tempted to walk away then and there, leaving Martha Bamforth's shrunken corpse for neighbours to find and the workhouse to bury. A little later, when she discovered the small bag of coins beneath the mattress, she chuckled with glee, for now she could take long overdue revenge, consigning the old woman to a pauper's grave and pocketing the meagre savings her grandmother had put by in order to avoid just such indignity. There was money enough to buy her a ticket on the railways she'd never explored and to keep her while she found employment. It was possible to get to Manchester or Birmingham or even London. She could start a new life in earnest, free at last from the encumbrances of the past. Surely she was owed no less?

Later she wondered why she hadn't walked away then. Why, having tipped the coins into her hand and felt their weight, she put them back, one by one, into the little bag with its faded embroidery, pulled the drawstring and slipped the bag in her pocket, before leaving the house to summon the doctor. Above all, why after she'd registered the death, did she present most of Martha's nest-egg to purchase a decent Christian burial? Why, at the moment of opportunity she'd so longed for, did she falter? Why, at such a juncture, did she for once ignore her own self-interest?

She couldn't answer these questions. She was certain she felt not a jot of guilt for the circumstances of her grandmother's lonely death. Yet perhaps the sight of the cotton bag, with the washed-out, uneven embroidery she'd painstakingly executed as a seven-year-old orphan, awoke some long forgotten hint of sentiment. Perhaps, rashly, she wanted to enjoy a few days of secret triumph, believing herself safe from Eb Pyle until the old woman was buried, enjoying the thought that, while he still lusted after her, she was about to desert him. Perhaps the physical abuse she'd suffered clouded her judgement while her battered body cried out for time to recuperate. Perhaps the vicious drama of the last few days had simply sapped her energy.

*****

The landlord gave her seven days' notice from the date of Martha Bamforth's death, as was to be expected, and she herself gave a week's notice at the button factory from the same date, ignoring Mr Copley's pop-eyed protests. This gave her three more days' work after the funeral, three more days' wages but three evenings of anxiety in case Eb came to call. Somewhat optimistically, she hoped he had decency enough to respect a full week of mourning for a bereaved granddaughter. She knew there was one great obstacle to confront in executing her scheme to disappear, because she owed it to Annie to tell her what she planned and to say goodbye. Too preoccupied with her own designs, she underestimated the impact her declaration would have.

'Next week? You'll be away from Sheffield next week? Chrissie, you can't. You mustn't go so soon. I want you by me in chapel when I'm wed. You're to hold my posy and be maid of honour. You know it's all arranged for Christmas Eve. You can't miss my wedding day.'

'I'm sorry. Truly. But I must go. If I stay in Sheffield I'll never be free of Eb. Next week I'll have no home to go to and no work. I've a few pence from Gran to get me away from town and I'll start anew. I must do it, Annie.'

She could not say that she believed her departure would also safeguard Will Turner and his family. The bride-to-be sobbed sadly but Chrissie was not to be persuaded.

*****

On the evening before her intended flight, she packed the carpetbag and set things tidy in the kitchen. The new tenants were welcome to the sticks of furniture she was leaving and she'd already promised herself that, when it was light, she would take Gran's abominable china dog into the yard and shatter it. To pass the time she sat in the kitchen, ineptly darning the toe of her stocking. She'd decided to go to Manchester because that could be done in a single train journey and she could afford the cost of the cheapest ticket. She was wondering what it might be like on the other side of the Pennine Hills when a crash on the window startled her back to her present surroundings. Furious to find a pane of glass was cracked, which she would have to pay for when the landlord's agent called in the morning, she flew to the door expecting to see some rascally urchin hiding in the shadows under the archway across the yard, ready to laugh at her discomfort. Instead her appearance was greeted by a cacophony of beaten saucepans and screeching women.

'Whore!'

'Harlot!'

'Filthy slag!'

Hurriedly she tried to slam the door in their faces but scraggy arms prevented her and four or five harpies rushed in, pinning her to the wall and tearing at her clothes while, behind the furious harridans, pale-faced Edie Pyle stood slyly smirking. Chrissie struggled and bit the hands which held her but her bruises were still tender and she lacked strength to resist effectively. When she cried out her assailants ripped a strip from her petticoat and gagged her with it; then they tore her dress apart and held her down, on the floor, while they taunted her. A lanky, hard-faced woman, whom she recognised from the incident outside the pie shop, ran rough hands over her breasts.

'Eh, what a beauty! Ever seen such tits? Bet thi Eb's sucked 'em, time enough, Edie. Who else has had 'ee, tha scum? How many other husbands have fucked 'ee? Can't get one of thi own, eh?'

'This is what tha likes, is it, lass?'

A grimy hand thrust itself between Chrissie's legs to the raucous amusement of the onlookers. She tried to writhe and free herself but they slapped her and held fast to her arms and ankles. One woman seized a wooden spoon from the table and rolled a dirty floor rag round it.

'This'll do. Push it up her, Edie. See if it's as good as thi old man's prick.'

The lanky woman had taken one of Gran's medicine bottles, left by the sink, and she smashed its neck against the stove. 'This'll do better, duck. Try this up her stinking arse.'

The gag choked Chrissie's screams but tears streamed down her cheeks at the excruciating pain. Then she saw the knife in Edie Pyle's hand and she closed her eyes, ready to die but furious at the ignominy of such a pathetic, futile way to lose her life, a neat perversion of what Gran had foretold.

The knife was not intended to kill, however, only to humiliate. Her head was jerked up from the floor by hands grasping her abundant curls and, triumphantly, Edie hacked at her lovely hair so that it fell about her in thick waving fronds which stuck to her sweat-soaked body. When the shearing was complete, they let her head drop back onto the flagstones and flung handfuls of hair in her face.

'Eh, she's shit herself!' one aggressor screamed with mirth. 'Thought us was set to cut thi throat, did 'ee love? No such luck, slut. Live with thi shame for all to see.'

'See who'll want thee now, flower. Wait on corner of street and see who'll take 'ee for a penny.'

They threw open the door and tumbled her into the muddy courtyard, leaving her there, immobile, as the rain turned to sleet.

*****

She crawled back into the house, dragging herself up the step on all fours, and rolled herself in her tattered skirt, to lie shivering before the embers of the fire. For a long time she could do nothing else and her mind drifted away. She imagined herself bleeding to death, until she realised that the flow of blood had lessened and was congealing. Stray ideas penetrated her pain – the women's capacity for vindictiveness towards one of their own kind who had offended against their code; and the knowledge that Edie Pyle would not have dared to wreak such revenge if Eb was likely to care two farthings about it.

Vaguely she comprehended that the beating he gave her at their last encounter should have alerted her. She had become, like Edie herself, an object for him to use with brutality when the mood took him and doubtless to discard when he chose. Probably he'd found some new bitch to sniff around, new shoulders to caress while he slipped a smart jacket over them, new skirts to lift, new breasts to fondle. Assuredly, he wouldn't want her with her broken body and mutilated hair, marked by the derision of neighbours. Maybe he'd explicitly sanctioned his wife's onslaught, encouraged the viciousness of the she-wolves.

Gran had been right to warn her about the risks she was running with a man like Eb. 'Stupid cow,' she'd called her granddaughter. That's what she was. Only an hour or two earlier she'd been amused to think she could walk away from him in triumph, deluding herself that she would control events and set her own terms. Now she was a laughing stock. Anger began to surge inside her and the anger re-awoke her resolve: in one thing, at least, she had been right. She must leave Tenter Croft. Now: during the night. If only her limbs would stop shaking with cold, with weakness, with fear. If she could get to her feet, staunch her wounds, force herself to walk. She must go.

Carefully she drew her knees under her and crouched while the throbbing behind her temples lessened. Perhaps she was not so very badly hurt. Encouraged, she reached up to clutch the mantelpiece and drag herself upright but, in doing so, she dislodged the loathsome china dog and the shock of its movement jolted her. Black and white shards skittered across the flagstones already stained with her blood, creating a gruesome mosaic of destruction. She clung to the shelf and cried aloud at the agony between her legs as she felt fresh moisture oozing there. With her teeth clamped over her lower lip to stifle further sounds of debility carrying next door, she sank onto a chair, summoning her remaining strength and her willpower.

Hours or minutes later, she could not tell, she pulled herself up the two flights of stairs to the garret which had been her room for eighteen months. The room where Jack had once slept, where he had cuddled and abused a little girl who loved him; where he had held her down for his friend to assault. Those ghosts were redundant now; she had new nightmares to plague her and she was light-headed with pain.

The grey December dawn was scarcely beginning to lighten the sky when she hobbled from the house, to make her way to Victoria railway station. She needed to carry the carpetbag across her chest because, if she took its handles in one hand and let it hang down, the pull on her injured nether-parts was unbearable. The muscles of her arms and shoulders protested at the awkward burden. She told herself she could manage but her progress was slow and irregular, so difficult was it to move her weight from one foot to the other. The sharp jabbing between her legs made her wonder if a splinter of glass from the broken bottle remained embedded within her.

She set herself to concentrate by counting her steps, looking ahead for features by which to mark her progress – a patch of mud by the roadside, a pile of rubbish, a heap of dung. As she staggered away from the crofts, the streets were already busy with men and women hurrying to their workplaces and they elbowed her aside if she was in their way, unaware that the lightest touch seemed to her like a hammer blow. While she struggled up the slope of Snig Hill, waves of nausea overcame her and she huddled in a corner, retching and shaking. When the spasm had passed, she dragged herself a few yards further, before stopping again to lean against a wall as her strength faded.

Across the road a woman with a strange jerky walk was tussling with a young boy. 'Shan't! Shan't!' he shouted, struggling away from Mary Brailsford's grasp. In his tantrum he ran across the road, dodged between the streams of people trudging purposefully in both directions and hurtled towards the spot where Chrissie was propped beside a drainpipe. As he ran, his cap fell off and his scarf came loose. A mass of blond curls broke free and his intelligent blue eyes looked straight at her.

Some distant part of her mind was still functioning, almost in slow motion. With stark precision she registered that this child's father was not the odious Ben Culley but her own adored, perverted Uncle Jack, whose image was stamped on the boy's handsome face.

Despite her pain she could still reason but wished she couldn't. This meant that before Jack corrupted his small trustful niece, explaining it as their shared secret, special and loving between them alone, he'd been sleeping with young Mary – and getting her with child. Maybe he'd only turned to Chrissie when Mary's pregnancy became known and there were murmurings among the neighbours. Maybe he'd always seen her as a second-best substitute. For Chrissie this was the cruellest betrayal of all. The illusion that she was special to him had made the other thing bearable. But there'd been nothing special between them, nothing special for Jack. That was why he sold her to his friend without compunction. He'd have pimped her more widely, as she grew older, if she hadn't told her resentful grandmother what he'd done.

The carpetbag crashed to the ground and she fell back against the wall, fingers splayed, slithering down. There was bile in her mouth and she could feel herself haemorrhaging. She could no longer resist. She sank onto the cobbles as the pulsating behind her forehead intensified and her distraught mind dissolved into welcome unconsciousness.

Chapter 10: December 1861

'She's a pleasant enough little lass. She means no harm. You should be flattered, you great dolt.'

My patience was often strained nowadays. It was nearly two months since I'd returned to Malin Bridge and in a fortnight it would be Christmas. Memories came to me of the previous year's festivities at the Hall. Bunches of holly festooned the porch, where the Bradfield singers clustered and sang carols special to the locality, before they were given plum cake and glasses of punch. Indoors, there'd been the spectacular sight of candles burning around a fir tree, which was decorated with loops of coloured ribbon and paper stars. I'd never seen such a thing before and Mrs Ibbotson told me the Queen's late husband, who had died so sadly in the summer, first introduced the custom from his native German lands. Father would not have approved of the good cheer in mistress's household.

Faced by my truculent brother, I thrust nostalgia aside to concentrate on the troublesome business in hand. Tom's chin jutted stubbornly towards me. 'She's a right menace, Sal. Makes me look daft with me mates. Makes eyes at me and moons about waiting for me to come by. I've got to get rid of her. Can't you talk to her? Tell her to clear off?'

'No, I can't. If anyone's to speak it has to be you. But you mustn't be rude to her. Tell her you're not ready to walk out with any girl, not for a year or two.'

'Tried that. Said she'd wait.'

I couldn't help grinning. Good for Lizzie! Though why anyone should find my spotty-faced sibling an object of romantic interest was a mystery.

'I've thought of leaving Da's forge,' Tom said quietly. 'Get a position in Sheffield. Plenty of openings there for apprentices and journeymen who already belong to the trade.'

'I'd be sorry if you went, Tom. Don't let little Lizzie Simmonite drive you to do anything rash that you might regret. Da would be furious. And think how you'd manage; you'd need lodgings and money in your pocket to get started and you wouldn't know anyone in town.'

'I'd find Chrissie Mallon. Be much easier if I were there all the time.'

'Don't talk rubbish. It's time you forgot her. She's probably wed by now – or employed in something worse...'

'You've no right to speak that way about her.' Tom's temper flared. 'Just because she's pretty and lively – and you're becoming a dried-up old maid!'

I didn't trust myself to reply, pushing him aside and running out of the house. I ran along the street and into the lane by the riverside. I didn't stop until I reached the dell down by the water, where I'd played as a child, surrounded by leafy undergrowth in the summer but now just a muddy space among dead branches. I sat on a frost-rimed tree-stump. Why did I let my brother's silly gibe hurt me? Little did he know! I drew out of my sleeve the treasured letter I'd received that morning.

'Dear Miss Webster,

As I wrote before to you, I was deeply grieved to learn of your mother's death. When I sent my condolences, I felt it was not proper to mention other matters. Now, however, writing to wish you well at this blessed Christmastide, may I make so bold to remind you of my declaration and, as I hope, our understanding. Mrs Ibbotson told me of your decision to remain at Malin Bridge for some time and care for your bereaved family and I respect that, indeed I do.

I would hope, however, Sarah (I may use your first name, mayn't I?), that I may call upon you at your home as soon as the time of your deepest mourning is past. I do so long to see you again and would gladly ride out to Malin

Bridge and address myself to your father, if you think fit, so that our position can be open and honest.

Please Miss Webster, Sarah, please let me have an answer soon. My heart is saddened without you.

Arthur Rawdon'

I kissed the paper with its solemn, sincere words and, in my mind, composed a suitably modest, but encouraging, reply.

*****

It was not only Tom whose footsteps were dogged by Lizzie Simmonite. She'd become my faithful acolyte, eager to hear about life at the Hall. The slight, whey-faced girl hovered at our door, asking if she could help with errands or cleaning, and she trudged with me to the market at Hillsborough, to carry the basket and wheedle the stall-holders into offering bargains. It appeared that, in despair of winning Tom's interest by direct means, she aspired to gain his sister's friendship for a more oblique assault on his affections. Perhaps Lizzie was more calculating than she looked. I found the situation both amusing and irritating but I was sorry for my lovelorn young neighbour. Lizzie and Tom were two of a kind, I thought: both adored the unattainable and appeared to relish the agony of rejection. Neither would abandon what was patently hopeless infatuation.

'Tom's away to Sheffield for the day,' I said when Lizzie joined me on the way to chapel on the Sunday before Christmas. 'Father's in a fury but Tom was set on it. Said he'd go to the service at Carver Street Chapel but I doubt he will.'

'Why was he so set on going, with snow on ground?'

Lizzie knew the answer perfectly well but I took the opportunity to speak explicitly. 'He's gone to look for that

97

good-for-nothing, Chrissie Mallon. It's the third time in as many weeks. I pray he won't find her but I wish he'd cease looking.'

Lizzie sighed pathetically and her eyes filled with tears, which they did very readily. I found this lachrymose weakness over trifles annoying. 'He's not worth your pining. He's only a lad still and he's stupid with it. Best put him out of your thoughts. Don't waste your time.'

'You're maybe right.' Lizzie's trembling voice attempted, but failed, to steady itself. 'But so long as I see him regular like, I can't help but...'

'Good morning, my good lasses.' The boom and rustle of Mrs Groomsley's arrival disrupted our conversation. 'No more chatter now. Us'll best compose ourselves for chapel. I'm glad your father's preaching today, Sarah. He's an awesome harrower of sin, the Lord be praised. Why, love, you'd do well to take that lace off your bonnet now you're come home. It's a mite unseemly for chapel.'

But not for church at High Bradfield, with Mrs Ibbotson, I thought fiercely although I said nothing. Despite his vehemence, or perhaps because of it, I absorbed little of father's sermon. I sat, demure and subdued, between sad Lizzie, constantly dabbing at her eyes and nose, and the self-confident matron who exuded superiority. I grieved anew for mother and for my lost life at the Hall, now I'd written to Mrs Ibbotson explaining I would not be able to return there. I'd written also in reply to Arthur's letter but I feared that my efforts to reconcile the excitement I felt at his constancy with the dictates of decorum might have made its message rather confused.

*****

98

It was well after dark when Tom returned home. Father had gone to preach in Owlerton that evening and I was sitting by the fireside with the Bible before me, obedient to his decree that no other occupation was suitable for the Sabbath. Even so I didn't know where I'd opened it. I was distressed by my brother's look of dejection as he stumbled through the door, beating the snow from his overcoat. He shook his wet scarf vaguely towards the fire, causing the flames to splutter and hiss.

'Tom, you'll be frozen. I'll get you some broth.'

'No, Sal. I don't want nowt.' He sank down on a stool and, horrifyingly, began to weep.

'What is it, Tom? What's the matter?'

Between gulps his words came indistinctly. 'She's gone, Sal. I've lost her. She never... She might...They said...'

'Don't take on so. Tell me straight, what's happened?'

With an effort, he drew himself up. 'I found where she'd been living, Sal. After all this time, got the address – Tenter Croft. Dreary place. Wish I'd found it afore. Came too late. She'd left. Neighbour said she were a bad lot, had to go. Her Gran passed away.'

He struggled to control himself and I didn't interrupt. 'Don't know what happened, Sal, but it sounds as if she were hurt, hurt bad. Neighbour could hardly hide her glee. Vindictive bitch! Said Chrissie were dead for all she cared. Any rate, seems she went one night, never came back. I asked people in the street but no one knew where she were. I even went to Infirmary and workhouse to see...'

'The workhouse? Surely, she wasn't...'

'Thought she might have been taken to one or t'other if she were hurt – or dead even. They said they've no record but I knew they weren't interested to check. She's likely gone right away from Sheffield. Oh, Sal, what'll I do?'

I bit back the obvious answer; it was too callous. Instead I put my arm round my brother's shoulders and sat quietly while he stifled his sobs. Now, surely, he must get over that wretched girl. Maybe poor Lizzie would have a chance after all, if she had the good sense to leave him alone and not pester him for a while. I didn't spend long pondering Chrissie's fate. I presumed the jade had spread lies once too often and reaped a just reward. Yet fleetingly the image came to me of that mischievous, laughing lass, with extraordinary clouds of auburn curls, who could keep her friends in fits of giggles with her audacious merriment.

*****

When Mrs Ibbotson's carriage drew up outside the house, I was sitting on mother's upright chair beside the window darning father's work clothes, struggling to force my needle through the coarse material and not to snag the thread. I flung down my sewing and ran out into the street, to greet my former mistress, in a flutter of joy and apprehension.

'Sarah, my dear. Why, you're taller, I swear. In so short a time.' Mrs Ibbotson's smile allayed my momentary alarm and I ushered her into the house.

'I'm come to see if you'll reconsider,' the old lady said when she'd been served with tea in one of the best china cups with crinkly rims. 'I'd like you back with me and I flatter myself you'd be glad to come if it weren't for your father and brother. Is that so?'

'Indeed, ma'am. If I had no other responsibilities, nothing would please me more. But I can't come. I must stay here. Father insists and it's my duty. I'm sorry.'

I faltered and Mrs Ibbotson looked at me sharply. 'Duty is a harsh mistress, my dear. You may serve her well but she may not requite you.'

'I know. I've thought about it long and hard. But I must stay. I've made my decision.'

100

My visitor sighed. 'If that's the case, I'll press you no more. I wanted to be sure before I make changes in the household and fill your position. I shall need to do so now. Susan has been filling your role while you've been away and I think she'll do well enough as a lady's maid. She'll not be the companion to me you'd become but she's willing and sensible. I'll need to look for a new parlour-maid in her place.'

'Do you have someone in mind, ma'am?' As Mrs Ibbotson shook her head, my words came tumbling out. 'I could recommend a girl, a neighbour here. Her family's quite respectable. She's young but presentable and I think she'd learn soon enough. Her name's Lizzie Simmonite.'

Mrs Ibbotson smiled in surprise. 'That's thoughtful. I'm much obliged. I've no one else in mind. I'll see this Lizzie.'

So it was arranged that, after Christmas, the carriage would call again at Malin Bridge to convey the new parlour-maid to the Hall. I spoke at length to her, urging the good sense of leaving Tom in peace while he struggled with his feelings of desolation, until Lizzie, somewhat half-heartedly, agreed to go. She admitted she was curious to see that different world Mrs Ibbotson inhabited, which I'd described so vividly. To Tom, his sister's success in ridding him of a perpetual irritant was unexpected but well appreciated and he was genuinely grateful. Yet I was troubled by the vacant look, which had come into his eyes since his last visit to Sheffield, and the new hardness in the way his mouth was set. He'd lost his teasing manner towards me and the friction between him and father was festering dangerously.

*****

On Christmas Eve the snow had turned to slush but the clouds hung low and threatening over the hills. As I went about my domestic preparations, I thought wanly that there would be little joy for our household in the absence of mother to preside at our celebration of Christ's Nativity. Mrs Groomsley would join us for the Christmas meal, as she had done for several years since she was widowed. In the past, mother's graceful, generous-minded presence had constrained our guest's censoriousness but I had no illusion I could fill her place in that respect. I feared the brooding atmosphere of disapproval would only enhance father's rigid melancholy and perhaps provoke Tom to unforgivable misbehaviour. Lost in my thoughts, I didn't hear the horseman dismount at the front of the house and was startled by the knock on the door.

Arthur Rawdon stood on the threshold, ruddy from his ride, or from embarrassment, hat in one hand and sprigs of holly in the other.

'Miss Webster,' he began, 'I've presumed to call on you. Mrs Ibbotson said I might bring this holly from her garden.' He looked about shyly for somewhere to put it, not liking to thrust the prickly branches into my hands.

I recovered from amazement and, inwardly exulted, begged him to enter. I took the holly and put it on a chair, then reached again for the crinkly-edged china on the dresser. The kettle was simmering and tea was quickly made, while courteous enquiries as to each other's health were exchanged. An awkward silence followed, for we were both abashed by our proximity, alone together, but I knew what would be correct behaviour and asked about progress on the dam. Arthur seized the opportunity to respond with enthusiasm.

'The embankment is started right across the valley bottom, a quarter of a mile wide. The base is to be fully five hundred feet thick and it will taper as it's built upwards to twelve feet at the top. You should see it, Miss Webster. Even during the winter there's activity everywhere: the labourers with barrows and trucks on rails, moving the stones for facing, and the masons shaping them for the curve of the wall. Mr Gunson, as resident engineer, is in charge of the construction now. Mr Leather seldom needs to visit to check on progress. The heart of the embankment will be puddle clay, that's waterproof, you see. We design engineers have computed how the clay is to be compacted and layered with fine gravel.'

The pride in his voice made me smile with amused affection. 'It must be satisfying to be part of a scheme so ambitious and worthwhile.'

'It is.' He paused, recollecting that he had ridden to Malin Bridge to speak of more personal matters, which did not come to his lips so readily. 'Miss Webster. Sarah. I received your letter. I don't find it easy to set words down on a page, to make them say what I mean. Numbers, calculations of stress and quantities, come to me more naturally. But I wished to speak in person. To say to you, that wherever you are, at the Hall or here or anywhere, I shall be waiting for you, as I promised, and I beg you will wait for me until we are of age and can be wed. Will you truly do so?'

My eyes must have glowed. 'Yes, Arthur, I will.'

'And may I call upon you here from time to time, when I can get away to Malin Bridge?'

'That is a question best addressed to me, sir!'

The outer door crashed against the wall as father strode into the room, stamping his boots on the flagstones and brushing the dust from his hands. The most neutral observer could tell he came as self-appointed spokesman for Heaven's wrath. 'Who is this smart fellow, Sarah, that you think it right to receive him alone in the house?'

Ignoring the rudeness of his words, I kept my voice calm. 'Father, this is Mr Arthur Rawdon, a relative of Mrs

Ibbotson's late husband. He has brought this holly which she's sent us.'

'We thank her,' father replied, emphasising the last word. He turned to Arthur with withering politeness, adopting exaggerated dialect he did not normally use. 'Tha sees, sir, us are not used to entertaining gentlemen in t'house. Us be humble Christian working folk, with a care for us daughter's reputation. Gentlemen may have different ideas.'

'I apologise, Mr Webster. I was thoughtless.' Arthur spoke in confusion. 'But I do assure you I intended no impropriety. I hope I too am a good Christian. My father is a clergyman.' As he caught my stricken look, Arthur's voice faded but he could not retract the misplaced statement. 'He is the vicar of a parish near Huddersfield,' he added faintly.

Father's voice thundered with the fulmination of his preaching. 'We are Methodists of the New Connection, governed by the living Word of God in all our doings. I've no more time for namby-pamby Anglican church-goers than for any other backsliders or sinners. Begging your pardon, sir'.

I squirmed with embarrassment at that sarcastic postscript and Arthur picked up his hat. 'I understand, Mr Webster,' he said coldly. 'I'm sorry I've offended you. I have the highest respect for Miss Webster and would not for the world have caused her distress. I shall not call here again.'

When he opened the door I made to follow him but father thrust me aside. 'You bide here, lass, and beg the Lord's forgiveness for your immodesty and rashness. If he comes again, you'll bar the door, d'you hear?'

'He said he would not come,' I protested, grieving at the apparent finality of Arthur's departure. He had promised to wait for me wherever I was but that was before this appalling encounter with father. Would his promise still hold? Would he write? How could I receive his letters without father's knowledge? How could he still love me after such boorish treatment?

Throughout Christmas, into the New Year and for many weeks, I agonised over these questions while going dutifully about my household tasks. I found no convincing answers and I received no communications.

Chapter 11: Easter 1862

A year ago, I thought sadly, sitting alone in the house after morning chapel, I had watched the first silvery buds begin to open high above the valley, while already on the lower slopes shimmering tinges of green revealed the earliest trees in leaf. A year ago a kindly mistress instructed me in new skills and praised my reading and diligence. A year ago I had waited in a stone-walled garden for the young horseman to ride past and pause to speak of the weather. Then, everything had seemed joyful and intriguing, full of promise for further happiness to come. Now spring had come again. Catkins were already hanging from heavy branches on the riverbanks and shoots were pushing their way through the moss-matted verge beside the lane. I didn't see them as harbingers of fresh delights this year. It was as if my life had come to a standstill, its routine of dreary dedication all I had to look forward to for years ahead, with no prospect of deeper fulfilment.

I could run the house with ease and I took some pleasure in emulating mother's high standards of housewifery. I cajoled and cosseted my melancholy brother, as he matured towards manhood and grew more self-assured in his defiance of father. I suffered father's strict intransigence without complaint, telling myself his increasing severity and short temper arose because he was grieving for his wife. He threw himself even more vehemently into the service of the chapel and between that and his work at the forge he seldom found time to be at home for anything except sleeping and eating. Even at table, his appetite was erratic.

A light tap at the door disturbed my reverie and I greeted my visitor with surprise. 'Lizzie! I didn't know you were come home. How are you?'

'Mrs Ibbotson's gone to her nephew at Penistone for Easter and I'm allowed home for three days to see everyone.' She took hold of my shoulders, holding me at arms' length. 'You're pale, lass, and skinny too. Are you ill?'

I shook my head. I'd been about to say how well Lizzie looked, her cheeks filled out and her hair dressed in a becoming style. 'Still mourning my mother,' I said simply. 'But tell me about things at the Hall.'

Our previous roles were now reversed and Lizzie prattled happily about the novelties she'd encountered in her mistress's fine house, the furnishings and ornaments, guests entertained, fellow servants, the manifold duties of a parlour-maid and her importance to the efficient running of the household. I was amused by this recital and pleased to hear that Mrs Ibbotson was in good health but I struggled to force back painful nostalgia. Ten minutes at least passed before Lizzie enquired after Tom.

'He's gone with father to Grenoside to see an old workmate who's ailing. They left after chapel. They'll be arguing all the way. They've little tolerance for each other these days.'

'I'll maybe see him before I go back to the Hall,' Lizzie said lightly. Then she exclaimed and took something from her drawstring bag. 'I was to give you this.'

I took the small packet, scarcely daring to breathe, and unfolded the paper. Inside lay a handful of rather crushed primroses. On the paper was written:

'I remember and am constant. I can bear this silence no longer.'

I looked searchingly at my visitor, unable to speak for the emotion choking me.

'Mr Rawdon asked if he might write to you. He seemed to think there'd be difficulty.'

'Only that my Da might object and forbid it.' I surprised myself with the scorn of my response and continued hurriedly. 'But I'd be glad if Mr Rawdon wished to write. I'd be grateful if you'd tell him. Father has usually left for the forge on a workday before the post-boy calls.'

Lizzie gave a wicked, knowing smile, an expression I would not previously have expected of her. 'Ooh! It's romantic, lass, and him a gentleman too.'

'You'll say nothing, will you, Lizzie, not to Tom or anyone?'

She giggled. 'You can trust me, love. I weren't born yesterday.'

*****

I'd been right to think the walk to Grenoside and back would be acrimonious. Father returned alone, in time for evening chapel, with clenched fists and fury in his eyes. I was profoundly grateful he was not preaching that night or even the most virtuous would have been blasted to perdition. I accompanied him to the service and didn't interrupt his brooding silence when we returned to the house.

'I'm off to my bed,' he said as soon as the door was shut. 'I've chapel business to attend to in morning. You'll not wait up for your brother, d'you hear me? He's to be let be until he repents.'

I nodded with a heavy heart and shortly afterwards went to my room, where I lay down but didn't sleep. A beam of moonlight glowed on the little jar of primroses and the sight filled me with joy; yet my delight was constrained by fear of father's mood towards my brother.

It was not until the first glimmer of dawn that I heard Tom stumble through the front door and the creak of the fireside chair told me he wouldn't be mounting the stairs to his bed. After another half-hour of disturbed rest, I roused myself to go down and prepare father's breakfast.

The day after Eastertide was a Saint Monday, observed as a holiday by most of the workplaces, but father wouldn't allow himself to rest. His routine was too engrained and backsliding would seem to him a serious transgression. Besides, he'd said he had chapel business to conduct.

To my surprise Tom was not slumped in the chair in drunken stupor but was on his knees, rekindling the kitchen fire. His face was drawn from lack of sleep but it bore no signs of inebriation. 'Morning, Sal. Is Da up yet?'

'I don't think so. Whatever's happened, Tom? He was mortal angry with you last night.'

'And so am I with him. I hate him, Sal, that's truth! I'm done with his lectures and his ranting. It's obvious we can't get on. Yet he won't let me go – won't pass me indentures to another master. He'll try to hold me here to be his dogsbody. I won't have it, Sal. I'll break his bloody neck if he tries to hold me.'

'Tom! What do you mean about your indentures?'

'I'm set on going to work in town, lass, well away from here. Make me own way. But if I haven't got me indentures I'll be outside the trade. No one'll be able to give me work without breaking union rules. He says I'm to stay 'till I've finished me apprenticeship. He's a bastard, a selfish bloody bastard!'

'For pity's sake, don't speak so! I can hear him up and about. He'll be down soon. Don't argue with him. Let you both simmer down.'

'I'll not be stopped, Sal.' Tom spoke defiantly but then he relaxed a little. 'Maybe you're right though. I'll bide out of his way for now. I'll tackle him again this evening. Maybe there's something could change his mind.'

He slipped through the door and I laid out the breakfast things noisily to disguise his departure, battling my horror of what might lay ahead.

109

*****

What lay ahead was not quite what I expected: not at all what I expected, not in a thousand years. It was, I thought afterwards, so startling, so appalling, it was like something from the Book of Revelation, even a portent for the horsemen of the Apocalypse to appear.

Father had disappeared for the day and Tom did not return until late afternoon. When he did so I thought the demons from Hell had taken possession of him, sent him stark raving mad. Flushed scarlet, he flung open the door with a shout that shook the rafters, so that neighbours several doors along the terrace must have quaked with apprehension. He ran forward, lifted me from the stool, where I was peeling potatoes, and swung me in the air, shouting again in jubilation.

'I've got him, Sal! I've got him! The dirty stinking hypocrite. If I'd known afore. Who'd have thought it? You'll not believe it. Foul stinking lecher, he is'

I froze as he set me back on my feet. 'What on earth are you talking about?'

'Our pious, righteous Da, that's what! Had me suspicions. Heard lads' gossip. So I followed him. Caught 'em at it. Up in her house, brazen as you please. At it hammer and tongs. Straddling her great bare belly – like a whale she is – with his little harpoon throbbing!'

'Stop it! Stop it! Don't say such things.'

I screamed, with my hands over my ears. I knew what he was going to say. I wanted to prevent him.

'Sorry, Sal. Forgot you'd be squeamish. But it's true. I saw 'em. They saw me too. There'll be the devil to pay. But he'll have to let me go away to town now, with me indentures and a good character too. I'll have him booted out of chapel otherwise. Can you believe it? Our Da and the Black Crow!'

110

'No! No! No!'

I ran out of the house as fast as my stockinged feet could carry me, down to the riverside, stumbling over roots, splashing my skirt with mud, catching my hair on low hanging branches – just as that other time. I didn't stop until I came to the fallen tree trunk where we'd been sitting and there I sank down and sobbed.

Nearly three years ago, wasn't it? Two carefree girls had sat there laughing together: idle chatter given a frisson of forbidden danger by Chrissie Mallon's giggling account of her Uncle George putting his hand up her skirt. I hadn't been sure I believed it but my friend told a good tale and I'd been tempted to indulge in some sinful speculation.

'How can you say such things?' I'd asked, aghast but enjoying it.

'Don't believe me then?' Chrissie's wonderful long curls had leapt and sparkled in the sunlight as she jumped up from the tree trunk.

'Your uncle's regular at chapel. Surely he wouldn't...?'

My friend started to run uphill, chuckling merrily, and I followed. I was worried our banter had gone too far. There were things that shouldn't be spoken of, certainly not joked about. Sometimes I thought Chrissie was thoroughly immoral and that frightened me. She must have been irritated by my guileless innocence. Breathless, she reached out for the branch of a spindly tree beside the hedgerow and clung to it for a moment, as if uncertain whether to go on, then she swung round to face me. Her eyes, narrowed against the sun, suddenly looked spiteful.

'What a goose you are. Thinking everyone's good because they go to chapel and say their prayers. You don't know half of it.' Then, gulping slightly, she spoke viciously. 'Can't see what's under your silly nose, can you? No more can your Ma.'

111

'What do you mean? What about my mother?'

'Only she's right dim not to know. Your precious, pious father's been bedding Mrs Groomsley this last twelvemonth.'

I'd been a step or two below Chrissie on the slope. I stopped abruptly, swaying from the impact of what had been said. 'That's a dreadful wicked lie,' I burst out. 'How can you say such a vile, sinful thing? My mother's poorly and my father would never commit such abomination.'

Chrissie gave a rippling, mocking laugh. 'He's a man, isn't he, for all his preachifying? D'you think he lives like a monk with his wife an invalid? Or does he come after you now your breasts are formed, and make you serve his turn? Has he put his prick, you know where?'

I'd been incapable of a response. I hurtled downhill, away from my tormentor, squelching through wet leaves, stumbling over mossy tussocks, catching my skirt on brambles, miring it with cow dung. When I reached the riverside, I ran on desperately, away from the village and the forge, into the woods, to hide in the thickest undergrowth I could find. I crouched there, hugging myself, trying to still my shaking limbs, swallowing the convulsive sobs which threatened to betray my hiding place and I stayed in the thicket until the sky darkened. Then I ventured to the riverbank and scooped handfuls of water to drench my face and it was not just tearstains I wanted to wash away. I felt unclean, soiled by Chrissie's words, the filthy thought they conveyed.

When I returned to the footpath, I met Tom, sent to search for me. His cheerful face and childish chatter were reassuring. As we entered the house, father came forward expressing relief that I was unharmed: I was so late, he'd been worrying. He didn't condemn me but returned to his task, which my arrival interrupted. Mother, sitting wrapped in her shawl in the big armchair, hugged me and stroked my hair while father poured gruel into a bowl and carried it to her. He put a gentle hand on her shoulder and, as mother smiled up at him wordlessly, I smiled too. All was as it always had been: slanderous falsehoods could be forgotten. So I'd thought.

From that day I shunned my erstwhile friend and, not long afterwards, I rejoiced when Mrs Ibbotson invited me to go to the Hall and start a new life. I thrust the horrible, lewd taunts out of my mind, dismissed the nightmares which recurred for some while afterwards and disowned the years of childish companionship. I branded Chrissie Mallon a malicious, perverted liar.

And now, I was sure, without a doubt, that on one matter at least she had been abominably correct.

Chapter 12: Easter - May 1862

There were three angels, from time to time, she thought. Mistily, through pain and fever, she'd glimpsed them, concerned and kindly, one face merging with another. At the height of her delirium she hadn't known who they were or why they cared about her but they were always there, soothing, ministering, strengthening. Three women. When she'd found herself smiling wanly at the irony of it being three women who restored her sanity and saved her life, after the depredations of those other females, she knew she would recover.

Of course one of the women, dear Annie, had been responsible for her relapse and the crisis of her illness but Chrissie did not blame her. After all, who could begrudge such a gentle, loving angel her wish to have a friend present at her wedding? So, on Christmas Eve, the invalid had been conveyed in Will Turner's reassuring arms the short distance to Carver Street Chapel, to hold the bride's posy and voice her good wishes in person to the joyful pair. Mrs Turner thought the outing unwise but, not wanting to jeopardise her daughter's happiness, she allowed herself to be persuaded by Chrissie's insistence that she felt well enough to go, frail though she was after those awful events in Tenter Croft. During the service, the bride's mother was too happily preoccupied to notice her patient shivering uncontrollably despite the thick shawl wrapped round her.

In the weeks that followed the wedding, both Annie and Mrs Turner suffered pangs of remorse for the serious deterioration in Chrissie's condition, blaming themselves for their selfish neglect of her welfare. The invalid herself did not hold them responsible. To her, scarcely aware of her surroundings, they were two of her blessed angels, on whom she depended for everything. At times it seemed to her she was fading from the world and the women by her bedside were indeed messengers from heaven come to claim her. Later, her confused mind remembered it would not be to heaven that she would be bound after her demise, unless physical torment in this world could cancel out sins committed here. She clung to that alluring idea and almost regretted slowly regaining her health.

It was perhaps to her third angel that Chrissie owed most. Mrs Crookes' appearance, at the moment of her collapse by West Bar, seemed the nearest she was ever likely to come to heavenly intervention. The explanation was in fact quite prosaic. Dan's mother was making her way, as she did every morning, towards the Public Dispensary Hospital in West Street, where she scrubbed the floors and washed the dishes. She'd gone over to the young woman, fallen unconscious on top of her carpetbag, and recognised her as Annie's friend who helped on the night of the Acorn Street bombing. She looked at the girl's shorn hair with disbelief and saw the fresh blood haemorrhaging through her skirt. Then, summoning the help of another passer-by, she half-dragged, half-carried, Chrissie to the dispensary.

Chrissie had lost a good deal of blood and the doctor kept her in a hospital bed for several days, insisting she must have absolute rest. He would not hear of her setting out anew for the railway station and she was too weak to do more than protest ineffectually. In any case, by that time Mrs Crookes had told Annie and Mrs Turner all she knew of the girl's predicament and, as a result, there'd been no question where she would go on discharge from medical care. So it came about that for the past four months Chrissie had been tended in the little house off Division Street where she rallied, suffered serious relapse and then recuperated.

After their marriage Annie and Dan went to live with Mrs Crookes in Acorn Street so, as her health improved, Chrissie shared a room with the younger Turner girls: Bessie, Mrs Turner's second daughter who had now taken

115

her elder sister's place at the button factory, and Lily who was about to leave home and become a kitchen maid in Broomhill. Will and his brothers shared the third room upstairs.

When she was strong enough, Chrissie helped Mrs Turner in the house and with the piles of mending three rumbustious boys created – where fine stitching was not essential. She saw little of Will who, most days, left early for the grinding shop and returned late after union meetings. She welcomed his absences to save her from the embarrassment she felt in front of him. She couldn't credit that she'd nestled in his arms on the way to and from Annie's wedding, deeming herself light-headed at the time. Now she was acutely aware that he must comprehend fully the reasons for her lodging with his family although he never referred to them. Sometimes she took a surreptitious glance towards him as he sat talking with his mother. He looked paler than she remembered, his face more clearly chiselled in the lamplight, and she thought him the most handsome man she'd ever seen. She tried to shrug away such pointless thoughts but did not wholly succeed.

Chrissie remained in the house most of the time when Mrs Turner went out, not liking to admit, even to herself, how afraid she was of encountering her attackers or being the object of derision by others who'd heard of her humiliation. Occasionally, with her shawl pulled over her forehead, she ventured to the New Market, off South Street, well away from the neighbourhood of Tenter Croft, but she still felt uneasy on these outings. She hadn't abandoned her resolve to leave Sheffield, for it was the only way to escape her miserable past, but the lethargy of weakness was reinforced by the unfamiliar comfort of Mrs Turner's kindness and the sanctuary of a home without violence.

On the Monday of Easter week, Will took time off from his work and it was proposed that the whole family should walk up to the reservoirs at Crookesmoor to breathe the fresh air and admire the view down the valley. Chrissie sought at once to excuse herself, pleading that the climb up Western Bank might be too strenuous for her.

'No, love, we'll take it slowly and rest now and then,' Mrs Turner said, suspecting the real reason for her guest's reluctance. 'Some country air'd be good for you, bring a bit more colour to your cheeks.'

Chrissie shook her head but, surprisingly, Will added his voice to his mother's. 'You can take my arm uphill, Miss Mallon. We'll all be there to help you.'

It was so unexpected and spoken with sincerity she could not persist in her refusal: not when she wanted so much to rest her arm on his again and lean a little on him for support. She accepted his offer before she could stop herself but it was stupid to permit futile fantasies to form in her mind. She had nothing to hope for from his politeness. She'd knowingly rejected conventional decorum and squandered any chance she might have had of respectability. Will knew her for what she was and she doubted he was a man who would seek the company of whores, even in secret.

The little party made their way pleasantly to the reservoirs where the boys ran off to play tag and hide-and-seek in the bushes while the others sat on the grass to watch. Bessie was in high spirits. She related how Mr Copley, once overseer of the women's workshop, whom Chrissie remembered very well, had now become manager of the whole button factory. She described him preening himself, even growing his side-whiskers in celebration. There was much sniggering as Bessie described his pointy rats' teeth and declared they looked ridiculous in the middle of such hairy abundance.

Chrissie learned for the first time that, after her sudden departure from the factory, Mr Copley had asked Annie if she knew what had happened to 'dear Miss Mallon'.

Later, after he heard of her illness – although not, of course, of its origin – he enquired as to her progress, questioning Annie and subsequently Bessie, when she arrived to work at the button lathes. More recently, before moving into his grand new managerial office, he'd requested Bessie to pass on his cordial good wishes both to her sister and to Miss Mallon. Promotion, it seemed, filled him with unctuous goodwill. Chrissie was troubled by this intelligence because, although Mr Copley had been harmless enough, he was part of the life she wished to forget and she didn't like to be reminded of his attentions. Moreover, if he had been able to confirm her whereabouts without difficulty, might not other, less inoffensive acquaintances discover her refuge?

Chrissie walked up and down beside her laughing companions, discontented and thoughtful. She did not notice Will move to her side and gave a start at the sound of his voice so close to her.

'Shall we climb a bit higher, Miss Mallon? The view of the Infirmary and St Philip's Church is better from up the slope.'

Strangely he seemed more out of breath than she was as they crested the ridge and she wondered, for a wild extravagant moment, whether he was creating an opportunity for them to sit together unobserved by his family. She looked at him and gave what she knew was a bewitching smile, slightly cross with herself that flirtation came so naturally even when it was wholly inappropriate.

'Sorry,' he said, coughing and spitting into the grass. 'Us grinders breathe in so much dust off our wheels it clogs up our lungs. Fresh air cleans it all out.'

She murmured sympathetically. Uncle George at Malin Bridge suffered the same way.

'Some of the new works have fans to blow the dust away but old grinding shops don't bother. To my mind the union should press for fans in every workplace but it's not seen as important by some. Too busy with their rattening.'

'Still going on then?' She forced herself to express interest.

'Always will, 'till we get the legal right to collect dues from union members and set down rules we can lawfully enforce in defence of trade. Without that, bullying louts can take over the union and run things for their own purposes: line their own pockets too, I shouldn't wonder.'

Chrissie stood up in irritation. She didn't wish to be reminded of Eb Pyle and his cronies. She'd witnessed the aftermath of the outrage at Acorn Street and knew only too well how abhorrent their violent activities could be. More despondently, she recognised the uselessness of trying to attract Will Turner with her well-tested charms. He must see her only as a shameful, loose woman, although his decency meant he would always behave courteously towards her because she was Annie's friend and his mother's guest. Another man in his place might simply throw her on her back to have his way with her. Despite everything, that unworthy thought excited her.

Chrissie looked down at Will's solemn, worried face and sighed. If she were to strip naked in front of him, he probably wouldn't notice. No, she corrected herself: he would notice and put his jacket round her shoulders to preserve her modesty. She felt bewildered.

*****

After the frustrating Easter outing Chrissie determined she must move on but she was at a loss how to do so without hurting Mrs Turner's feelings. The woman had been so good to her, so hospitable and loving, she'd given a glimpse of what a mother could be, and was willing to be, to a feckless good-for-nothing who was not her own daughter.

119

Chrissie sensed, rather than understood, that it was Mrs Turner's nature to look for the good in everyone and instinctively she responded with trust. The three boys regarded her as another elder sister to tease, while Bessie was quietly affectionate and reminded her of Annie.

Chrissie knew she should be on her knees thanking heaven that she'd found such an undeserved haven from her previous disreputable and dangerous existence. After all that had happened to her, the result of her own stupidity and self-satisfaction, she recognised that her ingratitude and restlessness were perverse. Yet the ordered domestic routine in the household sometimes felt constricting, as if it was forcing her into a way of life which was alien to her.

Above all, Will's indifference was intolerable. As her resilience reasserted itself, so did her yearning to be admired and courted by a man she found attractive. She wondered if he went with other men and was impervious to female beauty. Uncle Jack had told her of such men, living outside the law. Fine one he'd been to speak sneeringly of others! She tried to persuade herself Will was like that, so she might give up her vain obsession but, without certainty, she wasn't convinced. Although it was useless, she still looked through her eyelashes at him and pursed her lips fetchingly. Irrational hope persisted. Every day she resolved to leave the Turners, but still she lingered.

One day in early May she walked to the New Market, pleased that her hair had now grown enough for tiny curls to escape onto her forehead from beneath her tight-fitting bonnet. She was still wary of meeting anyone she knew but the crowded market hall provided a good setting for anonymity and she'd grown a little bolder in venturing out alone. Nevertheless she froze in terror when she heard her name called behind her. 'Chrissie! Chrissie!'

Footsteps were approaching. She was tempted to run, to duck between the stalls and hide herself where the throng was densest, but the man's voice that called was one she half-recognised and it was not Eb Pyle's. Slowly she turned.

'Oh, Chrissie, I thought you'd gone forever. Heard you'd left Sheffield.'

Tom Webster stood before her, bashful as always, clutching his cap which he had snatched from his head as he spoke. He had become a very presentable young man, muscular and tall. His teeth were dazzling.

'No, that were wrong, though I'd thought of going. But I were ill, taken quite bad. Friends took me in and got me better.'

She smiled as she gave her condensed version of events and Tom beamed back. 'I'm glad of that. You look beautiful. Ravishing.'

This was no longer a lovelorn youth to be trifled with, she thought, alert to his new maturity, and she sought to divert the conversation away from herself by asking his business in town. She was startled by his reply.

'Ma died. Live in Sheffield now, I do. Employed by Greaves at Sheaf Works. Had me apprenticeship transferred there. I've got lodgings here in South Street. Just on me way back to work after midday break.'

'You've left Malin Bridge then? Where's Sarah?'

'At home, poor lass. Old man's taken up with the Black Crow, would you believe! They're to wed come Whit Monday and me mother not eight months in her grave. Disgusting, I calls it. Sarah'll be their skivvy, shouldn't wonder.'

Chrissie was staring into the distance with unfocussed eyes, remembering and suddenly grieving for her lost friendship with the childhood companion who had been so naïve and so cruelly deceived. Now Sarah knew the truth.

'When you see her, Tom, tell Sarah I'm sorry. She'll understand. Will you do that?'

He nodded. 'I have to go now, Chrissie, due back at Greaves. Will you let me call on you? Where do you live now? Will you take a walk with me next Sunday?'

At once she became defensive. 'Oh, it's all sudden, Tom. I don't know. Really, I can't. I'm not free, that is I...'

'You've got a young man, have you?'

The desolation in Tom's voice was obvious but his misapprehension offered her a way of escape. 'Yes,' she said. 'I've got a young man.'

He swallowed and spoke huskily. 'I'm too late then. Just when I've found you. Mind, Chrissie, if owt goes wrong, you'll know where I am. Two doors along from here, lodging with Mrs Purkis. If you need help ever, you must find me. I'll always wait for you.'

His eyes were filled with tears as he hurried away from her and Chrissie herself was shaking. How easily lies came.

*****

That evening Will sat at home with sheets of figures spread in front of him on the kitchen table and he looked troubled.

'Put papers away, lad,' his mother said. 'You'll ruin your eyes.'

'Treasurer's sick and I said I'd check accounts. Can't make 'em add up right. I'm fair flummoxed. Needs fresh eyes and a clear head to make sense of 'em.'

'No good looking at me, son,' Mrs Turner laughed. 'Written too small for me to make out.'

'Is it just straight adding?' Chrissie spoke quietly, surprised to hear her own voice.

'Aye, but checking columns as well, to see each sum is entered twice, in and out like'

'I can do adding and I could look for figures. Never could multiply though.'

'Would you look at 'em for me?'

Chrissie moved to the table. There were a great many entries but she made her way through each column, checking the arithmetic ponderously. Then she saw what the problem was. 'Columns don't add up right because some figures have been switched across somehow.'

'Where? Show me, Chrissie.'

It was the first time he'd used her given name and she shivered. She pointed out where there seemed to be discrepancies, acutely conscious of how close he was as he peered where her finger moved across the columns. 'I don't know what it means,' she said, 'but that's why the totals are different.'

He gave a growl of delight. 'I know right enough. Downright thieving! That's what it is. Union dues switched from general fund to secretary's expenses. Money meant to pay men on the box, when they're out of work, used to line others' pockets. I'll get 'em for this, the bastards. Stealing from other workingmen! Men they're meant to stand up for. Damned shameful!' He paused and turned to look at her. 'I'm right grateful, Chrissie. That were good. You spotted it so quick.'

'I'm a bit rusty. Not done adding up like that for a long while. But I could always help if you wanted.'

'I'd like that fine, lass,' he said and his great dark eyes fixed on hers.

They didn't notice Mrs Turner's little sigh of contentment at the revelation that Chrissie could offer Will practical support as well as seduction. It would have astonished both of them that a mother might recognise, before her son did, where his affections could become

123

irrevocably, if unsuitably, engaged. But Mrs Turner believed in the perfectibility of all God's creation and she was determined to pray for the goodness, which must be somewhere in the girl's heart, to be fittingly redeemed from the abuse it had suffered.

Lacking Mrs Turner's insight, Chrissie was perplexed as she crept into bed beside Bessie. She was happy to have helped Will, glad he appreciated her assistance, but arithmetic, in her opinion, was unlikely to lead to amorousness. She also felt another niggling regret: she shouldn't have lied to Tom Webster.

Chapter 13: June 1862

I mulled over my wretched lot while I scrubbed the front step. My hands, which had become smooth and ladylike up at the Hall (aided by a little of Mrs Ibbotson's perfumed lotion) were now roughened and coarse. If that were all I had to trouble me it would be a petty concern but, looking at my broken nails and reddened skin, I saw them as visible symptoms of the anguish I'd suffered since Easter.

In the weeks up to that hateful, unholy wedding father and his betrothed treated me with careful civility, pretending, of course, that their companionship had blossomed only after mother's death. I kept my secret knowledge to myself but I despised them for their deception. After their courtship was publicly acknowledged, Mrs Groomsley came to call every evening and I was expected to sit with them in some strange parody of chaperoning the middle-aged, delinquent pair. I knew, as did all the neighbours, that when father escorted his paramour back to her house he lingered there some time but I tried to dismiss the scene from my imagination. I remembered too well my brother's description of what he'd interrupted when he observed their copulation and thereby expedited their nuptials.

Tom had been as good as his word. The day after he confronted the guilty couple, he obtained his indenture papers from father and set out for Sheffield, where he soon obtained work. I wished him good fortune in the town but I missed his quips and feared he'd abandoned Malin Bridge for ever. He hadn't attended the wedding. Only one workmate of father's was present with me, ostensibly because, father pontificated, it would not be seemly to mark his remarriage with undue celebrations, in view of the shortness of time since his first wife died. Seemly!

125

I squirmed to think of the blatant hypocrisy I was witnessing. I'd always been afraid of father's wrath and felt remorse for failing to meet his demanding standards of rectitude. I'd never loved him, as I loved my mother, but I'd regarded him as a being on another plane of righteousness from ordinary folk, beside whom I must forever be accounted unworthy. Now he'd forfeited my respect and left me bewildered. Not only had his despicable behaviour given the lie to his sanctimonious words but he seemed oblivious of the impact this had on his daughter. The incongruity between his continued expressions of piety and his unforgiving nature towards the transgressions of others was quite lost on him.

More decorous neighbours and acquaintances from chapel undoubtedly whispered in private about whited sepulchres and making an honest woman of one fallen from grace, but they said nothing to me on the subject. Those inclined to be more judgemental spoke to me pityingly and that was difficult to bear. Chrissie Mallon's Aunt Ada, recently widowed herself, laid her hand on my arm and whimpered at me sympathetically. 'Poor child! Poor child! What a den of iniquity you find yourself in – and to think Hephzibah Groomsley was my friend. Have courage in adversity, love. We all must.' Nauseating, maybe, but it showed she understood the situation.

Nastier was the ribald mirth of the village lads who may have hesitated to mock the principals in the scandalous liaison. They enjoyed the safer pleasure of teasing me.

'At it all the time are they, Sal, lass?'

'Gets it up her afore breakfast, does he?'

'How big are her tits, love? Big as cow's udder?'

Once, they would not have dared to taunt Sam Webster's daughter but in their eyes the aura of respectability had been removed from me and I was fair game for derision. Fair game for more direct mischief also, I feared, after I encountered the burly lad from the farm along the lane a week previously. I'd always thought he looked shifty and unpleasant but he'd only ever nodded at me in the past and grunted 'good-day'. This time had been very different. He crept up behind me, while I sat daydreaming on the bank beside the river, and pulled me roughly so that I fell back between his legs. His hands squeezed my breasts.

'Stop it! Let me go!' I screamed but he rolled on top of me and thrust his tongue into my mouth while scrabbling at my skirt. I bit his tongue hard and struggled free as he gulped with pain, but he was both quicker and stronger than me. He forced me to the ground again, slapping my face.

'Bleeding bitch! Think you're too grand for me? Your Da's free with his cock. You can have a bit of mine.' Mercifully, at that moment there was the distant murmur of voices along the path so, cursing, he let me go and ran off, promising to 'fuck'ee right and proper' next time. I'd felt tarnished and terrified.

After the wedding I quickly resolved that I must leave Malin Bridge. Any duty I may have had towards father was discharged and the changes were too great to bear. Mrs Hephzibah Webster had moved from her own house, with all her goods and chattels, and started to throw out anything in her husband's home which did not please her. The best crinkly-edged china, proudly displayed on the dresser by my mother, was now displaced and her beautifully embroidered tablecloths were superseded by plain starched linen. The framed text of *Vengeance is mine* had been allowed to remain on the landing but the delicate scene of Christ, suffering the little children to come to Him, had been ejected in favour of a second text telling, upliftingly, of the fires of Hell.

In my distress I'd written to Mrs Ibbotson, explaining my predicament and asking if my former mistress knew of any situation for which I could be

127

recommended. The old lady replied she would see what she could do but it might take some weeks to find something suitable, so I resigned myself to the necessity of patience. I sought to keep my own counsel, however painful I found the alterations imposed on the household, but sometimes the strain seemed unbearable. My self-imposed confinement made it worse. I'd always enjoyed rambling by the riverside but now I dared not venture outside the village, for fear of the farm lad who assaulted me and threatened worse to come. It was impossible to tell father of that incident because I knew he would see me as in some way blameworthy. He would never concede that his own reprehensible behaviour could have harmed me in any way.

Dismissing these troubling thoughts, I stood up, shook the water from my scrubbing brush and carried the bucket to the outside drain. It was a beautiful cloudless day, at odds with my sadness, and I forced myself to concentrate on memories of the Hall, not so far away up the valley, of my carefree days when I worked there, when I first met Arthur and when nature seemed in tune with my emotions. Dear, sweet Arthur! His short affectionate letters, coming regularly each week, gave me courage to endure my tribulations. Towards the end of the year he would become of age and, even though I would be only eighteen, perhaps if I'd already escaped from Malin Bridge I would be able to marry him. It was my dearest wish.

A new complication had arisen since I gained a stepmother. When I'd been left alone, while Tom and father were at the forge, it'd been easy enough to take delivery of Arthur's letters without their knowledge. I'd written to explain my changed circumstances and to ask Arthur to send his letters in future to arrive on a Wednesday morning, when the new Mrs Webster was away from the house on regular charitable visitations. He'd always complied with this request and today his next letter was due. It was with joy that I saw the post-boy approaching.

'Morning, miss. Letter from Bradfield for 'ee.'

'From the Hall again, I expect. Thank you.'

I smiled, taking the letter with casual unconcern. I didn't know if the post-boy could distinguish between letters from Mrs Ibbotson and those in different handwriting but he seemed disinterested so all was well. The short epistle was everything I could have wished: hesitant and gentle as Arthur was himself, expressing his grief that the changes at Malin Bridge saddened me, encouraging me to take comfort from the passing weeks. Then he signed himself boldly, as he'd never done before. *'Your own ever-loving Arthur'*! Clasping it to my heart I ran up to my room, to read and re-read and then put it, with his earlier letters (and those from Mrs Ibbotson), in the small trinket box I had claimed as my mother's treasured bequest.

*****

Later that day my stepmother asked me to take some broth to an elderly couple who lived a few doors along the street and I stayed there talking to them until I saw father returning from the forge. I walked back with him to our house and he went so far as to express approval of my visit to the needy but my pleasure at this rare endorsement was short-lived. Hephzibah Webster was waiting, standing majestically by the kitchen table.

'Sit, Samuel,' she boomed, 'and listen to what I have to say to this sinful child of yours before you decide what punishment is fitting. Sarah, come here.'

I didn't move but watched with horror as my stepmother drew from her apron pocket a sheaf of neatly folded letters, which she flung onto the table.

'What explanation do you have for these?'

129

My self-control was near to snapping. 'You can see what they are. Letters to me. Personal letters. You have no right to touch them.'

'I have every right, now I am your mother.'

'You are not my mother!'

'Silence, Sarah. How dare you speak so?' Father advanced. 'What are those letters?'

'Some are from Mrs Ibbotson and others from her relative, Mr Arthur Rawdon, whom you met when he called here. He told you he would not call again but he writes to me instead.'

'You did not tell me you were receiving letters. Do you reply to them?'

'Yes, father. Mr Rawdon is my friend.'

'A gentleman like that cannot be your friend, foolish lass.' Father sounded irritated but not at that moment condemnatory.

His wife required a more robust stance. 'Samuel, I asked you to listen. This gentleman is more than your daughter's friend, even if such a role were likely. Hear how he writes to her. *'Your own ever-loving Arthur'*. Ever-loving! What does he mean by that?'

'Not what you are thinking! There's nothing improper between us.'

'Nothing improper! To receive such letters! Samuel, your daughter has squandered her virtue. She is a wanton flibbertigibbet, unworthy to be under your roof.'

'You shouldn't judge by your own standards.' My-suppressed rage erupted. 'How dare you presume to lecture me when you deceived my mother with your adultery? You stole my father and now you steal my letters.'

'Sarah, go to your room!'

Father's voice was icy but he'd turned pale and I realised with surprise that his anger was tempered by other emotions. My fury had hit home and this knowledge drove

130

aside my usual timidity. I lunged forward, sweeping the letters into my skirt. 'I'll go to my room to collect my things. Then I will leave the house. That should please you, stepmother. I've no wish to bide here. Tom knew right enough what it would be like when you arrived. He left in time.'

'Sarah!' Father spoke softly as if his throat were constricted. 'Wait a bit. Hephzibah, I'll speak to my lass alone, if you please.'

His wife looked regally affronted but she turned and swept up the stairs. 'Do your duty, Samuel,' she snapped.

'What you said was sinful, Sarah,' Father began and, as I went to respond, he added quickly, 'but what we did was sinful too, I grant you. We seek God's forgiveness for it daily. You're young, lass, and can't understand such things. Hephzibah is my loving helpmate.'

'You betrayed my mother.' I was implacable and ironically I'd never before sounded so much like father. 'You do well to seek God's forgiveness.'

'We'll say no more, lass, and I'll not stop you leaving. But you can't go tonight. Wait till morning at least. Will you go to Tom in Sheffield? You could maybe keep house for him.'

'No. I shall go to Mrs Ibbotson. She's agreed to help me find a post as lady's maid in a good household. She may let me stay at the Hall until it's arranged.'

Father took a deep breath. 'That would be proper.'

I'd never heard him speak with such humility but, with my new-found rigour, I refused to show sympathy for the transgressor. 'Don't lecture me on propriety!'

'Pray God to keep you from passing hasty judgement.' Father regained a little of his preacher's certainty. 'Remember the word of the Lord! The text is always before us as we climb the stairs: '*Vengeance is mine. I will repay.*' It's not for you to judge. Hephzibah and I will seek the Lord's redemption in our own lives. Look for God's charity in yours and may He keep you in the paths of virtue, lass.'

'Amen,' I said with finality.

*****

Next morning, after writing a short note to Arthur Rawdon, I set out, with a small bundle of clothes and my precious letters, to walk the five miles up the valley to the Hall. The rest of my belongings were packed and ready to be sent on when I notified father where I would be staying. He stood at the door to watch me leave while Mrs Hephzibah Webster kept to the matrimonial bedchamber until her stepdaughter was gone.

I had a jumble of feelings – anger, elation, excitement, nervousness, pride, sorrow – but I concentrated on the practicalities of my journey. I was relieved when I'd passed beyond the furthest fields of the neighbouring farm without seeing my loutish attacker and I made my way cautiously while skirting the edge of Loxley Chase where, people said, thieving vagabonds used to lie in wait for travellers on foot. Rejoicing not to have encountered any such hazards, I eventually reached the village of Low Bradfield where Arthur had lodgings. I knew he would not be at home in the middle of a working day so I went boldly to the house beside the river and delivered my note to his landlady.

Beyond Low Bradfield the last section of the track led sharply uphill and I halted once or twice as I climbed, looking down on the monstrous barricade of the dam wall which now bisected the valley. I knew it was far from reaching its full intended height but already its bulk was prominent in the landscape and I marvelled at the volume of water it was designed to constrain. I marvelled also to think that Arthur was helping to design this formidable project and I glowed with pride that so talented a professional man had chosen me as his intended bride. Then, as I rounded a corner, the Hall and its walled garden were in sight, evoking such joyful memories.

I hurried forward, exultant to have returned, even if briefly, to that place of sanctuary. I rapped the knocker sharply and the door was opened by Lizzie Simmonite.

The parlour-maid had become quite attractive, although unrefined, and she was trimly efficient as she ushered me into the vestibule. She set aside my bundle and courteously invited me to sit, while she went to tell Mrs Ibbotson of my arrival. I noted Lizzie's transformation with mild amusement.

The old lady greeted me with surprise, concerned that I'd come alone on foot from Malin Bridge and alarmed at what might lay behind my sudden appearance. She listened with sadness as I explained in more detail what had happened at home. 'You must certainly stay here until you're suited, my dear,' she said, taking my hand. 'I have hopes that I've found a situation for you. I expect a reply in a day or two. It's with my own nephew who has come to live on the edge of Sheffield.'

'The doctor from Penistone?'

'No. It's his younger brother, Robert Strines, also a doctor. He's been practising in Manchester for a few years but some months ago he purchased a partnership in Ranmoor. I suspect he'll make a good living from the wealthy steel-masters and factory owners who live around there; although I gather he also does some work at the town's Infirmary serving the wider community. His wife's health has been fragile since they lost their new-born baby and the dampness of Lancashire didn't agree with her weak chest. It is she who's in need of a lady's maid. Her previous girl couldn't settle after their move and returned across the Pennines. I've recommended you to Mrs Strines.'

Full of excited thanks, I sat talking happily with Mrs Ibbotson for half an hour and, surprisingly, it was she who raised the subject I was too diffident to mention. 'It's a shame Mr Rawdon is away, my dear. I understand he's gone to Leeds for a week or more, to finalise some drawings and calculations in Mr Leather's offices. He'll be sorry if he misses seeing you.'

She gave me a knowing look but said no more and I looked down modestly, not daring to recognise compassion in her words. I too would be sorry to miss seeing Arthur although I'd been well aware I could not count on a meeting.

Later Lizzie showed me to a guestroom where I could stay until Mrs Strines' reply was come. The parlour-maid showed little inclination to gossip but I felt I should give her news of Tom. 'My brother's left home as well. He lives in Sheffield now, employed at Sheaf Works.'

'I hadn't heard.' Lizzie was either masking her interest or the old infatuation had truly faded. 'I wish him well.'

Lizzie turned back the cover on my bed, treating me respectfully as if I were an honoured visitor. 'Your Mr Rawdon's a rare gentleman, right enough.'

I was taken aback but not displeased to hear this attribution.

'You've seen him recently, Lizzie?'

'He stops sometimes of an evening when I'm in the garden behind house. Passes time of day right polite like.'

I felt the blood rush into my cheeks. It was stupid, I knew. I had no doubt of Arthur's devotion. I had in my trinket box all his letters and his latest ever-loving declaration. We had but to wait half a year and I was now confident father would permit us to wed when I was eighteen. He would see it as resolving his own guilt and the awkwardness he felt towards me. And yet...

Of course Arthur would politely acknowledge Mrs Ibbotson's parlour-maid, I reassured myself. I had nothing to concern myself with on his account. But why was Lizzie in the garden? Was she waiting there intentionally as I had done? Could it be the fickle minx had her own mischievous designs? The agonies of senseless, visceral jealousy were an unfamiliar burden to be endured.

Chapter 14: May - June 1862

'You don't need me to help now, Mrs Turner,' Chrissie began. 'With Lily gone into service and Ned starting at the grinding shop, you'll only have two little 'uns to care for. I'm just an extra mouth to feed.'

'But I like to have you here, lass, and you've nowhere to go. Besides, Will'd miss you bad.'

'Will? I don't think he'd notice!'

'Why'd you say that, love? You're a right help to him.'

'With a few sums.' Chrissie was annoyed. She would have preferred simply to slip away without farewells but she owed Mrs Turner so much, it seemed only fair to explain. Announcing her intentions was also the surest way of guaranteeing she'd carry them out. She'd already delayed her departure for longer than was sensible.

'More'n that. I know my lad. He's a deep one but he's taken to you. He don't do that easily.'

The conversation remained inconclusive and Chrissie did not specify when she would leave. She was angry with herself for prevaricating but the suggestion that Will might regret her departure was too troubling to disregard untested. It seemed completely improbable, yet Mrs Turner was surely the last person to indulge in baseless supposition on such a subject. It was puzzling she should share it with Chrissie herself. There might be mothers who believed a serious-minded son would benefit from the ministrations of a loose woman but it was not credible Mrs Turner was among them. It made no sense.

Nonetheless Chrissie was tantalized by the idea that Will might be attracted to her – might be induced to become her lover: a lover who would never be cruel, she was sure. Perhaps, she reflected, she needed to provoke him into declaring himself, one way or the other. With a different man she undoubtedly would have done so by now but she'd been deterred by Will's austere manner and apparent indifference. On the other hand, if it was encouragement he needed, this was no time for her to become unnaturally bashful.

She created her opportunity by waiting up until he returned home late in the evening, long after the light in the sky had faded and the others had gone to bed. On hearing the latch move, she glided towards the door but stopped instantly when she saw him stagger, ashen-faced, against the doorframe, coughing and clutching his chest. Quickly she fetched a beaker of water and made him sit down until his breathing eased.

'Thanks, Chrissie. Throat got dry after so much arguing at meeting. I went to see Secretary of the union, William Broadhead himself. Nasty piece of work, to my mind. I complained about the way accounts were being kept and what money were used for. There were a right set-to.'

'What happened?'

He looked at her gratefully. He wanted to talk, to share his anxieties, but he feared he would bore her.

'Broadhead's a bully, up to his neck in villainy, I shouldn't wonder. Can't prove anything. He's too well protected – got a bevy of henchmen to do his bidding. I had to make appointment to see him in backroom at the Green Man, bottom of West Bar. Kept waiting an hour or more but I weren't going to give up. Then he sits there like he were a judge, and me in the dock, with his mates ranged behind him. I told him there were false accounting. First, he said I were deluded so I showed him the figures. Then he says end justified the means. Calm as you like. Said money weren't for officers of the union but to pay expenses of the committee – meaning payment for them as carries out rattening and worse. Looked me straight in the eye and asked if I were for the union. When I said of course I were, he tells me to know what's good for me and keep quiet. Otherwise I'd be named

137

as obnoxious to the trade and have to take consequences. After that his cronies hustled me out – Eb Pyle were one of them.'

Chrissie shuddered but said nothing.

'Sorry, lass, shouldn't have mentioned him.'

'It's no surprise to hear he were there.'

'Aye but I weren't thinking.' Will covered his embarrassment by resuming his narrative. 'Thank God there're some in the unions wanting to do things properly but they're stymied – we've got no rights while unions aren't recognised in law. Filesmiths have right idea. Their secretary's a respectable type. He's written to the *Sheffield Independent* setting out the case for unions to have lawful control over members so they can enforce the rules. Us saw grinders have to put up with Broadhead and his menaces to make members toe the line. Police mostly turn a blind eye and when they do act they can't make charges stick. A man called Thomson were arrested for the Acorn Street outrage. Brought to trial, he were, but he's been acquitted at York Assizes.'

Chrissie had her own views as to the perpetrators of that atrocity. 'Maybe they got wrong man.'

'Happen they did.' Will was becoming agitated again, taking rapid shallow breaths. 'Tears me apart, it does. Thinking how Broadhead and his crew abuse men's trust. He threatened me with enquiry by the Investigating Committee if I didn't keep me mouth shut. Investigating Committee! That's the same lousy crowd. Judge and jury they are.'

He started coughing again and spat into a bowl before continuing but Chrissie didn't hear his words. His eyes followed hers to the reddish streak in his sputum and he smiled that bewitching smile which had attracted her on the Whit Walk a year ago.

'It's all right, lass. Nothing to worry about. Dust irritation. Grates on innards – bit of blood comes. Most

138

grinders spit blood sometimes. Dry grinders are worst, mark you. Not so bad for saw grinders – we grind with wet wheels. But in my shop wet and dry works alongside each other, so we all breathes in grit.'

'You shouldn't let union business upset you, Will. For all Broadhead and his mates are rotten, you'll not mend it. You need some other interest, less serious like.'

She smiled at him winsomely, daring to hope her patience as his confidante might draw them closer in a more tangible way. He stared at her and he seemed to have recovered after clearing his throat. 'Whit Week's nearly here again,' he said brightly. 'We could go for a walk, like last year.'

She laughed. 'I'd like that fine but not to Norfolk Park this time. There'd likely be people there I don't want to meet. But we don't have to wait till then, lad, if there were other ways I could help you. I think you need some diversion.'

His eyes were fixed on hers, as if he was absorbed in the intensity of their colour so, taking this as encouragement, she knelt beside him and took his hands. He did not withdraw them.

'You know what I am, Will. You can have me, if you've a mind to.'

He was trembling and she was afraid he would push her away, repelled by her advances, but when he hesitated, she drew his hands to her bosom, pressing herself against his fingers. After a moment he slipped to his knees beside her. Then, with his hands to her cheeks, he kissed her so lightly she was not sure if she'd imagined it.

'Don't throw yourself away on me, Chrissie,' he said, rising.

She gasped in disbelief and reached out to him but he was already on the stairs. She sat back on her heels, astonished by his words and the sadness in his voice, uncertain whether or not he had repulsed her in disgust: whether or not he spoke with dark sarcasm.

*****

Over the next few days neither Chrissie nor Will referred to what had taken place so ambiguously between them. She helped him look through more columns of figures and he expressed his thanks politely. She avoided flirtatious behaviour. She lowered her eyes without looking up through her lashes and she took care to set his broth on the table without bending forward so he could see down the top of her bodice. Yet she didn't sense he felt resentful or awkward with her. There was no evident strain when they spoke to each other. But they were always in company when they did so.

Chrissie feared Will would abandon the idea of their proposed outing after her rash offer of unwanted intimacy, so she was pleased when he told his mother what they planned. Unaccountably, as before, Mrs Turner expressed her delight and busied herself, first thing in the morning of Whit Monday, filling her son's knapsack with hunks of bread and cheese and onions. Then, as the banner-carrying, hymn-singing processions poured out of the town towards Norfolk Park on their annual walk, Chrissie and Will made their way in the opposite direction, climbing the hills to the north of Division Street, until they passed through the seemingly deserted village of Walkley. Outside the unexpectedly ornate building of the Primitive Methodist Chapel Will stopped, as if deep in thought, before speaking in a quiet, determined voice.

'That's where I was to have wed.'

Chrissie stared at him in amazement.

'Three year back. Fanny her name were. Prettiest little thing I'd ever seen. Her Da worked with mine. Known

140

her since she were small. She were seventeen and I were four years older when I spoke to her and we gave each other promises to wed. Then me Da took bad and it weren't right to think of marrying right away.' He paused.

'Didn't she wait for you?'

He shook his head. 'She were true as finest steel but we'd no sooner buried me Da when Fanny sickened. Four days she fought it but her frail little body were no match for the fever. Within a sennight I were back in cemetery with her family laying her to rest.'

'Oh, Will, I'm sorry. I never knew. Annie never said nowt about it.'

'Fanny and me hadn't said much because of Da being ill. I told Ma but Annie wouldn't have known the truth of it. I've not talked about it since.'

They walked in silence until they crested the ridge overlooking the Rivelin Valley where the wide panorama of woods and fields spread before them, down to the sheltered river. To their left the dale rose westwards to the steep moors while, to the east, further down the valley, Malin Bridge was screened from view. Chrissie was glad she couldn't see the village although she recognised with discomfort some of the lower slopes where she and Sarah Webster had played. She was relieved when Will struck off to the left towards less familiar ground and soon the track took them up onto a rocky outcrop.

Across the valley the spire of Stannington church rose like a tiny needle through the rim of tree-cover, silhouetted against the horizon. The rough pastureland of the moors was dotted with specks of grey, which could equally well be boulders or sheep, and here and there a glimmer of water shone through the undergrowth by the riverside. Absorbed in the peaceful view, they smiled at each other and sat down to eat Mrs Turner's carefully wrapped provisions.

'I've been a right fool,' Chrissie said softly, 'thinking you had no time for lasses. Flaunting meself and trying to bring you on t'other night. You must have been disgusted.'

He took her hand and she found the movement distressing. 'No, Chrissie. Never disgusted by you. Saddened.'

'Because I'm a filthy whore? Because I've been with others?'

'Because you've thrown yourself away on men who've use you callously. You're worth more'n that.'

'How can you say that? You know what I am.'

'I knows what you've been like, but I knows what you could be, if you'd a mind.'

She was irritated, thinking he was patronizing her or about to preach on the need for redemption and forgiveness. She hadn't expected him to be sanctimonious. 'What could I be then?' she snapped.

'My wife, Chrissie, if you wanted.'

She pulled away from him, trembling. 'Don't mock me, Will. I were wrong to tease you but I'm sorry for it.'

'I mean it, Chrissie. I'm mortal serious. When Fanny died I thought that were the end of my hopes for a loving wife, that there were no other lass in the world for me. Till I met you a year ago and then I knew different. I tried to set it aside, this new longing I had. It didn't seem likely you'd be interested in a solemn lad like me, who couldn't give you pretty things and wanted a livelong partner, not just a roll in the hay. You're so full of life. You could crook your little finger at any man to have him come running. But it's no use, Chrissie, no use at all. You're like no one I've known and I'm straight bowled over. I love you.'

'How can you say that? You know...'

'You said that before. Come here.'

He drew her to him, down into the newly budding heather, kissing her with none of the restraint he had

142

displayed previously. Her impetuosity matched his but their lovemaking was tender and she let her doubts slip away. Later, however, as they lay side by side, she smiled ironically to herself, amused that he'd thought it necessary to dress up his lust with words of decent propriety.

As if reading her thoughts he turned and kissed her softly. 'I meant every word, love. I want you for my wife. But I'm not so daft to think you'd like to have a grinder for husband. It's a hard way of life and you could do better'n that. I'll not press you. I know you need time to think on it. Don't answer now.'

Chrissie had started to tremble uncontrollably again. She was about to protest that Mrs Turner couldn't be expected to welcome a trollop into her family but she realised, as soon as she'd formed the thought, that this was exactly what the good woman had already done. Will's mother saw into her son's closed heart and wanted him to recognise what lay within it. Chrissie knew this was not a time for her usual wilfulness or a wholly frivolous riposte but neither must she be too intense.

She kissed Will. 'I'll think on it right enough, you great randy goat,' she whispered.

*****

They walked back over the hills hand in hand as dust fell, both wondering whether Will's mother would be able to see from their appearance what had happened between them, whether she might be looking out to see if it had happened. Mrs Turner, comfortably plump and homely, was not a great conversationist and all her family, except perhaps Annie, failed to discern her powers of perception. She missed little that affected them and judged astutely where their interests lay. She was the pivot on which the household turned.

The house was alive with activity when they arrived, the younger boys chasing each other around the room with whoops of excitement, while Bessie was hugging her mother. Annie and Dan, come to visit with the elder Mrs Crookes in tow, looked as if butter wouldn't melt in their mouths.

'You're to be an uncle, lad,' said the five-months bride archly to her brother, pecking his cheek. Then she flung her arms around Chrissie. 'And you'll hold the baby at christening, lass. You'll not refuse.'

Chrissie grinned, nodding, at her sheer unsuitability for such a role. She needed no further proof she'd already been embraced into the Turner family but she hadn't shed her own uncertainties. She knew doubts would creep back, insidiously, when her elation moderated. Will understood her too well, framing his unexpected proposal as he had and giving her time to reply.

Marriage? Respectable marriage was surely every girl's dream? Yet it was not, she'd believed, a future open to her. So how, when it was offered, could she hesitate? She was too clear-sighted, not deluded by romantic notions. She knew what marriage to a grinder would entail. Hardship. Toil. How could there be excitement? Boredom was more probable. The prospect of boredom unnerved her. She wanted Will in her bed night after night without question but was she ready for what else this proffered relationship might involve? Truly, she did not know.

*****

Two mornings later she was still pondering the question. Her desire for Will and her dread of being pinned down and trapped in drudgery battled with each other. The balance shifted from hour to hour.

She set out for the New Market in a reverie, scarcely glancing at her surroundings. At the corner of Division

144

Street a freshly painted gig was waiting but she wasn't aware of it and, as she turned the bend in the road beside it, the sound of her name being called was startling. She looked around fearfully and realised she was being addressed by the driver of the gig, a smartly turned-out fellow who raised his silk hat to her.

'Miss Chrissie Mallon! I rejoice to see you well. You'll remember me, Nathaniel Copley, at your service.'

'Mr Copley!'

'I'm afraid I alarmed you, calling out so rudely. I've waited in the hope of seeing you three or four mornings lately. I heard you were living nearby.'

She ignored the implications of this announcement. 'I heard you were made manager of the whole button factory.' She looked at the gig with admiration.

'I've had a double stroke of luck, Chrissie. I may call you so, I trust. Will you come for a ride and I'll tell you my good fortune?'

'I'm going to the market in South Street.'

'Then I'll take you there. Have no fear, lass, you'll get there safe and sound.'

It was too tempting, to be handed up into the fine vehicle and sit beside the elegantly attired man. She appraised him and decided he actually looked quite pleasing now his moustache was thicker and his luxuriant sideburns covered his pallid cheeks. Bessie had been wrong about his rats' teeth: they were less obvious beneath his whiskers.

'I mustn't be long.'

'Nor will you be, Chrissie. But let me tell you how it comes about that I'm sitting here in such comfortable array. I am indeed become manager of the factory but I've also received an unexpected inheritance from an aunt I hardly knew I had. My circumstances are greatly changed for the better. New horizons have opened. Been introduced to the Mayor. May seek a place on the town council myself.'

'I'm pleased for you, Mr Copley.' She was sure he didn't need her endorsement, so overwhelming was his pride and complacency.

Chrissie noticed that when they turned out from Division Street he switched the reins into one hand and, as the horse slowed its pace, his free hand slid to her thigh. She pulled away from him and he brought the gig to a halt.

'I've been searching for you, Chrissie, since my fortune changed.'

She stared at him without speaking.

'I've never forgotten you. Missed you at the factory. You must have known how I felt. When I had my good fortune I wished you were there. Tried to find you. Now I can make you an offer, fair and square.'

'What offer?'

'I'll set you up, Chrissie. In your own lodgings, decent and well supplied with nice dresses and fancy goods, with your own allowance, free to come and go. If...'

'If?' she repeated, both astonished and appalled.

'If you'll be my mistress, Chrissie. Strictly mine, you understand. I'll visit whenever I can, several days a week after leaving the factory, before I return home.'

'You've got a family?'

'Mrs Copley and five little ones. They'll know nothing. I'm acquainted with how these matters are conducted. The landlady of the lodgings I have in mind has been recommended to me by a respected gentleman. I understand she's a most discreet and proper person. She will tend to your needs – take care of anything that may befall.'

He was leaning close, the cologne on his whiskers nearly choking her, and he'd taken her hand. 'Will you accept?'

She pulled herself to the edge of the seat. 'I'm not free,' she said feebly.

'You're not wed?'

146

'No, but...'

'Then consider how what I offer will weigh against any other's proposition. Take a while to think and in the meantime I have this for you – a token, no strings. It's your own, come what may.'

She could not restrain a gasp of pleasure when he lifted a box from the floor of the gig and extracted a low-crowned blue hat with curling grey feathers. It was the height of fashion, which she had admired since she saw such hats on the Whit Walk last year. It would look glorious against her auburn hair. He bent forward and threw back her shawl, revealing her short curls. He was clearly surprised that she no longer had the long, coiled tresses he remembered but he smiled as her miniature ringlets blew around her face in the breeze. Brushing them from her forehead, he set the captivating hat on her head. The feathers fell gracefully beside one cheek. He stroked her neck.

'I can't take it.' Her protest was half-hearted.

'No strings,' he repeated and bent to kiss her throat. Again she made a weak protest. For a moment he smiled at her lasciviously, then he jerked the reins and they moved on, quickly covering the short distance to the market, where he handed her down from the gig with the utmost courtesy.

'My offer stands, Chrissie. I've already waited long months for you. I'll wait again if necessary. Send a message to me at the factory when you're ready. Let it say: *'Your blue hat awaits'*. Then I'll make all the arrangements and come for you. I'm offering you a comfortable life, lass. Think about it.'

He leaned from the gig and kissed her.

'I'll think.'

Chrissie hurried into the market, disorientated, blind to the crush of people and the stalls of produce. She leaned against a wall, shaking with incredulity. Why had this

147

happened? Why, at such a moment, compounding her uncertainty? Why hadn't she sent Nathaniel Copley curtly about his business? Why hadn't she rejected the low-crowned hat with its intriguing grey feathers? How could she even contemplate his offer when set against Will's honourable, true-loving proposal? She had no answers but she was thinking of the richly clad ladies she'd seen driving out to the Botanical Gardens in carriages last year, in their silks and velvets. She wondered if some of them were less respectable than they'd seemed. Assuredly they were not the wives of grinders!

She removed the hat carefully from her head and returned it to its box.

Chapter 15: June 1862

Mrs Ibbotson received her nephew's reply four days after I returned to the Hall. It was effusive and encouraging. He and his wife were deeply grateful to receive a recommendation regarding a possible lady's maid from his esteemed aunt, whose discernment was unquestionable. They would be ready to meet the girl at her earliest convenience. Subject only to Mrs Bella Strines confirming her suitability, Miss Webster could be engaged at once.

I smiled as Mrs Ibbotson read out the letter. 'I'll start out in the morning, ma'am,' I said, even as I remembered that Arthur Rawdon was not expected to return to Bradfield for another day or two.

'Saturday will be time enough, Sarah, and I'll accompany you in the carriage. You can present yourself to Mrs Strines while I reacquaint myself with young Robert. I've not seen him for several years, not since his wedding day, in fact, when Mr Ibbotson and I attended the celebrations in Penistone. He was newly qualified then and shortly to move with his wife to Manchester.'

'What is Mrs Strines like, ma'am?'

'I only saw her that once. She was a very pretty bride, small-boned, inclined to be frail, I shouldn't wonder. They made a handsome pair. Robert was a fine-looking young man; may have run to stoutness now, like his brother. He seemed devoted to his Bella. Such a sorrow they have no living children. There's still time perhaps but Mrs Strines was very ill after her last confinement and the baby died after a few days.'

'How sad. Poor lady!'

'You must help build up her spirits, Sarah. Now, I shall write at once so they may expect us on Saturday.' The old lady gave a playful grin. 'Perhaps Mr Rawdon will return before we depart. I'm sure he'd be glad to see you.'

*****

Arthur did not return and I was forced to write him a second note, explaining where I hoped to be living in future and referring him to Mrs Ibbotson for confirmation. I sent this to his lodgings where it would be waiting for him on his return, doubtless along with my earlier, hand-delivered letter describing my departure from Malin Bridge. I hadn't known he was away from Bradfield when I called there and it was unlikely the landlady would have forwarded my message to him without an explicit request. That Saturday morning I looked fondly at the house by the river, as we passed in the carriage, and peered along the track leading north from the village in case we should encounter Arthur returning from Leeds; but we did not.

Although we were not due to join Dr and Mrs Strines until three o'clock in the afternoon, we'd set out early so that Mrs Ibbotson could visit an old friend, now an invalid, who lived in Broomhall. This would conveniently permit me to call on my brother in South Street. I'd written to suggest this arrangement and, as he was due to work that day, he invited me to come during his midday break before he returned to Sheaf Works for the second shift. I duly presented myself to his landlady, Mrs Purkis, who stood blocking the door, appraising me closely.

'Sister, are 'ee?'

'Yes, ma'am.'

'Aye, I see likeness in the eyes. Come on in with 'ee. Don't normally allow young females inside. Respectable house, this is.'

I was amused by the idea of Mrs Purkis, as gatekeeper, protecting my brother's virtue. Then, as Tom came hastening out of his room to greet me, I could see that after three months in town he had become a quite likely target for the attentions of a certain type of young woman. Taller than ever, muscular, clear-eyed and modestly be-whiskered, he would be a desirable catch for any scheming hussy.

'Sal, lass! Good to see you. Come in. I've some bread and sausage ready.'

I thought he seemed more staid, less spontaneous, than usual. There were faint vertical lines above his nose, which made him look older, and there was an unfamiliar sadness in his expression.

'Tom, are you well?'

'Right enough. Sit you down. I were glad to hear you'd left father and that great cow. Found a good place in Ranmoor, have you?'

'I hope so.'

After we'd exchanged news and shared our meal, Tom stood up. 'Have to go soon, Sal, back to Greaves. Working extra shift, we're that busy. It's hard graft but I'm learning more than at Da's forge, earning more too.' He fingered his shiny new pocket watch hanging from his workaday waistcoat.

'Tom, there's something I wanted to ask you.' I must have sounded awkward and my brother looked at me quizzically. 'Do you know where Chrissie Mallon lives?'

He sank back in his chair as if he'd been punched in the stomach. 'Why'd you ask? Thought you hated her.'

'I was wrong. I did her an injustice. I thought she'd lied to me but I discovered she hadn't. What she told me was true. I'd like to apologise to her.'

'She's a bad lot, Sal. Have nowt to do with her.'

Astonished by this reversal of our attitudes towards Chrissie, I reached out to take my brother's hand. 'What do you mean, Tom? Have you seen her? You said she might have gone away.'

'Seen her twice. Spoke once.' There were tears in his eyes at his recollections but he pulled himself together hurriedly. 'Saw her couple of months back. She were looking lovely. Told me she'd got a young man. Sorry to hear that, I were.'

I sighed, accepting the explanation for Tom's air of melancholy as all too credible. It was bound to happen but he'd get over it.

'She asked after you again, Sal. I told her what had happened at home, about Da and the Black Crow. She asked particular that I should tell you she were sorry. Said you'd understand.'

I swallowed. I understood all too well. 'But you saw her again?'

'Aye. Saw her for what she is too. Her young man's no decent working lad but some toff with a smart gig. Just leaving me lodgings, I were, back to me shift at Greaves, when I saw them. Outside the New Market. He handed her down from the gig like she were some fine lady. Wearing a feathered hat, she were. He kissed her, right there in street. She's some man's fancy woman, kept in frills and furbelows. No wonder she's no time for the likes of me.'

His hand travelled again to his pocket watch and I fancied something glistening was intertwined in its chain: something very fine, like a hair. Surely it couldn't be? I dismissed the foolish idea. Tom was simply checking the time. We parted at the door of his lodgings and I walked to the house in Broomhall to re-join Mrs Ibbotson.

I felt immensely sad, sorry for Tom's rude awakening to the inadequacies of his fallen idol, regretting my own intransigence towards Chrissie. Illogically, it seemed possible that, if I hadn't rejected my childhood friend as a foul-mouthed liar, the mischievous, knowing girl might not have descended into the pit of immorality. Now I'd come too late to apologise and Chrissie had become a lost soul.

152

****

The three-storeyed, detached house was approached up a short drive through a well-stocked garden. While inevitably not so impressive as the Hall, in location or architecture, it was nonetheless solidly imposing. It was given extra cachet as a desirable residence for a rising professional man by its proximity to the fashionable church of St. John the Evangelist (a place of worship so over-patronised that a new building was proposed). Mrs Taylor, the housekeeper, greeted Mrs Ibbotson sedately and led her into the drawing room before taking me upstairs to Mrs Strines' private sitting room on the first floor. The heavy curtains were partly drawn but, through a gap, a beam of sunlight fell across the room illuminating the mistress of the house.

The delicate-looking lady, reclining on a chaise-longue, covered in a peacock-patterned wrap, was extraordinarily beautiful. Huge pale blue eyes gazed at me from a small symmetrical face with a dimpled chin. Soft swathes of impossibly fair curls tumbled from beneath a tiny but elaborately ribboned cap. Her voice was mellifluous.

'Come nearer, Miss Webster. Stand in the light so I can see you better.'

I obeyed and as if with an effort Mrs Strines raised her head from the velvet cushions. 'Turn round. Take off your bonnet.'

I did as bidden and stood, bonnet in hand, regretting my unremarkable features and dull brown hair, straight as a plumb-line, coiled into a knot at the back of my neck.

'You have been well trained by Mrs Ibbotson, I hear.'

'I try to be a credit to her, ma'am.'

The lady pulled herself up on the cushions, throwing out one arm dramatically from beneath the wrap. 'You left my husband's aunt on the death of your mother, I believe, but have now quitted your father's house.' The statement implied a question.

'He's married again, ma'am. They have no need for my assistance and I wished to resume my work as a lady's maid.'

'You speak well and your looks are seemly. Are you a good girl, Sarah?'

I was surprised by this direct enquiry and blushed, remembering the way my temper had flared at Malin Bridge and my misguided repudiation of Chrissie Mallon. 'I hope so, ma'am. I try to be.'

'Do you have a beau? I allow no followers at the house.'

Honesty seemed the best policy. 'I correspond with a young man, ma'am. We have an understanding although it's not publicly known. He isn't yet come of age. There's nothing improper in our friendship.' Honesty did not go so far as to refer to Arthur Rawdon as a young gentleman.

'I believe you, Sarah. You seem to me truthful and well meaning. God keep you so.'

'Amen.' It came mechanically.

'Well, my good girl, I'll take you as my maid if you are content to stay.'

'Oh, yes, indeed, ma'am.'

'Go now and ask Mrs Ibbotson to come up for a short while so I may greet her. Then I will rest. Later you can assist me to dress for dinner. Dr Strines and I dine away from home this evening.'

I found Mrs Ibbotson with the doctor, a handsome stylishly-dressed man in his late thirties, who had not run to stoutness despite his aunt's presentiment. I gave Mrs Strines' message and, as the old lady was escorted upstairs by the housekeeper, I moved to leave the drawing room at the same time.

'Sarah, isn't it?' I was surprised to hear myself addressed in a rich bass voice.

'Yes, sir.'

He looked me up and down and smiled pleasantly. I found myself smiling back and quickly lowered my head.

'Have a good care for my wife. She isn't strong.'

'Yes, sir.'

'You may wait here until Mrs Ibbotson returns. Sit down.'

'Thank you, sir.'

He left the room and I sank into the thick upholstery of the nearest chair. It was not so grand a household as that of my former mistress but it seemed welcoming and my new employers were considerate. I thought myself very fortunate. When Mrs Ibbotson returned, I accompanied her to the carriage and unloaded my own small bag of belongings.

'I hope you'll be happy here, Sarah. Did you like Mrs Strines?'

'She's very lovely and kindly too. She seems to me like a lady in a novel, almost ethereal, a little languid perhaps.'

'Languorous is the word, in my opinion!' The old lady laughed. 'She'll be a charming mistress, I'm sure, and you must try to cheer her. She's still mourning her baby.' Mrs Ibbotson climbed into the carriage and looked up at the house. 'My nephew is prospering in his profession.' She pursed her lips approvingly. 'I dare say his demeanour is pleasing to some of his wealthy patients, though I find it a mite ingratiating myself!'

I was delighted that Mrs Ibbotson sometimes shared such irreverent comments with me and we both laughed again.

'I'll not say more, Sarah, for this is to be your home and I believe they will be kind to you. Write to me sometimes and tell me how you fare. Be a good girl now you're out in the wicked world of Ranmoor.'

I was still smiling as the carriage drove out of sight. I turned to enter the doctor's fine house, vastly amused by Mrs Ibbotson's impish sense of humour. Wickedness in Ranmoor seemed highly improbable, I thought.

*****

Later that afternoon I enjoyed arranging Mrs Strines' remarkable hair. Soft as a baby's, it fell in a mass of corn-coloured curls so that, however it was pinned and looped, it always looked delightful. The pearls that were then interlaced through it gleamed richly, as did their counterparts at the lady's throat and wrist, where I dabbed a little of the heavy perfume which my new mistress said came from Paris. When I smoothed the folds of pale pink silk over the wire hoop of the crinoline, draping them carefully, I was gratified to be praised for my efforts.

Next morning more sober outfits were worn for attendance at church but Mrs Strines looked just as charming. I was proud to sit along the pew from her and the doctor, next to the housekeeper, and to note the respectful way they were addressed despite their recent arrival in the neighbourhood. The church had a large and distinguished-looking congregation and, after the service, the doctor was assiduous in greeting acquaintances and, no doubt, potential patients. His wife, accompanied by her maid, returned home before him so that she would not need to stand about while he conversed.

That afternoon the doctor went riding while Mrs Strines rested. She took out her embroidery and I marvelled at the tiny, perfectly executed, stitches. I remembered my mother's skilful needlework but knew it could not rival this delicate artistry.

'Would you read to me while I sew, Sarah?'

'Why, yes, ma'am.' I looked round for a Bible which would provide appropriate passages for reading on a Sunday.

'Do you read poetry?'

'A little, ma'am.'

'Read to me from this.'

She handed me a well-worn volume bound in stout drab boards, opened at the title page showing the names of three poems by John Keats.

'Read me the *Eve of St Agnes*.'

I had never encountered such a work before but I was soon enthralled by the tale of knights and ladies, the legend of the Eve on which a maiden might dream of her lover and the daring Porphyro who entered his enemy's house to gaze upon his beloved Madeline. The verse seemed to me to sing with its romance and sensuousness:

...her vespers done,
Of all its wreathed pearls her hair she frees;
Unclasps her warmed jewels one by one;
Loosens her fragrant bodice; by degrees
Her rich attire creeps rustling to her knees...

I remembered how, the previous evening, I'd helped my mistress undress, before leaving her with her husband. The poetry was so apt and beautiful but I was embarrassed at the thought that the chaste girl in the poem was observed all the while by the importunate young man. I shivered while I read how he gazed on the empty dress and crept to the bedside. The idea of the intruder breathing in the scent of the abandoned garment was strangely troubling. I was relieved to find he sought Madeline honourably, as his bride, and rejoiced when they rode away from her hostile kinsmen: *lovers fled away into the storm*. As I finished reading, I sighed.

I was surprised to see tears on Mrs Strines' cheeks for the lady must surely know the poem well. 'You have a gift for reading poetry, Sarah. Isn't it wonderful? Such passionate, pure love. Have you ever sought to dream of a lover on St Agnes' Eve?'

I blushed, uncertain how to answer, thinking what father would say about such ungodly behaviour.

'Not the young man with whom you correspond? Don't be shy. I'm only teasing you. But next St Agnes' Eve – it's in January, I believe – you must see if the spell is effective. You must lie in your bed, supine and naked, and see if the vision comes.'

I was disconcerted by my exotic mistress's imagination and by the excitement I'd felt myself while reading the poem. The contrast between the new household I'd joined and my family home at Malin Bridge was remarkable. Whatever sins of the flesh my hypocritical father had committed, he would never allow such poetry to be read in the house – least of all on the Sabbath. I rejoiced that I was no longer in thrall to his puritanical constraints but in service with employers of elegance and sophistication.

*****

The next day I was to learn that life in the house at Ranmoor was not entirely lived on a plane of artistic and romantic elevation. During the morning I encountered the doctor's assistant, Dick Jewitt, who came each day during the week to assist as required, sometimes accompanying Dr Strines on his rounds and, under instruction, making up the mixtures he prescribed. This young man was not appealing to look at, with a protruding jaw and thick lips below flaxen brows and bushy hair several shades darker than these excrescences. I was reminded of an unfortunate mongrel dog in my village with ill-assorted hybrid colouring but I

158

reproved myself for such a thought. Mr Jewitt was intent on being amiable.

'Miss Sarah, delighted to meet you. Doctor Strines said you'd come. You and me'll get along fine, I can see. Betsy, Mrs Strines' maid in Manchester, was a rare pal of mine. Your hand, miss. My, what pretty fingers.'

I withdrew my hand quickly when he attempted to stroke it and from then on I sought to avoid him as much as possible but, as the week progressed and I went about my work, it was often necessary to pass the doctor's consulting room and the adjoining pharmacy. I concluded it could be no coincidence that Mr Jewitt was almost always at the door when I went by. He sought to be helpful, offering to carry piles of laundry I was bringing from the scullery, but, when on one occasion I let him hold the door for me, he stroked my cheek as I passed and I had to ask him to desist.

Another time I protested because he'd put his hand on mine as I turned the doorknob to the drawing room and this led him to leer at me unpleasantly. 'Don't be standoffish, Miss Sarah,' he purred. 'We're meant to get along, you and me, serving the same household as we are. Can't resist those dainty fingers of yours.'

He raised my hand towards his lips but I pulled it away. 'Please don't touch me, Mr Jewitt. It's not proper.'

He smirked and walked away but, later as I was bending down to retrieve some swatches of silk, which had been left on a chair in the hall after Mrs Strines' dressmaker had called, I felt a sharp nip on my bottom. I twirled round, furious and upset, but the consulting room door was just shutting.

I reflected with annoyance that Dick Jewitt was a menace I must learn to tolerate for I would be too embarrassed to report his conduct to my mistress. I reassured myself that, as there were always other members of the household present in the house when he was at work, there was no need to be seriously afraid of what he might do. I must not over-react for that might provoke him to even worse behaviour. Even so, he was an irritant, a pest, disturbing my otherwise joyous Elysium.

Chapter 16: August 1862

Despite prolonged bouts of morning sickness Annie continued to visit her mother several times a week and sometimes the elder Mrs Crookes accompanied her. The pregnancy had become very visible and Chrissie felt sorry that her friend's figure was coarsened and distorted. The younger Mrs Crookes revelled in her expectation of maternity, as did both prospective grandmothers, but Chrissie could not share their ebullience, did not understand why any woman should so eagerly embrace a life of domestic drudgery and thraldom.

Chrissie kept her truculence to herself but it fed her misgivings about her own future. Over the past few weeks she'd studied Mrs Turner's daily life, trying to see herself, day after day for years ahead, toiling to keep pokey rooms sparkling clean, to launder and polish, to darn and make do and, probably, to feed increasing numbers of small mouths. She'd grudgingly kept house for Aunt Ada and, still less willingly, for old Martha Bamforth, although that had been offset by the companionship of the button factory. In these cases, however, there'd been a realistic chance of escape, in due course, to something more adventurous and alluring, at least something less humdrum. She now spent her time helping people of whom she'd grown fond, but she feared what became routine would inevitably pall.

Marriage, she thought, would follow a predictable pattern. She too would become thickened, her belly distended from childbirth, her breasts sagging from giving suck, her eyes dull with tiredness as she hauled herself up the stairs, hand over hand on the banisters, each weary night. Could she find joy in motherhood that seemed so antipathetic to her at present? Will too would change as he grew older, losing his thick curls, his complexion greyer, wracked by coughing and shortness of breath, tormented by physical weakness and perpetual union annoyances. Would she still love him? Would he love her?

In the here and now their passion for each other blossomed richly. There were few occasions they could be alone in the house but, like many other courting couples, on summer evenings they made their way out of town to the meadows with long grass and shady bushes where they could lie together, persuading themselves they were unseen. She was content for this rapture to continue, unsullied by thoughts of practicality and settled domesticity. Will did not press her to commit to matrimony but she, while hating the idea of compulsion, agreed that, if she were to find herself in the family way, she would wed him without delay. She teased him then, when his fervour was intense, suggesting he was set on getting her with child to exact fulfilment of her promise. Yet as she continued barren, she wondered secretly whether her mauling by Edie Pyle's companions had damaged her irreparably and she would never bear a child. Inconsistently, given her repugnance towards childbirth, this possibility gave her no comfort. She thought of Aunt Ada and Uncle George. A childless marriage might be sterile in more ways than one.

As the weeks passed Will was more than ever absorbed by disputes within the union and between trades, yet he spoke less freely about them, answering in discouraging monosyllables to her questions. Chrissie found this worrying, because in the past he'd seemed to welcome the chance to speak to her of his concerns. She worried that, despite his restraint in not urging her to commit herself, or perhaps because of it, he was suffering from her reluctance to formalise their engagement. She suspected Will's mother also felt the stress of waiting for the announcement the older woman so obviously wanted.

During a period of unusually hot weather Mrs Turner strained her back lifting a tub of laundry and needed to rest.

She was fretful that Annie had not visited for a whole week and Chrissie offered to go to Acorn Street next morning to check that all was well.

'You've not gone that way for a while, love, have you?'

Chrissie appreciated the delicacy with which Mrs Turner alluded to her continuing avoidance of that part of the town in the vicinity of Tenter Croft and West Bar.

'I'll do well enough now, I reckon. Be good to see Annie.' Hastily she changed the subject, looking directly at Will's mother. 'You've been happy with your family over the years, haven't you? With all your work and troubles, you're always cheerful.'

Mrs Turner smiled broadly, arms akimbo, clearly recognising the reason for Chrissie's unexpected enquiry. 'I have right enough, lass. Nothing's made me happier than me children. Mean the world to me they do.'

'You've had a hard life though.'

'Not over yet, love, thank the Lord! It's had its troubles but none worse than most. Everyone has troubles. No use to dwell on it, you have to get over them. When Will's Da died I doubted I'd manage. But I had to, you see. Eight mouths to feed and only Will earning but we all rallied round. Annie went to button factory. I took in sewing and Bessie helped me. We got through.'

'How old was your husband when he died?'

'Forty-one all but a month or two. Not a bad age for a grinder, all things considered. Some goes much younger.'

'Was he ill long?'

'Years really. Came on him slowly. Usually does. Grinders' disease they calls it. Clogs their lungs so they can't breathe proper.'

Chrissie nodded, thinking of Will. If his father's experience was any guide, he might have sixteen years left, maybe more. It seemed a reassuringly long time. Nothing to

163

worry about. Sixteen years: while his coughing grew worse and his strength diminished, while she watched and struggled to make ends meet and lost her figure and her looks. Sixteen years of her life mapped out irrevocably.

Later, while Mrs Turner dozed, Chrissie went to the tiny bedroom she shared with Bessie and drew her threadbare carpetbag from under the bedstead. Carefully she lifted the box hidden under an old shawl and took out the low-crowned blue hat with grey feathers. She put it on and looked at herself in the small cracked mirror on the wall. It suited her so exactly. It was bewitching. Who'd have thought Mr Copley would have such impeccable taste?

*****

Next morning she made her way to Acorn Street by a somewhat circuitous route, avoiding the vicinity of Tenter Croft. In spite of the heat she pulled her shawl forward and scurried with small steps, instead of her normal fluid stride, annoyed with herself for this attempt at disguise. She was relieved to reach the Crookes' front door without incident and knocked quickly, scarcely glancing at the house nearby which had been the scene of the outrage on the night her grandmother died.

Annie opened the door. She looked well, her cheeks fuller than of late, but the fleeting glimpse of happiness in her eyes was rapidly replaced by something like awkwardness or embarrassment. 'Chrissie!'

'Surprised to see me? Your mother's right worried about you, not coming for days. Have you been ill?'

'I'm well enough, nowt wrong with me nor baby.' Annie still stood in the doorway as if reluctant to let Chrissie enter.

'Then why've you not come? What's the matter, lass? Can I come in?'

164

Without speaking Annie let her pass and followed her into the kitchen. There was no sign of the elder Mrs Crookes.

'I'm glad you came, love, though I'd not expected it. Tell Ma I'm sorry not to see her, that I miss her bad. But I thought she'd realise, know I couldn't go there now, on account of all what happened.'

'What are you talking about? Why can't you come? What's happened?'

Embarrassment was replaced by doubt in Annie's voice. 'You don't know? He's not said?'

'He? What? You mean Will?'

'You really don't know!' Annie sank onto a straight-backed chair by the hearth. 'Oh, I'm right sorry. I didn't want to worry Ma more'n she must be. Took it for granted Will'd have told her.' Her hands were scrabbling at her apron, twisting the material before smoothing it again.

'Tell me what's happened. Will's said nowt but he's been unusual quiet these last few days.'

'He and Dan have had a great to-do. Came to blows, shouldn't wonder, though Dan don't say. Over union business as usual. Dan got furious with what the unions were doing, said they were pack of charlatans or worse, feathering own nests from subs of honest men.'

'But Will thinks the same way! He had it out with his union secretary months back. Showed how money'd been switched about in the accounts, though it didn't do much good. Will agrees with Dan. Why should they argue?'

'Dan's gone further. He says Will's a milksop, set on changing union from inside, talking fine but doing nowt. Dan's had enough waiting. Says unions don't stand up for workers who want to get ahead, make something of themselves. Unions want members all kowtowing to what the officials say. Set unfair rules to stop men joining the

165

trade. Come to head now, it has. Dan's walked out of his union. That's what riled Will most. Now they don't speak.'

'And Dan's forbidden you to visit your mother?'

'Not forbidden exactly, he wouldn't do that, but I knows he wouldn't like it. Not when Will might be there, any rate.'

'Will isn't at home during the day!'

'No, love, I know.' Annie's lips had begun to tremble and her eyes were filling with tears. Her apron was screwed into a ball. 'But now we've got the other problem.'

'What other problem?'

'Hurt his hand, he has. Two days back. His wheel cracked and a bit flew off. Cut hand at base of thumb, nasty deep cut. Been off work and this morning the cut looked real angry, turning septic. He's gone to Dispensary. Mrs Crookes' gone with him. I'm right worried.'

Even while she spoke, they heard the creak of the front door and they both turned as Dan and his mother came in. Seeing his right hand heavily bandaged, Annie ran to him.

'What's doctor say, love?'

'Cleaned it up, put ointment on it. Says I'm not to use it for a few days and go to see him again. Hopes it'll mend all right.'

'Hopes?'

'Aye, lass. If it turns bad, I'll lose me hand.' He spoke lightly, with a laugh, soothing Annie in his arms. Then he acknowledged Chrissie.

'Thank you for coming. Annie's missing her mother but she don't like to visit. Neither of us wants to see Will.'

'She must come round in the mornings like she used to. Mrs Turner's strained her back and can't get out just now. She's worried for Annie and it seems she's good cause.'

'We'll manage. Tell her we're fine enough.'

'But you're not! If your hand...'

Chrissie stopped, catching the fierceness in Dan's eyes. She understood he did not want to discuss his injury further in front of his wife, so she extracted a promise that Annie was free to call on her mother and said goodbye. The elder Mrs Crookes came with her to the door.

'I think you've got some credit with Will Turner, lass. See if you can get him to understand Dan's side o' things. Annie's taken it so to heart and I'm fearful for the baby.'

'He can be pig-headed where the union's concerned,' Chrissie said doubtfully.

The older woman sniffed, 'Aye, lass, they all can. No sense, men.'

*****

Returning, bravely, along West Bar, Chrissie remembered her collapse there, eight months previously, remembered how the unmasking of Mary Brailsford's son, her uncle's son, had proved more than her maltreated body could bear. It was strange how, after she was assaulted, it was that petty incident, the final affront to her self-esteem, which crushed her remaining strength. Lost in painful recollections, she stared blankly at the woman rounding the corner towards her, as if it was only to be expected that she should imagine seeing again that wraith-like childhood friend with her uneven gait. Then she stiffened, rousing herself, realising this was no hallucination. Mary was equally startled, staring at Chrissie as if she too was a spectre, before turning aside to pass by without acknowledgement.

'Stop, Mary! It's all right. There's nowt to hide now. I know it were Jack got your lad on you. I've nowt against you.'

'I thought you were dead, Chrissie. Saw you here on pavement, blood soaking through your skirt. Thought someone'd done for you.'

'Nearly had. But I lived, as you see. Where's your lad? What's his name?'

'Bertie. I've boarded him out with folk in the Shambles, down by the Ponds. He'll learn their trade in slaughterhouse – butchers they are.'

'So soon? He's no more'n a little 'un.'

'I'm to be wed, Chrissie, come next Saturday. Moving out to Darnall. Sid don't want no other man's by-blow in house but he's happy enough to take me without the lad. Besides, I've another on way.' She patted her stomach complacently.

'I've wondered about what Jack did to you. Did he force you and give you baubles to keep quiet?'

The bride-to-be gazed at Chrissie in disbelief. 'Didn't you know, love? T'were well known all around, your Uncle Jack and that Ben Culley was after all the little lasses. Right twisted pair they were, God rest 'em; got their deserts, they did. Funny how things goes though. It's Ben Culley's young brother, Sid, I'm to wed. Solid and steady as a rock, he is.'

'I'm glad, Mary. Good luck to you.'

Chrissie continued on her way, unwilling to prolong their conversation or to dwell on what she'd just learned. She'd laid that part of her life to rest eight months ago. Further revelations, embellishing her childhood history of delusion and betrayal, were meaningless. Yet the blade of new comprehension cut her deeply.

*****

It was not difficult to get Mrs Turner to take to her bed early that evening as her back was painful and the younger boys were already asleep. Bessie, when she returned from visiting a friend after work, was also tired and Ned, who'd recently discovered the attractions of the alehouse, trundled upstairs bleary-eyed, with Chrissie's encouragement. Then she embarked on her solitary vigil, waiting for Will once more. It was very late when he eventually crept in, surprised to see her sitting in the dark, lit only by a dull gleam of moonlight through the window.

'Chrissie! Why're you up so late?' He sounded almost accusatory.

'Waiting for you, Will. I need to speak to you. I've seen Annie.' No point in beating about the bush.

'She came here?'

'No. I went to Acorn Street. Your Ma's been fair frazzled fretting about her not coming to visit. Why didn't you tell us what had happened?'

'Union business.' The incontrovertible, unanswerable assertion.

'Will, it's their business too, your Ma's and Annie's. They're caught in middle.'

He sat down heavily. 'Can't help it. Defence of trade's sacred. If that goes, we all goes with it. Union's the best safeguard. Keeps up the wages what feeds us. Dan's trying to opt out, have his cake and eat it. Can't do that.'

'But you know there's corruption in the union, things done you don't agree with. Why turn on Dan when he says same thing?'

'You know nowt, Chrissie. 'Not your business. Dan's turned traitor to the trade.'

The harshness of his tone was bitter to her, as cruel as if he had struck her across the face, but she would not be browbeaten. 'You've been happy to talk to me about the union afore.'

'Well, I'm not now. Keep your nose out of it, lass, and tell Annie to do same. She can come and see Ma when I'm at work but there's to be no women's gossip about the union. D'you hear me, Chrissie?'

169

He'd never spoken to her in this way before and she bridled at his words. 'Who d'you think you're talking to, Will Turner? I'm not your bloody wife to order about!'

His mouth quivered and he took her hands. 'We mustn't quarrel, lass, but try to understand. I love you and wants to wed, but you must trust me to know best in some things.'

'Especially about the bloody union!'

'I wish you wouldn't speak so crude.'

'Oh! Sorry, I'm sure! It's me background. Never taught to be respectable, I weren't.'

Her sarcasm was lost on him but he attempted to draw her onto his knee. She stood rigidly in front of him, rejecting his advances, unwilling to be mollified by caresses. She would make one more effort to persuade him.

'Dan's hurt his hand. Off work. May be serious. His wheel cracked.'

'It happens.' Will shrugged, taking out his pipe and starting to clean it.

'That all you can say? Annie's your sister!' She was infuriated by his nonchalance. Then the horrifying thought came to her and she froze, her eyes fixed on him, enormous and luminous. 'Perhaps the wheel cracking weren't no accident!'

He set down his pipe, glaring back at her. Slowly he rose and took hold of her upper arms. 'What does that mean?'

'You told me yourself there's worse than rattening done sometimes. What if the nuts on his wheel were jammed on purpose so it would shatter when he tried to turn it?'

'You think I'd do such a thing?'

'Not you, Will, but others in your bleeding union.'

'Don't say that!' He released her and turned away, his voice gruff. 'But if it was true, he'd have brought it on himself. He'll get no sick money from the union. He's outside union now. A knobstick!'

His coldness appalled her and she spat out her response. 'Eb Pyle called you by that name once, Will. Aren't you ashamed to use it of Dan?'

He span round, lines of fury creasing his forehead. 'He called you a floozy too!'

'Perhaps he were right on both counts!'

She rushed to the stairs, desperate to escape, heedless of what she was saying, wanting to hurt him, but Will caught her arm. His face was stricken and he started to cough.

'Chrissie, don't say that. Don't do this. I shouldn't have said what I did but don't set yourself up against the union.'

'Goodnight, Will.' She tossed her head and marched up the stairs, upright and scornful. The shadows hid her tears.

Chapter 17: August 1862

Mrs Taylor, the housekeeper-cook at Ranmoor, seemed to take a fancy to me early on, perhaps appreciating my modest demeanour and genteel diction. She sometimes invited me to join her for tea in her snug, heavily-furnished room in the attic, next to my own, when Mrs Strines did not need attendance. She was immensely proud of the household she served and an enthusiastic chronicler of the virtues displayed by the doctor and his wife, especially the doctor.

'Fair broke my heart, it did, when their little mite died,' she said mournfully, as she had on several previous occasions. 'Only three days old, he was: the image of his father.'

'I pray Mrs Strines may fall for another baby.'

'Amen, my dear. Doctor goes to her bed every night. None could be more attentive. She's such a little thing, though. Narrow hipped, not made for easy child-bearing. More's the pity. The doctor's such a fine man, so respected and admired. Half his lady patients are in love with him. He deserves children – handsome sons, like himself, and charming daughters. You're fortunate to have such employers, Sarah. We both are.'

I was cheered by Mrs Taylor's confidences, indelicate though some were. Our tête-à-têtes made me feel valued and secure and I ventured to mention the single blot on my domestic landscape. 'Mr Jewitt has been with the doctor some time, I think?'

She looked at me sharply. 'Come to us three years ago in Manchester. Good enough assistant, I suppose. He'll not become a doctor himself: without the talent or the connections.' She pursed her thin lips. 'Has he been troubling you, Sarah?'

172

'Not troubling exactly, Mrs Taylor. I make no complaint, you understand, but he does pay me attentions I don't welcome. I wish he were a little more distant.'

'My judgement would be he means no harm but the doctor will tolerate no nonsense from him, believe me. Don't concern yourself but leave the matter with me, dear.'

I had no wish to pursue the subject further, reassured by the housekeeper's words, but I wondered what she had in mind. Perhaps Mrs Taylor would speak to Dick Jewitt herself, although it fell well outside her sphere of responsibility. Nevertheless, I thought her formidable enough to undertake such a task and sufficiently intimidating to moderate the young man's behaviour, so I was satisfied to leave things in her hands.

*****

Mrs Strines' spirits rallied somewhat and she seemed happy when I read to her from her favourite volumes of poetry and the latest instalments of novels printed in the penny journals. Sometimes she would sing, in her clear soaring voice, and I listened entranced, marvelling how such a powerful sound could emanate from so slight a form. Mrs Strines and the doctor went out often in the evening, when they were not entertaining company themselves, and I was astonished by the whirl of activity which comprised their social life.

My own little world was contented. My collection of treasured letters grew by the week and Arthur Rawdon's declarations of devotion were enchanting, although scarcely so romantically ardent as those in the works of fiction I read to my mistress. I received occasional misspelt and stilted letters from my brother and I wished he would cease to mope after losing his last hope of wretched, unreliable Chrissie Mallon – I didn't care to be reminded of Chrissie.

Steadfastly, I did not correspond with my father and stepmother and I dismissed them from my thoughts.

One evening Doctor and Mrs Strines returned early from the theatre as the lady had developed a severe headache. I attended her, gave her the cordial which soothed her when she was afflicted in this way and left her to rest. I was returning to my own room when there were screams outside the house and a pounding on the front door. I heard Mrs Taylor bustling to answer it and then all was pandemonium, with shrieks and groans and shouts for the doctor to come at once. Cautiously, I leaned over the banisters and peered down.

A portly woman, greatly distraught, supported a tall, rake-thin man across the threshold. He was clutching a battered felt hat and his face was streaming with blood. I'd seen the pair in church, with their unassuming daughter, but did not know their names. I hurried down the stairs to help as the doctor, in his smoking jacket, came from his study. The injured man's wife was screeching and sobbing, her words incoherent and hysterical.

'Shall I run to Mr Jewitt's lodgings to fetch him here to help?' Mrs Taylor asked the doctor as he examined his patient.

'No, thank you. You'd best take this good lady and get her some tea. Good strong sweet tea. I don't think Mr Paterson is as badly hurt as all that. Can you make it into my consulting room, good fellow? Sarah, would you mind assisting me? You're not afraid of a little blood?'

'No, sir.' I had no time to be amazed that I should be asked to help Dr Strines. I opened the door for him to enter the consulting room, while he supported Mr Paterson, who seemed liable to crumple at the knees, and the housekeeper led the tearful Mrs Paterson down to the kitchen. The doctor inspected the man's head more closely and, indicating a pile of clean cloths, asked me to soak some in water to make a cold compress. He wiped away congealing blood from the patient's forehead and cheek and then picked up the misshapen hat which had fallen to the floor. A small ragged hole was visible in the brim.

'You've had a lucky escape, my friend. The bullet went through the edge of your hat and scraped your forehead but the wound is not deep and will heal easily.'

Fresh blood was still seeping down Mr Paterson's chin and I was not surprised that the doctor instructed him to open his mouth. I was surprised to be addressed directly as I fetched more wet cloths. 'Do you know, Sarah, why there's so much blood from this other wound?'

'I think the gentleman may have bitten his tongue, sir. That makes a lot of bleeding.'

'Capital! You're brighter than some of my students at the Infirmary! How do you know that?'

'My brother bit his tongue badly once, when he fell out of a tree he was climbing.'

'Well remembered. Here, Mr Paterson, you see our excellent lady's maid has it all correctly. In the shock of being fired on, your teeth have given your tongue a rather nasty gash. It'll be sore for a day or two but will quickly mend. The soft flesh there restores itself rapidly. What you need is a little brandy to steady your nerves.'

As the patient took the glass, he grew calmer and slowly described what had happened. He and his wife had been driving home in their gig, passing a nearby plantation at the side of the road, when a shot rang out and he had lurched forward, believing himself seriously injured. Mrs Paterson, with great presence of mind, had seized the reins and driven straight to Dr Strines' but the sight of so much blood had reinforced their belief that her husband was near to death, the victim of attempted murder.

'Are there any with such a vicious grudge against you, Mr Paterson? It could perhaps have been an unlucky shot by lads out rabbit shooting. It's a clear night for such mischief.'

'I'd like to think it were lads, doctor, but I fear not. I've a small grinding shop and I've had arguments with union men seeking work there. Won't entertain them, I won't. Only cause trouble. Try to tell masters how to run their business. I've had threats lately. That was no accident.'

The doctor escorted Mr and Mrs Paterson the short distance to their home and returned on foot to find me still rinsing out the bloodied cloths in his pharmacy. I'd been recalling to myself all that had occurred, proud to have been of use to Dr Strines and full of respect for his professional aplomb and reassuring manner.

'You shouldn't have troubled with these, my dear. Mr Jewitt could have seen to them in the morning. But I'm glad you're here so I can thank you for your help.'

'I did little, sir.' I could feel myself blushing.

'A level headed assistant is what a doctor needs in such a case. The main requirement is to give confidence to the patient whose nerves have been shaken. He was little harmed physically.'

'Could it have been intended murder, sir? Is such a thing possible?'

'I'm afraid it is, Sarah, although I can't be certain that was the case. There's been trouble enough in the town from maverick members of the unions who don't recoil from using violence to support their cause. At the Infirmary a poor woman died last year after a bombing at a house where she lodged in Acorn Street. A second woman, wife of the intended victim, I believe, is still receiving treatment for her injuries.'

'I didn't know, sir.'

'Don't be afraid, my dear. This is as near as such dangers will come to you here. You're safe with us in Ranmoor and we're greatly pleased with you.'

He opened the door and held the lamp for me to see my way across the hall. I passed him as he was speaking and he pressed my hand lightly with his final words. For a long time afterwards I cradled my palm, which had been so favoured by his pleasantly firm and courteous touch. I knew that henceforth I would yield nothing to Mrs Taylor in the extent of my admiration for Dr Strines.

*****

Next morning I encountered Dick Jewitt in the hall outside the pharmacy door. In the week or two since I mentioned his attentions to Mrs Taylor, I'd found his behaviour towards me less worrying. He'd taken to rolling his eyes and clasping his heart when he saw me alone and I knew he would take my hand if he had the opportunity, but I kept my distance and nothing untoward had ensued. On this occasion he succeeded in surprising me, emerging from behind the hallstand where he'd been screened by the coats of Dr Strines' patients.

'Coolheaded and capable, as well as beautiful!' he exclaimed, stepping forward with hands clenched to his chest. 'I must have a care for my position. Dr Strines is full of your skill in assisting him with the unfortunate Mr Paterson. Says I must look to my laurels for I have a rival in the house, potentially as able and talented as myself!'

He struck a dramatic pose, head thrown back with one hand to his brow, and I couldn't help but laugh at his histrionics. He peered at me through his fingers.

'Dr Strines is amused to tease both of us, I think,' I said, suppressing the foolish excitement I felt at hearing the doctor had praised my modest efforts, albeit in jest.

'Oh, I'm happy, Miss Sarah. I've made you smile at last. Such radiance! And that little flush of mirth creeping into your cheeks. I'm smitten beyond all reason.'

177

'You will recover I'm sure, Mr Jewitt. And you need not fear too greatly for your position. I have no wish to spend my days mixing potions and the like. Mrs Strines' cordial is the limit of my ambition.'

'Wit, modesty and charm!' He opened the drawing room door and let me pass unmolested.

I was pleased with myself for countering his impudence in a jocular manner. Maybe this was how to handle him. After all, his attentions could only be light-hearted, for he had called me beautiful and I knew I was not. It was part of a game, I decided, which could provide innocent amusement: I was learning the ways of the world. Nonetheless, I was relieved Mr Jewitt attributed my blushing to enjoyment of his tragedian's posture, because I knew well it derived from joy that the doctor had expressed appreciation of me and I wished no one to know that.

*****

Arthur's letter, which I received a few days after the stirring events of that evening, was tantalisingly obscure. It spoke of a possible surprise, which he might be able to spring on me, and of the piece of good fortune, which he hoped would soon be his. I stroked the paper and set it in my trinket box along with my other treasures but, caught up in my duties for the rest of the day, I didn't give the mystery much further thought, content to await its resolution.

The next Saturday afternoon I was reading to Mrs Strines, seeking to put interest and excitement into one of Mr Wordsworth's more ponderous works, when I heard sounds of arrival downstairs and surmised that the doctor was entertaining one of his medical friends who called from time to time. Shortly afterwards, however, my recital was interrupted by Mrs Taylor entering and speaking softly to our mistress, whereupon Mrs Strines sighed.

'The doctor asks that you attend in the drawing room, Sarah. A visitor has come whom he thinks you would wish to meet.'

Wondering if Mrs Ibbotson was paying an unexpected call, I hurried downstairs but when I opened the drawing room door it was no gracious old lady who greeted me. The doctor and his companion both stood as I entered and Arthur Rawdon extended his hand.

'Mr Rawdon is my kinsman by marriage, Sarah. I think you may know this and I believe you are acquainted with the gentleman.' There may have been a hint of amusement in the doctor's voice but I was too confused to notice.

'Sarah, how good it is to see you.'

'Mr Rawdon, Arthur...'

The doctor laughed loudly. 'I am the intruder here, I know. My presence is profoundly *de trop*, as the French would say. Don't let Mrs Strines know that I've left you alone with a personal visitor, Sarah, for you're aware such callers to the house are not allowed. But I have an urgent need to consult some diagnostic notes, forgive me.'

He left the room chuckling and Arthur moved forward to take both my hands.

'You look glowing. Life in Ranmoor suits you.'

'I'm fortunate and happy in my position but all the more so to see you. How have you managed to come?'

'I claimed a remote kinsman's privilege, although I've never met Dr Strines before. I needed to see you so much.'

'Your letter spoke of a surprise. I never thought to see you here in person.'

He slipped his arm around my waist and I smiled with nervous pleasure at this unprecedented effrontery, although I wasn't sure if such intimacy was quite proper.

'I must use our time alone to speak quickly, Sarah. My father is ailing and I've made so bold as to tell him that,

179

when I'm come of age at the end of the year, I mean to marry. As I knew would be the case, he wasn't enthusiastic but he's cheered by the idea that he might see a grandchild before he weakens too greatly so he will give us his blessing.'

My surge of anxiety was perplexing. 'I'm glad, Arthur. Oh, I'm sorry about your father. The unexpected sight of you here has taken me so unawares I don't know what to say...'

Gently he held me to him and kissed my lips with gossamer lightness. 'Will you accept my ring, Sarah, as token of our engagement?' He held out a small gold circlet with a single turquoise stone.

'I won't be allowed to wear it in the house.'

'But you will take it?'

'Yes, Arthur. With all my heart.'

Again his lips brushed mine and I put my arms around his neck, nestling against his chest, satisfied that such behaviour was sanctioned by convention for a formally betrothed couple. Then a prolonged and noisy coughing outside the door prevented any further proximity and we were standing several feet apart when the doctor re-entered the room.

'My young cousin-in-law tells me he's been engaged in the design of the great dam at Dale Dyke and is shortly to move to another project.'

'My other news, Sarah, which I referred to in my letter. My role in the work at Dale Dyke will be finished before the end of the year, although construction will continue more than another twelvemonth. When I've completed my indentures, I'm to move onto designs for the Agden reservoir, which is to be built further up the valley, and I will have two assistants in my new role.'

'That's good fortune indeed. Will you remain at Low Bradfield?'

180

Arthur smiled broadly. 'With my greater salary I propose to take larger lodgings there, beside the river. They're modest but decently appointed and they'll suit very well, I think.'

I lowered my head to hide an awkward smile, for I knew he meant the lodgings would suit both of us very well and the prospect both entranced and alarmed me. I was strangely relieved when he left shortly afterwards, bidding goodbye formally, but I held his ring hidden in my clenched hand, treasuring the sensation of its solidity pressed into my palm.

As Mrs Taylor showed Arthur out, I expressed gratitude to the doctor for allowing us to meet but I was disconcerted to see he found the situation vastly entertaining.

'A worthy young man, I think, Sarah, but perhaps a smidgeon too restrained in the circumstances.' He reached out and lightly touched my cap. 'Not a hair out of place, not a ribbon askew. I would hope for a little more ardour, in your position. Go to your mistress now and resume reading those passionate romances she so enjoys. Don't mention your own admirer. I wouldn't like to perturb her. She's grown fond of you and won't wish to contemplate your leaving.'

My heart was thudding when I re-joined Mrs Strines but the lady was now asleep and I had nothing to do but sit in silence. I tried to read more of Mr Wordsworth to myself but I couldn't concentrate. Inexplicably my thoughts turned to the story of young Porphyro on St Agnes' Eve, breathing in the odour of his beloved from her abandoned gown. I couldn't quite imagine Arthur Rawdon doing that and, most improperly, I wished I could.

Chapter 18: September 1862

After a week or two of clear, bright weather the familiar autumnal mist had settled in the bowl of the river valleys. Over the lower slopes of the hills it hung like a dirty muslin curtain, although sometimes their crests were visible as if through tears in the gauze. It exuded penetrating dampness to chill rheumy bones and straighten curls which owed more to tongs heated on the stove than Mother Nature. In the centre of the town, where Sheffield's many rivers ran together, it was far more pernicious. Freighted by industrial smoke and dust, studded with the residues of metal grinding and belching furnaces, its yellow opacity filled the streets, concealing whatever lay two paces ahead. Its sulphurous fumes clogged the windpipes of young and old alike.

Mrs Turner was horrified to see Annie at the door on such a day, hustling her inside and chiding her for venturing out in the fog.

'I had to come, Ma. I wanted you to know things have taken a turn for the better. Doctor said this morning Dan's hand were good enough to use now and the dear lad's to be back at his grinding shop tomorrow. Oh, Ma, it's such a mercy.'

Mrs Turner hugged her daughter while Chrissie mashed fresh tea. They all knew how hard it had been for the family at Acorn Street with their breadwinner off work for more than three weeks and no support from union funds. Even after the infection in Dan's hand cleared, he'd been told he must not risk opening up the wound again and they were forced to wait, subsisting as best they could, until he could resume employment. Their own limited savings had been soon expended. Mrs Turner offered what little she could afford and plied Annie, on her visits, with nourishing broths and puddings to keep up her strength, while the elder Mrs Crookes sold two cherished silver-plated clasps which her late husband had given her on their wedding day twenty-five years ago. No one could imagine how they would have managed, even for a further week, without recourse to relief from the Guardians of the Poor, a demeaning outlook they all dreaded.

Settled by the fireside, Annie smiled gloriously, her cheeks rosy with pleasure, and Chrissie acknowledged to herself, somewhat reluctantly, that now the morning sickness had passed, pregnancy seemed to suit her friend.

'What's Dan got to say about the union? Will he pay up his natty money and hold his tongue in future?'

Her questions sounded harsher than she intended and Mrs Turner frowned, shaking her head in warning not to pursue this subject. Annie, however, was not content to let the provocation pass.

'No, he won't, Chrissie. And you can tell Will so too, if you like. Nowt can be mended between them. Dan still holds to his principles and I'm with him whatever comes.'

'All right, lass. I'll not press point.'

'Aye, that's right,' echoed Mrs Turner. 'Unions be men's business.'

So Will made clear perpetually, Chrissie thought, giving a grimace.

Since their hurtful argument three weeks earlier, she'd avoided being alone with him and, in company, he scarcely conversed. She'd noticed he was eating less than usual, although he seemed always thirsty, and she hoped this loss of appetite was a sign of his contrition for the way he'd spoken to her. Perhaps his pride prevented him from making a move towards their reconciliation and she wondered whether she should offer an olive branch, although she was loath to be the one to yield first. Now, with Dan recovered and able to resume work, the friction between herself and Will should be eased so she decided she would give him an opening to apologise. She admitted to

183

herself ruefully that she was aching for her lover's embrace more than she would wish to tell him.

*****

Will came home early that evening. Chrissie had expected this in view of the putrid fog outside and, determined on rapprochement, she'd tidied her wayward hair and pinched her cheeks to bring more ruddiness to them. She was stirring vegetables into the stockpot, while Mrs Turner kneaded dough, when the door crashed open and he stumbled across the threshold, sinking to his knees on the flagstones, swathed in a lingering trail of bilious-coloured mist.

'Will!'

Doubled up with frantic coughing, he clutched his chest and gasped for breath. His face was grey and deep furrows ran upwards from his mouth, bisecting his cheeks, to the dark sockets of his eyes. He was shivering and his hands were icy.

'Has fog got to you? We must get you to bed, love. Drink this.'

As Chrissie helped him to the stairs, she was conscious that Mrs Turner had not moved. Will's mother was standing rigidly still, with floured hands dangling, a look of haunted desperation on her face. Then, seeing the girl struggle to support her son, she rallied herself and between them they hauled him to his bed.

'He's chilled to the bone. We must get doctor. I'll go.'

'No, Chrissie, you're not to go out in this weather. Ned can go when he comes home.' There was a frightening note of resignation in her voice.

Will had taken Chrissie's hand in his. His speech came with difficulty. 'Sit with me, love, will you? Till my breath comes easier.'

She sat by his side all night. Slowly his hand grew warm in hers and then became burning hot. She watched his face change in the lamplight as crimson streaks spread beside his nose and across his cheekbones, while sweat glistened on his forehead and collected in the hollow of his throat. In his fever he tossed and turned, muttering wordlessly, and once he started up with a horrifying growl which seemed to come from the pit of his stomach. Bessie and Mrs Turner brought wet rags to cool his brow and they urged Chrissie to take some rest but she would not. She sat bolt upright, her eyes fastened on Will, struggling silently with her inner demons, confronting the depths of her own distress.

Young Ned did not return home all night and at first light Bessie set off for the Public Dispensary. By then Will's sweating had diminished and he was sleeping more peacefully but Mrs Turner had come to stand, with her hand on Chrissie's shoulder. The agony of comprehension was etched on her face.

'I've seen this afore, Chrissie,' she whispered. 'Will's Da were stricken like this. But he were nigh twenty years older.'

'Will's strong. It's just the fog. Got to his throat. He'll be right enough with rest.' Her resolute words belied her own terror.

The doctor listened to their accounts of Will's collapse and looked carefully at his dark sputum, spotted with pus and particles of grit and metal. He asked the patient how long he'd experienced shortness of breath and coughing and whether there'd been previous night sweats. Will confirmed that all these occurrences were longstanding and, at this disclosure, Mrs Turner covered her face with her hands. Chrissie winced and noted that, as the doctor drew back the bedcover to examine Will's chest and back, his expression was grave.

185

'Chest expansion in a young man should be a good deal better than this and there's a creaking sound under the right nipple I don't like. Below the clavicle here there's a considerable depression. You're a grinder, Mr Turner?'

'Wet grinder – saws.' It came in a reedy tone.

'But working with dry grinders, I fancy, cheek by jowl?'

Will nodded.

'Well, Mr Turner, I fear the disease is well set in and this is not good in a young man. I've made a study of such cases and I can't give you false cheer. Your best hope to halt the malady's progress is either to abstain from your work and find some other employment or, at the very least, to move away from the vicinity of dry grinders. The first alternative is much your best course of action.'

'Cannot do it, sir. I've a family to feed.'

The doctor had heard the tale so many times. Grinders' earnings were not easily matched in other trades. He patted Will's arm. 'I can give you some physic which will ease your breathing a little but you must do something to help yourself, you understand. You're not to think of venturing out until the fog clears and you're to avoid smoke and fumes at all costs. Get your wheel moved so you're near a window and away from the dry grinders. You're basically a strong fellow and if you take care you may hold things at bay.'

When Mrs Turner showed the doctor downstairs, Will lay back on the bolster with his eyes closed, but Chrissie saw his hand was shaking and pressed it firmly. Her decision was made. 'You'll do as doctor says, Will Turner, and you'll get better, d'you hear me?'

He opened his eyes, moist with tears, and looked at her sadly. 'Me strength's gone, Chrissie. I can feel it.'

'Then you'd better get it back again, lad. You'll be no use to me as husband if you've lost your vigour.'

186

He stared, holding her gaze. His pale lips twitched slightly. 'D'you mean it?'

'Had chance to think things through last night, looking at you so poorly. I know now I couldn't bear to lose you, Will Turner, with your precious union and all. Sat here all the time knowing that, knowing I love you proper. If it helps to get you better, I suppose I'd have to wed you.'

A tear ran into the furrow in his cheek and his shoulders shook but his voice was firmer. 'I'll hold you to that, love, I promise.'

*****

Now she had taken her decision Chrissie felt a sense of relief. Her previous aimlessness gave way before absolute commitment to the mission she adopted as fervently as a postulant preparing to take her conventual vows. She would dedicate herself to restoring Will's health and thenceforward she would shower on him all the devotion she possessed, all the devotion she'd disregarded and recklessly misdirected in the past. They agreed their understanding would remain secret between them for a few days, until Will was feeling better and could share the burden of Mrs Turner's delight. Chrissie welcomed this respite. She knew the rest of the household would assume her air of distraction resulted from lack of sleep and she was glad to foster this illusion.

She went out to market despite the persisting murk and thought it appropriate that the fog shrouded her movements, just as she sought to veil her newly burgeoning hopes. Even so, it didn't prove possible to dispel all memories of her earlier life and in West Street next morning, through the swirling gloom, she glimpsed a lanky figure, in demure bonnet and heavy skirt, who caused her a tremor of sheer fright. The woman reminded her of Edie Pyle's most vicious associate: her foul-mouthed, bottle-wielding assailant. They passed each other at a distance of several paces, at the limits of their misted vision, and Chrissie could not be certain it was the woman she feared, but she was reassured to know her own identity must have been similarly obscured. The incident was upsetting and she recognised how vulnerable she was, not just to the hostility of others but also to her own haunted imagination.

*****

'Troubles never come singly,' Mrs Turner grieved, holding Annie's hand. 'I sometimes wonder what we've done to become so unlucky. Oh, lass, what'll you do? Why've you waited three days to tell us? To lose his job after all the other troubles!'

'I couldn't bear to come so soon after you'd seen me happy at the thought of Dan back at work. Fools' paradise that were, right enough. Anyway you didn't tell me Will were ill neither.'

'Didn't want to worry you, love. You've got the baby to think about.'

The elder Mrs Crookes moved forward and put her arm round Annie's mother. The three women hung together, clasping each other, each trying to comfort the others and stifle her own tears.

'I could try to speak to the saw grinders' secretary, Annie.' Will's husky voice caused them to turn to where he was sitting, swathed in a rug, by the hearth. They'd thought he was asleep. 'Get him to ask fender grinders whether the union would put Dan on the box if I paid the subs he owes.'

'Will, would you really do that?'

'Don't get your hopes up though, lass. Dan's turned his back on the union. They've no cause to help him.'

He started to catch his breath and splutter so Mrs Turner, clucking nervously, broke away from her daughter to cosset her son.

Chrissie had unaccountably hurried upstairs, just after Annie explained that Dan had been turned off work and would get no unemployment money from the union, but her voice now sounded from the landing as she reappeared.

'Will, you can't go crawling to the secretary after all you've said to him about fraud in the accounts. Broadhead wants nowt better than to defy you. Union wouldn't agree, any road. Annie said his master turned Dan out for very reason that he weren't in the union. Union won't have him back on your say-so.'

'It's true, lad. Union put pressure on the master while Dan were off sick. Threatened to blow up whole forge if he took Dan back. There's nowt you can do.' Annie had gone over to crouch beside her brother. 'But it were good of you to offer. Specially after your quarrel with him.'

Chrissie joined them at the fireside and held out her hand, opening her fingers to reveal a small embossed silver locket on a delicate chain. 'It won't be worth much but it'll maybe help with rent for a bit. I've no use for it. Eb Pyle gave it me.'

She had contemplated donating the blue hat as well but persuaded herself it would be difficult to recover even a fraction of its value, second-hand. The locket was the only saleable thing she possessed and Annie was aware of that.

'Oh, Chrissie, you're so kind but I can't take it. You're a good friend but I can't put a claim on you like that.'

At this, Chrissie looked at Will with her eyebrows raised and, grinning, he nodded. 'Not as a friend maybe but perhaps as a sister, love.'

Mrs Turner gave a little gasp.

Chrissie moved behind Will's chair, her free hand holding his shoulder. 'We'd thought to wait till he were full better before telling you all but now he's on the mend and we reckon a bit of good news wouldn't come amiss. We're to wed as soon as he can totter up the aisle.'

Laughing at her affectionate mockery, Will took her hand and drew her round beside him. The others embraced them both, twittering in excitement at the pleasure of being distracted temporarily from their troubles. Huddled in the midst of his jubilant womenfolk, Will turned to Annie, speaking in a stronger voice without pausing.

'Never thought to say this, lass, and it goes against the grain, but Dan's best chance of work is to go to one of them new steelworks down in the Don Valley. Some of 'em takes non-union men. They're large enough to thumb their noses at the likes of Broadhead and his crew. Other grinders and cutlery men have gone there. It's hard graft feeding crucible furnaces but Dan's a strong lad and it's not bad money.'

Annie beamed at her brother. 'Dan said that himself but I thought you'd cast us both off forever if he did it.'

Will was holding Chrissie's hand closely to his chest. 'I still believe the union's the best defence for the likes of us and I'll always stand up for it. But maybe I've been thinking a bit, on what else has to be considered now this lass has been daft enough to say she'll take me. I'll hold no more grudges. Life's too short!'

Mrs Turner and the two Mrs Crookes exclaimed in delight and bustled about to refill the kettle and rinse out teacups. Chrissie forced a smile when they looked at her with gratitude, as if her benign influence had brought about this change of heart in Will. She knew otherwise. His last words had been no casual, trite expression. Her hand could feel the feeble movement in his lungs and she could hear the faint clicking of his respiration. She alone knew that, in accepting him, she had accepted also the challenge to confront and avert the death sentence Fate had decreed for him.

Chapter 19: September 1862

Mrs Strines had introduced me to the works of William Shakespeare and, although I didn't understand all the complicated phrases and allusions, I soon revelled in the sonorous cadences of his tragedies and the mirthful misadventures of more light-hearted scenes. One evening the lady was at her most whimsical, looking at me soulfully.

'Read me Portia's speech in the courtroom from 'The Merchant of Venice'. The one about mercy. It touches me so deeply.'

I took up the heavy leather-bound volume.
'The quality of mercy is not strained.
It droppeth as the gentle dew from heaven
Upon the earth beneath. It is twice blessed.
It blesses he who gives and him who takes.'

'Oh, how true, how true!' Mrs Strines exclaimed. 'Mercy and forgiveness. The offender rejoices that the transgression is pardoned but the merciful person, who forgives the penitent, is blessed above all others.'

'Our Lord preached forgiveness, ma'am.' I was surprised my quixotic mistress looked to a secular drama for the virtues of mercy.

'Indeed He did, Sarah. But forgiveness is not just a spiritual exercise. It can restore a soul in anguish. It can soothe dissent and bring unforeseen rewards to the giver. It can move mountains!'

I forbore from saying that Holy Scripture attributed the mountain-moving miracle to faith, not forgiveness. Who was I to query Mrs Strines' delight in what was virtuous and sanctified? I was, as ever, puzzled by the lady's capricious enthusiasms and felt stolidly unimaginative when I encountered them. Her next words were still more unexpected.

'I have a mind to venture into town tomorrow. I shall take the gig and you must accompany me. It's the doctor's birthday next week and I wish to give him a particular present. I shall call upon a colleague of his who can help me in the matter. While I'm so engaged you may visit Gray's Exchange, the drapery establishment, and purchase some new braiding for my lavender gown. You remember we mentioned it needed refreshing. The doctor is to believe we are both going to Gray's Exchange, do you understand?'

'Yes, ma'am.' I was pleased by the stratagem, appreciating that the deceit would be justified by Mrs Strines' beneficent intentions. Doubtless she would secure some new piece of medical equipment for her husband's birthday. I had never set foot in Gray's Exchange, although I knew the store was frequented by the most respectable and affluent in society, so I was flattered and excited to be charged with going there alone.

*****

Mrs Strines duly set me down from the gig at the lofty arcaded entrance to the emporium and arranged to meet me there again in an hour's time. I stared for a moment at the grand Italianate façade and then, with head held high despite my nervousness, I entered its portals. Bemused at first by the profusion of merchandise, I timidly sought direction to the haberdashery counter where, after some indecision, I found appropriate braiding. I enjoyed the politeness of the assistant when I explained I was purchasing it for my mistress, Mrs Robert Strines of Ranmoor. After this success I amused myself looking at the displays of Nottingham lace, buckskin gloves and painted fans. I gasped at the great rolls of velvet, silks and fine cottons which the salesmen unwound with a flourish, spinning out the material against their measuring rods and

193

cutting it deftly to the requisite length. I'd never seen such a collection of worldly adornments and luxurious furbelows and my pleasure at viewing them made me feel gloriously guilty.

Realising I had time in hand before I was due to meet my mistress, I left Gray's Exchange to walk along the narrow High Street, to admire the miscellany of hatters, bootmakers, hosiers and silversmiths displaying their wares. A glimpse of the clock on the Town Hall tower in Waingate confirmed I had time to venture further and I continued my walk to the busy concourse fronting the portico of Norfolk Market Hall on Hay Market. I was wary of straying too far beyond this in case I encountered violent ne'er-do-wells in the rougher parts of central Sheffield, intent on causing affray and murder.

I stood transfixed by the columns of water spurting from the central basin of the fountain in the square: artificial cascades which shot upwards from a stone bowl. I was familiar with small waterfalls on the Loxley and the Rivelin Rivers, and the man-made weirs at dams feeding the waterwheels. In those cases water poured downwards as was natural. Here it was propelled upwards, defying gravity. I admired this technical skill and thought fondly of the engineers who designed the fountain and its mechanisms.

Around me a great variety of people came and went: stylish ladies and gentlemen, modest maidservants like me, decently clad working folk and a few overdressed women, flaunting their finery, who I felt sure were of dubious repute and to be avoided. As I turned back towards the High Street, I saw two young women arm-in- arm and laughing happily; the shorter one was noticeably pregnant. They were plainly but neatly dressed, carrying baskets, and I put them down in my mind as respectable housewives about their domestic business.

When they drew nearer I caught my breath, disbelieving what I saw, for the taller woman had withdrawn her hand from her companion to adjust her shawl and a tumble of auburn curls fell onto her forehead, while her trill of infectious, self-assured merriment caught the attention of other passers-by. I'd only ever seen one person with vivid burnished hair like that and eyes with sparkling violet irises, which caught the sunlight. I'd only ever heard one mischievous laugh to turn heads so easily. Yet I felt sure this was no rich man's kept woman. Tom thought he'd seen her wearing a flamboyant feathered hat, handed down amorously from a gig, but surely that wasn't possible? He must have been mistaken. At all events, here without a doubt was my rascally, sometimes outrageous, school friend, who knew more of the world than was good for her and who was now looking straight at me, recognition dawning in her beautiful eyes.

'Sarah!' Chrissie Mallon held out her arms with a glowing smile.

'Chrissie!' I didn't move at first, still baffled, and she misinterpreted my reticence.

'Are you still angry with me for what I said all that time ago? I always did speak out of turn, you know.'

I shook my head and reached out my hand. 'I know now what you said was true. I'm just so surprised to see you. Tom told me you were...' I checked myself quickly. 'Tom said he'd seen you.'

'Few months back now. I asked him to let you know I were sorry at what'd happened. He said you were still at Malin Bridge then. You're not now, I see.'

I stood rather stiffly, smoothing the dark skirt of my servant's dress. 'I'm lady's maid to a doctor's wife in Ranmoor.'

'I'm glad you've left your father and your...'

'Please don't speak of them. How are you, Chrissie?'

195

'I'm right well, though I were ill a while back but here's the angel who helped me recover. This is Annie, my old workmate who's soon to be my sister, and here's Sarah who I grew up with when I were at me aunt's house.'

I found Annie's guileless smile very pleasing and returned her hug appreciatively. 'Your sister? You mean?'

'I'm to be wed soon, to Annie's brother, Will. He's a saw grinder. I've lodged with his family since me Gran died.'

'I'm delighted for you. Tom told me you'd got a young man. He was rather downcast about it.'

I noticed Annie look quizzically at Chrissie and hastened to correct any misapprehension. 'Tom's my young brother. He's been infatuated with Chrissie since he was a little lad. I fear she only used to tease him.'

'Would I ever?'

We all laughed, more at ease with each other. Chrissie turned to Annie.

'He's a nice lad, is Tom. Do for our Bessie.' She fended off her friend's playful slap. 'How about you, Sarah? Have you got an admirer? You look so smart.'

I'd told no one else but I was suddenly eager to share my secret. I could feel my cheeks burning. 'Yes, I have. I'm promised but it's not publicly known. I hope to wed in the New Year.'

'Your mistress don't know!'

'No, indeed. I'm not allowed followers.' The chimes of a clock were sounding. 'Oh, Chrissie, I must go. I'm due to meet her at noon. I'm very pleased to have seen you.'

'You must come to my wedding, Sarah. Tom too, if he's a mind to. Where does your doctor live in Ranmoor, so I can let you know time and place? What's the doctor's name?'

'Dr Strines, by St John's Church. Goodbye Chrissie, Annie.'

I lifted my skirts and hurried back towards Gray's Exchange. I was not too concerned about my lateness, for I doubted Mrs Strines would be prompt, and I arrived at the store several minutes before the gig appeared. The doctor's wife greeted me radiantly and was enchanted with the braiding, although she scarcely gave it a glance, and she let the horse pace slowly uphill away from the centre of town. We didn't converse but sat together abstractedly, each lost in her own thoughts, ignorant of the other's preoccupation.

In my mind I was exploring every nuance of my meeting with Chrissie Mallon, bewildered how to reconcile what I'd heard and seen with Tom's account. He must have been wrong: although it beggared belief he would mistake another woman for the girl he'd idolised for so long. I had my own reasons for wanting to credit that my childhood friend had not left the paths of virtue and was to be a respectable married woman, with a skilled grinder for her husband. I was reassured by Annie, with her open honest look, nodding confirmation of what her future sister-in-law had said. Experience showed that Chrissie's apparent lies were not always falsehoods and it might be that her overwhelming beauty and exuberance caused her to be misjudged. If this was the case, I had no need to blame myself for her presumed fall from grace. My guilt was assuaged.

*****

On the morning of the doctor's birthday he saw only one patient at the house, so that he would have time to spend with his wife before leaving on his home visits. He ushered the woman out with courtesy but some impatience, giving a sigh of relief when she had gone. She was Miss Prudence Paterson, to whom he had first been introduced when he escorted her parents to their home after the shooting incident. Since then a succession of minor ailments had led her to seek frequent consultations with him. After

197

shutting the door on her, he hurried to the kitchen, for he had declared that on this special day he would take up his wife's breakfast tray himself.

After he had collected the tray, Mrs Taylor murmured appreciatively. 'Bless me, the doctor's a good man, right enough. Though some might think it more fitting he should be the one served on his birthday.'

I'd been ready to take up Mrs Strines' breakfast myself. I grinned but wouldn't endorse any implied criticism of my mistress, who customarily rose late. As the doctor had taken over my usual function by waiting on his wife, there was time for me to ask the housekeeper a particular question. When I'd tried to do so previously, Mrs Taylor moved the conversation onto different topics so I was resolved to secure an answer on this occasion. I planned to approach the issue obliquely. I offered to help by creaming sugar and butter in the mixing bowl while the older woman assembled the other ingredients for a celebratory pudding.

'You're a good lass, Sarah. That hoity-toity Betsy never offered to help me.'

'What was she like? She served the mistress for several years, didn't she?'

Mrs Taylor grunted. 'Seemed nice enough at first,' she said after a pause, 'but then it came to light, what a flighty little thing she was. Caused no end of trouble. Had to go.'

I saw my opportunity. 'Mr Jewitt mentioned he was quite friendly with her, a rare pal, he said'

The housekeeper snorted. 'A pal! Good deal more, I should say! She led him on shamelessly, little hussy.'

I looked guardedly at Mrs Taylor. 'Mr Jewitt may not have been wholly averse, I think. He was forward enough at my first meeting with him. But he's been more restrained towards me of late, since I mentioned my discomfort to you in fact. I'm grateful.'

198

Mrs Taylor did not concede that thanks were due to her but she looked pleased. 'Glad to hear it, my dear. I don't think he's the sort to persist where he's not wanted. Looks for a bit of encouragement, he does. Most men do. Mind you, give them an inch, they'll take a mile. Remember that, Sarah. But I've reason to believe Mr Jewitt's attention is directed otherwise at the moment – been seen walking out with the housemaid at the vicarage. Not as ladylike as you but a neat enough little thing.'

My exclamation of delight at this news was interrupted by the throwing open of the kitchen door and the eruption into the room of Dr Strines. His face was ruddy, his cravat loose and he was jubilant.

'Mrs Taylor, Sarah, rejoice with me!'

He flung his arms round the housekeeper and embraced her warmly, lifting her buxom form clean off the floor.

'Mrs Strines is with child again! She went last week to see my colleague in town. He says all is well. Deception was practised on me! I thought she had gone to purchase fripperies with Sarah.'

He turned to me, seizing me by the elbows and twirling me round, while I still clutched the mixing spoon heavy with glutinous fats, and as we pirouetted he bent and kissed me full on the lips. Then he set me down, taking my free hand and Mrs Taylor's arm.

'We must resolve she shall not lose the child this time. We three will have a care for her like never before. All her whims are to be indulged and nothing must be allowed to perturb her. Is that agreed?'

He drew both of us to him, his arms slipped round our waists as we promised to do all within our power to sustain a healthy confinement. My lips burned and I couldn't prevent myself trembling beneath the doctor's hand. He must have felt my palpitation but I could do nothing. For me the momentous news of Mrs Strines' pregnancy was matched, terrifyingly, by some strange but no less momentous, awakening within myself.

Chapter 20: September - October 1862

When Chrissie and Annie made their way into the market hall after meeting Sarah, the mother-to-be looked up at her companion archly. 'Sarah said you'd told her brother you had a young man but I thought it were a few months back you met Tom.'

Chrissie laughed. 'It's all true, lass. White lie, it were, I told him then. I said it to discourage the lad – weren't good for him to be maundering after me now he's a grown man. But it were Will I had in mind as me young man, love, though he hadn't spoken for me at the time. Scarcely noticed me existence, I thought.'

'You're a scheming minx, Chrissie Mallon!'

'Oh, I hope so, Annie! I hope so. But I mean to be a devoted wife as Chrissie Turner.'

She meant it with all her heart. It was the bargain she'd offered Fate in return for Will's life.

*****

Will's health improved in the next few weeks and he returned to work at the grinding shop. He was well regarded there by both the owner of the forge and his workmates so they helped him move to a position beneath the window, across the room from the dry grinders. In the balmy late autumn days which followed the dispersal of the heavy fog, he relished the light breeze bringing in fresher air from the street, even though it carried with it the dust and smoke which were endemic in the town. Unfortunately, when the incessant rains came, it was necessary to shut the window and he felt again the grit in his nostrils and the phlegmy congestion building up in his chest. The doctor's advice echoed in his mind.

Whenever he had the opportunity, he walked with Chrissie on the hills, where he could breathe more easily, and they talked of moving from the centre of town, out to one of the nearby villages where the air was purer. They fixed their wedding day for Christmas Eve, by which time, if all went well, Annie and Dan's baby would have been born and Mrs Turner would be free to concentrate her maternal devotion on her eldest son.

Since accepting Will's proposal, Chrissie had thrown herself into the role of helpmeet and bride-to-be but sometimes, when a stray remnant of her old perversity came to her, she wondered if she was simply acting a part, carried along by her genuine concern for her lover and by the idea that some adverse deity required propitiation. At such moments her existence, current and prospective, seemed unreal or not intended – alien to her natural restlessness – a sacrifice which she was bound to offer but might yet regret. When these fancies passed, as they did, she shrugged off her doubts and redoubled her efforts to deserve the reward of her future husband's recovery.

One Saturday, to celebrate his birthday, Will surprised Chrissie by announcing they were to visit Mr Youdan's music-hall where barrel dancers, trapeze artists, performing dogs, tightrope walkers and jugglers were all appearing. Her excitement was great for she'd never seen an entertainment of this kind and she remembered how she gawped at the billboards on West Bar when she first returned to Sheffield. As they entered the vast entrance hall of the theatre, with its gaudy refreshment stall and tavern, she gazed around entranced, for it seemed to her the miscellany of people milling about in the foyer would be amusement enough to watch. Then they climbed to the high gallery and for a moment she was alarmed by the steeply tiered seats, imagining that if someone lost their footing they would tumble, head over heels, down the precipice to certain doom.

Below them a seething mass of working men, women and children filled the pit while, alongside where they sat on the wooden benches of the gallery, the crowd pressed forward, exhaling pungent breath and nudging those already seated to squeeze closer together. It was clear many had already visited the tavern. The volume of rowdy, raucous conversation was deafening, as gibes and laughter resounded against the domed ceiling. A haze of tobacco smoke hung in the air and Will began to cough, although no more strenuously than many others in the audience who were tamping their pipes and, down in the circle, lighting their cigars. After the curtain was drawn back and the performance started, a succession of entertainers displayed their impressive skills of balance, grace and adroitness, while the onlookers participated vociferously with catcalls, witticisms, applause and laughter. Chrissie was enthralled and she added to the din with her own shrieks of excitement and suspense, clapping frantically and joining the cries for more.

At the end of the performance, as they made their way down the stairs and back to the entrance foyer, she clung to Will's arm, still shaking with merriment. The melody of the vocalist's final song was running in her head and she was glowing with her enjoyment of the evening. They drew level with the throng emerging from the pit and let themselves be carried forward in a surge towards the tavern. When Will made a drinking gesture with his free hand she nodded happily. Then, all of a sudden, her gaiety evaporated. Dragging on his arm, she tried to pull him away and to whisper the cause of her distress but, buffeted by the crowd behind them, they had no chance to turn and Will could not make out what she mouthed in the surrounding hubbub. Too late he realised what she had seen.

Ebenezer Pyle, grown paunchier and flushed of face, was standing at the bar guffawing loudly, with his arm around the well-corseted waist of a colourful young woman. Her low-cut gown of crimson taffeta, which had seen better days, displayed her prominent bosom to great effect. A multi-hued corsage of silk flowers was draped from shoulder to décolletage and a purple wrap of gauzy material hung limply, looped over her elbows. Her russet hair, which too evidently owed little to nature, was piled high and topped by a silvery ornament, sparkling ostentatiously.

Despite the charms of his companion, Eb was more observant than Will and set down his beer jug with a thud. To do him justice, he paled at the sight of Chrissie but his greeting gave no hint of remorse.

'Christ Almighty! The bitch has returned to her turd. I were told tha was seen in town, fucking slut. Didn't know tha was with this slop o' dishwater. Heard the disease'd got him. Doubt he can get it up thee proper now, love, in his poorly state. Lost his spunk I reckon. Can't keep thee in pretty trinkets either, eh?'

He dragged his over-dressed lady friend forward pointing to the artificial pearls at her throat and the decoration in her hair. 'See these, Chrissie. Don't tha wish tha had 'em? By Christ! Eb Pyle weren't good enough for thee, were he? Now see what tha'rt come to – whore to a spineless weakling, gasping for his breath.'

Chrissie and Will stood silently while he ranted. They could not move away because of the tight-packed crowd but they compelled themselves not to respond, aware of heads turning towards the confrontation, until at Eb's last words Will could restrain himself no longer.

'Take that back! She's my promised wife!'

Chrissie shut her eyes, knowing this admission was ill-advised while Eb roared with sarcastic laughter, slapping the counter so that beer spilled from other men's tankards and more eyes turned, antagonistically, towards him.

'Don't be mardy, love. She's nowt to fret about.' Eb's companion stroked his arm, pressing herself against him, but he thrust her aside.

'Shut thi noise.'

Then, in one fierce movement Eb pushed Will in the chest, so that he staggered backwards into the people behind, and dragged Chrissie into his arms, kissing her aggressively despite her scratches to his face. At this assault a cacophony of shouts erupted, a woman screamed and burly spectators seized the assailant by the shoulders, wresting him from his victims. As he was manhandled away, he glared menacingly at Chrissie.

'I'll have thee again, tha fucking cow,' he hissed. 'Thi husband'll not stop me!'

Miraculously the crowd parted so the ruffian could be escorted, none too gently, from the premises, with his affronted lady friend following as best she could, silk petals scattering from her corsage after it caught on the sleeve of a bystander. Will was doubled over, clutching his chest and spitting blood, while Chrissie sank to her knees beside him, hoping desperately he had not heard Eb's threat. A woman brought water and he sipped it. Then, slowly he stood up, wiped his mouth, straightened his jacket and, declining further assistance, offered his arm to his fiancée. Several by-standers went with them to the front of the theatre, concerned to see them safely on their way, clamouring with their advice.

'You should lay charges, lad.'

'He's a wrong 'un, that 'un.'

'Take care, lass. He'll not give up easy.'

'Is your chest bad, love?' Chrissie asked after they turned the corner, out of earshot.

'Better now. Just lost me puff for a bit.' His voice became desolate. 'Chrissie, I'm no use to you. I can't protect you. He were right when he called me a weakling. Can't stop scum like that molesting you.'

'I've known worse,' she said grimly. 'You'll get better, Will. I've told you before.'

She was confident the determination in her voice sounded convincing.

*****

It was not difficult to persuade Mrs Turner that they should move away from the centre of town after they were married. The more salubrious surroundings of a nearby village, such as Walkley, Heeley or even Malin Bridge, offered obvious advantages to her son, with his congested lungs, but she was not tempted to join them in leaving the district where she'd been born. Bessie and Ned worked nearby and she would continue to keep house for them while the younger boys were still receiving schooling, in between running errands to earn a few pennies. Practical as ever, she declared she would take in a paying lodger, if need be, to help ends meet. For Chrissie there was a second urgent reason to move away although she spoke of her fears to no one. Since the encounter at the music-hall she lived in dread that Eb Pyle would try to make good his threat. Escape from central Sheffield would be the only reliable way to thwart him.

Reluctantly, for the sake of his health, Will started to look for employment further afield but for a skilled saw grinder there were few out-of-town opportunities. In the villages, most grinders were less well-paid, working on smaller edge-tools, such as knives, scissors and files. Besides, to switch between specialist trades was not straightforward, given the attitude of rival unions with their constraints on the admission of newcomers, and Will would never betray his principles by taking work as a jobbing grinder. He prided himself that saw grinders were the elite among their comrades and Chrissie knew it would be hard for him to compromise his commitment and his dignity by accepting another role.

There might be one possible solution and on a Saturday afternoon they walked out the few miles along the turnpike road to Abbeydale. There the grouped works on the River Sheaf specialised in making large tools including scythes, grass hooks and hay knives, all prestige items. Even on a dull October day the countryside seemed pleasant and reviving, not least to Chrissie who, in other circumstances, would have wrinkled her nose at the thought of leaving the livelier attractions of the town. Dominating the village was an industrial complex with waterwheels, smithies, a tilt forge and a grinding shop. Nearby were workers' cottages, warehouses and stables, all solidly built and well maintained. It was very different from conditions in the centre of Sheffield. Will looked around thoughtfully and spoke to two men fishing above the dam who answered his questions with enthusiastic praise for life at Abbeydale. If he could secure employment there, it might be the key to resolve their difficulties.

Will seemed satisfied but he was silent as they started on their journey back and, as his pace grew slower, Chrissie looked at him sideways and saw he was labouring harder with each step. She urged him to rest and later to ask for seats in one of the carts which were trundling towards town. Accepting that he had not walked so far since his illness, he did not resist the suggestion and waved down a passing vehicle.

The wagoner who accommodated them was jovial and talkative but their other travelling companions, not of their choosing, were two large pigs on their way to the slaughterhouse. The animals at the back of the cart were restless, unused to this mode of transport, so they snorted, grunted and nuzzled their fellow passengers. Will, recovering his breath, was unconcerned but Chrissie feared their slobbering would soil her clothes and drew as far away from the animals as she could. She was glad when they reached the butchers' sheds and could alight, bidding farewell to the driver with gratitude and the porkers with relief.

Although Slaughter Lane was not far in distance from the gentility of Norfolk Market's spacious square, it was miserably different in appearance and odour. The stench from the boiling-house for tripe mingled with that of steaming refuse, heaped in putrefying piles outside the sheds; but it did not deter two urchins who played happily with handfuls of discarded offal. Underfoot, the broken paving was threaded by streams of blood and faeces which percolated from the slaughterhouses and oozed towards the river. The weird, unearthly screeches of terrified beasts sounded from inside the rickety buildings while muffled expletives confirmed that few half-day holidays were being taken in the Shambles that Saturday.

Dimly at first Chrissie became aware of other screams, human in origin, and the smell of something else, foul and cloying. Instinctively she shivered and, when they rounded a bend, they saw that one of the shabbier sheds was on fire and people were running to fetch buckets. The billowing smoke was intensifying and flames were beginning to take hold, fed by the fatty carcases stored in the building. She shuddered.

'Come away, love. Smoke'll do you no good.'

Chrissie took Will's arm to draw him uphill away from the conflagration but his attention had been drawn to an upper window under the eaves of the abattoir.

'There's someone in there. Up in garret. Good God, it's a child! Poor little mite. Must be a butcher's boy, maybe left alone in the shed.'

She looked up to the tiny casement. Intermittently through the smoke she could see the petrified small face, with its halo of blond curls, pressed to the glass and small hands battering uselessly on the unyielding panes. Men were shouting to fetch a ladder; others declared it was too late, the building was near collapse. Chrissie, rooted to the spot, began to shake uncontrollably and Will stared at her, pulling her arm.

'Don't watch, love. Can't do anything. Let's go on.'

She knew it would be wiser to say nothing but some atavistic compulsion tugged at her heart. Her voice sounded strange, forced, as if coming from far away, from the pitiable history of Uncle Jack, Ben Culley and Mary Brailsford. She owed that wretched child her acknowledgement.

'That little lad's my cousin.'

'Your cousin?'

'My uncle's son, Bertie. No, Will. Don't!'

She shrieked and flung herself forward, grabbing for his coat, but the strong hands of spectators drew her back as Will dashed into the smoke-filled shed. A torrent of sparks marked his arrival through the door and at once flames shot up towards the fragile roof, hissing and crackling. Chrissie struggled, cursing those who held her, and she begged someone, anyone, for the love of God, to help Will. She cursed herself most of all for her stupidity in divulging a meaningless relationship, sullied by betrayal, which Will had interpreted as a plea.

'No use, lass. Too late. Your man should've had more sense. Little lad's a goner. He will be too, shouldn't wonder.'

A roaring noise made everyone look up and they heard the snap of the beam when part of the roof fell in. The resulting display of pyrotechnics was dazzling. One wall began to crumble, but the panes of the narrow window under the eaves still held fast although there was no face to be seen there now. Then, through the swirling smoke inside the door, a figure carrying something stumbled forward.

'Will! For God's sake, help him!'

Several men ran to assist, releasing her, as Will staggered across the threshold. He'd pulled his muffler up round his face but he was gasping for breath. His coat was scorched and his hair singed; soot and grease covered his clothes. His face was ashen and he stared at Chrissie blankly, holding out the small inert body he was clutching.

'I'm sorry, love. I'm sorry. Your cousin... Couldn't save him. No use. I'm no use...'

He slumped forward, choking, as one man took the little corpse from his arms and another stopped his fall, lowering him gently to the ground.

'Get doctor.'

'Take him in cart to Dispensary.'

'Never should've gone in there.'

'Hero, he is, I reckon.'

Chrissie was oblivious to the cries around her. She knew why Will had risked his life. Why he longed to prove his strength was sufficient to help her kin, of whom he knew nothing. But it was futile. Their plans were doomed. Their optimism obliterated. Bent over him, kissing his insensible lips, she saw her hopes smashed, her future shattered, her bargain with Fate cruelly rejected.

Chapter 21: October - November 1862

'The doctor's like no other man on earth, I swear, my dear. Who else would subdue his natural instincts for the sake of his wife and unborn child? Saintly, he is, no less.'

I was helping Mrs Taylor move Dr Strines' things into a spare room while she indulged in her favoured pastime of singing his praises.

'Mistress says he moved into another room before her last confinement, so he wouldn't trouble her as time went on.'

'So he did. He has some fancy notion that exercising his conjugal rights might imperil her health or the baby's. Did you ever hear such a thing? Of course, he's a doctor so he should know but it stands to reason a man can't be expected to live like a bachelor while his wife's with child. Spend half their life like monks, they would!'

I considered this conversation rather improper, alluding to matters best left unsaid, but I warmed to the idea that Dr Strines was noble and self-sacrificing. I regarded another aspect of the regime he'd imposed for his wife's sake as regrettable, for he insisted his Bella should not sing while she was carrying. He thought the strain of her passionate recitals might be too great when she needed to conserve her strength and Mrs Strines accepted her husband's stipulation without protest. She'd become very capricious, babbling about forgiveness and grace, begging me to be virtuous, generous-spirited and humble, but I put these vagaries down to the effects of pregnancy on one of such a sensitive disposition. I understood how greatly both the doctor and his wife longed for the birth of a healthy child and, vicariously, I shared their hopes and fears, as did Mrs Taylor.

In recent weeks Mr Jewitt had appeared self-absorbed, taciturn and surly. I wondered if his courtship of

211

the housemaid at the vicarage was not prospering and I worried he might turn his attentions towards me once more. My qualms were reinforced one morning when he leered at me silently, as we passed in the hallway, and ran his tongue round his lips so that they glistened with saliva. Then he smiled sardonically and continued on his way.

Mrs Strines rested a good deal and I spent much of my time reading aloud to her or stitching quietly while she dozed. I chided myself on these occasions that, when my mind wandered from the task in hand, it tended to fasten on thoughts of the paragon who was Dr Robert Strines. I marvelled at his dedicated sense of duty, his renowned skill as a doctor, his consideration as a husband, and I couldn't help remembering the guilty excitement I'd felt when he held my waist and kissed me in his jubilation about his wife's pregnancy. I admitted to myself the dreadful secret that I worshipped my employer and the still more dreadful realisation that what I felt for dear, devoted Arthur Rawdon appeared feeble by comparison. Disconcerting as this knowledge was, I reassured myself that it was in no way dangerous, known only to me, merely a fantasy like one in a romantic poem.

One afternoon, on Mrs Taylor's half-day, the housekeeper had gone to visit her sister, the doctor was out at the Infirmary and Mrs Strines was asleep. I'd been pressing my mistress's linen and was carrying a pile of immaculate ruffles and lace up the stairs from the scullery. I knew the doctor had gone out on horseback and I let my imagination picture him as he rode through the town, acknowledging the admiring glances of acquaintances and bringing cheer and recovery to the poor folk in the hospital. The click of the pharmacy door jolted me back to reality and I was flustered to see Dick Jewitt emerging.

'My, but you're looking pretty today, Miss Sarah. What a becoming flush on your cheeks. Have I caught you daydreaming of a lover?'

'Please don't tease me, Mr Jewitt.'

'Oh, I don't tease, Miss Sarah. I'm deeply in earnest. Never more so. We're alone, my dear, and it's time we had a little chat, you and I. Don't you think?'

He laid hands on my pile of linen as if to take it from me.

'Please let go, Mr Jewitt. I must take this upstairs.'

'Not until we've concluded our business, Miss Sarah.'

'What business? I have no business with you.'

'Oh but you have, my dear. I have a debt owed me and you can help me secure my reparations.'

'What are you talking about? Let go!'

He jerked the laundry from my hands and set it on the hallstand. Then he clapped his hand over my mouth and pushed me against the wall.

'Don't call out or you'll wake Mrs Strines and we wouldn't want her alarmed, would we? What would Dr Strines say if she suffered a miscarriage because of your carelessness?'

I shook my head but struggled fiercely as panic seized me. Despite my efforts, he dragged me into the pharmacy and through into the doctor's consulting room. There he lifted me onto the couch and, unfastening his trousers, flung himself beside me.

'Tit for tat, an eye for an eye, tooth for tooth. You know your scriptures, Miss Sarah?'

'Let me go! Stop it, Mr Jewitt. What do you mean?'

'I mean to enjoy you before he does, Miss Sarah. This time he can have my leavings.'

He thrust his hand under my skirt. In terror I remembered my tussle with the farmer's lad at Malin Bridge and tried to bite his other hand but he kept it out of reach of my thrashing head and grasped both my wrists with his broad fingers.

'Just let yourself go limp, my dear. It won't hurt so much. It'll be an honour to take your maidenhood, little virgin. Here, see this.'

I shut my eyes when he exposed himself and I prayed desperately for heaven's assistance as he threw up my skirt. Then, astonishingly, as he came down on me, the miracle I piously implored was manifested. The door flew open, thudding against the wall, rattling the windowpanes, vibrating the medicine bottles on the shelf, and my saviour was at hand.

'How dare you, sir!'

The horsewhip cracked across Mr Jewitt's bare buttocks and he tumbled, whimpering, to the floor.

'Get out!'

The doctor's injunction was obeyed instantly. Dazed, shivering with relief and adoration, I shook down my skirt and slid from the couch. I put out a hand to steady myself against the cupboard as a wave of dizziness swept over me.

'Did he hurt you, Sarah?'

'No, sir. Thank you. But if you hadn't come in...'

'Poor child! Thank God I returned early. When I saw the pile of linen askew in the hall, I feared something was amiss. The wretch has terrified you.'

He reached out to take my arm and drew me to him. Scarcely knowing what I did, I hid my face against his chest and he enfolded me in his arms until my trembling ceased.

'He shall leave the house, Sarah. He shall harass you no more.'

'I only ask that he doesn't try...'

My eyes filled with tears at the embarrassment of speaking to the doctor of such a thing, afraid that he would think I was in part responsible for my predicament, aware that he must have seen my naked thighs. He put his hand to my cheek.

'Don't cry, Sarah. You've had a dreadful shock. I'll give you something to calm your nerves. You're a good girl and you've been horribly assaulted. My trust has been abused and I must apologise to you for the unspeakable behaviour of my assistant.'

I drank the liquid he gave me and looked up at him in wonder as he smoothed my disordered hair. He wiped a tear from my eyelashes and bent to kiss my forehead solemnly.

'Go to Mrs Strines now, Sarah. You won't distress her by mentioning this intolerable business, will you?'

'No, sir. I promise.'

'Good girl.' He stroked my cheek again and opened the door for me to leave.

Only much later did I remember some of the strange things Mr Jewitt said. At the time they made no sense to me.

*****

I said nothing to the housekeeper about the incident and passed no comment when Mrs Taylor exclaimed in surprise at Mr Jewitt's sudden departure from the doctor's service. I answered her enquiring looks with a carefully vacuous expression but I was not confident my insouciance was convincing. Mercifully, Mrs Strines was oblivious of the turbulent events in her household. My own peace of mind was far from restored but it was not only Dick Jewitt's attempt on my virtue which disturbed me, horrifying though that had been. In my direst need I had prayed to God for rescue and, incredibly, He had answered through the immediate intervention of His undoubted agent on earth, Robert Strines. What this might signify I couldn't fathom but I comprehended the boundless devotion I felt to my deliverer.

A day or two later, when I heard banging at the tradesman's entrance, I deemed it to be the impertinent lad who brought fresh produce from the dairy along the road, but Mrs Taylor's cry of concern corrected that impression. I opened the kitchen door to see what had happened and a well-built young man in working clothes ran towards me.

'Tom!'

'Sal, oh Sal, lass!'

Mrs Taylor discreetly closed the door on us as my brother sank onto a stool. 'Got a lift from a carter part of way, then I ran," he panted. "It's bad news, Sal, sad news from Malin Bridge. I'm on my way there.'

I stared at him in silence. I didn't want to hear what he'd come to tell me.

'Been an accident at the forge. Da's hurt bad. Wheel split. Half flew off and pinned his legs to ground. Crushed 'em, like.'

'He's still alive?' I asked mechanically.

'Was when message were sent me. I'm off to see him. I can walk over the tops to the Rivelin from here. I'll be there by nightfall. Thought you should know, so you can go to him too. You could get a ride with the carter this afternoon if you'd a mind to.'

'I can't leave my mistress.' I sounded prim.

'But he may be dying, Sal. He'll want to see you.'

'I'm not going, Tom. Give him my wishes for his recovery. Say I'll pray for him. But I will not enter his house again. I will not meet his wife.'

My brother gasped. 'You've become awful cold, Sal. At such a time shouldn't we let bygones be...?'

'No! Don't try to persuade me, Tom. I won't go. I'll get you some broth; then you can be on your way.'

216

He knew better than to persist against his implacable sister so he shrugged and took the broth I fetched. While he spooned it, I changed the subject pointedly and told of my meeting with Chrissie and that young woman's forthcoming nuptials.

'Marrying a grinder?' He sounded incredulous.

'She said so and her new sister-in-law was with her, respectable young woman she looked.'

'Well, it don't tally with what I saw but I'm glad if she's to wed decent like.'

When Tom set off again it seemed for a moment as if he was going to ask me to reconsider my refusal to go to Malin Bridge but the look I gave him was one of defiance, so he didn't raise the subject and simply pressed my hand.

'Don't let yourself be so unfeeling, Sal. Seems you've become hard as stone. Don't judge others so harsh. We're all human.'

I smiled thinly and waved him on his way. Then I stumbled indoors and clutched the dresser for support as revulsion and guilt overcame me. Unfeeling! Thank God my brother didn't know the strength of my feelings and where they were indecorously directed.

*****

The letter from Mrs Ibbotson set out her invitation to Dr and Mrs Strines, asking them to visit the Hall for a week at Christmastide and to bring me with them. She mentioned that her nephew from Penistone, Dr Stephen Strines, would also be present with his wife and Arthur Rawdon would join the party, after calling on his father in Huddersfield. The old lady probably guessed it would be deemed inadvisable for my mistress to travel so far in her delicate state and, as an alternative, asked if I would be permitted to visit for a day or two alone.

217

Arthur's concurrent letter begged me to come to the Hall so that he could make his formal proposal to me in the place where our first happy encounters occurred. Our engagement could then be announced to the assembly. He swore his undying love and assured me that his father was reconciled to the idea of our marriage. I folded the paper and put it away in my mother's box. I didn't untie the wide ribbon which enclosed Arthur's treasured ring; I hadn't done so for several weeks and felt uncomfortable to see it there. I didn't want to meet him so soon, to have to confront the reality of our engagement, publicly declared. I wanted to be left a little longer to indulge my harmless infatuation in daydreams. Surely, there was no need to hurry? I persuaded myself it was unmannerly of Arthur to press me so earnestly to reply.

I was surprised when Mrs Taylor told me the doctor would like to see me in his study but the housekeeper, who missed little, mentioned he had received a letter from Mrs Ibbotson. I didn't relish the prospect of discussing the invitation to the Hall with Dr Strines and I was nervous at entering the private realm of his study, where I'd never been before. He rose as I entered and removed books from an armchair so I could sit, a courtesy that embarrassed me. A nearby couch was also piled high with volumes.

'How are you today, Sarah?' He sounded business-like.

'Well, thank you, sir.'

'You know of Mrs Ibbotson's invitation to us all?'

I confirmed that I did.

'Of course it's impossible for Mrs Strines to make the journey and I wouldn't consider leaving her at such a time. However, although my wife would miss your services, you're free to go for a few days, if you wish. I think you may have other matters to discuss at the Hall.'

218

His direct look seemed to bore into me and I took a deep breath. 'I don't wish to go, sir. I don't wish to leave Mrs Strines.'

I heard his sigh as he seated himself, facing me across his desk. 'I believe Arthur Rawdon is anxious to see you. Aren't you anxious to see him?'

My predicament in answering was evident and I took refuge once more in primness. 'Indeed, sir, but there's no hurry. I owe my duty to Mrs Strines, especially at this time.'

'And to me, Sarah? Do you owe duty to me too?'

He smiled, suddenly animated. He had risen and come to the side of the desk. He perched there, stretching his long legs towards me.

'Why, yes, sir. You are my employer – and my saviour.' My voice cracked a little and I covered my face with my hands.

'I didn't mean to remind you of that lout, Jewitt. That wasn't what I meant.' He moved to stand beside my chair and I looked up at him in bewilderment. 'I'm a lonely man, Sarah, during my wife's confinement. Do you understand?'

I sat motionless, not believing what I'd heard, uncertain how to interpret his words, not daring to be certain. He took my hands and drew me up in front of him. He held me by the waist. 'I am grown devilish fond of you, little Sarah.'

'Please, sir, don't...'

'I shall do nothing to harm you, Sarah, believe me. I shall do nothing against your will. But let me kiss you.'

He bent over me, cupping my face in his hands, and he kissed me with passion I'd never experienced. Timidly I raised my arms to embrace him and he kissed me again. Then he released me. 'Now you'd best go, Sarah. Mrs Taylor will be wondering what discourse can be keeping you so long.'

He opened the door and, half-blindly, I left the room. I knew I'd come to an uncharted wilderness where nothing was as it seemed. The doctor had said he was fond of me! I groped my way downstairs to the kitchen, grateful to find Mrs Taylor was not there, and I splashed water on my burning face. When I was calmer, I went up to my mistress, solicitous to indulge her fancies, but I was appalled to realise how easily I could dissemble outwardly. In my heart, by contrast, the truth was crystal clear, for the one thing I could never hide from myself was my overwhelming love for Robert Strines.

Chapter 22: November - December 1862

Annie had miscalculated the term of her pregnancy. Mrs Turner suspected it for some time as her daughter's bulk grew larger and she could no longer manage to walk the distance to Division Street. Then one day in late November, while her mother was visiting the Crookes' household, the young woman's pains began. Two tense grandmothers-to-be made her comfortable and settled down to give encouragement and advice, often contradictory, until it was time to send for the midwife. It was likely to be a lengthy business and Mrs Turner gave the lad next-door a halfpenny to take a message to her family, saying she would stay with Annie until the birth.

Chrissie received the message and offered the lad a drink before his return journey. When he'd gone she took a stool to sit beside Will's armchair, where he rested nowadays gazing blankly at the flames in the grate, coughing and gasping for breath, especially when the sweating came. The flesh had fallen away from his face so completely that his jaw and cheekbones protruded through the paper-thin film of skin. His deep eye-sockets were blotched with unhealthy yellow and brown pigmentation. A living cadaver, Chrissie thought bitterly: the kindest outcome for him would be early release from his suffering.

And for herself? She would not let herself consider her own future. Her whole purpose was to bring solace to her stricken lover, to be with him until the last – and then...? Who knew what she would do then? She'd tried to make a bargain with Fate but Fate held all the cards. It was her bitter history which was destroying Will – it was her fault. Why, when she recognised that pathetic butcher's lad as the child Uncle Jack got on Mary Brailsford, had she not held her tongue? If she hadn't named the boy as her cousin, Will would never have entered the inferno so pointlessly. He'd wanted to show he could protect her, and anyone he thought she cared for, but his lungs had collapsed under the impact of the smoke. The cruel irony was not lost on her. Fate, which for a short time seemed to offer the hope of happiness, had snatched away that illusion. It left her less able to cope with adversity than in the past because misfortune had lost its former familiarity.

Will smiled at her as she took his hand. 'Did you hear what the lad said? Annie's time has come and your mother's staying with her.'

He inclined his head. With an effort he managed to speak, hoarsely, while his free hand darted to and fro tangling the fringe of the rug which covered him. 'How're we doing for money, love?'

She'd dreaded this question from him. When it became apparent, after the fire at the slaughterhouse, that Will would never be able to work again, she'd discussed the problem with Mrs Turner and Bessie, insisting she must get paid employment to supplement the family's income. At this, Bessie offered to speak to the manager about taking her on again at the button factory but Chrissie couldn't tell the Turners why this was impossible, why she could never appeal to Mr Copley, other than by offering herself to him. She dismissed Bessie's suggestion brusquely, with no adequate reason, and spoke of going out to do cleaning at the big houses in Broomhill but Mrs Turner rejected that idea.

'You need to stay with Will, Chrissie. It's you he wants to see when he opens his eyes. You're all he's got to ease his pain.'

Instead, Mrs Turner proposed that Freddie, the next-to-youngest of her brood, should start work at the grinding shop, even though he was barely twelve years old and had been praised by the schoolmaster as a promising scholar. Now Chrissie had to tell Will what was intended and, as she feared, he became agitated, with each shuddering cough bringing up blood-stained phlegm and pus.

'No! Not Freddie!' he rasped. 'He's a bright 'un. Could do a clerk's job. He's not to be a grinder, over my dead body!'

They gazed at each other in horror, shocked by his ill-chosen exclamation.

After a while Chrissie went to answer a sharp knock at the front door, expecting it to be another messenger from the Crookes' house, but she found herself confronted by a slight, beady-eyed man who twitched nervously. She knew exactly where she'd seen him before – twice – on the evening she and Annie observed the bands hidden in a gulley by ratteners and on the night of the Acorn Street bombing. He was Eb Pyle's weasel-like comrade and fellow ne'er-do-well.

'Come to see Will Turner, love. From union.'

Warily, she admitted him, checking as she closed the door that no one else was lurking outside. She indicated the parlour and the little man skittered across the hall into the snug room where the invalid was sitting but he stopped abruptly at the sight of Will's wasted figure and haggard face.

'Eh, lad! I'm right sorry to see thee so bad. After thi heroics and all.'

'Joe.' Will's started coughing again as his visitor sat down. Chrissie stood watching from the doorway.

'Been sent to report to union how tha'rt doing.'

'On me last legs, as you can see.'

'Nay, don't say so. But tha don't look too good. Union committee heard tha were bad. Decided to put thee on t'box as tha can't be earning.'

Will's surprise caused him to gulp for breath, unable to speak, and Chrissie came swiftly to his side. 'I thought the box were to pay men out of work for the time being.' She addressed the visitor coldly. 'Will can't hope to work again. We didn't think he qualified to go on box.'

Joe stood up, eying her closely. 'Will Turner's been a true union man all his life, if a bit too soft for his own good at times. Committee's decided to provide for him and his kin while he's so incapacitated.'

He pronounced the last word carefully and smirked at Chrissie knowingly. She held the door to the hall open for him to leave.

'He's not to be tired. Doctor said. You'd best go now.'

She escorted him to the front door and opened it but he grinned and laid a scraggy hand on her arm. He was more like a slimy snake than a weasel, she decided.

'Eb Pyle wishes thee well, lass. Asked me to tell 'ee.'

'He sent you?'

'Big man in union, he is. Able to decide who goes on box. Said tha'd understand.'

She was ready with a tart rejoinder but, seeing Bessie returning from her morning shift, she held her tongue. Joe peered appreciatively at the younger girl and smacked his lips as she passed, so Chrissie hustled him out of the door and shut it firmly, slipping the bolt. She gave Bessie news of her sister and packed her off upstairs with bread and cheese, saying she needed to speak privately with Will. Then she took her place beside him, her stomach churning.

'Chrissie,' he whispered. 'Now you see the value of the union. We'll make do without Freddie having to go to the grinding shop.' He managed to smile, almost roguishly. 'You'll have to take back your rude words about the union.'

She swallowed the bile which had risen in her throat and kissed him lightly.

'Aye, love. Maybe you're right. Union looks after its own, I don't doubt.'

*****

224

Annie was brought to bed of a bonny son with an assertive cry who looked likely to flourish. She herself ailed for a few days but then rallied and escaped the fearful childbed fever, so dreaded by those around her. After a week Mrs Turner returned home triumphantly, bearing the news that the baby was to be named Willie, in honour of his uncle, and a request that Chrissie should visit soon to see the infant. There was no change in Will's condition and he urged her to walk round to Acorn Street to see his nephew but she did so with a heavy heart, taking the roundabout route which avoided the neighbourhood of Tenter Croft. She was anxious to see Annie, recovered from the unpleasant business of childbirth, but she had little interest in viewing a mewling child.

Annie was pale but glowing with happiness, prattling about every explicit detail of her confinement, which made her listener cringe with distaste. The object of her proud rejoicing lay peacefully in his cradle throughout this recital. His prospective aunt hoped that he would continue to slumber, so his doting parent would be loath to disturb him, but eventually he opened his eyes and began a high-pitched wailing. Chrissie looked anxiously at his mother.

'He wants milk. You'll not mind me putting him to the breast.'

It was a long while since Chrissie had watched an intimate maternal scene and she was intrigued by the pleasure it seemed to give both participants. Annie relished the naturalness of nursing her baby, as if she had done so many times before, and when Willie had taken his fill, she lifted him gently onto her shoulder to wind him, as instructed by the elder Mrs Crookes and Mrs Turner. Then she wiped a milky dribble from his lips and held him out to her visitor.

'Hold him a bit, love.'

225

Gingerly, Chrissie took the small bundle and looked at the boy's crumpled face. He had Annie's charming turned-up nose, a perfect miniature copy, and perhaps Dan's forehead and beefy neck, but his clear blue eyes reminded her of Will, of Will as he had been a few months ago. She stared at him and felt herself tremble as some primeval urge rose within her, choking her voice and causing the muscles of her belly to tighten. Lower down, she knew, she was quivering.

Willie started to whimper and brought her to her senses. She held him out apologetically to his mother. 'Knows I'm not his Ma, right enough.'

'You might have held him too tight. Keep being told he's not made of bone china. He'll not break.'

'He's lovely, Annie. He's beautiful.'

She marvelled at her own words, still more at her feelings, but later, as she walked back to Division Street, she tried to dismiss the revelation she'd experienced, for the rapture of that brief moment was now overlaid with terrible despair. Too late she had learned how greatly she longed to bear Will Turner's child. Too late: for she knew it could never be.

*****

Several men from the saw grinders' union visited Will over the next fortnight. Because of his growing weakness he did not always recognise or respond to them but, with one or two close workmates, he managed to smile and nod his head acknowledging their awkward attempts at humour. Although she would not admit it, Chrissie was exhausted by caring for him, nursing him day and night, allowing herself to think of nothing but his welfare. For Mrs Turner it was a huge relief to have her never-to-be daughter-in-law on hand, sparing her some measure of the pain she

226

suffered in watching her son die in the same way as his father. It enabled her to escape to Acorn Street, to tutor her daughter in the minutiae of motherhood, to pamper her amazing grandson and to argue, in friendly fashion, with the elder Mrs Crookes, about the desirability of administering new-fangled gripe water.

When she went to answer the door one Sunday morning in the middle of December, after other visitors had already left, Chrissie was concerned Will should not be troubled further. She knew he ought to be resting and she was ready to doze a little herself but irritation at the thought of another caller was quickly replaced by sheer terror for, there on the step, in his best suit and a cleaner neckerchief than usual, stood Eb Pyle, his paunch bulging under his waistcoat. He put out his foot to stop her slamming the door.

'Come from union, love. Remember.'

He looked her up and down, ogling, and as he stepped into the hall he ran his hands rapidly from her shoulders down to her bosom.

'Stop that!'

'Hold meself in patience, I will, love. Never tha fret. Where's thi handsome fancy man?' He laughed, sounding almost good-natured and followed her into the parlour, but he recoiled when he saw Will slumped asleep in his chair, wheezing noisily. The invalid's body was pathetically emaciated, his face gaunt, and his lungs creaked with every intake of breath. 'Not have long to wait now, I reckon.'

'Get out, Eb.'

'Might give him helping hand if I punched him in chest and cracked a rib or two. What d'tha think, eh?'

'You'll hang for it, if you put a finger on him.'

'Who'll lay charges? His lungs are all done up any road. No one'd believe thee if tha made complaint, Chrissie Mallon, not with thi past, tha knows.

He was smirking at her, amused by the situation, and he clenched his right hand. As he took a step towards Will, Chrissie threw herself on to him, battering his chest with her fists, only to realise this was the reaction he wanted to provoke. He caught hold of her with a jubilant guffaw, bending her backwards from the waist, and thrust his groin against her. Will moved his head and mumbled inarticulately in his sleep. She slapped Eb's face.

'Bastard! Got no decency!'

He laughed, pulling her away from Will into the hall. 'Decency! To hear the slut! Never think she were my bitch, to fuck as I liked. Never tha mind, lass, I haven't come to clout that putrid bag of bones. It's thee I've come to speak to. Just to get things clear, like. I want thee back, Chrissie.'

'Never!'

'Remember tha owes me for all I've done for that useless stud and his family.'

'After all you and your wife did to me?'

To her surprise Eb's expression softened. 'I were sorry they did that. Edie suffered for it, I can tell 'ee. Won't see out of one eye again.' He ran his fingers down her throat. 'Come back to me, Chrissie. I'll treat thee proper. When I saw thee with Will Turner at t'music-hall, I knew I wanted thee like no other. Play straight with me and I'll not hurt thee again. Come back. I'll buy thee pretty things.'

His ingratiating, wheedling tone frightened her more than his habitual menace.

Will's croaking voice called from the parlour. 'Chrissie! Who's there?'

'Get out, Eb.'

'I'll go, love. But once he's dead and buried I'll be back. Tha'll come where tha belongs.'

'Get out!' She slammed the door and hurried back to her fiancé but he looked at her desolately. 'When I'm gone,

Chrissie,' he wheezed, 'have a care for yourself. Promise me, love. Do whatever's best for you.'

Equally desolate, she nodded.

*****

Will died in Chrissie's arms one week before the day they'd fixed on for their wedding. Later Mrs Turner and Bessie, with Ned's help, carried her away from the corpse she continued to embrace and the bereft mother shook her head as she touched Chrissie's icy cheek.

'Poor lass, she loved him so well. It's bitter gall. She put all her energy into nursing him. Poor lass. Whatever'll become of her now? Only the Good Lord knows.'

Chapter 23: December 1862

Arthur's letter was unaccustomedly edgy, even petulant. He chided me for declining Mrs Ibbotson's invitation and failed to understand how I could not be spared from my employers' home for a day or two. I gazed vacantly at his final sentences, more articulate and direct than usual:

It seems to me you too readily place the Strineses' convenience before your own and mine. I had hoped we might announce our betrothal to the company at the Hall but I must accept, regretfully, that you feel it more appropriate to remain at Ranmoor. It falls to me, therefore, to seek you out and, after Christmas, I will do so. Neither Doctor nor Mrs Strines shall prevent me claiming you as my promised bride.

I thought of Arthur's placid face and diffident manner and could not visualise him defying the doctor. I didn't question that he loved me as best he could. He was honest and kind and I would always feel affection for him but I doubted he was capable of the ardour against which any other must now be judged.

Each day for the last two weeks I'd longed only for the snatched moments when I encountered Dr Strines alone and he fondled me. I was delighted that he seemed to be at home more often than had been his custom and, denying to myself that it was anything but coincidence, I managed to contrive that I was outside his study or consulting room just at the times he might emerge and we would be, briefly, undisturbed. I half-recognised this insanity could not last but I felt enveloped in a cocoon of delicious adoration. I wanted no metamorphosis into reality.

I wondered at myself from time to time, puzzled that my guilt was not more compelling, since my behaviour was at odds with my whole upbringing and the strict morality I'd accepted. Yet the doctor told me often how necessary I was to his well-being and I was surely stealing nothing from Mrs Strines, for he was lovingly attentive to his pregnant wife. Besides, the sin on my part, if such it was, must be a tiny one, I thought, compared with my father's adultery – he had proclaimed himself penitent but continued sinning. So I let my thoughts drift on, reassured by the mildness of my own transgression and irritated that Arthur Rawdon's words threatened to disrupt my rapturous secret world.

Next day I received a second letter and the sight of my brother's ill-formed writing jolted me with alarm that new unwelcome news would intrude into my private heaven. Fortunately it was not as woeful as I feared but it was startling.

Dear Sal

I hope this finds you well. Glad to say Da is out of danger and like to live. But doctor says he won't never walk again seeing as how his legs are crushed. Our Step-Ma cares for him in everything. As Da cannot work more, I been asked if I wanted his place at the forge in Rivelin Valley and I said yes. There be nowt for me in Sheffield now. I have taken lodgings with Chrissie Mallon's Aunt Ada. She has heard nowt of Chrissie since she left Malin Bridge so I knew more'n her.

Our Da has been changed by his accident. Says it were God's punishment for sin. He would be glad to see you Sal. It would be kind if you visited him.

Your loving brother, Tom

Waves of conflicting emotion swept over me: amazement at Tom's change of heart towards our father, regret for Da's serious injury and irrational annoyance that the sinner viewed his accident as deserved retribution. For a moment it came to me that his contrition contrasted with my own ambivalent moral position but I didn't want to think about such things. I stuffed the letter away in my box.

231

Later that afternoon I settled Mrs Strines for her usual rest in the upstairs sitting room, while Mrs Taylor was busy in the basement kitchen and the doctor's new assistant, a self-effacing married man, was just leaving the house. When the front door closed, I slipped quietly into the hall to linger outside the consulting room and almost at once Robert Strines emerged and drew me inside. He seemed particularly agitated and he held me so closely I thought I would suffocate but he sensed my unease and relaxed his hold. His voice was husky.

'Don't be afraid, Sarah. I mean you no harm but will you do something for me?'

I looked at him fearfully, aghast at what he might want.

'I'm a man who needs the companionship of women. Sometimes I cannot bear having no one to touch me. Will you help me?'

'I, I don't know.' I wished I didn't sound so inane.

He took my hands. 'I don't ask you to do more than hold me, here.'

I felt his rigid member through the thick material of his trousers and heard him sigh as my fingers rested lightly on his crotch. At first I tried to remain calm but, as the movement of his body intensified, I tore my hands away and fled through the door, running, stumbling upstairs to my sleeping mistress. For a long time I sat, in near darkness, my heart thumping, petrified by the destruction of what I had persuaded myself was harmless flirtation, a kissing, cuddling flirtation, but no more. I quailed at the awful responsibility of choice which might now lie before me: choice between betrayal of my precious virtue and consummation of my sinful, burgeoning desire.

*****

Christmas Day dawned dank and gloomy and everyone was well wrapped as we attended the church of St John the Evangelist. Mrs Strines looked immensely elegant in her quilted bonnet and a new velvet mantle with a tasselled cape. Her pregnancy scarcely showed under the bulky folds and she seemed to glide over the rough paths, in her fine kid-leather shoes, unperturbed by potholes and loose stones. I marvelled anew at my mistress's grace as I followed my employers and sat, with the housekeeper, along the pew from them. I noticed Miss Paterson across the aisle, beside her parents, coyly acknowledging the doctor's bow, and I felt a moment's sympathy for the heavy-featured woman who was so obviously besotted with her physician.

All members of the doctor's household attended the celebratory meal during the early afternoon and feasted on Mrs Taylor's exquisite roast goose. After the plum pudding the doctor proposed a toast, in port wine, to Christmas and to his wife, asking that she share with the servants the news she had given him on their return from St John's.

Mrs Strines blushed, smiling. 'Oh, Robert, they will think me foolish.'

'Not at all, my love. Go on.'

'Why it is simply that I have felt the baby move – for the first time with certainty – and it was in church. I feel sure this is a blessed omen.'

'Amen, ma'am.' Mrs Taylor clasped her hands and looked up to Heaven.

'I'm so pleased, ma'am.' I beamed wholeheartedly at my mistress. I knew the doctor was looking at me but I willed myself not to glance towards him. The last few days had been a purgatory of doubt and misgivings for me. I'd ceased to loiter in the hall and the doctor had not attempted to seek me out, although he was genial towards me in company. I was uncertain what conclusions to draw from the ambiguity of my situation but could find no comfort in the alternatives. Perhaps the doctor had accepted my dread of greater intimacy and I was excused from deciding my own fate but, if that were true, my blissful dream had been demolished and this too was insupportable.

Before Mrs Taylor cleared the table, the carol singers came to the door with their seasonal songs, accompanied by fiddle and flute, and were invited inside to share titbits of plum pudding and lubricate their throats. After they had gone, Dr Strines suggested more carols should be sung, domestically, round the piano in the drawing room, and he acquiesced when his wife begged to be allowed to take part. He confessed he was longing to hear the trill of his nightingale again but he stipulated she must put no strain on her chest. During the recital he insisted we all take a little more port wine to loosen our vocal cords and, when the piano lid was closed, he produced a box of sugared fruits for us to share. He popped a fruit into each of the women's mouths and I hardly knew how to hold myself steady when he selected a candied plum for me, so large it hardly fitted into my mouth. I was forced to chew, with desperate rapidity, while the others laughed amicably at my embarrassment.

The doctor would not let Mrs Taylor attend to the dishes but said she must remain while he told entertaining stories of eccentric patients and marvellous phenomena. He described amazing cures and extraordinary discoveries and he made us giggle when he mimicked Miss Paterson's cow-like expression as she explained her latest ailment to him.

'A pathetic hypochondriac,' he chortled, 'or a frustrated spinster, much the same.'

'Robert!' his wife declared. 'She is enamoured of you. Sore stricken, alas!'

He kissed Bella Strines' hand, bowing with elaborate ease. 'Have no fear, my dear. I have no mind for bovine dalliance.' His wife pressed his hand to her cheek, smiling.

I thought the subject in very poor taste. I went hot and cold at the thought the doctor might mock my infatuation in the same way but it seemed unlikely he would speak about me to his wife.

After that we played "Consequences" and guessing games, trying to finish rhymes which the doctor started – always the ebullient life and soul of the small party. By early evening, however, the others began to tire and it was no surprise when Mrs Strines said she was fatigued and would go to her bed. I stood up to accompany her upstairs.

'Come back when my wife is settled,' the doctor called jovially. 'You must join Mrs Taylor and me in a hand of cards.'

I started to demur but Mrs Strines answered on my behalf, promising I would soon be free to return. I took my time, however, not wishing to connive with whatever might befall, for my head was not entirely clear and I felt both uneasy and exhilarated. When I did creep back downstairs, tentatively, I was mildly disgruntled to find the doctor and his housekeeper engrossed in a game of bezique.

'My wife has kept you uncommonly long, Sarah, despite her protestations. Come, sit down. We've nearly finished this round and Mrs Taylor is about to vanquish me ignominiously.'

I joined them in a further hand of cards playing as best I could, being a novice at such amusements which would have been forbidden in my father's house, and I found it difficult to concentrate. In between rounds, and ignoring our protests, the doctor refilled all our glasses. I sipped slowly but Mrs Taylor, who was unusually flushed, drank with enthusiasm and soon began to yawn. 'If you'll excuse me, doctor,' she said at the end of the next game, 'I'm that tired. I'll just take the dirty things from the dining room down to the kitchen, then I'll turn in. You'll forgive me, sir.'

'I'm remiss in having kept you so long. You've toiled hard today and given us a magnificent repast. Leave the things where they are. Sarah and I will see to them. May you sleep soundly, Mrs Taylor.'

I was conscious of the housekeeper's questioning look and felt it incumbent upon me to confirm these arrangements. 'Don't worry: I'll take everything down to the kitchen. Goodnight, Mrs Taylor.'

'Bless you, dear. Goodnight.'

Despite my polite protest the doctor was as good as his word, carrying dishes downstairs, emptying tureens and chatting inconsequentially in a loud voice. He made no attempt to touch me. His merriment was reassuring and I felt increasingly light-headed, losing my nervousness as I shared his inoffensive mirth but, perversely, I was also disappointed. When there was no more to do, I surveyed the dining room, now emptied of its dirty crockery. 'That's everything.' My tone was flat. 'Thank you, sir. Goodnight.'

'Join me in one more glass of port, Sarah. Please.'

My heart leapt and my mind convulsed. I looked at him doubtfully, willing myself to decline but I could not. I sipped from the glass he gave me and set it down on the sideboard, conscious he was watching me intently. 'I must go, sir.'

'Why must you, Sarah? Are you afraid of me?'

I didn't know how to reply, uncertain myself of the true answer.

'I think you like me a little, do you not?' He had come close and I knew I must escape.

'Yes, sir,' I whispered.

He took me in his arms and kissed my forehead. 'Say, yes, Robert.'

I shut my eyes. My head was befuddled but I felt his fingers on the buttons of my dress. 'Yes, Robert.'

'Sweet, dear little Sarah, I need you so badly. You know I would do nothing ever to hurt my wife. I worship her. But I have my own passions too. Will you lie with me, little love? The hearthrug is soft and I will be tender. There shall be no harm in it for you.'

I did not resist as he lifted me onto the rug and drew down the dress from my shoulders. 'Tell me what you feel for me, Sarah.'

I put my arms round his neck and held him to me as he nuzzled my breasts. There was only one answer. 'I love you, sir. Robert.'

'Then all is as it should be,' he said.

Chapter 24: December 1862

Next morning as I brushed my mistress's hair, I caught sight of my own puffy eyes and drawn cheeks in the mirror. I was appalled to see how my appearance reflected the shame I felt, rather than the exultation which also battled within me. This seemed symbolic. When I faltered in my brushing, Mrs Strines reached up and touched my hand.

'We were all merry yesterday, Sarah, were we not? Perhaps a little too much port wine was consumed.'

My flush must have spread from my neckline to my forehead. 'Yes, ma'am.'

'The doctor can be rather naughty in plying his subservient household with intoxicating drink. I fear Mrs Taylor will have a sore head. Fortunately we need little from her by way of cookery today. We have many cold victuals left to finish. That's why she's able to visit her sister this afternoon.'

'Mrs Taylor is going out?'

'Yes, and I fancy I shall be weary again after so much excitement yesterday. You may have an hour or two to yourself.'

'Thank you, ma'am.' I brushed more strenuously to subdue my trembling hand and hoped Mrs Strines could not hear the frantic beating of my heart.

When her toilette was complete my mistress stood and stretched with gazelle-like grace, before settling on the chaise-longue with her arms flung up onto the cushion above her head. Her swelling stomach showed more prominently under the soft fabric of her day gown and I glanced away, remembering Mrs Ibbotson's epithet – 'languorous' described Bella Strines perfectly.

'Read to me, Sarah. Let us continue with that work by Sir Walter Scott we began the other day if your clever little tongue can master the rustic Scots language.'

I was glad my mind was to be occupied by a task requiring concentration. I'd enjoyed the adventures of Waverley and Ivanhoe, by Sir Walter, which we'd already read together. I picked up the volume of Tales of my Landlord, second series, "The Heart of Midlothian", and turned to Chapter X, but as I read the complicated sentences, peppered with conversation in the Scots dialect, I grew more and more distressed. To my horror it became apparent that the delightful and vivacious Effie Deans had squandered her virtue to an unnamed seducer and, still worse, had been made pregnant. My voice quavered as I read how neighbours and fellow servants '*remarked with malicious curiosity or degrading pity, the disfigured shape, loose dress and pale cheeks of the delinquent*'. I prayed Mrs Strines would attribute my emotion solely to the pathos of the story.

At the end of the chapter after Effie had been apprehended for child murder, I set down the book and glanced shyly at my mistress. 'It's very sad, ma'am.'

'Sad and shocking. I cannot comprehend such vulgar immorality.'

I felt as if the earth must open up beneath me. Surely this comment showed Mrs Strines must know of my disgraceful behaviour. But how could she? Dr Strines was scarcely likely to have confessed. It could only be a horrible coincidence. Even more terrifying was the thought that I might have suffered Effie Deans' fate. Was it possible that a single falling from grace could have caused me to be with child? I wasn't sure.

Later, sharing cold ham and mutton with Mrs Taylor in the kitchen, I sensed that the housekeeper was regarding me intently and I fancied my ignominy must be written on my face. Sir Walter's description of the fellow servants' curiosity rang in my ears. It was a relief when the older woman was summoned to serve dessert in the dining room and I could escape upstairs, trying to control my palpitations.

When Mrs Strines returned to her sitting room after the meal, I was glad she required no more reading aloud but was content for us to sit with our sewing. We were stitching the small caps and long dresses which the expected infant would require and I concentrated fiercely on my simple embroidery, while my mistress used her needle effortlessly, making tiny gathers in the yoke of a flannel gown. After an hour Mrs Strines said she would rest and I went readily to my own room in the attic where I sank onto my bed, sitting there as if frozen, staring at the whitewashed wall. I treasured the opportunity to be alone and felt safer in my cell-like sanctuary, closed in from the awful realities outside, but my mind was in tumult.

What should I do? When would I know for certain if I was pregnant? Could I dissemble with my mistress and Mrs Taylor to dispel suspicion? Could they truly be suspicious already? Was it my guilty imagining? Cutting across this agonised self-questioning came the most desperate, dominating doubts: would the doctor seek to make love to me again? Did he sincerely feel affection for me? If he had need of me, could I deny him?

I didn't know how long I'd sat there, attempting to quell my fears, when I was startled by a bell ringing. It was not my mistress's bell. It came from the ground floor. It was not my duty to answer it but Mrs Taylor was out... Shocked understanding came to me. The doctor was ringing for attendance and he knew the housekeeper was not at home. He was ringing for me. I wondered if I should ignore it. What would happen if I dared to disregard the summons? Wasn't it possible the doctor had a legitimate reason for ringing? That some household task needed to be performed? But, if that was not the case, if he wanted me for his own gratification, what must my answer be? Slowly I tip-toed to

240

the narrow upper stairs, with their bare wooden treads, and descended to the grand sweeping staircase covered with a runner of deep-woven carpet.

Dr Strines was at the door of his study, dressed casually in shirtsleeves and waistcoat, with no cravat. Through the study door I saw he had cleared the leather sofa of the piles of books which had rested there on my previous visit. He drew me into the room and sat beside me on the couch, his arm enfolding my waist.

'You're well, Sarah?'

'I think so, sir.'

He smiled. 'You don't hold last night against me?'

I struggled to say what I knew I must. 'It was wrong, sir. It was sinful.'

'I don't hold so rigid a definition of sin as Methodists of the New Connection.'

I felt he was mocking me and tried to stand but he pulled me onto his knee. 'Perhaps we were all a little overcome by the port wine.'

'I think so, sir. I'm sorry for it.'

'Sorry! I'm not sorry, Sarah. I've taken no strong drink today and I'm as eager to make love to you as I was yesterday.' His hands were busy with the fastenings on my dress. 'Don't you want me to please you again?'

'Sir, it's wrong.'

'Robert.'

'Please let me go.'

'Just one kiss.'

I knew I would yield and he knew so too, arousing me and taking his pleasure with absolute self-assurance. Afterwards I lay in his arms, realising I had no power of resistance against him. I was his creature to fashion and destroy as he would and, at that moment, I didn't wish it otherwise. When he rose to tidy himself, I stood and moved meekly to the door.

'Wait, Sarah, I had another purpose in ringing for you. Sit down.'

He walked round to the chair at his desk and faced me, business-like, as if he had summoned me for no other reason than to speak to me formally. 'A letter was hand-delivered here this morning. It's addressed to me but the contents concern you.' He lifted the folded paper from his desk and my heart fluttered as I recognised Arthur's writing. He saw that I recognised it. 'Mr Rawdon writes that he wishes to call on Saturday morning and to address himself to you. He seeks my permission, as your employer, to permit this meeting so that he may openly ask for your hand in marriage.'

I felt myself go cold. I didn't know what to say. I stared silently at the doctor.

'I trust you will accept him, Sarah, in fulfilment of your promise. But, for my wife's sake, I would ask that you tell Mr Rawdon you wish to delay your wedding until after she is brought to bed around Eastertide. We shall then engage a nurse for the child and it will be convenient to make other dispositions in the household at the same time.'

I could not believe he was speaking to me in this quiet dispassionate way, setting out these calculated terms as a matter of expediency, he who not fifteen minutes earlier had made love to me with such intensity. He smiled.

'We shall have four more months together, Sarah, you and I, then Arthur will benefit from a newly knowledgeable and confident wife. I suspect he's inexperienced in these delicate affairs. We do him a favour, my little love, to fit you to instruct him subtly and with discretion. Meanwhile we may be comfortable together, knowing your future is safe and you have insurance against misadventure.'

He came round to where I was sitting dumbfounded and took me in his arms. 'I'm damned fond of you, little

242

kitten. It'll be devilish hard to let you go but we must be sensible.' He smoothed my hair and kissed my brow. 'You'll ask him to delay your marriage until the child is born? Of course convention accepts that an engaged couple have certain latitude in their behaviour and you will be wise to encourage him accordingly. You understand? You'll answer him as I suggest?' I read the desire in his eyes. 'I shall contrive to come to you as often as I may, Sarah.'

'I will answer him,' I whispered.

I returned to my mistress in a flurry of confusion, marvelling at the doctor's need for me and the trickery he proposed should be practised on Arthur Rawdon. Even so it was not until I saw the volume of Sir Walter Scott's work lying on the table and remembered the fate of Effie Deans that the full enormity of what was being suggested dawned on me. The possible scale of the trickery was unspeakably monstrous.

*****

The drawing room had been made available for Arthur's visit and Dr Strines diplomatically absented himself, permitting Mrs Taylor to receive the visitor and announce him to me formally, as if I were the lady of the house. I was relieved he did not rush forward to embrace me but I was puzzled that he stood looking at me awkwardly as if it was he who had a difficult pronouncement to make. For a chilling moment I imagined he must know of my transgression and was about to upbraid me as a depraved, fallen woman. 'What is it, Arthur?' I asked sharply, wanting to bring matters to a head without delay. 'Is something wrong?'

He looked at me ruefully. 'It isn't as I wished this occasion to be, Sarah. I've planned it for so long, what I would say, how I would kneel before you to ask for your

243

hand. Now I must preface that joyful request with a confession and beg your forgiveness.'

My eyes were fixed on him and I spoke very quietly. 'What do you mean?'

'It was perhaps not a very big misdemeanour but I should not have committed it. I must lay it before you and crave absolution before I can have the right to speak those other words.'

I didn't respond, nervous that this unexpected introduction would cause me to depart from my own carefully prepared script. He sank to his knees, flushed with embarrassment.

'At Christmas, at the Hall, we had much jollity and recreation. Mrs Ibbotson is most hospitable and her relations from Penistone are amiable company. She invited all her servants to join in some frivolous pastimes and there was a game of blind-man's-buff through all the reception rooms. We'd supped very well and perhaps drank a little too freely and in the excitement of the moment...'

He faltered and I stood up in amazed suspense, disbelieving what he must be about to say.

He stood before me wringing his hands. 'In the shadow, behind the curtains, I kissed Lizzie Simmonite. Oh, Sarah, I'm so ashamed.'

'Kissed? Do you mean simply kissed? No more?' I sounded clinical and he looked surprised.

'A long kiss, I fear. But no more! Sarah, you don't believe I could have come here at all, to seek your hand, if I'd sinned more grievously? You cannot surely think I could be such a villain?'

I sighed. 'No, Arthur, I don't think that. I know you are honest and honourable. Insofar as I have the right, I forgive you freely.'

'Oh, my dear, generous, loving Sarah.'

He moved towards me but I held up my hand, reverting to the words I had practised in my head. 'Don't say more, Arthur. I must speak first to prevent you. What I have to say is painful for us both.'

'You wish to delay our wedding? I thought you might want to remain here until Mrs Strines' child is safely delivered. I understand your sense of duty and admire it. I will wait willingly, dear love. What are a few more months?'

His earnest interruption nearly distracted me but I kept rigorously to what I had to say. 'No, it isn't that. I don't ask for delay. I cannot marry you, Arthur. I free you from our understanding and must return your ring. I ask you not to think too unkindly of me.'

I held out the small circlet with its turquoise stone, cupped in my hand, but he did not move to take it. His face was contorted with disbelief.

'Sarah? Why? What has happened? I beg you take back your words. My father has consented. He awaits our announcement. There's no impediment.'

As he made no attempt to retrieve the ring, I set it on a side table and crossed to the door, grasping the handle, striving to show dignity and self-possession. 'I'm sorry, Arthur. It's my final word. Our marriage would not be fitting. I am not worthy of you.'

He covered his face with his hands, but I understood very well what he must be thinking. I said I was not worthy of him but he would deem it mere delicacy of expression. He would not doubt my true meaning – that it was he who had rendered himself unworthy. He would dread having to tell his father he'd been rejected, since the only explanation he could give would be to acknowledge his peccadillo with Lizzie Simmonite. It was unkind to put him in this humiliating position but I could not have foreseen the nature of our conversation. I slipped out of the room.

Mrs Taylor took him his coat and hat and she told me afterwards he picked up something from the side-table, clenching his fist over it. I knew he must be mortified and furious with himself for his stupidity, while I was ashamed to have hurt him so cruelly. Yet I believed I had no choice. I had done what was right.

Chapter 25: December 1862

In the days between Will's death and his burial, Chrissie spent most of her waking hours sitting vacant-faced in the parlour staring at his empty chair. Her mind seemed to work in slow motion, setting aside matters which were insoluble or too painful to confront. She felt the strength which had sustained her was extinguished and, with it, her resolution and her resilience. For much of the time she wished herself in the grave with her lover, freed from the need to consider her future and take action. It irked her that she'd glimpsed what real happiness might consist of before, in a cruel twist, it was snatched away by malignant Fate. Now part of her was ready to concede defeat. Yet, in the stubborn core of her being, something refused to bow to such a callous decree and slowly her capacity for rational thought returned.

Mrs Turner recognised her anguish and sought to protect her from well-meaning attempts by Bessie and the boys to divert her with their chatter. For long hours, the older woman sat quietly alongside Chrissie, waiting for the announcement she knew would be made. On the day before the funeral it came.

'I need to leave you, Mrs Turner. I can't stay here longer, with Will gone.'

'I know, dear. I understand. Where will you go?'

Chrissie did not reply but posed her own question, to which there was an inevitable answer. 'How will you manage without the union money?'

'They've sent a bit more. Enough for a week or two. It's good of them.'

'The union won't help longer'n that.'

If Mrs Turner was surprised by this emphatic assertion, she didn't challenge it. 'Freddie'll start work at the grinders' shop in New Year,' she said softly. 'We'll manage with the extra wage.'

Chrissie suppressed a useless sigh at the idea that clever young Freddie was doomed to join Ned in the trade that had killed their father and brother. There was nothing she could do to prevent it. Will had told her to have a care for herself and she tried to anchor her thoughts on the need to carry out his wishes, as best she could, treating it as a sacred duty. It was pointless to imagine she might sacrifice herself in order to secure more money from the union for the Turners. She knew that, whatever martyrdom she accepted, she could place no reliance on Eb Pyle's goodwill. In any case nothing on earth would lead her to submit to him again. The safest defence she could provide for her surrogate family was to disappear from their lives, leaving them in ignorance of her whereabouts.

Preposterously, for a short time, she contemplated throwing herself into the arms of young Tom Webster. He would welcome her with genuine devotion, she was sure, but she must not spread the pernicious poison she seemed to carry with her into the life of another blameless admirer. He was a Sheffield grinder, albeit working for one of the large employers. Eb Pyle would find a way of wielding sinister influence against him. An inexperienced lad would be far less able to withstand it than Will had been, when in health. Tom could offer her no certain protection and, if she went to him, she would ruin his life.

With cool detachment she reached her decision. She would venture all on a single throw of the dice. Six months or more had passed since the offer was made and it might no longer stand. So be it. She lacked the energy to leave the town and seek a new beginning elsewhere – as she had once planned – to battle poverty, slave for a pittance and struggle to avoid falling prey to another Eb. Her striking colouring and delicate features would prove a magnet wherever she went, but she no longer had the spirit to relish the implications. She needed to use her frail assets to win a measure of security and only a man in a superior station of life could offer her that. If Nathaniel Copley still wanted her, she would become his mistress and accept his terms. If he did not, she would throw herself from Lady's Bridge into the surging waters of the River Don.

Painstakingly she formed the letters on a scrap of paper and addressed it to Mr Copley: *'Your blue hat awaits.'* Then she added a message of her own: *'Come soon if you want me.'*

Pressing a penny into the hand of the youngest Turner boy she asked him to take the note to the button factory after his sister and her workmates had started their shift. She said he should wait for a reply and he must never breathe a word of this adventure to anyone. She led him to believe it would lead to Bessie's advancement. Now, after Mrs Turner had gone to market, she sat waiting for the boy to return but he'd been gone for two hours and she began to despair. Perhaps Mr Copley was away from the factory, gone out of Sheffield for Christmas. Perhaps he'd received her message and torn it up with contempt, ignoring her messenger who waited uselessly for an answer. She felt tears of degradation pricking her eyes, degradation and failure.

When the front door opened at last she was resigned to seeing Mrs Turner, with her basket of bread and cabbages, but it was the little lad who bounded in and gave a triumphant shout, reawakening her hope. 'Saw him meself, I did! Fine gentleman, with great ginger whiskers. Gave me a sixpence! Said I was a 'missory of Cupid'. What's that?'

Chrissie smiled, not recognising the word 'emissary' herself. Her heart was thudding. 'Did he give you a reply?'

The boy held out a sealed letter and she patted his head gratefully. Turning away from him she opened the paper and, struggling over some words, she read its contents to herself.

'*Let bells ring out. Let choirs sing anthems of rejoicing. Mrs Burkinshaw will meet you two days hence, on the corner of Division Street, at nine in the morning. Wear the blue hat.*'

It was almost poetic. She had not expected that. She dismissed a momentary regret that he should send a stranger to meet her, recognising how discretion required this subterfuge. She would have to get used to such contrivances in her new shadowy life. It was the price of her escape from desolation and ever-present menace: escape to what, she did not care to contemplate.

*****

A bevy of Will's workmates called to voice their condolences to his family, after they returned from the chapel, and Chrissie stood alongside the others, nodding acknowledgement, shaking their hands. She saw Eb Pyle among the throng and when he approached her, while the Turners were occupied with relatives from Heeley, she forced herself to appear unruffled.

'Well I'm blowed! The bride who never was, no less. Morning, Chrissie.'

She did not reply.

'I'm coming for 'ee first thing tomorrow morning, love. Me mate Joe's missus has a room for thee, Lea Croft they live. Nice and handy for me to visit. Suit us very well. Tha could go back to button factory if tha'd a mind to.'

She said nothing. Could he really believe she would move into Lea Croft, a set of dwellings even fouler than those of nearby Tenter Croft? That she would face the local women who had tortured her? That she would become his whore again, suffering his abuse? Despite her attempt at self-control, she could not keep a flicker of distaste from her expression.

He did not miss it and his voice was gruff. 'Joe's taken a fancy to thi little friend there.' He pointed at Bessie, standing by her mother, her modest face downcast. 'Be a pity if she came to harm, eh?'

Chrissie spoke crisply as if concluding a transaction with a tradesman. 'Make it noon tomorrow, Eb. I've promised to help Mrs Turner clear up.'

'Make me take time off work. Living round Division Street's given thee airs and graces seemingly. Never mind, lass, we'll soon have that put to rights when my cock's where it ought to be. Getting juicy between the legs already, eh?'

'Noon!'

'All right, tha fucking bitch. Noon it is.'

He gave a small bow, smirking at her, and moved away. Bessie crossed beside her and took her arm. 'Who's that nasty looking man, Chrissie?'

'A saw grinder. One of those in the union Will had no time for. No one you need to worry about.' Chrissie put her arm round the younger girl and hugged her.

*****

She bade a tearful goodbye to the younger Turners as they left the house early next morning for work and school. Then, on the doorstep with her bag at her feet, she spoke earnestly to their mother, giving her a folded paper.

'Midday, a man'll come asking for me. He were at funeral – belongs to Will's union. Give him this note, will you. It tells him I'm gone and I've not told you where. He'll blather a bit and curse me but he'll not bother you more. I've told him I've got a protector.'

'Oh, lass!' Mrs Turner clasped Chrissie to her. 'Are you sure about what you're doing, going away like this?'

'I'm sure. It's best. Bless you. I must go now.'

251

Only when she had coaxed Mrs Turner back into the house and shut the front door, did she extract the blue hat from its box.

A closed cab was waiting on the corner of Division Street and, as she drew near, the door opened and a buxom woman of indeterminate years leaned out to address her. 'Miss Mallon? Get in. Hannah Burkinshaw. Please to meet you.'

Mrs Burkinshaw's copious skirts spilled over most of the seat as Chrissie squeezed in beside her. She wore a heavy pleated mantle and an elaborate frilly bonnet beneath which her jowls wobbled alarmingly. After her initial greeting she sat in silence.

'Are we going far?' Chrissie asked, in case conversation was expected of her.

'Mile or two.' Mrs Burkinshaw inclined her head towards the leather panel separating them from the cab's driver. 'Talk when we get there.'

Chrissie shrank back from the window when she saw they were passing the market on South Street, where Mr Copley had set her down after their meeting and where she once encountered Tom Webster, who said he lodged nearby. Then they were heading uphill, past low terraced dwellings and a large private cemetery, before the houses became grander and more scattered. After that she lost track of the twists and turns of their route until they approached a formidable building behind high gates. For a moment she feared they were going to turn in there, that she'd been tricked and her journey was a macabre jest.

Mrs Burkinshaw seemed to sense her unease. 'Nether Edge workhouse,' she said crisply. 'Not far to go now.'

Still apprehensive, Chrissie wondered if this single statement contained a hidden meaning. Would the path she'd chosen lead inexorably to the workhouse when her charms had faded and Mr Copley cast her aside? The workhouse or a whorehouse? She shuddered. Perhaps the engulfing waters of the River Don would have been preferable.

She was reassured when they drew up before an isolated stone villa, shaded by trees, set on a triangular plot between two converging roads and she followed her escort into the house, noting appreciatively the comfortable furnishings of hall and staircase. As they came to the landing on the second floor a timid looking child of twelve or thirteen scurried into an adjacent room but no introduction was made. Then they climbed a further flight of stairs and Mrs Burkinshaw, panting, flung open the door facing them. 'This is your room, Miss Mallon.'

The heavily-built woman sank down on an upholstered chair to catch her breath while Chrissie stood staring at, what seemed to her, unimaginable luxury. In addition to the armchair there was a horsehair sofa, much smarter than the one Aunt Ada and Uncle George had prized, a heavy mahogany table with two upright chairs, a tall mirror on a stand, an ornate carved cupboard and a corner cabinet, full of knickknacks, topped by an aspidistra in a pot. A worn but serviceable carpet covered the centre of the floor and there was wallpaper on the walls, sprinkled with washed-out flowers of an indeterminate genus. Mrs Burkinshaw indicated an alcove, screened by a curtain, which Chrissie drew back. A double bed, with a purple counterpane and matching tester, filled most of the space, except for a plain wooden table on which stood a washing set with jug and bowl.

'Mr Copley said to say he'll be calling this evening. If you wants anything else than what's here, you should consult him. In meantime there's a dress in cupboard for you to wear. Maybe a bit large seeing as you're so slender but Mr Copley's asked for a dressmaker to call tomorrow to fit you up proper.'

253

Chrissie gazed round the room again as she tried to comprehend what Mrs Burkinshaw was saying. 'This is me own room?'

'Aye, it's all for you.'

'Do others live in the house?'

'Three other young ladies, like yourself: Miss Sykes, Miss Brammall and Miss Hawley, ladies of some refinement, you know. You'll meet 'em at meals in the dining room. Us all eats together. Save when one of the gentlemen asks for a private dinner tray when he visits. I'll send something up for you today though. You'll want to rest and prepare yourself before Mr Copley comes. He'll be eager to see you, I'm thinking.'

Sudden alarm, like that she'd felt at the sight of the workhouse, swept over Chrissie. 'Where have you brought me, Mrs Burkinshaw? What is this place?'

The woman's jowls waggled forbiddingly. Her eyes narrowed. 'What do you think?'

Chrissie stood rigidly. 'If it's a bawdy house, I been duped. I'll not go with all and sundry.'

'Shame on you, Miss Mallon, to think of such a thing! It's a respectable guesthouse, this is. Each of my young ladies has a gentleman who visits and, like as not, her friend pays the rent. If he does I'll not quibble. I live downstairs and look after the establishment and do the cooking. A girl comes to clean and helps with the dishes.'

The landlady hauled herself upright from the chair. Her tone had become caustic. 'I hope you'll fit in well, Miss Mallon. I've not done business with Mr Copley afore and maybe you're not well informed. You're clean, I trust?'

Chrissie looked at her witheringly. 'I've no sores between me legs, if that's what you mean.'

Mrs Burkinshaw responded with distaste. 'No need to be vulgar. I look for some delicacy in my house. I dare say you're overwrought so I'll make allowances. There's two

254

things to remember if your residence here is to be convenient to all.' She approached Chrissie, taking hold of her chin and turning her face from side to side to catch the feeble sunlight from the window. 'You're handsome lass, right enough; so keep a civil tongue and don't go causing difficulties in the house. Remember it's Mr Copley who provides for you. If you should see any of the other gentlemen what calls, keep your eyes down and don't get into conversation. Miss Sykes has a sharp jealous temper, in particular.'

Chrissie nodded blankly. 'There's something else for me to note?'

'Aye, lass. Something a bit intimate.' She held out a paper bag. 'Put one of these inside before your gentleman calls – it'll take care of you knows what – pessaries they're called. Won't hurt you. Things can still go wrong, so if you has reason to think you're in trouble, if you gets my meaning, you're to let me know at once. Us'll deal with it. Soonest said, soonest mended. Understand?'

*****

Left alone, Chrissie took the dress from the cupboard and put it on, folding her old workaday clothes and stowing them in her bag. The new gown was made of green silk with lace flounces at the neckline and on the sleeves. As Mrs Burkinshaw surmised, it hung loosely and the bodice dipped deeply to display the swell of her breasts. She looked at herself in the mirror and felt nothing: no pleasure, no excitement, no embarrassment. Her senses were numb. Later, with some repugnance, she inserted a pessary.

Mr Copley came soon after five o'clock. She heard him hurrying up the stairs then the door swung back on its hinges and he was there, standing as if awestruck, gaping as she moved towards him. His extravagant whiskers certainly

255

improved his thin face, although they were awkwardly multi-coloured, with the sideboards darker than his ginger moustache and thinning hair.

'Chrissie!'

'Should I call you Nathaniel now I'm to be your whore?' She was trying to sound good-natured and hadn't planned the note of bitterness in her voice.

'Don't say that. You'll be my mistress, not that other thing. I shall respect and esteem you. I've wanted you so long and I'll cherish you. Don't feel sour you've taken me as your protector.'

She was surprised by his sensitivity. She would be honest with him. 'I were to have wed by Christmas but my man took ill, grinders' disease. Buried him yesterday. Dangerous lout's been after me, threatening all sorts. That's why I've come. Can't deceive you.'

'You'll not regret it, Chrissie. You'll be safe here and I'll care for you, as richly as I can. I'll make you a small allowance and Mrs Burkinshaw'll do as she's bid for you.'

She bowed her head in acquiescence. The landlady had set out glasses and wine. 'Will you have something to drink?'

He moved forward to hold her. 'Later.' He thrust his moist whiskery mouth into her décolletage and his spiky teeth nipped her bosom; then he drew her towards the alcove. His excitement was so great that, as he penetrated her, he could not contain himself and he was immediately apologetic. His contrition amused her and she stroked his hair.

'Don't fret, love. There'll be times enough to get it right.'

'Chrissie, you're wonderful.'

She lay still while he pawed her, marvelling that she should find herself consoling this unattractive adulterer, but as she closed her eyes she smiled. In such unlikely circumstances it seemed she had found the haven she needed, where she could rest her wearied mind and body and see if recuperation of her devastated heart would be possible.

Chapter 26: December 1862 - January 1863

Next morning, as promised, Chrissie met two of her fellow residents at Mrs Burkinshaw's guesthouse. She quickly found it comical that their landlady had referred to them as ladies of refinement, although she didn't doubt they had pretensions in that direction. Miss Hester Sykes was the elder by a year or two. She was a stylish, fleshy woman, with a mass of dark hair piled elaborately on her head, who wore pearls to breakfast. She exuded a superior air and it was clear Miss Matilda Brammall customarily deferred to her. This second lady was flaxen haired and willowy but she wore a perpetually worried expression which creased her forehead and pinched the corners of her mouth unbecomingly. She was anxious to assert her companion's precedence among the occupants of the house.

'Hester has the whole of the first floor, as is right. The Duke treats her most royally.' It was Miss Brammall's affectation to speak with gentility, when she remembered.

'The Duke?'

Chrissie's astonishment was well appreciated by Miss Sykes. 'Not a real duke, love,' she said throatily. 'Us calls him that as he don't want his name bandied about, you know. He's a steel-master, a coming man in the Cutlers' Company, no less. Tilda's friend belongs there too.'

'In a smaller way of business altogether,' Miss Brammall added earnestly, making clear it was not her place to challenge Miss Sykes's reflected pre-eminence. 'The Duke sends an open carriage sometimes so she can take the air in style. Hester lets us ride with her. So good of her.'

Miss Sykes turned her short-sighted gaze towards Chrissie. 'Your gentleman's not kept a friend here before, Miss Mallon. Old Bodger, as us called him, took ill one night when he were here with Nancy, up in her room. Mrs

258

Burkinshaw hustled him out to his gig and he were found in it a mile away next morning, dead as a doornail.'

'What happened to Nancy?'

Miss Brammall shuffled her feet and crumbled the bread on her plate. Miss Sykes drew herself up magisterially. 'Gone back on streets, shouldn't wonder. Little slattern, she were.'

Chrissie thought it best to change the subject. 'Mrs B said there were four of us here.'

'Dolly Hawley's been poorly for a while. Having meals in her room. Mr Gregory's not been to visit much neither.'

'Fine gentleman, he is," Miss Brammall burst out enthusiastically. "Wouldn't mind a bit of him myself.'

Her giggle was cut short by Hester's frown. 'Us has our little jokes, Miss Mallon, but us all knows what's right between us. Is your room comfortable? Bit small, I suppose, up in garret.'

'It'll suit.' Chrissie realised she was being firmly put in her place as the newcomer to this strange household. She did not feel comfortable but there were compensations. 'Breakfast were good. Is all the food like that?'

'We're not stinted.' Hester patted her ample stomach appreciatively. 'The Duke likes a little plumpness here and there.' She chuckled and rose in a ripple of muslin. 'I wish you good-day, ladies.'

Chrissie turned to Miss Brammall who seemed eager to chat further. 'You can call me Tilda, Miss Mallon. Mrs Burkinshaw's a right good cook.'

'I'm Chrissie, love. Mrs B said there's a girl who cleans too, so we don't even need to see to our own rooms.'

'Mrs Burkinshaw's sense of humour, duck. The girl's about forty and covered in moles.'

'Oh! I thought she were that pale little thing I saw yesterday on the landing.'

Tilda pushed her plate aside and fluttered her hands awkwardly. 'Lord love us! You must have seen Dolly. Me and her have rooms on second floor.'

Chrissie felt the colour rise in her cheeks. 'She didn't look no more'n thirteen, maybe less.'

'Mr Gregory likes 'em young. Don't keep 'em long neither. Reckon Dolly'll be going soon. Found herself in a spot of bother. Mrs Burkinshaw sorted it out. I'll be going now, Chrissie. Like to do my embroidery in the morning when there's a bit of sun.'

Returned to her room, Chrissie hugged herself to stop the trembling, unable to dismiss Dolly's white face from her mind. Hester and Tilda were grown women, as she was. Their presence in Mrs Burkinshaw's house resulted from choices they'd made and which her two companions at least seemed to find wholly congenial. Dolly could have had no such luxury of choice. No doubt she'd been forced into her degraded way of life as Chrissie herself might have been, if things had turned out differently years ago. She felt a deep loathing for the fine Mr Gregory.

The dressmaker deftly altered the over-large gown to display Chrissie's figure to best advantage and took fittings for two day dresses and an elaborate crinoline for 'entertaining'. The girl's hair had not yet reached her shoulders but it was now long enough to pin up beneath a little confection of lace and ribbons, which disguised the unfashionable shortness of her curls, and when the seamstress had gone Chrissie remained looking in the mirror, content with what she saw. Nevertheless the sight of herself in elegant lady's attire highlighted the unreality of her situation and she felt as if she was playing some elaborate game of dressing-up in a land of make-believe. That was not inappropriate, she concluded with clear-sighted sarcasm, because she now inhabited a twilight world no respectable person would acknowledge.

260

That evening Mr Copley found her appearance so exquisite his manhood was cowed and he was quite unable to make love to her but again she found herself easing his embarrassment and winning his gratitude. He described the weekly allowance he would provide for her.

'I don't need so much to keep meself pretty for you, Nathaniel, but I'd like you to use half of it to help the friends who cared for me when I were sick and took me into their home.'

He did not mask his surprise. 'Won't you want to save yourself a nest-egg, Chrissie? I'm told most ladies here like to do that.'

'I'll manage with half the sum. I'd like to help Mrs Turner – Annie and Bessie's mother. There's a lad in their family who's bright enough to be a clerk if he gets more schooling.'

'That's a kind thought. If that's what you want, you could ask Mrs Burkinshaw to send your money to them.'

'I'd rather Mrs B don't know. I can't tell you why but I don't feel I could trust her with it.'

He looked thoughtful. 'You're maybe right. Put what you want to give them aside and I'll see it delivered privately to their house, whenever you wish.'

She kissed him. 'Thank you, Nathaniel. You're good to me.' She meant it sincerely.

*****

The gentlemen visitors did not call at Mrs Burkinshaw's house over the Christmas period, being properly engaged in domestic festivities at home with their families. This was the pattern every year and the landlady decreed she and her lodgers would hold their own celebration, with goose and plum pudding, like those other upright households. The ladies duly donned their finery and

261

joined their hostess in the dining room, decked in pearls and paste, ruching and rouge. Even timid Dolly came, in an unsuitably flimsy dress, and sat silently watching the antics of the others as the merriment grew and the gin flowed.

Miss Sykes was inclined to be petulant, as the Duke had been less generous than usual with his Christmas gift to her. Miss Brammall was amused by this and became bolder after she took a third glass from the landlady. She adopted her most cultured accent.

'Losing your touch, Hester? Maybe it's those grey hairs showing behind your ear.'

Miss Sykes rounded on her furiously. 'You're one to talk, you skinny cow! Your wrinkles get deeper by the day. Bosom's sagging too.'

Tilda gave a little scream and rose unsteadily from her chair while Mrs Burkinshaw interposed herself between them to prevent physical assault. Their bickering continued but became more desultory as their glasses were refilled and they grew sleepy. Chrissie moved to sit by Dolly, hoping to coax her to talk, for she'd failed previously to exchange more than a word or two with the child.

'Are you feeling better, Dolly? You don't look so pale.'

'Bit better.'

'What were wrong, love?'

Dolly cast a terrified glance across the room to where Mrs Burkinshaw was beginning to nod. She shook her head at Chrissie.

'How long've you been here?'

'Since summer last year.'

'Where'd you come from?'

Dolly's voice came in a whisper. 'Home were in Sharrow. Ma and me were ill with the fever. Ma died but I got better, more's the pity. Took me to workhouse. Then Mr Gregory said he'd take care of me. Brought me here.'

'Where'd you meet Mr Gregory?'

'At workhouse. He's some high-up, Guardian of the Poor or something. Saw me there.'

When the child began to cry Chrissie was afraid her sniffling would wake the others and led her into the hall. 'What happened to you, love? Tilda said Mrs B sorted it out.'

Dolly was shaking and bit her lip. 'Don't say I told you. I fell for a baby but I didn't know what were wrong. Didn't tell Mrs Burkinshaw when I should have. She were that mardy with me.'

'What did she do?'

'She got baby out. It hurt terrible and I were that ill they said I nearly died. Wish I had too.'

'What did Mr Gregory say?'

'He were mortal angry I hadn't told Mrs Burkinshaw at once. Said I were a stupid bitch.' Her frail body shook convulsively.

Chrissie took Dolly to her room and settled her with a dose of the laudanum Mrs Burkinshaw had supplied, soothing the child's puckered brow until she slept. Then she returned to the dining room and helped herself to two more glasses of gin, until the image of that terrified young face faded from her mind. She fell into a restless sleep for a while before joining the others, newly woken, in an incoherent game of cards. She forced herself to laugh at their badinage and accepted a glass of a fiendishly intoxicating liqueur which Mrs Burkinshaw produced when Hester and Tilda started to exchange increasingly smutty insults. By the time Chrissie pulled herself up the banisters to her own room she had forgotten Dolly's troubles, thinking only of the remarkable luxury she now enjoyed.

'Look at me now, Gran,' she said out loud, twirling around in grave danger of losing her balance. 'Slut, you called me! See me room with its drapes and upholstery? And me in a crinoline with folderols and flounces? What'd you think of that? Said I'd come to a sticky end, didn't you? Like as not I will! But now I've got food and lodging you couldn't imagine: feathers and silks and dainty shoes, all for letting a pathetic lecher up me arse a few days a week. Fucking cow, you called me! See me now!'

She sank down onto the armchair in giggles, kicking out her legs so that the hoop of her skirt billowed up in front and she could see her stocking tops in the long mirror, white against the shadows thrown by the oil lamp. She shivered suddenly and turned to look round at the empty room behind her.

'Thought I saw you, watching me, Will,' she gasped. 'Oh, why'd you leave me, lad? Why'd you have to go?'

*****

As the weeks passed Chrissie felt her spirit reviving. Certainly she'd never been so pampered and cosseted, so well fed, so smartly dressed and so little occupied with day-to-day necessities. She might have been lulled into a cosy lassitude, basking in the indulgences of her half-world but as her emotional exhaustion lessened, she grew restless and dissatisfied. It was not Mr Copley's fault. She became almost fond of his silly foibles. His adoration for her hadn't diminished and it could still lead him, variously, to premature ejaculation or impotence, as if she were some goddess before whom he fell into a state of nervous prostration. Yet, for all his adulation, she suspected he wanted her as much to boast about privately as to cherish. It ratified his new standing in society to be known, among a circle of discreet intimates, to keep a mistress, to be a regular man-about-town. Chrissie was also aware that he found her more tolerant than Mrs Copley, despite or perhaps because of the five Copley children, with regard to the diverting activities she would permit. At all events, Mr

264

Copley caused her no anxiety. The problem was that her privileged existence was becoming unendurably tedious.

Tilda spent her days with her embroidery and Hester fancied herself a skilful artist, sketching and painting pallid still-life arrangements in the way she fancied gentlewomen passed their time. Chrissie took no pleasure in such pursuits and made a crimson stain on the carpet when she tried her hand with Miss Sykes's watercolours. She found herself taking stock of her position, remembering her high hopes when she left Malin Bridge and the ignorant overconfidence with which she'd encouraged men to admire her. She thought with annoyance of how she'd thrown herself at Eb Pyle and all that ensued from that. She should have trusted her grandmother's judgement on their vicious, possessive neighbour, but the old woman had betrayed her as a child and forfeited her respect. The past could not be changed.

She longed to know how Annie and Dan were and how their little son was progressing but it was inconceivable she might contact them. They must never know of the life she'd chosen. She agonised that Freddie was probably already an apprenticed grinder and that Bessie was being harassed by Eb's obnoxious crony, Joe. Inexplicably, she thought of Sarah Webster, safe in the doctor's genteel household in Ranmoor, preparing to wed in the New Year. She thought of loyal, devoted Tom and wondered if he'd now reconciled himself to a life with Lizzie Simmonite or some other colourless local girl. As the days passed, she began to chafe at the restrictions of her circumscribed life, with its veil of secrecy shielding it from public view.

On one occasion she joined Hester and Tilda for a drive in the Duke's open carriage and at first she enjoyed the cold air on her face and the sight of hedgerows and fields. As they travelled on, however, her companions' continual chatter grew irksome and, when they came to a nearby farm, a gaggle of youths started to point at them and shout.

'Look! It's trollops from t'whorehouse!'

'How many's that fat 'un had, dost think?'

'Wouldn't mind that redhead meself.'

Hester thumped the side of the carriage and the coachman cracked his whip in the air. 'Ignorant whelps!' he shouted.

The boys ran off but a small urchin with a vacant expression limped after them, piping mechanically. 'Cart o' whores! Cart o' whores!'

Mrs Burkinshaw's efforts to portray her house as one of decorous respectability were given little credence in the neighbourhood, it seemed.

*****

When the heavy snow came in the middle of January Chrissie could restrain herself no longer. She crept out from the side door, dragging Dolly with her, and encouraged the girl to throw snowballs. They ran about on the open ground behind the house, plunging knee-deep in the drifts, and she was grateful to hear her young companion shrieking with glee as they tried to hit each other with their soggy missiles. While Dolly dodged to and fro round the corner of the house, Chrissie rolled a snowball which was particularly large and firm and she hurled it with all her strength. Her aim was sure but at that very moment a horseman rounded the bend and the projectile landed not on Dolly, who had prudently withdrawn indoors at the sight of the visitor, but directly on the paunch of the notable local citizen known in Mrs Burkinshaw's household as the Duke.

'How dare you!'

'Beg pardon, sir. I thought you was the child.'

'What child? You're impertinent. I'll have you whipped.'

'You'll do no such thing. It were honest mistake.'

266

Their angry confrontation quickly drew the landlady to the door and she bustled forward to placate Hester's friend and upbraid Chrissie.

'What are you doing out in the snow, Miss Mallon? Whatever are you thinking of?'

'I were throwing snowballs, Mrs Burkinshaw. It were fun but I happened to misthrow and hit the gentleman here. I'm sorry.'

She knew she must not mention Dolly as there was a chance the girl had managed to evade observation. The Duke was not impressed.

'She spoke to me with insolence, ma'am. I trust you'll teach her some manners.'

'You'll come to my sitting room directly, Miss Mallon.'

While the disgruntled visitor stormed up the stairs to shout at a startled Hester, Chrissie followed Mrs Burkinshaw into her private quarters.

'Miss Mallon, this will not do. You've behaved unseemly and offended a gentleman I much esteem.'

'One who pays you well.' Too late Chrissie bit her tongue.

'He said you was insolent and I well believe it. I've been watching you, Miss Mallon. You're stirring up trouble, encouraging that good-for-nothing, Dolly, and now you've assaulted Miss Sykes's friend!'

'Assaulted! With a snowball?'

'Enough of your cheek. Go to your room. I'll have to make complaint to Mr Copley. He'll not take it kindly that you've distressed such an important person in the town. I give you warning, if such a thing happens again, I'll be bound to ask him to remove you. Where'll you go then, I'd like to know?'

To that Chrissie had no answer and she withdrew with rigid docility.

Chapter 27: January 1863

In the days after Christmas I struggled with my confused emotions, guilt battling with joy, terror with recklessness. The one constant, reassuring certainty was that I had behaved correctly to release Arthur Rawdon from our engagement, dissociating myself from the wicked deception Robert Strines had proposed. I knew I was in a state of sin before God and would be an outcast in the eyes of decent society but I could neither repent nor redeem myself while my tempter was at hand. My passion for Robert Strines was the most overwhelming feeling I'd ever experienced; it drove away my customary common sense and routed my commitment to morality. That he desired me was a cause for jubilation and I didn't hold him uniquely blameworthy, for I saw myself as a partner in our transgression. That this madness must end, and might do so in shameful disaster, was not something I could bear to contemplate.

At New Year Mrs Strines became unwell. It was no more than a bad cold but she feared the violence of her sneezing and the harshness of her cough might endanger the baby. Unusually she became peevish with the doctor, declaring that his visits to the Infirmary might cause him to carry back with him the miasma of sickness from those he tended. Who knew what dreadful infections might be visited on the household? She wanted no one but me to attend her and required me to sleep on the couch in the adjoining sitting-room whence I could easily be summoned. The doctor humoured his wife without complaint but, after preparing sleeping draughts for the restless invalid, he took advantage of my proximity to his own room to pay nightly visits to my bed.

After a week my mistress's cold cleared but I had begun to cough and splutter so I was sent back to my room on the upper floor. Mrs Taylor was required to attend Mrs

Strines, in case I should make our mistress ill again, and I was kept in effective isolation until my symptoms lessened. It was unthinkable that the doctor would visit the servants' quarters and I languished, with streaming nose and rheumy eyes, pining for the man I loved and considering distractedly the intractable difficulties of my situation.

By the middle of the month, when I was released from seclusion, the weather had become a potent subject of conversation. Heavy snow over several days had blocked roads and covered crystalline ponds. Icicles hung dramatically from gables and lintels while the garden, under a pristine blanket two feet deep, gleamed in faint sunlight beneath trees which bowed their laden branches to touch the frozen ground. The damp clothes of those foolhardy enough to venture outside became rigid within seconds. Indoors, fires were well banked up in the reception rooms but the cold penetrated every unheated cranny and draughty passage.

Resuming my usual routine, with Mrs Strines in better health and spirits, I agonised about how and when the doctor would contrive to meet me privately again, for I was disconcerted to find him looking at me strangely and he made no attempt to encounter me alone. Miserably I contemplated the possibility that he'd tired of me, or even that he'd resolved to abjure his sinfulness. Perhaps his wife's illness had jolted him to regret his infidelity. If so, I must steel myself to accept and respect his sacrifice. If, on the other hand, he'd merely cast me aside as a worthless minx, whom he'd enjoyed but could now casually discard, I knew I would be distraught beyond remedy. I had to believe in the existence of genuine sentiment between us to mitigate our immorality.

For several days the enveloping snow enforced our confinement to the house and its immediate surroundings. The doctor was able to visit his patients in Ranmoor on foot but he did not attempt the journey across town to the Infirmary. The first sign that communications with the wider world were being re-established came when the post-boy trudged his way through the drifts to deliver letters, some of which had been delayed for several days at the office. The doctor opened one such at the breakfast table, with an air of cheerful expectation, while I was helping Mrs Strines adjust her wrap as we prepared to leave the room.

'God damn it!'

The doctor was not given to such impious exclamations and his wife turned in surprise.

'Bella sit down and Sarah too. This concerns you also. It's a letter from my brother, Stephen. He spent Christmas at the Hall, as you know, and it seems he thought our aunt somewhat unwell though not a cause for anxiety. Then, more than a week after he'd returned to Penistone, he was summoned back to the Hall by an urgent message from the housekeeper. On arrival he found Mrs Ibbotson had suffered an apoplexy and was fading fast. His letter urges me to come at once to pay my respects and to bring Sarah, whom the old lady has expressed a wish to see. Because the post has been delayed, I fear we may come too late.'

'You will not think of venturing to the Hall in these conditions, Robert? You've scarcely been close to your aunt.' My mistress's voice was as frosty as the air outside.

'I must do what is right, my love. You wouldn't have me behave uncharitably. There is some indication of a thaw beginning and the roads are being cleared. In a day or two it should be possible to take the gig. You would wish to come, Sarah?'

I was gratified by his kindly tone. 'Indeed, sir, I'll happily set off on foot today if I might get there sooner. I pray Mrs Ibbotson may yet rally.'

'What nonsense, Sarah,' Mrs Strines intervened crisply. 'How could you think of walking such a distance in

270

this weather? I'm afraid you must accept your old mistress has probably succumbed by now. It is no one's fault.'

'Please, ma'am, I wish to go.'

'Of course she does, Bella. She's loyal and owes much to Mrs Ibbotson. Do you think you could sit with me on my horse, Sarah? We could ride there and back within the day or, if conditions are very difficult, spend the night at the Hall. That way we will both have fulfilled our duty. You must not object to that, my sweet.'

Mrs Strines pouted prettily and sighed but gave her agreement. She found me an old hooded cloak to keep me warm and bade me return as quickly as possible because Mrs Taylor had no idea how to dress a lady's hair properly. It was bad enough to have endured a week without my services while I had a cold, without being further deprived. My mistress clearly thought herself greatly inconvenienced.

I'd never been on horseback before and I was very nervous but the doctor was full of reassurance. He promised the horse was sure-footed and, because of the snow, we would proceed slowly and carefully, keeping to the drove roads and tracks where local people had cleared the worst drifts. I needed no second invitation to cling tightly to his waist, nestling my head against his thick coat, and little by little I grew brave enough to look round as we crossed the moors. The extensive view, glistening and peaceful under its muffling coverlet, calmed me. There seemed no end to the ranges of hills and shrouded valleys I could see: an infinity of whiteness broken here and there by the black edges of exposed rock-faces. I rejoiced to be alone in this magical world with the man I loved and I wished the ride to go on forever.

On stretches where the snow was well trodden the ground was slippery but the doctor was experienced at riding on difficult terrain and he guided our mount confidently. The sharp descent into the Rivelin Valley

271

alarmed me but Robert was exhilarated and we picked up speed as we entered the riverside woods, hurling up splodges of slush where dripping trees had softened the compacted layer underfoot. By the waterside he reined the horse to a halt and dismounted, lifting me down beside him.

'We need a rest before we tackle the climb up the next ridge.'

The doctor broke the ice below the bank so the horse could drink from the stream. Then he brushed loose snow from a rocky knoll and sat down, pulling me beside him. He kissed me.

'You have the makings of an accomplished horsewoman, little love.'

I smiled, happy to hear him speak to me tenderly again, and I snuggled against him. I let myself imagine he might make love to me in that secluded spot, despite the freezing temperature and darkening sky, but I remembered to speak with more fitting solemnity. 'I'm too worried for Mrs Ibbotson to be over-concerned by what would terrify me otherwise.'

'Good girl.' He stroked my cheek. 'I confess, Sarah, I was perplexed why there'd not been earlier communications from the Hall. I expected a grand declaration of your engagement to Arthur Rawdon and epistles of congratulation from my aunt. Now I understand. With admirable discretion your betrothed has hesitated to make an announcement because of Mrs Ibbotson's illness. I suspect we may find Arthur himself at the Hall and all can then be spoken of openly.'

This misapprehension had to be corrected and I took a deep breath. 'No sir, Robert. He is not my betrothed. I have refused him.'

'What!' Dr Strines sprang up, dislodging clouds of powdery snow from the bush beside us. 'What on earth do you mean? Why did you not tell me?'

'I did what was right, Robert. I couldn't deceive him. He's honest and true.'

'You little fool! How can you be so naïve? Didn't you understand what I advised you?'

I was stung by his harshness and stood up to face him. 'I understood too well. It was unworthy to think of practising such a trick on him.'

'Unworthy! You call me unworthy now, do you?'

He seized my arms and shook me roughly, then pushed me away.

'I didn't say you were unworthy, sir.'

He took hold of my arm, wrenching me forward. 'Are you with child?'

'I don't think so, sir.'

'Thank God for that! But you cannot yet be certain. Now listen, Sarah, I'm sorry if I've hurt you in my annoyance but your action was foolhardy, thoughtless. It may still be redeemable. You must tell Arthur you were wrong to reject him. That it was modesty, shyness – whatever girls say – that made you do so. He'll forgive you.'

'You're asking me to lie and deceive him, Robert.'

'Maid servants are not meant to have such scruples, little kitten, when they choose to please their master so entirely.' He caressed me. 'Do as I say and we'll have pleasure in each other for a few more months. Come now, we'd best remount and be on our way. Do as I say and all will be well.'

There was no further conversation for the rest of our ponderous journey and as we neared the Hall, my humiliation and raw misery at Robert Strines' callousness was subsumed into grief for Mrs Ibbotson's affliction.

*****

The bell was answered by Mrs Staniforth, the housekeeper. She bobbed to the doctor and took me by the hands.

'Dr Strines, sir, your brother's with mistress now. She'll be so glad you've come, Sarah. When she could speak, she asked for you often.'

We hurried up the stairs and Robert's elder brother, Stephen, greeted us on the landing. 'I guessed my letter was delayed. It's good you're come. Our aunt is gravely ill but she has rallied a little, somewhat to my surprise. She's remarkably resilient for an elderly lady who's suffered so severe an attack. She's sleeping but you may both see her. She asked for you several times, Sarah.'

Mrs Ibbotson's wizened face, under her lacy nightcap, was grey and her mouth distorted. I couldn't restrain a gasp of distress to see her so stricken and, ignoring the presence of the two doctors, I bent low to whisper in the patient's ear.

'It's Sarah, ma'am. The weather delayed us coming from Ranmoor. I'm sorry to see you so poorly.'

For a moment there was no reaction, then one eyelid quivered slightly and the right side of Mrs Ibbotson's lips curled into a contented half-smile.

'Stay with her, Sarah,' said the elder Dr Strines. 'Your presence may do her more good than our attendance. Come, Robert, a glass of something warming will be of benefit after your journey.'

An hour or so later Robert Strines returned to Mrs Ibbotson's room. I was still sitting by the bed but I had removed my cloak and been supplied with a tray of food. He felt the invalid's pulse and then turned to me.

'There is a chance she will recover, Sarah, although how fully must be in doubt. I'm in agreement with my brother that your company may be helpful to her. I propose to return at once to Ranmoor and I shall explain to Mrs

274

Strines that I've bidden you stay here until my aunt is out of danger or has passed away. The outcome should be clear in a few days. I will assure my wife you protested you should return to her but I overrode your protests on my aunt's behalf.'

I noted how carefully he chose his words, as if he might be overheard by his brother. Then he leaned towards me across the bed and spoke softly. 'Arthur Rawdon is expected back from a visit to his father two days hence. Take your opportunity. Good day, Sarah.'

I stared after him with the misted eyes of disillusion and resumed my vigil.

*****

For the next two days, under the guidance of Dr Stephen Strines, I cared for my former mistress. I had a bed made up beside the patient's, so I could be always at hand, and I took my meals in the sickroom. Susan, my successor as lady's maid, was relieved to have me assume the role of nurse and waited good-naturedly on both of us. During the daytime I freed Mrs Ibbotson's right hand from the heavy bedclothes and held it gently, while I read to her, hoping that an eyelid would flicker again or a lip twitch slightly. Mrs Staniforth sat beside me sometimes and we chatted companionably in low voices. I learned that in the New Year, just before their mistress's collapse, Lizzie Simmonite had been given permission to leave the Hall for a week to visit her family. Her return had probably been delayed by the snow.

Alone with the unresponsive Mrs Ibbotson, in the afternoon of my second day at the Hall, I stood by the window, looking down to the vast dam slashing its way across the valley. I could see figures with barrows and pickaxes, still busy on the scaffolding despite the weather, working with pulleys and lifting gear to haul the facing stone up the height of the embankment. It was possible to imagine how the structure would look when it was complete and soon after that the dale upstream would be filled with water. I remembered how the key to the stability of the edifice was the puddle clay wall, which Arthur had described when he spoke so proudly of his profession. I found sight of the dam troubling but could not tell if this was simply because of its intrusiveness in such a beautiful setting or whether its associations with my spurned admirer had tainted its image in my eyes.

'I do not like to see it, Sarah.'

I span round in disbelief that the feeble, fluting voice was real. Mrs Ibbotson's eyes were open although the left side of her face seemed strangely rigid.

'Oh, ma'am!' I rushed to the bed and knelt clasping her wizened hand.

'I'm glad you're here, my dear. I think I shall mend.'

The words were difficult to distinguish, spoken from one side of the old lady's mouth, but I grasped their meaning with joy. The patient soon fell asleep but the elder Dr Strines confirmed that her brief return to consciousness and lucidity was encouraging. He praised my dedication and diligence and I smiled with pleasure, thinking how little the stolid and reliable doctor from Penistone resembled his brother, my now tarnished idol.

That evening I was reading to myself, reassured by the gentle rhythm of Mrs Ibbotson's breathing, when I heard sounds of arrival and women's voices downstairs. I was relieved they did not seem to mark Arthur Rawdon's return. I had no intention of reopening the issue of our engagement, as Robert Strines demanded, but I dreaded having to see Arthur for fear he would ask me to reconsider my rejection. The light tap on the bedroom door made me jump but, rather than call out and risk disturbing the old lady, I went to open it. I was pleased to see it was Lizzie Simmonite standing demurely outside, still enveloped in a travelling cape with the hood thrown back to reveal her fair hair piled high in an elegant fashion. Her cheeks were unusually flushed.

'Lizzie!'

'Oh, Sarah, I'm so sorry mistress is that ill. She were only a bit unwell when I left. How is she?'

'A little better. Dr Strines has hopes she may recover. How are your family?'

'Oh, they're very well. We...I saw them two weeks ago.' She took my arm and drew me onto the landing. 'I have to tell you something. I didn't think to find you here but you must know. You can't mind since you refused him but it's right awkward. I hope you won't be mardy.'

I stood very still, feeling the blood drain from my face and my fingertips become icy. 'What are you saying, Lizzie?'

'It were like this. When he came back to the Hall at New Year, after he'd been over to Ranmoor, Mr Rawdon were very down in dumps. He told me you'd refused him and I suppose I tried to comfort him a bit like. Then, two weeks back, he asked me to be his wife and I said "yes". Us went to Malin Bridge and he asked me Da, all proper, you know. Then he took me on to Huddersfield so his father could give his blessing. He's a bit poorly, the reverend gentleman, but he were right glad to meet me, though I think he thought I were you, or you was me, if you sees what I mean. T'any rate we got snowed up there a few days before we could come back and the wedding's all fixed now for Easter Day.'

Lizzie slid her left hand from the folds of her cape and held it out for me to admire. There, on the third finger, gleamed a little circlet of gold with a single turquoise. Chilled to the bone, scarcely capable of speech, I embraced the future Mrs Rawdon.

277

Chapter 28: February - April 1863

As the snow cleared, Chrissie began to take short walks in the neighbourhood, sometimes accompanied by Tilda Brammall. She found much of her companion's incessant prattling tedious but sought to turn it to advantage and learn more of the household she'd entered. This was hard work as Tilda's answers frequently digressed from the question posed and she was equally curious about Chrissie's background, especially her recent reprimand. Chrissie persisted.

'You say Mrs B were left the house by her patron when he died?'

'Years back. Old gent took her off streets and set her up to rent out rooms. Smitten he was. Like Hester and the Duke, you know. But she's not so happy now. After all this time, he's given her the clap, would you believe?'

'Hester?'

'Aye. Mrs Burkinshaw's given her ointment. But she's that riled. Says he must have been with some filthy bitch he met at the music-hall. Used to take Hester there sometimes. My gent don't never take me out. Too cautious like. You were lucky Mr Copley stuck up for 'ee after the Duke complained.'

'I told him it were accident, as it were. Nathaniel believed me and he made apology to the Duke. Pompous swine! Read Nat a lecture about proper behaviour.'

Tilda cackled coarsely. 'Proper behaviour! You should know what he asks Hester to do.'

Chrissie did not wish to know and she caught Tilda by the arm, lowering her voice. 'How old d'you think Dolly is?'

Miss Brammall looked round anxiously. 'I don't ask, Chrissie. No more should you. She were old enough to get bun in oven. Some girls look young. Others look older than they are.' She grew more enthusiastic, losing her affected tone. 'I mean, would you believe, Hester's only two years more'n me? She's becoming raddled already while my complexion's clear.'

'I doubt Dolly's barely thirteen and she's been here at least a year. It's obscene.'

'Oh, come on, Chrissie! Hadn't you had your first fellow afore then? I'd had two or three, love.'

'I were hoodwinked and forced; and so were Dolly. Mrs B fusses about how we behave, not upsetting the fine gentlemen and all, yet she lets Mr Gregory do what he does to no more'n a child.'

'Pays her well, don't he? Guardian of the Poor and Town Trustee, I've heard. You don't say 'No' to the likes of him. Not if you're Mrs Burkinshaw. Besides, she told me once the law says it's all right if a girl's twelve or more.'

'I'd still like some of his upright friends to know!'

'Chrissie,' Tilda spoke urgently, pulling her companion's shawl. 'Don't talk like that. Don't even whisper. Us learns to keep mouths shut here, if we knows what's good for us. Now let me tell you how my gent first took up with me at the sight of my pretty ankle. It were one day in the Wicker when I were on errand...'

She wittered on but Chrissie was no longer listening.

*****

Tilda had been right to speak appreciatively of Mr Copley's support in the difficulty with the Duke, Chrissie realised. He was not at all a bad sort; he never became violent and he still gazed at her as if she was something precious, to be treasured. She was fortunate. She came to value his visits and to welcome the way he talked to her about the factory, his family and his growing ambitions to make his mark in the town. He told her that Bessie Turner

279

was looking well and had been noticed, after work, walking towards Division Street in company with a pleasant, up-standing lad who operated one of the heavy lathes. Chrissie felt relief, hoping that any threat from Eb Pyle's distasteful crony, Joe, had receded.

One day, at the beginning of March, Mr Copley came earlier than usual, before she was fully prepared for him. He was justifiably pleased with himself for he brought her most welcome news. He had asked his workers whether they knew a lad who might be able to come in on Saturdays to help with the paperwork, which was falling behindhand. Bessie had mentioned her young brother, not yet apprenticed as a grinder but likely to be so after Easter. Freddie had duly attended for interview. The manager had been impressed by the lad's neat handwriting and facility with numbers and engaged him for the task at a very reasonable rate.

'I trust he can stay at his schooling now, till he's thirteen at least, and if he fulfils his promise I'll engage him in the office then, full-time.'

'I'm grateful, Nathaniel. It's so kind of you.'

'Not kind, lass, or only a little. Canny too, for the lad's bright and should prove a good investment. I'm a businessman first and foremost, Chrissie. I've an eye for quality, wouldn't you say?'

He pulled her to him and started to unhook her bodice as she looked at him with genuine affection.

*****

Some days later Chrissie became aware of Mrs Burkinshaw's raised voice on the floor below her and then of Dolly sobbing. She went out of her room to peer over the banisters and was just in time to see the burly woman hustling the child down the stairs. Dolly was wrapped in a shawl and clutched a small bundle. Chrissie called out to her

280

but it was the landlady who turned, glaring, and answered with robust disapproval.

'Go back in your room, Miss Mallon. This is nowt to do with you.'

'Where's Dolly going?'

'Back to workhouse where she came from. She don't suit no more.'

Chrissie started to run down the stairs.

'Do I have to tell you again, Miss Mallon. D'you want Mr Copley to have further complaints about 'ee?'

'I'd rather be in workhouse, Chrissie. He won't hurt me there.' Dolly's plaintiff voice sounded from the doorway. 'Bye, Chrissie.'

Defeated, she went back into her room and watched through the window as the pair climbed into a closed cab and drove away. She tried fiercely to cheer herself. Perhaps Dolly might be put out to work. If only she could find a position in a decent household her ejection from Mrs B's establishment would be to her benefit. It was not impossible. Chrissie needed, for her own sake, to believe the child might be fortunate because she hated her inability to help.

Later, as she idly plaited some strands of raffia to make an unnecessary tablemat, she heard the cab return. She recognised the landlady's voice paying the driver and then, as bridles clattered and the vehicle drove off, she was aware of the woman speaking again, in peremptory tones. She sidled to the window and gasped in revulsion at what she saw. The small girl, thinly clad in the biting wind, was plainly younger than Dolly, nine or ten at the most. She stood rooted to the spot, oblivious of Mrs Burkinshaw's furious cries, wide-eyed with fright. With an oath, inaudible to Chrissie but unmistakeably blasphemous, the woman swept the child into her arms and marched to the front door, shouting for the housemaid.

Chrissie heard movements on the floor below and interpreted their meaning with appalled certainty. The maid was bringing buckets of water so the child could be thoroughly dunked to remove any trace or aroma of the workhouse. Mrs Burkinshaw was bustling about, brushing the newcomer's tangled hair, pinning up one of Dolly's overlarge gowns, to do for now, delivering her familiar lecture on appropriate behaviour. How much could that little waif comprehend of the snide innuendo and veiled threats? Chrissie felt nauseous and, more than ever, fretted at her impotence, tearing the raffia into shreds and throwing it into the grate.

In the late afternoon, when the three ladies joined Mrs Burkinshaw for their usual meal, there was no sign of the new guest. Their hostess was in jubilant mood and, producing the gin bottle, proclaimed they must celebrate Miss Sykes's birthday, due in a few days' time. Chrissie was surprised by this premature festivity but, glad to be distracted from the anger and distress she felt, she accepted a glass and smiled benignly when Hester and Tilda started their habitual bickering. She heard distant sounds as someone was admitted to the house by the maid and told herself that the Duke must have arrived earlier than usual. Tilda's raucous merriment diverted her attention for a while although she wondered why Hester had not been summoned from their gathering to join her visitor. Then she heard the child screaming and she knew the real reason why Mrs Burkinshaw's lodgers had been beguiled with alcohol and jollity.

She stood up, eyes blazing, to confront the landlady. 'You bitch! He's raping that little scrap and you just sit there laughing!'

'Chrissie, don't interfere, love,' Tilda fluttered.

'Thank you, Miss Brammall, for your wise words. Miss Mallon, sit down and take another drink. I warn you! You're becoming obnoxious to me.'

'Obnoxious to the trade.' Chrissie could hear Will's worried voice as he told her of Broadhead's threats when he challenged the union's accounts. Obnoxious to the trade – to her trade of harlotry, into which, at that moment, a little girl was being initiated with brutality. She subsided onto her chair and poured another glass of gin which she drank quickly. Then she crumpled forward and vomited into her lap.

*****

That night an unexpected frost formed. Next day the silvery filigree on trees and bushes, railings and windowpanes, was caught by the strengthening sun and reflected into Chrissie's garret room. She admired nature's artistry and sourly contrasted its frozen beauty with the icy inhumanity in Mrs Burkinshaw's house. She'd rarely felt so incensed on another's behalf. It had always been her way to have regard to her own interests and let others look after themselves. Now she was obsessed by the thought of that wretched little creature in the room below, violated and degraded by a man whose reputation and social standing were irreproachable in the polite world which knew nothing of the house in Nether Edge. When Mr Copley came, she could not restrain herself from telling him what she had seen and heard, hoping against her better judgement that he might take some action to rescue the child, but his rebuff was immediate.

'Chrissie, I won't listen to this. What you're saying is slanderous, maligning a great gentleman of this town. I doubt the girl is as young as you say and she was probably corrupted years ago. It's all wicked surmise. You've let your imagination run away with you. Those of us who depend on Mrs Burkinshaw's good offices must behave with discretion and mutual understanding. You know that. You'll not say another word on this, d'you hear?'

She'd never heard him so displeased and, lacking an alternative, she accepted his reprimand meekly. Later that evening she knew it was not her fancy that his lovemaking had a new fervour, as if he wished to confirm her submission to his decree. She understood her inconvenient scruples needed to be crushed and she must, obediently, play the passive role required of a well-to-do man's plaything.

Her mind would not relinquish the subject so readily. The child never joined the rest of the household in the dining room and Chrissie guessed the landlady was keeping her out of sight lest her extreme youth should be more clearly revealed. Mr Gregory was assiduous in his visits and, although she no longer screamed when he was with her, the little girl sobbed each night after he'd left. Chrissie continued to rail silently at her helplessness, vainly trying to distract herself with futile pastimes and idle conversations, but slowly she formed an idea and the compulsion grew to put it into effect. In all probability it would be useless but she must make the attempt. If it led to her rejection by Nathaniel and her banishment from Mrs Burkinshaw's house, so it would have to be.

Carefully she wrote her letter, racking her brains to make the spelling as accurate as possible.

Sorry to trubble you, sir. I heard of you as a good man and a doctor. Plees help a child, no more'n nine I'd say who is held prisner at Mrs Birkinshor's house at Nether Ege A gent plesures himself with her. Takes her by fors. No one els will help her. Plees can you?

She signed it '*a welwisher*' and, remembering what Sarah Webster had said, when they met near Norfolk Market Hall, she addressed it to Dr Strines, by St John's Church at

Ranmoor. When next she took a walk from the house, she accosted a local lad, gave him a penny and asked him to take the letter to the post-boy. Now she could only wait.

*****

Two weeks later, as she was dressing to receive her lover, Chrissie tore the lace bow that hung from the plunging neckline of her finest dress. She hastened downstairs to Tilda's room to borrow a similar accessory, which she knew that lady possessed, and when she stepped back onto the stairs leading up to the top floor, she heard the other door on the landing open. Fully aware it was unforgivably rash, she turned to see Mr Gregory emerge.

He was without question a fine-looking man, tall, immaculately dressed and suavely elegant. He swept off the silk hat he had just set on his head, removed the lit cigar from his mouth and pursed his thick lips.

'Miss Mallon, if I mistake not. Nathaniel Copley has exquisite taste, I'm bound to concede. I congratulate him.'

'Mr Gregory.' She inclined her head. Then she fixed her violet eyes fully upon him. 'I hear you're a great man. I wonder you should fuck a child.'

'You insolent slut! How dare you!'

'I dare, sir, as others won't. It should be said straight. You're no more'n a vile rapist!'

'By God, you filthy trollop! You think you can pass judgement on your betters?'

Wrenching her by the wrist, he pulled her down the step and twisted her arm behind her back. Pain shot to her shoulder and she stamped furiously on his foot but her soft shoe had little impact on best calf leather. He forced her arm further and she was alarmed he would break a bone so, with all her strength, she kicked her voluminous skirt to the side and, as nearly as she could, she kneed him in the groin. He

285

gave a furious cry, letting go of her throbbing arm, but before she could escape, he thrust forward with his cigar and stubbed it onto her bosom. She screamed.

Mrs Burkinshaw and Mr Copley were already on the lower flight of stairs hastening towards them, shouting at Chrissie, as she recoiled with pain and sank onto the floor.

'Copley, I fear your lady friend is no better than a common whore. She threw herself upon me with a most indecent proposition. I was forced to defend myself.' Mr Gregory pulled down his cuff and waved his cigar ruefully. 'I trust you will chastise her appropriately and I'll thank you to keep her under better control and out of my way.'

He swept down the lower stairs, permitting Mrs Burkinshaw to fawn upon him with abject apologies. Mr Copley stood staring at Chrissie while she cringed in pain and misery.

'It isn't true, Nathaniel. I never offered myself. He attacked me.'

She looked up. Her protector was pop-eyed with terror. 'What did you say to him?'

'I said he were a vile rapist.'

'Oh Chrissie, you'll destroy me. I need Mr Gregory's support for a seat on the town council. How can you be so wilful, so vulgar?'

He turned back, thundering down the stairs, and left the house. She heard his voice, outside, high pitched with embarrassment, imploring Mr Gregory's forgiveness.

*****

For the next week Chrissie kept to her room, unvisited, awaiting the dismissal she was certain must come. Through her window she saw the buds opening in the garden, the clusters of primroses among the decaying leaves, and she heard the birds singing their assertive choruses at daybreak. Drawing up the sash she breathed in the mild air of burgeoning spring and she sighed, with a mixture of wavering joy and undeniable panic, for she was now sure she was carrying Nathaniel Copley's child

Chapter 29: February - March 1863

Towards the end of February Dr Stephen Strines pronounced his aunt not merely out of danger but on the road to recovery. He warned she might never regain full strength in her left arm and her left leg might drag slightly when she started to walk again but her fluency of speech had returned and her mental powers were unimpaired. He had already engaged a nurse to stay with Mrs Ibbotson for as long as necessary during convalescence and he was content to leave future care in her hands and those of the local doctor.

I had undertaken to go back to Ranmoor when the old lady was sufficiently recovered but I was torn about my situation. I'd slipped into a degree of my old contentment at the Hall but there was no justification for me remaining there. Besides, I dreaded having to meet Arthur Rawdon again, as I assuredly would if I lingered, despite his tactful absence so far. Above all, regardless of my guilt, I longed to be enfolded in Robert Strines' arms once more although, after his hurtful words to me on our journey, I saw more clearly the wretchedness of my infatuation. I was still love-struck but I acknowledged the hopelessness of my deluded rapture. My eyes had been opened to imperfections never previously suspected but I clung to the belief that the doctor's feelings for me were sincere. I was deeply confused. I wasn't willing to confess the truth to myself that he'd behaved shamefully towards me, but I couldn't deny he had the basest of intentions with regard to Arthur.

It was a relief that, even as she became more talkative, Mrs Ibbotson said nothing to me about my personal position until, on the evening before my departure, this reticence ended. The old lady was sitting in an armchair beside her bed. She had been reminiscing happily about the travels she'd undertaken, with her late husband, years ago before the Queen had even come to the throne. After a pause she turned to look directly at me.

'My recollection is still not very clear of the days after Christmas, just before I suffered my seizure, but I call to mind some sad news. Was it a dream that I had, a figment of my disordered imagination, or did Arthur Rawdon tell me something I did not like to hear?'

I knew I was blushing. 'Your memory isn't at fault, ma'am. I'm pleased it's so much restored. It is true I freed Arthur from our engagement.'

When Mrs Ibbotson said nothing but stared at me in incomprehension, I felt compelled to add, 'I'd recognised I wasn't worthy of him.'

'Rubbish!' The vehemence of the exclamation shook the old lady's frail body and her hand began to tremble. I rushed to her side.

'Please don't distress yourself, ma'am. I don't regret it. I'd come to realise our engagement was not appropriate.'

'So now he's to marry a semi-literate parlour-maid?' During her recuperation little had escaped her.

'Lizzie is a good, well-meaning lass.'

'And you are not?'

The sharpness of the interrogation stung me. I turned away, unable to answer that perceptive, double-edged question.

'Something has happened, Sarah, hasn't it? Something you don't wish to speak of? I won't press you but I have great misgivings. Tell me one thing honestly, my dear. Are you in trouble?'

I shook my head, blessing Mrs Ibbotson's delicacy. 'No, ma'am.'

'Thank heaven, but I think it unfortunate you ever went to Ranmoor. I was responsible for that.'

'I doubt I shall stay there after Mrs Strines is delivered of her child but you have nothing to reproach yourself with. You've always been so good to me.'

The old lady sighed. 'God keep you safe, Sarah, but mind you have a care for yourself as well. Think carefully about your position.'

I inclined my head as if accepting her guidance. She understood far too much.

*****

Mrs Ibbotson arranged that her carriage would convey me to Ranmoor, taking the main route along the well-used valley roads. This took us through Malin Bridge where I shrank back from the window, anxious not to see or be seen by anyone I knew in the village. Tom would be working at the forge but our stepmother might be in the street and I could not bring myself to visit our stricken, paralysed father. Not until we passed beyond Hillsborough did I relax and look out to admire the sparkling scenery under its silver canopy of frost.

Further on, I realised we were passing beside the imposing buildings of the Infirmary and I wondered if Dr Strines was there, tending his less affluent patients. I peered out intently when the carriage halted to let vehicles in front of us turn through the gates. To my amazement, I caught sight of a figure I thought I recognised crossing the courtyard. Once more I pulled back from the window but watched carefully as the young man came more fully into view. I was not mistaken. It was Dick Jewitt. He was well turned out, in formal office clothes without a top coat, carrying a sheaf of papers and looking quite at home in the establishment. I'd thought him dismissed from Ranmoor in disgrace, as he deserved to be. Could he really have secured employment in the Infirmary, where Dr Strines practised?

Surely the doctor must know of this? Had he not protested? He'd been outraged by Mr Jewitt's assault on me, surely? What could be the explanation?

I pondered this mystery as we drove on and, unaccountably I remembered Mr Jewitt's strange words when he attacked me: his talk of reparations and the doctor having his 'leavings this time'. Slowly, a horrible scenario formed in my mind. It must be the product of a fevered imagination, I thought, but, if it were true, it would humiliate and torture me. Had I been too credulous to comprehend his meaning or had I chosen wilfully to ignore the significance of what he said? Had I pushed his words aside? My shame was compounded.

My moment of return to Ranmoor was not auspicious. When I invited Mrs Ibbotson's coachman to take some refreshment in the kitchen, I could already hear shouts from the doctor's consulting room and I hurried directly to Mrs Strines, anxious that my mistress should not be distressed by the hubbub. The welcome she gave me was genuine.

'Sarah, at last you are come! I don't know how I've managed so long without you. Have you ever seen such a bird's nest as Mrs Taylor has made of my hair? And I'm grown so gross. See how monstrous I'm become! The doctor insists he can hear but one heart in my belly but I declare I believe I shall spawn three or four gigantic infants.'

'You look lovely, ma'am and I'll soon have your curls in place. You're not in the least monstrous, quite trim so near your time.'

'Bless you, Sarah. I've so missed you. You shall read to me again this evening. Pin up my hair first then you may take your things to your room. Oh, I do wish that disagreeable man would stop shouting.'

'Who is it, ma'am?' I took up the hairbrush.

291

'Some bad-tempered patient. He was here the other day. My husband said it was nothing to concern me but I declare the thought of unpleasantness gives me a headache. Ah! Already you are unravelling the tangles.'

After subduing my mistress's errant curls, I withdrew with a promise to bring the tea tray in an hour. I had just put my bag in my room when I heard the crash of the front door and feet hastening away from the house. I couldn't identify the thickly muffled man I glimpsed from the window so I hurried to the kitchen to ask Mrs Taylor the reason for this unusual disturbance. I found the housekeeper bursting with indignation.

'Oh, Sarah, I've never known the like. That was Mr Paterson, the gentleman you helped Dr Strines attend to after he'd been shot at.'

'But why was he so angry? He used to be full of praise for the doctor.'

'I'm not sure I should tell you, Sarah, you being a young unmarried girl, but I'm that riled I must speak out. Mr Paterson's making wicked, evil accusations against the doctor. Says he... No, I can't bring myself to say it.'

'Say what, Mrs Taylor?' My tone was brusque.

'That slanderer says the doctor interfered with his daughter when he was examining her the other day. Can you imagine? Miss Paterson complained to her father but it's all in her head, wishful thinking, if you ask me. She's hysterical. Oh, the poor doctor!'

I took a cup of tea from Mrs Taylor thoughtfully, sitting opposite her across the table. The coincidence was extraordinary. 'I dare say you're right about Miss Paterson's hysteria but it's a serious accusation.' I set down my cup carefully. 'Have such things been said about the doctor before?'

The housekeeper gave a start, spilling some of her tea into the saucer. 'What a question!' She looked profoundly uncomfortable and this enhanced my growing suspicions.

'Why did Dr Strines leave Manchester? Had something similar occurred?'

Mrs Taylor had turned very red. She spoke in a whisper. 'How do you know, Sarah? It was all hushed up and settled privately. It was another fanciful old maid, with no pretensions to beauty. Just like Miss Paterson she took a shine to the doctor. He can't help it; he's so handsome and kindly. Those feeble-minded spinsters have fantasies about him. But it would have been a dreadful scandal. She was with child and she accused the doctor of being the father. Poor man, it was very shocking for him. He couldn't risk it being made public for his wife's sake, as well as his reputation. He'd have been ruined. He arranged the move to Sheffield. He made some provision for that despicable woman too. So generous!'

'You don't believe he was the father?'

'Of course not! How can you say such a thing?'

The disclosure fitted too well with my wild conjectures in the carriage. With a heavy heart I continued my inquisition. 'What about Betsy? She fell for a baby, didn't she? Was he that child's father?'

The housekeeper was speechless for a moment. Her jowls wobbled as she tried to marshal her thoughts and respond to my unexpected challenge. She pursed her lips. 'Betsy claimed Dick Jewitt was the father.'

'But perhaps he wasn't? Maybe Dr Strines seduced her and then encouraged her to give herself to Mr Jewitt so the wretched young man could take the blame. He'd know Mr Jewitt was fond of her.' My mind was whirring and the words tumbled from my mouth. 'If Mr Jewitt found out the truth, he could have a hold over the doctor. Maybe that's why he's employed at the Infirmary, despite being dismissed

293

from here. I saw him there as we passed in the carriage. I couldn't believe it. But if Doctor Strines needs to keep him quiet, he might have arranged it.' My voice dropped to a whisper as I voiced the final possibility. 'Either that or the two are hand in glove sharing their prey.'

'Sarah! Have you lost your senses? What a pack of lies! Where have you got such dreadful ideas from?'

'I've been trying to understand, to make things fall into place: things that didn't make sense.'

I couldn't prevent tears running down my cheeks and Mrs Taylor stared at me aghast. 'How can you say such vile things about the doctor? How can you even imagine them possible?'

'Because it all rings true. When he assaulted me, Mr Jewitt spoke of the doctor's "leavings". What else could that mean?' I rose to my feet. 'In my experience, it rings true.'

'Sarah! What are you saying? Surely the doctor hasn't...?'

I ran blindly from the kitchen. The love which had seemed sacred, although illicit, was now revealed as abominably profane. Like unnumbered others, I'd been deceived, trifled with, manipulated, never loved. My virtue had been to him a trivial matter, to be sullied without compunction to satisfy his basest instincts. My future, and that of the guileless, honourable man to whom I'd been engaged, were bagatelles to be casually shrugged aside when they became inconveniences. How could I ever have believed otherwise?

*****

In the days that followed I was attentive to Mrs Strines' every need, engulfed by waves of guilt and sympathy for the doctor's ill-used wife. It was incomprehensible that he should allow himself to be beguiled by predatory hysterics, and seek to take advantage of foolish besotted maidens, while he had the wondrous and cultured Bella in blessed matrimony. I wondered how far my mistress knew herself betrayed. I surmised she might not be wholly ignorant. Perhaps her frequent melancholy was not the romantic affectation of a sensitive spirit but the result of unspeakable, recurrent treachery which she could not escape.

I was sitting with the doctor's wife, as we both embroidered corners of a quilted shawl, when a tight-lipped Mrs Taylor announced that Mrs Paterson had called and was enquiring whether Mrs Strines was at home. I was so much alarmed that I nearly spoke on the lady's behalf to decline the visit, but permission had already been given to admit the visitor. Dr Strines was not in the house.

'I hope Mrs Paterson will not upset you, ma'am. Please have her shown out if she's troublesome.'

'Never fear, I will. And you shall stay with me. But I'm intrigued to know why she's calling on me.'

The portly newcomer looked as if she had dressed in haste and she was not at ease. She accepted a chair but sat, bolt-upright, on the edge of her seat and twisted her gloves as she spoke. 'Mrs Strines, it is good of you to see me. I was apprehensive you would not. My husband has behaved so badly to the doctor, I'm ashamed. I wanted to say to you myself, he was grievously misguided. He has wronged the doctor terribly. Oh dear, I'm torn apart by what has happened.'

My mistress sat very still but the vein at her temple was throbbing. 'What do you mean, Mrs Paterson? In what way was your husband misguided? I know the doctor has been sorely tried by his recent visits.'

'Oh, Mrs Strines, it was all falsehood. I got to the bottom of it when I heard – I wasn't privy to it at first – but woman's intuition, you know. My daughter is not quite well in her mind. She always fancies she has some illness or other. But that she should have traduced the doctor... such a good man... that she should say he touched...'

Bella Strines' crystal tones cut across the tremulous recital. 'And it was not true? She now accepts it was not true?'

'She's confused, poor child, but her maid was with her throughout the examination. We didn't know that at first. Her maid swears the doctor behaved, as always, with total propriety. Oh, I'm so ashamed.'

My mistress pulled herself up from her chair. 'I'm obliged that you should call to tell me this. I'm sure my husband will wish for a personal apology from Mr Paterson but, beyond that, we shall say no more about it. I can see it was a most unfortunate mistake but it could have had fearful consequences for a professional gentleman. May I suggest you consult some other physician as to your daughter's health in future?'

She rang the bell for the housekeeper to show her visitor out, charming as ever. Nonetheless, after Mrs Paterson had left, expressing obsequious gratitude, Mrs Strines sank onto the chaise-longue, white with the strain of polite pretence.

I knelt beside her. 'Ma'am, are you all right?'

'I will be. I will master my weakness. I have done so before.'

'I was sorry to hear all Mrs Paterson said.' I tried to speak judiciously. 'I'm glad her daughter's maid has refuted the slander.'

'So am I, Sarah; so am I.' Her voice acquired a bitter edge. 'A fortuitous resolution of events indeed, is it not? One dare not suppose that the doctor might have compromised the maid as well as the mistress.'

My mouth fell open but my mistress closed her eyes, shutting within herself the world-weary cynicism she had allowed me to glimpse.

*****

When she heard her husband return to the house, Mrs Strines summoned Mrs Taylor to ask him to come to her sitting room, whereupon I moved swiftly to the door.

'Don't go, Sarah. I wish you to be here.'

There was nothing to be gleaned from her smooth tone but I withdrew to the far corner by the window, and was tempted to hide myself in the heavy curtains which hung down to the floor. I was petrified by the thought of what was to come.

Robert Strines entered his wife's room jauntily, blowing a kiss. 'My precious, is all well?'

She regarded him coldly. 'No, husband, it is not. Mrs Paterson has called on me.'

The doctor's jaw jutted upwards and he clenched his hands. 'She had no right to distress you, my love. It's outrageous. What did she say?'

'I'm not distressed. She explained her daughter had made false allegations which their maid has now denied. I've asked that Mr Paterson call upon you to apologise.'

The doctor relaxed. 'That's most welcome news, my angel, but she shouldn't have troubled you. I sought to keep such damaging nonsense from you in your condition. Still, I'm relieved to know Miss Paterson's defamatory accusations have been confirmed as no more than the poor woman's delusions.'

He moved to embrace his wife but she held up both hands to deter him. 'I'm well aware they were not mere delusions, Robert. Let us be very clear. How many other

297

adoring acolytes have you dallied with while I've been conveniently encumbered with your child?'

Dr Strines flinched, shaken by the coarseness behind my mistress's silken tones. I clung to the brocaded drapes fearing I would faint in terror at what must now be revealed. I would be exposed as another devotee, a slut who would be dismissed from the house without a character. That must be why I'd been compelled to witness this scene.

'Oh, Bella, I've failed you.' The doctor was on his knees, grovelling at his wife's feet. His sudden self-abasement was astonishing. 'Yet again I'm a miserable sinner, begging mercy and forgiveness. You know me, my love. Too easily I'm filled with vulgar depravity when they entice me, even though no one but you rules my heart. These others are nothing to me. They offer themselves and I am weak. They are worthless creatures. You are my bright goddess. My idol, my life'

Mrs Strines seemed unsurprised by his posture or his torrent of confessional words. 'Go, Robert. I wish to hear no more. Leave me for now.'

'Dearest love, have pity on my weakness. I'm distraught.'

He moved on his knees to the door and crept onto the landing with histrionic self-abnegation. His wife had turned away from him and clutched her stomach. She straightened and crossed to where I was standing, still grasping the curtains, awaiting my fate. Her eyes held mine.

'*The quality of mercy is not strained.* You remember, Sarah? *It blesses he who gives and him who takes.* Isn't that fortunate? It is incumbent on me to forgive the man to whom I am bound, whose child I bear, whose chattel I am; and I shall do so. But it will be in my own good time. That latitude at least is granted me.'

She put out one hand to grip my shoulder and held me at arms' length. 'I trust you have found this episode instructive. Now leave me.'

Chilled by her tartness and in bewildered incomprehension, I fled from the room.

Chapter 30: April - May 1863

The household maintained a veneer of ordinary life for the next fortnight but under the surface there were currents of passion which I could not fathom and did not dare contemplate. After the confrontation with her husband Mrs Strines took to her bed for much of each day. She ate and drank what was brought to her and didn't seem unwell but she spoke little, except to ask me to attend to her requirements and read from Mr Wordsworth's most solemn works. She listened with a rapt expression, sighing gently from time to time but she passed no comment. I was glad to be occupied, concentrating on the sense of difficult passages, trying to keep the tremor from my voice when the words gripped my imagination with their pertinence.

Dr Strines went about his work as usual, seeing patients at the house and the Infirmary and visiting others in their homes but, when he returned in the evening, he ate alone and seemed distracted from everyday matters. He sat staring at the newspaper without turning the pages and he neglected his correspondence, so that a growing pile of unopened letters accumulated on the table. He only took up his pen to send messages to his wife, begging that she admit him, and invariably she wrote two words on these notes, to be returned to him: '*Not yet*'. I moved about the house silently, trying to avoid the doctor and, when inevitably I encountered him, I lowered my eyes and passed with only a small bob of acknowledgement. To my relief, he did not try to detain me.

I was deeply perplexed. The extraordinary sequence of events seemed unreal, leading from my own extravagant deductions concerning Mr Jewitt, through Miss Paterson's hysterical imaginings to the bizarre marital scene. I could not grasp where the truth lay, nor what were the intentions of the principals in that scene, but I was sure I too was trapped in their web of artifice, unable to escape unless they released me. Was I to become their scapegoat: my disgrace the means to reunite them? I did not know what to expect and my disquiet intensified day by day.

My reserve and sense of guilt prevented me from asking anything of Mrs Strines but after a week I broached my concern for our employers with Mrs Taylor. At first the housekeeper denied that anything was amiss but, driven to rashness, I persisted.

'I won't betray their confidences but I was compelled to observe a most distressing exchange between the doctor and our mistress. Since then I know they don't meet. Mrs Strines does not wish it and the doctor doesn't insist. It's as if they're persecuting each other. I'm profoundly uncomfortable and can't imagine what will happen. Please, Mrs Taylor, will you tell me whether anything like this has occurred before?'

At first the housekeeper did not reply but concentrated on shuffling jars to and fro on a shelf until I feared she would completely ignore me. Then she turned, peered at me and, with a sigh, sat down.

'It's a bad business you're caught up in, Sarah, no mistake. You shouldn't have to fret on their behalf. And there's no need. They'll sort it out themselves. They always do.'

I held her gaze. 'Always? More than once before?'

Mrs Taylor nodded, biting her lip. 'As you say we must respect their confidences but they have their own way of resolving problems. It's like a game they play, performing roles they've played before.'

'It's a hideous game then. Especially for Mrs Strines if the situation happens repeatedly. How can she bear it? Maybe that's why she seeks refuge in literature – stories which resonate with her own pain.'

301

'The play-acting gives her power, though. Power she doesn't have otherwise. The doctor accepts that.' The housekeeper sounded disapproving.

'You mean the power to grant mercy: to forgive?'

'She knows how to turn it to advantage, mark my words. Don't worry, dear, they'll be reconciled and she'll have the poor doctor cowering at her feet. That'll give her satisfaction.'

I gasped but swallowed my annoyance. Perhaps it signified some milepost in my maturity but I could not feel sorry for Robert Strines. Had Mrs Taylor no jot of sympathy for Mrs Strines? Had she forgotten what I'd implied to her about my own involvement with the doctor? That was unlikely, but she must have dismissed the inconvenient idea from her mind.

I thanked the housekeeper for her advice and slipped away, pretending to be reassured, but her words had done nothing to lessen my dread of the dénouement to come. Meanwhile the charade continued and the tension grew.

I guessed the stalemate was about to be resolved one afternoon when Mrs Strines asked for her hair to be dressed in her favourite style, laced with pearls. Then she settled herself on the chaise-longue, draped in her finest silk wrap, her expression solemn, her hands loose on her pronounced bump. Sure enough, after the doctor returned to the house, she invited him to join her and, as on the previous occasion, she told me to remain at her side. I was filled with despair at this request and braced myself to endure the finale, which must surely end in my dismissal, but I was taken aback by the mannered exchange which took place.

The doctor entered silently, all humble contrition and, as before, he knelt before his wife. His face seemed to have lost its chiselled lines; he looked grey and pudgy and his voice sounded weary. 'Have pity on me, Bella.'

'Pity? Do I have the luxury of conferring pity on my lord and master? I am his bondwoman, powerless, surely? He may roam where he will and I am bound to receive him back joyously.'

'But with true forgiveness, Bella, I beg you.'

'Ha! Forgiveness? I knew we would come to that: the blessing on she who confers it. How many times, Robert? What use is it that you ask forgiveness for sins past? What of those to come?'

'What on earth do you mean? Am I to repent sins not yet committed? Surely I must seek to sin no more.'

'I don't ask the impossible! One wiser than us put this predicament in sacred words. It is written in a Hymn to God the Father. I pray heaven I may not blaspheme in suggesting you seek forgiveness from me in similar terms. Sarah, take up that book of Dr John Donne's poems on the side table. I have put a marker in the page. Read those lines I have marked.'

I took the volume with trembling hands, afraid I might drop the embroidered bookmark without finding the place. Glancing through the verse, I was astounded how dreadfully apposite it was and how spiteful Mrs Strines had become, compelling her husband to repent trespasses yet to come – and in front of her culpable maid. Steadying my voice, I read as if I were making my own confession.

> '*Wilt thou forgive that sin, where I begun,*
> *Which is my sin, though it were done before?*
> *Wilt thou forgive those sins through which I run?*
> *And do them still, though still I do deplore?*
> *When thou hast done, thou hast not done,*
> *For I have more.*'

Robert Strines' face turned a sickly yellow. He bowed his head. 'Amen,' he said in a husky growl. 'I accept your censure.'

His wife sat up, pulling her pillow into a more comfortable position. She smiled thinly. 'Thank you, Sarah. As ever you read beautifully. You may leave us now.'

While I hastened to the door in desperate relief, the lady reached out her hand to her husband and he moved towards her. I sensed there was layer upon layer of meaning in his apparent submission but it was not for me to unpick. Rather, I wondered who had been most humiliated by that carefully staged and over-charged scene. I could not fail to view it as retribution I deserved. Yet, inexplicably, I deduced that I had also been reprieved.

*****

Next morning Mrs Strines' labour began. It was earlier than expected and the doctor sent urgently for the accoucheur he had engaged. He favoured a man-midwife, who had received some medical training, rather than the usual old woman with no formal learning but years of experience to guide her. Even though his wife's previous pregnancy had ended tragically the doctor's confidence in the efficacy of a male colleague was unshaken. He also summoned the nursemaid who was to care for the child if all went well, while Mrs Taylor and I were on hand to assist as necessary.

The labour was prolonged and difficult, causing Mrs Strines to cry out with each contraction, until in the early evening, with Dr Strines' permission, the 'midwife' applied chloroform to a pad of cotton and placed it over her nose so she subsided into unconsciousness. I welcomed this respite, for my mistress had been clinging to my hand as the spasms grew more intense and at one point she had bitten my fingers distractedly. She'd insisted that I stayed with her despite my ignorance and unmarried status.

Later the accoucheur announced that the birth was imminent and called for hot water. He poured liquid from a bottle into it and washed his hands but, as time went on without further progress, he began to look concerned and asked me to bring his leather bag to the bedside. He loosened the covers on one side of the bed.

'Is something wrong, sir?'

He looked at me quickly, recognising my unease. 'I hope all may yet be well. The baby's head is clearly visible in the birth canal but it is large and your mistress is delicately built. She and the child need a little help.'

He extracted a long instrument with wires and curved blades, like a pair of giant sugar tongs, from the bag. I couldn't prevent a gasp of terror when I saw it.

'Don't be alarmed,' the man said. 'I've had success with this many times. Would you raise the lady's left knee for me?'

Gently he slipped the wires forward and after careful positioning he secured a grip. I was profoundly grateful I couldn't see what he was doing, as the covers were hanging down on my side of the bed, but I fancied I could hear the crunch of bone and feared for the infant's skull. I started to pray silently. Then, after what seemed an eternity of suspense, I watched in wonder as the instrument was slowly withdrawn and a scrawny, bloodied child was eased away from its mother. The accoucheur wiped its head, mottled but intact, clamped the cord and handed the baby to the nursemaid to wash, at which indignity it emitted a piercing cry and all present, other than the insensible mother, exclaimed with relief.

Dr Strines had been banned from his wife's room, notwithstanding he was a medical man, because the accoucheur declared childbirth was no place for a father, whoever he was. Nonetheless, at the sound of the new-born's cry the doctor rushed through the door, shaking with emotion.

'Congratulations, Dr Strines, you have a son, a healthy boy so far as I can see and likely to thrive.'

'Thank God! Thank God! And Bella?' He turned to my mistress who lay unmoving and I stood back.

'Nothing to worry about. It's been a hard birth but she'll do. Look, she's stirring.'

Robert covered his wife's face with kisses, telling her repeatedly of their child's safe delivery and his love for her, until the accoucheur took hold of him by the shoulders and led him firmly from the room.

The baby, now cleanly wrapped by the nursemaid, with a little cap covering his bruised, bald head, was laid in his mother's arms and Bella Strines' weary face was transfigured by a smile of sincere elation. The blissful scene was a revelation, negating all false posturing, and I could no longer hold back my tears.

*****

The nursemaid took charge of the infant while Mrs Strines, inevitably weak after her ordeal, was expected to remain in bed for two weeks and must be closely watched for any sign of fever. Dr Strines was full of praise for his colleague's skill and explained that, before the delivery, the accoucheur had washed his hands in chlorinated water, a technique introduced a few years previously in Vienna which seemed to lessen the chance of infection. Nevertheless it could not be regarded as fool-proof and anxiety would persist for several days during which my mistress must be kept quiet and isolated.

I waited on her tirelessly but I felt drained of emotion after the searing experiences of the past weeks. My mind was made up and I resolved to give in my notice as

306

soon as Mrs Strines was strong enough to deal with changes in the household. I prepared an advertisement to place in a respectable journal, announcing my availability as a lady's maid with good references.

Meanwhile the doctor seemed unabashed by all that had happened but uninhibitedly jubilant at the birth of his son. He was filled with energy and turned at last to his neglected pile of correspondence. He was holding two documents when he burst into the kitchen where Mrs Taylor was busy baking and chatting with me.

'I've been remiss in not attending to my letters,' he said breezily. 'There's one here from my brother with news of Mrs Ibbotson, Sarah. You'll be glad to know she's progressing slowly. He's recommended she should spend the summer by the sea where the air will be beneficial. He's hopeful she'll take his advice.'

I expressed pleasure but was privately sorry the old lady would be far away when she might have been consulted on potential employers of lady's maids. Dr Strines unfolded the other untidy-looking missive and gave a cough.

'This note is strange and worrying. It's ill written and I don't know who sent it but it makes very serious allegations concerning wicked usage of a child. The writer says she – I suspect it is a she – knows of me as someone who might help.'

'There's hundreds would know you, doctor, and look to you for assistance.' Mrs Taylor's staunch adulation of her master had survived the buffeting of recent weeks undiminished.

'It's no one who knows me personally, I think, nor my correct address. "Dr Strines, by St John's Church at Ranmoor" is rather imprecise. It's written in a badly formed hand and has quaint spelling – 'p l e e s' for 'please' and so on.' He held the letter up but far enough away for us not to be able to read any troubling details it contained. 'I don't

307

suppose either of you has any idea who sent it?' We shook our heads. 'No, I didn't expect you would. By the sound of it the writer has knowledge of some sort of house of doubtful repute, probably a servant who's worried about what goes on there. I shouldn't have mentioned it.'

'What will you do about it, sir?' It was the first time in weeks I'd spoken to him unbidden.

'I'll pass it to the Chief Constable. It needs investigation but I fear, if there've been misdemeanours, the offenders' tracks will be well covered.'

The doctor left the kitchen and Mrs Taylor shook her head, muttering about evil in the world. I said nothing but I was recalling an encounter outside Norfolk Market Hall months back, when I'd mentioned my employers and where they lived. I also remembered a school friend from long ago, whose writing was as erratic as her spelling was rudimentary, and who particularly struggled to put the vowels correctly in the word 'please'. Was it possible that Chrissie Mallon, now duly married, was working as servant in some dubious establishment or had Tom been right all the time about her occupation? How easily suspicions came where Chrissie was concerned. Had that misguided young woman descended so far into the pit of immorality that she'd become a common prostitute? Was this so-called husband she'd spoken of no more than a pimp or brothel-keeper? I did not want to learn the answers. I knew little of a shadowy world scarcely hinted at in my hearing, but I drew my own conclusions.

*****

Mercifully, as the days passed, Mrs Strines stayed free of the deadly childbed fever. Her husband prescribed an iron tonic and one of Dr James's Powders to strengthen her and the bloom returned to her cheeks. All the same, it was her new resolve and dedication which were most striking. She still found pleasure in her books when her son was sleeping but it became clear that from now on the centre of her world would be Robin, the diminutive by which the boy was to be called. What unspoken compromises she made in her mind I could not know but she had found a new and fulfilling equilibrium in her life.

I rejoiced for her and for myself as her composure made it easier to speak of my decision to leave Ranmoor. She did not demur. She made clear there was no requirement for me to go but she implied tactfully that I might have good reason for choosing to depart. Her kindness overwhelmed me and, however rashly, at that moment I felt impelled to make a full confession of my sinful behaviour.

With bowed head I began, 'Oh, ma'am, I can't deceive you. I need to tell…'

'Tell me nothing, Sarah.' Bella Strines sounded imperiously severe. 'I don't wish to hear. The past is closed to me. I live now for my son. You have been an excellent maid and played your part in a becoming manner. It is enough.'

I did not dare question what she meant or imagine the possibility of her complicity with a part devised for me. I was content to accept absolution, the weight of my burden finally lifted. I didn't relish the need to join a new household, with all its unknown hardships and pitfalls, but I saw it as the price of my pardon. I had learned harsh lessons but my gratitude to the complex, puzzling woman I'd served was heartfelt.

*****

I placed my advertisement in the ladies' journal and awaited replies. Only one response came in the next few days and it was not especially encouraging: '*A distinguished lady in the town is currently seeking to engage an experienced and high class lady's maid, of excellent character. If Miss Webster cares to attend for interview on Friday afternoon at 3 p.m., at her own expense, she may be considered along with two or three others, subject to references.*'

It came from an address in Broomhall, which Mrs Taylor said was a grand mansion. I felt sure I would not pass muster there but, supressing my misgivings, I confirmed I would attend. Yet it was not to be.

On the day before the impending interview, to my surprise, Dr Strines hailed me jovially from the breakfast table. 'There's a letter for you, Sarah. Although the hand is shaky, I think it may be from my aunt.'

I was disconcerted when the doctor stroked my fingers as he gave me the letter, incredulous that he could behave flirtatiously with me after all that had occurred. I pulled my hand away and hurried to my own room, where I looked sadly at how Mrs Ibbotson's elegant writing had deteriorated. Still, I unfolded the letter with pleasure to think the old lady was at least well enough to put pen to paper again. Her message was momentous.

'*At last, dear Sarah, I can summon sufficient control to make my words legible. My recuperation continues. I am in Scarborough where I shall stay until the colder weather comes. I take the (revolting) waters at the spa and breathe the excessively brisk air. I am told these things do me good.*

I no longer have need of a nurse to attend me and scarcely any requirement for a lady's maid. Susan travelled here with me but wishes to return to the Hall (I know she has a beau in the area). She is happy to resume her role as parlour-maid now that wretched Lizzie Simmonite is wed beyond her station. What I have great need for, my dear, is

310

a loving maid-companion, to read to me and talk with intelligently.

When you came to me in my illness, I knew all was not well with you in Ranmoor and you said you might leave your position when Mrs Strines was delivered. If it suits you now to make a change in your situation, nothing would give me greater joy than to welcome you back, not as a mere servant but as a valued friend.'

I fell to my knees, thanking Heaven, but surely I did not deserve this beneficence. Whatever was required of me in return for this good fortune, I was ready to comply.

The next days passed in a whirl. Letters were sent to and fro, train times confirmed, the journey planned and a small trunk of clothes dispatched in advance. My mistress and Mrs Taylor wiped away tears as they made their farewells and Dr Strines insisted he would take me to the station in the gig. As our parting would be in public, I did not object.

Outside the sombre frontage of Victoria Station, he lifted me down from the vehicle and for a moment pressed himself to me. 'I shall miss you, little Sarah,' he said while I stood rigidly in front of him.

'I shall remember you, sir, and I wish you and Mrs Strines every happiness.'

'Oh, so solemn, little minx. I shall remember you too with much pleasure – your smooth slim thighs and the easy way you responded to my promptings.'

'Please, sir. This isn't proper.'

'Oh, and your captivating prudery. Your prim rectitude which meant nothing when your blood was pounding. Goodbye, little love. Can you feel? I am hard for you even now.' He kissed my forehead with genteel decorum.

I snatched up my bag and hurried into the station without looking back.

311

From Sheffield to Rotherham (change), to Doncaster (don't change), to York (change), then on to Scarborough: it was a complicated journey for one who had never travelled on a train before, even accompanied. I sat nervously upright until I became accustomed to the noisy rhythm of the conveyance, then gradually relaxed. I looked out in fascination at the acres of industrial buildings and narrow-fronted houses, followed by miles of agricultural plain, before the coastal moors came in sight. With every rotation of the wheels I was being taken further from all that was familiar and so much that had been shameful. I felt disgust at what the doctor had said at the station, disgust and sinful excitement too, for he still had power to arouse me in a way I abominated but could not deny.

Were all men philandering deceivers? I thought of my father and his treachery to my mother. Even gentle Arthur had proved weak and malleable. Dear Tom, at least, had been honest and true in his ill-considered devotion to Chrissie Mallon but that was mere youthful foolishness. Perhaps he too would prove unreliable as he grew older.

No, I decided, I wanted no more dealings with Adam's perfidious posterity. But neither could I ever exonerate myself from culpability. I had connived and gloried in my fall from grace. Throughout the rest of my life I must strive to expiate my guilt.

312

Chapter 31: May 1863

Chrissie contemplated her situation for several days, considering and discarding half a dozen courses of action. Mr Copley had still not visited or sent a message. Daily she expected a smirking Hannah Burkinshaw to announce that the rent for her room was no longer being paid and she was to be ejected from the house. If – when – that happened she would have few options. She had a little money saved from her allowance but it would not last long. She would have to seek employment, away from Sheffield, and manage as best she could, perhaps by pretending she was a respectable widow although no one would believe that convenient fiction. No doubt when her pregnancy was advanced she would be directed to the workhouse but never, she vowed, would she throw herself on the mercy of the parish, with the likes of Mr Gregory assessing her deserts. Yet what alternative was there? A shameful idea presented itself transiently, as her mind churned over this depressing predicament, but she dismissed it firmly.

The one constant in her mental meanderings was the certainty that she wanted to bear her child, for the revelation she experienced when she took Annie's son in her arms had returned. The yearning to have Will's baby had come too late, frustrated by his declining health, and at that time she'd convinced herself she was barren. The newfound joy that this was not so, that she had conceived, made her resolve to love the infant as if it were Will's own.

If only Nathaniel would forgive her for the altercation with Mr Gregory and resume his visits. If only he would contrive somehow that she could stay under his protection, with the baby, either at Mrs Burkinshaw's or elsewhere. She knew some men had second families, hidden away from lawful wives and public scrutiny. If only that could be arranged, she told herself, she would cherish him

313

gratefully as her lover and cause him no further problems. She would curb her tongue, be docile and obedient to his wishes. If only that could be.

When at last she heard his footsteps on the stairs, she was filled with trepidation. What future had he come to bring her? Would she be expelled without ever telling him she was to bear his child? Was her dream of reprieve and reconciliation remotely possible? As he entered the room, she rose hurriedly to face him, in desperate suspense. His expression was severe but, as he looked at her without speaking for a moment, the annoyance faded from his eyes and his whiskers twitched.

'You're more beautiful than ever, Chrissie, and I'm glad of it. I've paid Mrs Burkinshaw a great deal of money to overlook your unfortunate behaviour and I've sworn to support Mr Gregory in proposing a property transaction much to his benefit, which others in positions of trust may oppose. You're a costly investment, Miss Mallon, but when I see you I know the dividends I reap are reward enough.'

'Nathaniel! You're not casting me off?' She curled herself against him. 'I don't deserve your kindness.'

'Maybe not. You've bewitched me, you villainous creature. Mrs Burkinshaw and Mr Gregory must think me a feeble fellow to put up with your mischief but you still captivate me. I'm under your spell and I've no wish to break it.'

He buried his face in the curve of her throat and drew down the top of her dress to kiss the livid mark where the cigar had burned her soft skin.

'Come,' she said, drawing him towards the bed in its alcove, 'I'll reward you with all the black magic a witch possesses. And I have something to tell you.'

He smiled at her happily but resisted the invitation. 'I can't stay this evening, for all your enchantments, evil sorceress. I have to attend the meeting at which Mr

Gregory's proposal is to be discussed. I need to fulfil my commitment to him. But tomorrow I'll come and my time will be for you alone, I promise.'

'I'll be waiting, Nat, on fire for you. We'll make it a time to remember.' Her radiant smile was unforced.

*****

She rose later than usual next morning, having little appetite for breakfast in the last few days. She put on a loose robe and sat by her mirror, peering anxiously at the faint hollows beneath her eyes, before applying rose-tinted lotion to her cheeks. She was aware of movement outside her door before it was flung open unceremoniously, without the courtesy of a knock.

'Mrs Burkinshaw, what...?'

The woman strode forward, dragging Chrissie to her feet, and ripped open the fastenings of her gown so her naked body was displayed. Then she struck the girl viciously across her face. 'You slut! When did you know?'

Chrissie grasped the edges of her robe together, struggling to control her fury and not to retaliate. She was certain her condition was not yet visible. 'Know what? Why did you hit me?'

'Where are your soiled cloths then? The girl tells me you've had no blood-stained cloths for nigh two months. I've thrashed her for not telling me afore, when she had no cloths to wash out weeks ago. You're carrying, aren't 'ee?'

'What if I am?'

'You was told clear enough to let me know if you got yourself into trouble. You stupid bitch! I'd have thought you knew better.' She produced a bulky device from the bag hanging at her waist. 'You'll use this at once. Let's hope you're not too far gone.'

315

Chrissie stared at the object with its long nozzle and bulbous rubber ball. 'What is it?'

'Called a douche. Stick it up your front passage and squeeze the liquid in. It's filled with acid water to flush the thing out. If it don't work, I'll have to see to you meself, like I did for that daft chit, Dolly.'

Chrissie was trembling frantically. 'I don't want...'

'Don't argue. Thought I made meself plain when you came to the house. Here, use it now or I'll do it for you.' She advanced on Chrissie, brandishing the instrument.

'I'll do it myself, when you're gone. I were going to tell Mr Copley this evening.'

'What?' the landlady's explosion of wrath shook the rafters. 'You'll never say a word to him, d'you hear? The gentlemen know I'll deal with any unfortunate occurrences. They're not to be bothered. It's women's business. Get on the bed and open your legs – you knows how to do that well enough. Be best if I do it.'

'No. I'll do it. Let me alone!'

'I'll give you five minutes. Use every last drop.'

Mrs Burkinshaw thrust the syringe into the girl's hand and marched out of the room with a ferocious snort. Chrissie had already decided what she would do. She rushed to the aspidistra on the corner cabinet and squeezed hard on the rubber ball, emptying the liquid into the china pot, relieved to see the dry earth soak it up. Then she splashed herself between her legs with water from the washstand and lay on the bed holding the deflated douche.

When the landlady returned to inspect, she nodded approval. 'Feel anything inside?'

'Don't know. Sort of burning maybe.'

'Good. I made it up strong seeing you'd left it so late. Should all come away in next few hours. Tell me if it don't work and don't you dare say a word to Mr Copley.'

316

*****

Chrissie was everything her lover desired that evening, both seductive and submissive, and she encouraged him so effectively that he was able to take her twice in succession. Only then, as they lay together restfully with her head on his shoulder, did she stroke his cheek and whisper in his ear. 'Said I had something to tell you, Nat. Can you guess?'

'Have you bought a new dress?'

'No, something more special, love.' She fingered his moustache. 'I'm carrying your child, Nat.'

'What!' For the second time that day the same shouted word echoed in the rafters. He sat up, pulling away from her. 'Haven't you seen Mrs Burkinshaw?'

'I've seen her. She gave me a douche to get rid of it.'

'Don't talk about such filthy things. It's for you and her to manage. I don't need to hear. Just do what's necessary.'

'I want the child, Nat. I've not used the douche.'

He was goggle-eyed with terror. 'What are you saying, Chrissie?'

'I want to bear your child. I'll love it and be a proper mother.'

'You're mad!'

'We'll be like a second family for you. You love your children with Mrs Copley. You'll just have one more, with me, and I'll...'

'How dare you! How dare you speak of my family in the same breath as your bastard!'

Her indignation erupted. 'T'will be your child too.'

'How do I know that, trollop? I shall not acknowledge it. How do I know you've not been with others?'

317

'What here? With Mrs B keeping guard?' She laughed at the preposterous notion.

'Mr Gregory said you'd propositioned him.'

She was standing facing him across the bed, incredulity stamped on her pale face. 'Nat, you can't believe that. You're overwrought. I never thought the news would shock you so. I thought you'd love our child, as I will.'

He pulled on his trousers, buttoning awkwardly with clumsy fingers. 'Mrs Burkinshaw told me such things would not happen. That she looked after any problems. I made clear I would never accept a child, was not able to provide for one; my means are not limitless. I've been deceived by the pair of you.'

'Is that your last word, Nat? If so I'll leave in morning. I'll make no claim on you, don't fret.' She spoke with unusual dignity.

He came round the bed and held her to him, giving her cause to hope he would relent. She could feel his hammering heartbeat. 'Get rid of it, Chrissie. So we can be as we have been. I worship you, lass. Don't force me to lose you.'

'I want your child, Nat.'

'I'll kill you first!'

He bared his pointy teeth and flung her onto the bed, his hands at her throat. He pinned her down with his knee as she thrashed about trying to tear his thumbs from her windpipe, until she began to choke. Then he leapt back from her, staring in panic as she rolled on her side, gasping for breath.

'Chrissie!'

She drew herself up into a sitting position, her voice constricted as she gulped air into her lungs. 'That's right, Nat. Kill us both, me and the child. Be free of us both.'

'You've made me a murderer, a would-be murderer.' He staggered to a chair, appalled that he was capable of such violence. They sat in frozen silence, looking at each other, slowly comprehending the enormity of what had happened. Chrissie was the first to move. Shakily she stood and handed Mr Copley his jacket.

'I'll leave all the things you've given me. Thank you for use of them.'

Her bitter gratitude stung him and he flinched. 'Take what you want, Chrissie. The things I've given you are yours.'

'Don't doubt Mrs B'll have me pursued as a thief.'

'I'll speak to her. Here, she won't know of this. A parting gift.' He took a small sheaf of banknotes from his pocket.

There was tenderness in her look as she took the money. 'You're still generous, Nat.'

'And you're cruel, Chrissie. To put some puking brat ahead of me after all I've done for you and would do still. I wish it dead and you writhing in agony.'

He flung open the door and then he hesitated, turning back to her again with plaintive eyes. 'If it's stillborn, come back to me.'

She flung herself forward, slamming the door behind him. Then she leaned back against the jamb, listening bleakly to his receding steps.

*****

She took the two day dresses, the money and the jewellery, leaving the fancy evening gowns and trimmings. She had as much as she could carry. She slipped from the house in the early morning, aware that Mrs Burkinshaw was watching from her sitting room where the door was open a chink, but first she put a note under Tilda's door, regretting she could not say goodbye in person. As she walked out into the street the chilly breeze blew back her shawl and she stopped to adjust it. Then, purposefully, she set off downhill to find her way back to the centre of the town.

During that sleepless night she'd thought again of resorting to the shameful expedient she dismissed from her mind before announcing her pregnancy, but she still had qualms. In the small hours she'd been tormented by the horror of Mr Copley's brutal response, the shattering of her silly illusion that he would cherish her and their child. She wondered if she was indeed insane to reject Mrs Burkinshaw's ministrations to get rid of the intruder in her womb. She knew women in her situation, favoured, 'kept' women, with access to the confidential services of someone like her landlady, often resorted to such attempts. She knew also such attempts could be dangerous, and sometimes killed the wretched woman as well as the infant, but it was not fear for herself which reinforced her repugnance to take that course of action. It was the mysterious, innate desire to bear her child surging within her, overpowering reason. And it was anger.

Her anger was all embracing. It was directed towards everyone and everything that had shaped her destiny. The catalogue, which started with her absent father and her mother who had died too soon, ran on through hateful grandmother and perverted uncle to her own rash self-confidence and poor judgement. When, after leaving Malin Bridge, she sought to make a new life, relying on her unusual beauty and youthful vanity, she'd thrown herself at the abhorrent Eb Pyle – of all people – and she had paid for it dearly. When she found her true soul-mate, after stupidly vacillating in rebellion against what marriage to him would entail, her thoughtlessness led him to dash into a choking inferno, where the smoke destroyed his ravaged lungs, and she'd been forced to witness his gradual annihilation. When she sought respite in the arms of a kindly benefactor, who offered her comfort and solace, he had been exposed as self-serving and pusillanimous. Her fate was malignant or it was farcical.

While she tramped on downhill, the blustery wind grew stronger across the open slope beside the smart private cemetery. She glanced with annoyance at the elaborate headstones, with their embellished scrolls and drooping angels, and she thought of Will's unmarked grave in the public cemetery on the other side of town. Mrs Turner had said he would not have wanted them to spend money on a stone and there was no need anyway, for his memory was forever in their hearts. Dear Mrs Turner.

At the bottom of Cemetery Road, where it crossed the Porter Brook, she sat down on the parapet to rest. She glanced idly at the rushing water, at the collected debris caught against the sides of the bridge and in the bushes on the bank. Driftwood. That's what I am, she thought sourly: driftwood, tumbled along in the current, cast up where it happens to rest, clinging onto ledges and in crevices which offer short-lived support, then hurled again into the stream. She watched a twig whirled round and round in a miniature eddy and observed that a small green leaf still sprouted from its fractured side, a leaf which would never fully open but moulder and die. Life sprouted in her too and she would not abandon it to the vagaries of life's vortex. She would do what was necessary to safeguard its future. Her resolution was made. However hideously manipulative and shameful it might be, she would provide a secure resting place for herself and her child.

*****

Passing the New Market, she saw several men emerge from the door on South Street, setting off for the morning shift, but Tom Webster was not among them. Undeterred, she knocked and the door was opened by a

321

forbidding matron who appraised her sternly from head to foot.

'What dost tha want?' Mrs Purkis snapped.

'Does Tom Webster still live here?'

'No, he don't.'

The door moved towards her but Chrissie grabbed the knob and prevented it shutting. 'Could you tell me where he lives now?'

'No, I couldn't. He's a decent young man. He don't want likes of thee troubling him. Get away!'

The door was pushed with such violence that Chrissie was compelled to step back or risk injury. It crashed shut and she heard the bolt slide into place. She stared at the blank woodwork and turned away disconsolately. She would get nothing out of that grim gatekeeper. Why had the woman assumed so readily she was a ne'er-do-well? Surely her appearance was modest and unremarkable? Perhaps the landlady protected all her lodgers and the reputation of her house in that way. At least she had not said Tom was sick or hurt or wed – but perhaps he was.

She did not like the idea but she would have to enquire as to Tom's whereabouts from his sister who, she feared, would question her motives for the enquiry. This was a risk she must take. It would necessitate a journey uphill to Ranmoor and, if Sarah was already married and moved elsewhere, who knew how many miles she would have to trail in search of Tom's new address. Already she was feeling tired, so she set off to see if she could find a carrier going in the right direction and in this she was lucky.

*****

Mrs Taylor opened the door and looked doubtfully at the visitor who knocked.

'Is Sarah Webster here, ma'am?'

As the housekeeper shook her head an inner door creaked and voices were heard. Dr Strines escorted his patient to the threshold and Chrissie stepped aside to let a frail old lady pass. She had not expected to encounter the doctor but she was quickly conscious of him scrutinising her and she looked directly into his face, only to read the nature of his interest with distaste. He was good-looking, elegant, polished and he reminded her unpleasantly of Mr Gregory. She knew at once he was not a man to be trusted.

'What does this young woman want, Mrs Taylor?'

'Asking for Miss Sarah, sir.'

The doctor's eyes were lingering on the swell of Chrissie's breasts under the plain material of her dress. 'She's left our household. Gone to Scarborough to re-join her former mistress.'

'It were actually her brother I wanted to enquire after. Do you know his address, please?'

Chrissie spoke to Mrs Taylor, uncomfortable under the doctor's gaze, guessing he would welcome some pretext to detain her. It was he who answered.

'I know nothing of her brother. Are you a friend of Sarah's?'

'Since childhood.' Flustered by Sarah's return to Mrs Ibbotson, annoyed by the doctor's leer, she let temptation overcome her. She looked up at him archly, through her lashes. 'I sent you a letter, sir, a while back, though I didn't sign it.'

The housekeeper was watching their exchange keenly and raised her eyebrows at mention of the letter. Upstairs a sweet voice was crooning a lullaby.

'Come into my study for a moment, young woman.'

He ushered her courteously into his room and pulled a chair forward for her to sit. 'I know the letter you speak of and I regret there was some delay in my attending to it. I've forwarded it to the Chief Constable. He will investigate. Is the child you mentioned still at the house?'

'Yes, sir.'

'The child is no more than nine, you say?'

'I'm sure so.'

'Carnal knowledge of a girl under ten is, by Act of Parliament, made a felony. That's serious but there's often difficulty in obtaining clear evidence in such cases. The landlady may claim the girl as her grandchild and swear she is virtuous. The girl may be too fearful to make complaint.'

'I understand. But what's happening is foul. I couldn't let it be.'

'Quite right. That's commendable.' Suavely he moved forward to pat her hand and she recognised the desire in his eyes. 'You are employed at the house?'

'I've left there.'

'That's for the best, my dear.' His voice was soothing, ingratiating. 'You were a servant, a maid, there?'

'No, sir, I lived there.' She rose and he took a step back, the muscles of his jaw taut with uncertainty. She enjoyed his discomfort. 'My protector paid the rent, you see.'

He flushed scarlet. 'How dare you come to this house! A common whore! How dare you!' He flung open the door. 'Mrs Taylor, show this female out from the tradesman's door. She's no more than a harlot. She has no business in a respectable house.'

Chrissie ran the tip of her tongue around her lips and gave a small ironic curtsey. 'You'd be acquainted with those of my calling, sir?'

'How dare you!'

She brushed against him as she passed. 'You're repetitive, love,' she said huskily, amused to see that he was trembling.

Mrs Taylor hurried her downstairs and opened the backdoor noisily. 'Get out, you baggage!' she exclaimed.

Then touching Chrissie's arm gently she whispered, 'Sarah had a letter from her brother a while back. Their father had been hurt in an accident and her brother took over his job, back in the village they came from.'

'Malin Bridge?' She could scarcely speak for surprise.

'That's it.'

'Thank you, ma'am. I'm right grateful to you.'

Mrs Taylor gave a curt nod. 'Be off with you now.'

Chrissie turned away from the house, resolute and clear what she must do. Nonetheless, she wondered fleetingly how sweet, innocent Sarah had coped with that sanctimonious, dissolute master.

*****

She had to walk a mile before she found a carter bound for the centre of town and she was shaken about on the vehicle's bare boards, amid piles of kindling wood, as it trundled slowly downhill. On arrival, she struggled through the bustling streets to Snig Hill, anxious not to meet any of her old acquaintances, but her good fortune held and she found a carrier able to take her all the way to Hillsborough. It had been a long exhausting day and as she sat beside the loquacious wagoner, who mercifully sought no response to his monologue, her composure faded and she was seized with panic. What would she do when she reached Malin Bridge? Would Tom be living with his father and stepmother? It was inconceivable she should throw herself on the mercy of the Black Crow. Would Tom still want her? Was this to be the final rejection?

The last half mile on foot to the village, following the River Loxley upstream from the bridge at Hillsborough, was almost more than she could manage. Worn out and near despair, she dragged herself along the road, struggling with the weight of her bag, which numbed her fingers and pulled the tendons of arm and shoulder. She would not call at the Websters' home, of that she was sure. As a last resort she might have to seek a night's rest at Aunt Ada's, bitter humiliation though that would be. What a fool she had been to come, clutching at an illusory straw.

It was turning to dusk when she approached the Stag Inn, where she'd waited so excitedly three years earlier to leave the village for ever. She noticed men emerging onto the road from the riverside track, where the Rivelin came in to join the waters of the Loxley, and she hung back by the side of the inn, realising they were workers on their way home from the wheels and forges beside the tributary. Tom would come that way.

When they had gone, she peered to make certain no one else was in sight and started out along the track. Round the first bend, she put her bag under a bush and hauled herself up the slope to a tumbledown shack, where she'd played hide and seek with Sarah. Then, in the shadow of its dilapidated walls, she waited. Several more men appeared, smoking and laughing but, afterwards as the sky darkened, there was no further sound of human activity, only the cries of the waterfowl and roosting starlings. She feared she had missed Tom and must defer a meeting until the next day. She pondered whether she might sleep in the shelter of the battered shed, in preference to facing Aunt Ada, but she was very hungry.

Then she heard the crack of a twig, slow footsteps advancing, and she saw him. He was ambling contentedly, looking across the river where a fish had surfaced, a young man of consequence, at ease with himself, confident in his skills and his position in the world. Here was no callow youth to be wheedled and seduced. Her heart beat faster. She let him pass a little beyond the shack before she called.

'Tom!'

He swivelled round looking in wonder up the slope, where her voice had come from, and the expression on his face gave her courage. He stood stock still while she descended, heedless of how she snagged her shawl on the brambles and muddied her skirt. Only at that point, whispering in awe, did he speak her name.

'Chrissie!'

'Tom. Oh, Tom...'

Now she'd found him she didn't know what to say but it did not matter, for his cry of triumph lifted a skein of duck from the water and caused the rooks in the trees above them to circle and add their own raucous counterpoint to his greeting.

'Chrissie! Chrissie! You're come! You're come home. Oh, Chrissie.'

And he took her in his arms.

Chapter 32: Summer 1863

Mrs Ibbotson sent her carriage to meet me at Scarborough railway station, to convey me the short distance to the lodgings she had taken for the summer. These were superbly situated, adjoining the fashionable Crown Hotel, overlooking South Bay and just above the imposing new spa buildings which nestled at a lower level against the cliff. I took in few of these details on my arrival but I registered with pleasure that the invalid was able to rise from her chair and pull herself upright with the help of a heavy stick. Mrs Ibbotson greeted me warmly and I stammered a suitable reply, expressing joy at her improved appearance. Then, still grasping my travelling bag against my side, I spoke the words formulated in my mind during the journey.

'Ma'am, I'm sorry. I shouldn't have come. It isn't right for me to be here. I'll leave at once.'

The old lady sighed. 'You will do no such thing, Sarah. You are tired and overwrought. You're not used to journeying and I've no doubt there are matters which have distressed you. Susan will show you to your room and bring you a supper tray. We'll speak further in the morning.'

Faced with Mrs Ibbotson's determination and my own weariness, I acquiesced. Next morning, from the window of my room, I watched the risen sun across the softly rippling water and marvelled at this immensity of sea which I'd never seen before. I stared at the expanse of beach, the sands dotted with rocky islets to the south of the bay, the rugged headland in the other direction and the bevy of fishing boats setting off on the tide from the harbour below the town. Then I dressed myself again in the travelling clothes I'd worn the previous day and made my way to the sitting room. Mrs Ibbotson was already seated at the breakfast table pouring tea. She replaced the pot carefully on its china stand.

'Good morning, Sarah. I trust you're well rested.'

'Thank you, ma'am, and I'm sorry for my bad manners yesterday. I was brusque and ungrateful. It was so good of you to offer me a situation and in Sheffield it seemed to me everything I could wish for. But I do not deserve...'

I paused and Mrs Ibbotson raised her eyebrows, motioning me to sit. I remained standing and drew breath to continue. 'Ma'am, it isn't right that I should re-join your household. I'm not as I was. I would bring disgrace and shame with me. I can't stay.'

'What rubbish!' The old lady raised her hands. 'Do you think that as I reach the seventy fifth anniversary of my birth, I am concerned with such considerations? You've not changed in the essentials I look for – an intelligent sensible companion. If you've done what you should not, in the eyes of narrow moralists, it's no concern of mine. I grew up in a different age. When I was a girl in the Prince Regent's day attitudes were rather more accommodating. What passes now for conventional morality is somewhat overrated in my opinion.'

'Ma'am, I mustn't deceive you. I've sinned grievously.'

'So have we all, my dear, in our different ways; and few, I suspect, more than that blandly dissembling younger nephew of mine.'

I blanched and set down my bag. 'You know, ma'am?'

'I guessed and I hold myself to some degree responsible for your exposure to temptation. I sensed there was something not quite as it should be at Ranmoor, when I took you there, but I didn't realise what a blackguard the man was.'

'He's not so much to blame, ma'am. He never forced me.' My voice sank to a whisper. 'I loved him deeply.'

Ponderously she rose, leaning on the table-top. 'And that's why you rejected young Arthur?'

329

'I couldn't trifle with him, ma'am, and I didn't feel for him what I felt for – the other.'

'Oh, my dear, you've been greatly wronged; but also richly blessed to feel such powerful emotion, however misplaced. It doesn't come to all, you know. Many a devoted wife has never known passion – although that may be all to the good. Passion is not the best foundation for matrimony – deep affection is much more reliable.'

I stood tongue-tied and then slowly advanced to kneel before Mrs Ibbotson. 'You're so good and understanding, ma'am.'

'Nonsense! I'm a selfish and resolute old woman who wants to secure the services of the maid-companion of her choice. Get up. You've witnessed too many histrionics at Ranmoor, I think.' She paused, stretching out her hand to make me rise. 'Will you stay? Please, for my sake.'

'With all my heart, ma'am, if it's what you truly want.'

I was now in tears, as Mrs Ibbotson embraced me, but I had one more protestation to make. 'I promise you, ma'am, I'll let no more immodest emotions sweep me away. My brother once said I was as hard as stone – towards my father. Now I shall be still more unforgiving towards myself.'

Mrs Ibbotson smiled. 'I hope you will not stifle your heart entirely,' and, when I began to insist, she took my hand. 'Enough, my dear. Time will tell.'

*****

The genteel, undemanding monotony of life at Scarborough, in an invalid's household, was in all respects welcome to me. In the next few weeks I often sat peacefully beside my mistress, reading or sewing, with the double doors open onto our small balcony fronted by decorative wrought iron railings, so we could glance from time to time

330

at the miscellany of ships near the harbour and the walkers strolling along the beach. When Mrs Ibbotson felt strong enough, I helped her down the steep slope to the spa, where she took the waters and rested in the Promenade Lounge while the band played outside. Then the carriage would come down to carry us back, by a winding route, up the cliff.

I learned that, since the opening of the railway, Scarborough had become a destination for families with a lower station in life than those who had first frequented the spa. Trippers came from Leeds and Bradford, bringing an air of boisterous bustle to the town, and the huge assembly hall in the spa complex, which seated 2000, catered for a variety of tastes, most popularly with a music-hall. More discriminating and cultured visitors, who still favoured the resort in their hundreds, attended elegant recitals at the Town Hall and classical performances at the Theatre Royal, where I sat, round-eyed with amazement, as I listened for the first time to an orchestra playing Rossini overtures and Mozart symphonies. The music raised my spirits and I rejoiced to see that my mistress enjoyed this entertainment and might wish to attend future concerts. I understood my new role as Mrs Ibbotson's companion gave me a subtly different status in society from that of a mere maid and, as I consciously adopted ladylike behaviour, I grew in self-confidence.

Sometimes, on errands or for my own amusement, I walked across the Cliff Bridge into the centre of the town. The iron bridge spanned the Mill Beck, racing its way down a deep wooded valley to the sea, and there were fine views over its balustrade in all directions. At the town end of the bridge, contractors had begun to construct a fine hotel, to be perched on the very cliff-top, and from there one could descend to the harbour with its triple piers and brick lighthouse. I was entranced by this unfamiliar world, watching as fishermen unloaded their catches on the

331

quayside and trading vessels brought in timber, coal and brandy. I learned they set sail again carrying plump hams, salt fish and firkins of local butter for the folk in far off cities. Twice a week the packet-boat, plying between London and Edinburgh, called with special deliveries of cargo and travellers who sometimes looked relieved to step ashore – even in summer the North Sea could be unpredictable and choppy.

On her visits to the spa, Mrs Ibbotson became friendly with the wife of a well-to-do businessman from Newcastle who was staying with her husband at the Crown Hotel, in the hope that the spa waters and the sea air would bring about some improvement in her crippling rheumatics. Mr Ashington patiently pushed his wife up and down Scarborough's steep streets in a basket-weave contrivance on wheels which, I was told, had first been introduced in the town of Bath. They were a pleasant, unpretentious couple and I was glad when, on a balmy June day, my mistress invited them to ride in her carriage for a drive around the headland to see the ruins of the ancient castle which surmounted it.

We admired the recently renovated church of St Mary before proceeding into the castle yard and there we all exclaimed delightedly at the picturesque remains of the Norman fortress, romantically embellished with ferns growing from cracks in the mortar and small trees rooted in the crumbling stone walls. The views from the castle extended beyond the headland to the North Bay sands and Mr Ashington and I descended from the carriage to walk nearer the cliff edge and see more of the coast. The old gentleman had bristling eyebrows, which gave his face a puckish appearance, and he enjoyed identifying various ships on the sea.

332

'See that one turning the point towards the harbour? From Newcastle she is, carrying coal, built in the very yard I have an interest in.'

'You have a shipyard, Mr Ashington?'

'Joint interest with my brother. Our father started the business. He'd been a miner but he saw there was money to be made in shipping coal to where it's needed so he raised a loan, with others, to hire a little vessel and went on from there. Bought out his partners, he did. Then when Joshua and I joined him from school we began to build ships as well as operate them. Small yard, it is, but prosperous. My elder son's taken up the reins now, though I still keep an eye on things.'

'Your father was very enterprising.'

'He was, Miss Webster, and we try to do him credit. Risen from very little, we are; now we employ scores of men. I don't forget where we came from but Henry's further away from the start of it, he's my elder lad, building himself a fine new house on the edge of town and found himself a fancy, highfalutin wife. Still, we have young Charles to keep us on the straight and narrow.'

'Your younger son?'

'Aye, good lad. Intelligent. Takes after his mother for finer feelings. Been at the university in Durham. Now he's set on going into the church, would you believe?'

I wasn't called on to reply as we had re-joined the others and it was agreed the carriage should take us down to the harbour, so Mrs Ibbotson and Mrs Ashington could see the fishing fleet at close quarters. On arrival, Mr Ashington and I were again set down to walk along the old pier towards the lighthouse.

'Sea's smooth as silk today, Miss Webster. It's not often like that. There's usually some swell. But I suppose you've not seen it in a real fury, coming from Sheffield?'

'No, indeed. It's the first time I've been to the coast but I've read of shipwrecks and disasters out in the ocean.'

'Not just away from the land either. When the lifeboat was first launched here, more than fifty years ago, it came to grief right in sight of the town, over against the sea wall below where the spa is now, across the bay there. Smashed to pieces and two of the crew lost, along with three spectators on the shore.'

'How dreadful!'

'Fearsome, the power of water can be, Miss Webster. Those who know the sea well never underestimate it.'

*****

On arrival back at Mrs Ibbotson's lodgings, I was given a letter which had been sent on from Ranmoor and, recognising my brother's script, I eyed it anxiously. I hadn't yet told Tom of my changed circumstances and I worried his reason for writing would relate to our father's declining health. My guess was wrong but I exclaimed in disbelief as I read the extraordinary message.

Dear Sal

This is to tell you of my joyful news. I can scarce form my words for happiness. A few weeks back my beloved Chrissie came to me and on Saturday we was wed in chapel. She's Chrissie Mallon no longer but Chrissie Webster and I'm happiest man in world. She sends her regards and we hopes you will rejoice with us and visit when you are back in Sheffield.

Your loving brother Tom

'Not bad news, Sarah?' said Mrs Ibbotson, watching my stricken expression and trembling hands.

'I hope not, ma'am. My brother has wed a girl he's long admired though she never showed interest in him. She

334

was my childhood friend but I've sometimes doubted her honesty and still don't know what to make of her.'

'But your brother loves her?'

'No question of that. But it's so sudden and he's quite young. That she should go to him when she'd always ignored him – it's very strange! And I'd heard she was to wed another. Poor Tom is besotted.'

'Then it's not for us to judge but wish them well.'

So I wrote with cordial greetings, invoking blessings on their life together, but my amiable expressions of goodwill did not dispel the misgivings in my mind.

*****

Several weeks later when Mrs Ibbotson and I arrived at the spa building we found Mrs Ashington flushed and animated, waving at us from her bath-chair.

'My son, Charles, is to join us here for a few days,' she called. 'He'll arrive tomorrow. It's quite a surprise. He's preparing for his ordination as deacon, but it seems he can contrive to leave his studies for a short while and he's taken pity on his old parents to pay us a visit. He's such a good lad.'

It was arranged that we would all attend the concert at the Town Hall two days hence so the ladies from the West Riding of Yorkshire could meet the young man from Newcastle. I didn't relish the prospect. I was comfortable with my sedate companions and feared the intrusion of a younger man, however worthy, would disrupt our quiet contentment. I dreaded above all that he might pay me unwanted attention, as the only other young person in the party, and I would find that intolerable. It was therefore reassuring to find that Charles Ashington was earnest, diffidently courteous, profoundly serious and undeniably boring. He was moreover of only medium height, stockily

335

built, with a square head and eyes set too far apart to be attractive.

Three days later I was invited, as Mrs Ibbotson's companion, to join a dinner with the Ashingtons in a private room at the Crown Hotel. I found myself sitting next to the younger gentleman and managed to converse with him unaffectedly and without strain. He spoke at some length, learnedly, on the complex divisions within the Anglican Church and I found his explanations easy to follow and more interesting than I would have expected. I concluded that the haven of emotional safety I'd found in Scarborough was under no threat from him and I was greatly relieved.

*****

On the morning after the dinner the weather changed. The long spell of sunlit days was replaced by squally rain while raging seas crashed against the defensive walls behind the beaches. My mistress and I stayed indoors, regarding the storm through closed windows, snug in our comfortable lodgings.

When the landlady brought up the post, Mrs Ibbotson read one letter with evident displeasure.

'Really, this is unacceptable, Sarah, and I apologise. My nephew writes from Ranmoor...'

'Oh, are they well, Mrs Strines and the baby...? Beg pardon, ma'am.'

'All are thriving, I'm pleased to say, but it is they who should beg pardon. My nephew encloses a letter addressed to you, received at his house nearly two months ago, soon after your brother's which he forwarded. Somehow this one was mislaid and only lately discovered being used as a bookmark in some volume of poetry Mrs Strines was perusing. It seems she had intended to add a note of personal good wishes to pass on to you but it escaped her mind. I hope the letter contains nothing urgent, Sarah.'

I took the envelope, looking blankly at the carefully formed, rather childish writing. It was unfamiliar to me. The letter was dated at the beginning of June. Its contents were disturbing.

Dear Miss Webster

I hope you will forgive my writing to you. Tis a desperate last attempt to see if I can find my friend Chrissie Mallon. You may remember meeting me with her by Norfolk Market Hall last year. She were to have wed my brother but he became mortal sick and sadly passed away in December. Shortly after that Chrissie left my mother's house where she lodged all of a sudden and without saying where she were going. I have been worried since that she did not get in touch but my baby were poorly for a while and I were too harassed to make enquiries. Now I have asked around the neighbourhood and learned nothing.

I mind Chrissie was your friend from years ago and wondered if you might know where she has gone. If you can let me know, I shall be very grateful.

Yours respectfully

Annie Crookes

(My young brother who is a clerk helped me with my letter)

I folded the paper and put it in my pocket. 'It isn't urgent, ma'am. Simply news of an old friend.'

My calm words satisfied Mrs Ibbotson but did nothing to reassure me. I ran through the chronology in my mind. Chrissie had been bereaved and disappeared in December but, from what Tom had written, she had not gone to him until May. Where had she been until then? Where had she been when that strange letter was sent to Doctor Strines, before little Robin's birth, with serious allegations concerning a house of doubtful repute? I had suspected then and I suspected still it had come from Chrissie. I winced.

Later, recalling the good impression Annie had made on me at our meeting, I penned a brief reply. I explained the reason for the delay and how my brother had written to say Chrissie was at Malin Bridge but I did not refer to their nuptials. That was for Chrissie to tell her friend, if she so wished. I didn't want to be involved.

*****

In the afternoon the rain slackened, although the wind was if anything more intense. Clusters of people were gathering along the sea wall, below the spa buildings, observing the furious waves and jumping away excitedly from the clouds of spray. I received permission to leave Mrs Ibbotson in order to view the spectacle more closely and I made my way down the cliff path to join the crowd. I stood well back, daunted by the ferocity of the water but enjoying the delight of several children who screamed with glee as they narrowly avoided a soaking when the waves swept over the coping. One small lad of five or six tried to climb onto the top of the wall but his father wisely restrained him.

The man was accompanied by a woman who clutched a baby, swathed in a shawl, and held the hand of a toddler. As a plume of spray fell over them, this little girl squealed and suddenly broke free from her mother, running unsteadily between the onlookers, to tumble over at my feet. I stooped to lift and comfort the whimpering child, as the woman hastily gave the baby to its father and hurried after her daughter. The incident caused other heads to turn back from the sea for a moment but, as I smiled at the grateful woman and held out the chastened run-away, I glimpsed a rapid movement by the wall and screamed.

It happened in a flash. The small lad, freed momentarily from his father's supervision, leapt onto the wall just as a huge wave thundered against it, sweeping water over the feet of the bystanders and, as it receded, carrying the boy into the tumultuous sea. Instantly the man thrust the baby into a neighbour's arms and flung himself after his son. While pandemonium broke out around me, I sought to prevent the hysterical woman from following her husband. I remembered Mr Ashington's tale of the lifeboat disaster near the same spot and feared I was to witness a similar outcome. The onlookers crowded forward.

'There's the lad! He's floundering.'

'Heaven help 'em.'

'The waves'll take the boy.'

'He's got him! Look! His Da's grabbed the lad's shoulder.'

Satisfaction that the man had managed to grasp his son was soon muted for there seemed no way he could fight his way back to the wall, against the tide, with the boy thrashing about in his arms. Then, from somewhere out of my sight, a rope was thrown and, despite the swirling water, the father caught hold of it.

'Take hold of the rope, lads, and help drag them in!'

Three or four men obeyed this direction and I saw a sturdy figure, stripped to his waistcoat, coiling the loose end of the rope around his middle to anchor it, while he and his assistants exerted all their strength to pull the half-drowned victims ashore. Fortunately, the father was a muscular fellow and he succeeded in maintaining his grip, even lifting his son slightly for a rescuer to take hold of the boy when they reached the wall. Then he himself was dragged ashore. The little lad was terrified and spluttering but not seriously hurt by his ordeal and he was bundled into a blanket brought from the spa. The man's right hand was badly chafed by the rope but his eyes shone with pride as the reunited family

339

were hurried away into the building. While the onlookers began to move away, I walked over to the young man who was unhitching the rope from his waist.

'Mr Ashington,' I said appreciatively, 'that was bravely done.'

'My physique often led me to be anchor-man in tug-of-war battles at school. But it was your quick eyes, Miss Webster, which alerted everyone and gave time for us to get the rope, before the waves drew them under for good.'

I smiled acknowledgement and turned to go but Charles Ashington spoke again. 'We're both suffering from the shock of witnessing near disaster, Miss Webster. I think a pot of tea is called for to steady our nerves. Will you walk across Cliff Bridge to a small teashop I've visited with my mother? It's a very respectable place.'

I was amused by his punctilious regard for propriety and in spite of my apprehension I knew it would be churlish to refuse. I walked beside him timidly, while he described more fully his exertions on the sports field and, afterwards, sitting at a table in the smart, bow-fronted window of the teashop in Bar Street, I listened to his eager plans to serve, in due course, as incumbent at a church in a poor district of Newcastle.

'That's my vocation, Miss Webster, to serve the working people who live in such insalubrious areas. I've asked that when I'm ordained curate, I may be appointed to such a post but city parishes are often too impoverished to support more than one clergyman.'

'I hope you're fortunate, Mr Ashington. I do indeed.' I was acutely conscious how unsuitable a companion at the tea-table I was for a high-minded cleric.

When he had escorted me back to Mrs Ibbotson's lodgings he bade me farewell for he was to leave the town early next morning. He politely expressed his pleasure in meeting me and I wished him well for his future, relieved that I wouldn't have to face the embarrassment of encountering him again.

*****

Mr and Mrs Ashington departed from Scarborough in the last week of August and I missed their company more than my brief acquaintance with their son. Mrs Ibbotson had decided to stay at the resort for a further two weeks before returning home and I was glad of this, thinking ruefully that life at the Hall would now seem duller than it had when I first lived there. I would miss the concerts, theatrical entertainments and society I'd learned to enjoy at the spa town but I resolved to discipline myself, thinking that an existence of quiet reclusiveness was appropriate for one in my situation.

Two days before we were due to leave, I received another letter from Tom and I opened it nervously, fearing some unpleasant disclosure, but my anxiety was misplaced.

Dear Sal

Should have written afore. Glad to let you know Chrissie is carrying and doing well. Right big and bonny she is. What do you think of your brother as a father? I can scarce grind my knives for excitement. Our Da is pleased as punch and I hope you will be too. We've taken rooms at Little Matlock and are right comfortable there. I hope if you return to the Hall for winter you will see us before long.

Your loving brother Tom

I smiled at the lad's enthusiasm and was happy that a child should cement that improbable, impetuous union.

Chapter 33: July - October 1863

'What are you staring at? Go away.'

Mrs Chrissie Webster eyed the small boy with a mixture of annoyance and alarm. She had not suffered the daily sickness she remembered Annie enduring in the early months of her pregnancy but she often felt nauseous and irritable. The lad was a strange little fellow. His enquiring face was turned insistently towards her and he'd accompanied her all the way down the lane. She let her light shawl drape more loosely over her arms. Surely it was not her condition, carefully shrouded by the fullness of her dress, which intrigued him?

'D'you hear me? Go away. What do you want?'

'You're so beautiful, miss. Your hair's such a colour.'

Her expression softened and she smiled beneficently on the child, ruffling his curls. 'And you're a real charmer, love.'

'Would tha say that to me if I complimented thee? My son has great perception. No wonder he gave me the slip. Come here, tha varmint.'

She turned at the sound of the deep voice behind her as the boy ran back and was scooped up in the man's arms. The newcomer was strongly built, respectably clad and he had a dangerous twinkle in his dark eyes. He strode round in front of her.

'My words were for the child, sir.'

He sighed extravagantly. 'I see tha wears a wedding band. My pardon on my son's behalf, ma'am. He addressed thee incorrectly.'

She shrugged her shoulders and moved to continue on her way.

'John Bettison, thi servant, ma'am, farmer from over t'hill at Wadsley. Come to visit my sister who keeps inn at Loxley village. Dost tha know her?'

She nodded. He was still blocking her way. 'I'm wife to Tom Webster, knife grinder of Little Matlock. Pleased to meet you.'

He let her pass but reached out to catch one of her straggling curls. 'The lad's right. Thi hair's magnificent. Thi husband's a lucky man.'

She hurried away from him, disconcerted but flattered. It seemed her charms had not yet deserted her despite the thickening of her body, of which she at least was well aware. That was pleasing but, now she had committed herself to wifely virtue and maternal dedication, she didn't covet the thrill of idle banter with a good-looking stranger. Surely, she didn't?

Chrissie said nothing of the trivial encounter to Tom that evening. She had other news to share, for she'd received a reply to the letter she sent a week previously to Annie. It was the first contact she'd made with her friend since leaving Mrs Turner's house after Will's death. She'd announced her marriage and her pregnancy, with careful vagueness as to dates, and asked if Annie and Dan would be able to make an excursion to meet Tom before the days drew in once more. Young Mrs Crookes had responded eagerly, overjoyed for Chrissie and anxious to meet her husband. She'd discovered there was a horse-drawn omnibus to Hillsborough and they would be able to come on Saturday week, at the beginning of September; from there they could walk to Malin Bridge – perhaps Mr and Mrs Webster would be able to meet them? They would leave Willie with Dan's mother for fear the jolting of the vehicle would upset him as he was liable to throw up for the least reason.

Chrissie smiled at Tom. 'I'm right happy they're coming. You'll like them.'

'They'll maybe think I'm a poor substitute for Annie's brother.'

'Don't do yourself down, love. You're my husband and they'll like you very well.'

'I'm a lucky man, Chrissie.'

He often said this, endearingly, but on that occasion the similar words spoken by Farmer Bettison echoed in her head. She dismissed the recollection.

'I'm right glad they're coming,' she repeated. She was especially glad they were coming soon, before she grew much larger.

*****

They met each other by the riverside between Hillsborough and Malin Bridge and stopped for refreshment at the inn before walking on towards Little Matlock, where Tom and Chrissie had taken rooms on the ground floor of an elderly widower's house. The hamlet was perched on a narrow spit of land directly below the cliff where Acorn Hill shelved steeply down to the river. It was across the Loxley from the track to Malin Bridge and approached by a footbridge beside a mill. Their rent was low in return for Chrissie cleaning and cooking for their landlord, Mr Woodhouse, who lived on the floor above them.

Dan and Tom warmed to each other at once and the younger man soon invited his visitor to climb the hill and walk over to see the forge in the Rivelin Valley where he worked, leaving their wives to chatter. As the men disappeared through the door, Annie threw her arms around her friend.

'Oh, Chrissie, I can't tell you how worried I were about 'ee. If Willie hadn't been so sick I'd have scoured the town looking. In the end I wrote to Tom's sister in case she'd heard where you were.'

'Sarah?'

344

'Never had a reply though. Didn't have exact address at Ranmoor so maybe the letter never reached her.'

Memories flooded back into Chrissie's mind: Sarah outside Norfolk Market Hall mentioning where she lived; her own letter to Dr Strines about that sad, abused child; the doctor's diabolical hypocrisy when she encountered him.

'Sarah left Ranmoor months back. Re-joined her old mistress and went to Scarborough for the summer. Probably your letter were never sent on.'

'Don't matter now! When your letter came I were so happy. Tom's a good man.' Annie looked at Chrissie and giggled. 'Didn't waste your time, the pair of you!'

Mrs Webster gave her a playful slap. 'Maybe twins on the way,' she said complacently.

'Oh, aye, heard that afore!'

They laughed and hugged, then spoke of other things. Annie reported news of her family: Mrs Turner's pride in Freddie's progress now he was engaged full-time as a clerk at the button factory; Bessie's forthcoming nuptials to a pleasant young man they all liked; and Ned's growing maturity since he'd become the man of the household. They did not mention Will but sat, holding hands, thinking of him.

As Tom and Chrissie walked back, arm in arm, from saying goodbye to their visitors at Hillsborough, he stroked her fingers. 'I can see why you likes them and they love you clear enough.'

'They're dear friends, to both of us now, Tom.'

'It were good to have them come. I hope Sarah'll be back from Scarborough soon so we can see her too. Can I write and tell her of the baby yet?'

Unaccountably, Chrissie had resisted telling Sarah after she made her first tentative announcement to Tom. Now she looked down, unusually bashful. She was not looking forward to her sister-in-law's scrutiny but she comforted herself that Sarah might not be familiar with the exact evolution of an expectant mother's appearance.

'The baby seems all right and nowt's gone wrong,' she said quietly, 'so, yes, write and tell her.'

Tom smiled blissfully.

*****

Tom's stepmother viewed his bride suspiciously, remembering the impudent, badly behaved young girl who had rolled her vivid eyes at anything at all prepossessing in trousers and disappeared into the bushes with a good many. In the intervening period, Hephzibah had deduced, from guarded remarks which her friend Ada made, that shameful things had gone on in the woman's house, years ago, involving that vulgar flibbertigibbet and her uncle, the late, unlamented George. Ada seemed reluctant to say more but Hephzibah shuddered to think her stepson had been so deluded as to bind himself to a scandalous hussy with a sordid history.

She was surprised when she realised Samuel Webster was prepared to be more tolerant and not a little irritated that he responded favourably to his daughter-in-law's ingratiating smiles while she listened to his sermons and accepted his mild admonitions with charm. Fawning artifice, Hephzibah thought it, but she could understand that her husband, whose paralysis made him largely housebound, enjoyed visits from a caller at such pains to please him. When the forthcoming arrival of a grandchild was announced, she resigned herself to accept Samuel's delight and was honest enough to recognise that she, who had remained childless, also experienced some personal pleasure at the prospect of becoming, to all intents and purposes, a grandmother. She resolved to assume the righteous burden of ensuring the child was inculcated with proper standards of Christian behaviour.

The senior Mrs Webster pursed her lips, noting the rather rapid swelling of Chrissie's belly after the marriage, but Hephzibah was not best placed to be censorious about pre-nuptial intimacy, so she said nothing.

Young Mrs Webster's contacts with her Aunt Ada were not so cordial but Chrissie was careful to behave with decorous correctness when she met her relative. Fortunately Ada had developed a fondness for her former lodger and, while she regretted that he'd been beguiled into taking an inappropriate wife, she couldn't bring herself to disown Tom, so she made a show of frosty courtesy towards her niece.

'You don't deserve your fortune with such a good man, my lass. Mind you shows yourself grateful and does his bidding, obedient like. Pray Heaven you've left your giddy ways behind and quitted the paths of evil. Remember the Word of God: wives submit yourselves unto your own husbands as unto the Lord.'

Chrissie bowed her head and mumbled, 'Ephesians 6, verse 22,' as she gained familiarity with this much quoted text.

As for Tom himself, he remained on an exalted plane of happiness, glorying that Chrissie had come to him, proud that he was the chosen husband of this irresistible beauty. Other men's envy only reinforced his contentment. He didn't attempt to curb his wife's vivacity or independent spirit; he was triumphantly uxorious. He still spent summer evenings kicking a ball about with the young men of the district and, with them, frequenting the numerous alehouses in the nearby hamlets and villages; but he was always eager to return home, for she would be waiting, an amusing, irreverent companion whose sensuousness could always distract him from mundane cares. As the weeks progressed and he put his hands on her stomach to feel the child move, he was overcome with humility and a burgeoning sense of responsibility.

Chrissie recognised the strength of Tom's devotion and respected him for his limitless faith in her. She was profoundly grateful to him and content with the action she'd taken, even though it sometimes seemed inevitable that her duplicity would be exposed and her fragile security shattered. She lived simultaneously on different levels of reality. With Tom she was the loving wife, carrying their firstborn. Consigned to her memory, with a vestige of distaste, was the fact that the child was Nathaniel Copley's. In her secret heart, which alone she listened to with sincerity, she regarded Will as the true father and she wanted no other.

In late September Tom was offered a place at the Rowell Bridge grinding mill, upstream on the River Loxley from Little Matlock, nearer their home than the forge across the hill, on the Rivelin, where his father had always worked. He was now a fully-fledged self-employed grinder, as was common in the neighbourhood, and the move to Rowell Bridge would offer several advantages. He explained to Chrissie that the water supply on the rivers, necessary to drive the wheels, was becoming unreliable in dry weather, as industrial use in the valleys increased and drinking water was siphoned off for the town, but he'd heard the great new reservoir at Dale Dyke would ensure a more regular flow down the Loxley.

'Be able to keep me production up more constant like and make sure me income is regular.'

'That'd be right welcome,' she agreed. 'You must do what suits you best.'

So they walked to Rowell Bridge together one evening, to see the mill and find out more about the opening of the new dam. They duly chatted to the mill owner who told them that up in the hills, at the head of the valley, the reservoir was already filling with water and the mills and forges on the Loxley would benefit from its regulated outflow during the following year. Tom confirmed his readiness to take a wheel at the grinding mill.

Afterwards they lingered for a while on the bridge over the river and Chrissie sat on the parapet to rest before walking home. She remembered how she'd sat, in near despair, overlooking the Porter Brook after leaving the house at Nether Edge. This time she did not look down at the water but, instead, smiled at her husband and turned her head to admire the russet and ruby glow in the western sky.

At the sound of a vehicle clattering towards them down the hill, she drew in her skirts and Tom flattened himself against the stone wall as a shiny new brougham, with the hood thrown back, came alongside and slowed. The young woman sitting beside the driver leaned forward. She was wearing a fashionable straw bonnet, fussy with silk flowers and ribbons, which did not quite suit her unremarkable features.

'Tom Webster!' she squealed excitedly, forgetting genteel forms of speech and motioning her companion to rein the horse to a standstill. 'How good to see 'ee! You've heard I'm wed, I'm sure. This is me husband, Mr Arthur Rawdon.'

'Lizzie...Mrs Rawdon, Mr Rawdon, pleased to meet you.'

'This is Sarah Webster's brother Tom, my love. You're recently wed too, I believe. I heard as much. Chrissie, my dear, congratulations.'

As Lizzie turned graciously from one to the other, alternately simpering and patronising, Chrissie noted how Arthur looked embarrassed. She'd never met him before but she'd learned about Sarah's old liking for him from Tom and knew he once called at Malin Bridge when Samuel Webster had driven him away. He looked pleasant enough but likely to be spineless, she thought. Mrs Rawdon was still in full flow, chattering with calculated condescension.

'I see you're expecting, Mrs Webster. Another cause for joy! Not too long to go either, by the looks of it. Oh, my dear, I must tell you, Mr Rawdon and I are also to be blessed with a little one. Not so soon as you, Chrissie, but in the New Year. Us were only wed at Easter, you know.'

Who would have thought silly, insipid Lizzie Simmonite would become this smooth-tongued, insinuating bitch! Chrissie was certain the young woman knew well enough she and Tom had married in early June. 'My best wishes to you,' she said, coolly polite.

Arthur rallied himself sufficiently to speak to Tom. 'Do you still live at Malin Bridge, Mr Webster?'

'No, us has our home at Little Matlock. And you, sir?'

'We've taken a house at Low Bradfield, by the water's edge. I'm mainly employed on designs for new reservoirs further up the valley beyond Dale Dyke but I've grown to love the Loxley and am happy to live here.'

'Arthur's making a great name for himself, you know. Such a clever fellow, he is. Have us own brougham now, as you sees, and soon us plan to...'

'I've heard today from Mrs Ibbotson.'

Lizzie looked momentarily affronted as her husband's words interrupted hers but she composed herself with a small moue of resignation, regretting that she had let her newly acquired accent slip. Arthur was still addressing Tom.

'My aunt is returning to the Hall next week. Your sister will be coming with her.'

'That's good news. I haven't seen Sarah for many months.'

'Nor I.'

Chrissie detected the faint hint of regret in Arthur's brief comment. So did Lizzie.

'No doubt we'll see your aunt's attendant in due course, my love. Such a shame for her, she'll be shut away from company in that remote mansion with an ageing invalid. A shame, I think, she left the doctor's house at Ranmoor. Don't you agree, Mrs Webster? Must have been much more amusement for her there in a younger household.'

Chrissie thought grimly of Dr Strines and said nothing. Arthur had drawn up the reins, ready to move on from the bridge.

'You'll excuse us, Mrs Webster. We must be on our way.'

Chrissie inclined her head while Lizzie bestowed on her a slight contemptuous flutter of a wave. As the Rawdons drove off she took Tom's arm. 'When you were children, I thought you might make a pair with Lizzie one day.'

'You ninny! Never had eyes for anyone but you. I surely don't envy Mr Rawdon, any road!'

'Not sure if he's best pleased himself. Married in haste, if you asks me.'

'Like us, Chrissie?'

She snuggled against him.

*****

The leaves were turning in a riot of fire-bright radiance and the sunlight angled low across her path as Chrissie returned from buying bread in Malin Bridge. She tired easily these days and, on the uneven cobbled path, she needed to take care not to turn her unreliable ankle and stumble. Nothing must imperil her child. She dreaded the possibility of a genuinely premature birth when her delivery

351

at full-term needed to be seen as premature. She sat down on a tree stump cradling her stomach.

A stone splashed in the river nearby and a mallard took off in a flurry of wings and water. 'Nearly got him!'

The little boy ran round the bend towards her, shrieking with pleasure. He saw her and stopped abruptly. 'Da, it's that lady. The beautiful one with red hair.'

Farmer Bettison followed his son, sweeping off his cap. He was bronzed and very handsome. 'Mrs Webster, I'm delighted to see thee. The colour is golden-brown; auburn they call it, lad, not red. Altogether more subtle and fetching. Run on and see if tha can flush a rabbit. Can I carry thi basket, Mrs Webster?'

'I'm going t'other way. Thank you.'

'I'll walk with thee, if tha'll let me. Glad to be of help.'

He'd come very close. She could see his Adam's apple bulging in his throat. He reached out to take the basket.

'No, thank you. Good-day, Mr Bettison.'

He seized her wrist. 'I've heard a story or two about thee, Mrs Webster, from men in the village who were lads when tha wast a lass there. I doubt tha'rt that different now. Come next spring, when tha's farrowed, I'll look out for 'ee. Tha might care to come with me to one of my barns up t'hill. I'll give thee a good time, love.'

'You'll do no such thing! Good morning, Mr Bettison.'

Chrissie pulled her arm away and hoisted the basket higher against her chest. She turned her back and strode on, with as much dignity as she could muster in view of her cumbersome gait. She was annoyed. Why did men make that sickly, deceiving offer: 'a good time'? How dare he think she could be seduced by such a hackneyed proposition? Yet, if truth were told, she was a little gratified.

Chapter 34: October 1863

Mrs Ibbotson and I stood high on the hillside above the Hall. The old lady was leaning hard on her walking stick but she'd managed the climb despite the impediment of her left leg which still dragged when she moved. In front of us was the cottage, occupied until recently by the Ibbotsons' former housekeeper who had passed away while we were in Scarborough.

'Mrs Burns never wanted changes made or even new guttering. But it doesn't look in bad condition and she kept the place neat inside. I'll get the builder in Bradfield to see what can be done to improve it before I seek another tenant. It's a lonely spot.'

I had turned away from the isolated building and stared further afield, far down into the valley, at the vast pool of water gleaming in the sunlight behind the grey stone of the retaining wall.

'The reservoir is filling fast. It looks glassy flat. Not like the sea which always shows a gentle swell even when it's calm weather.'

Mrs Ibbotson was amused by my veneer of well-travelled experience but, reluctantly, followed my gaze. 'Such peacefulness may be deceptive. When the winds whip through the hills from Bleaklow I don't doubt the water will be churned up furiously. The dam must hold back a tremendous weight.' She put her hand on my arm. 'I think we might exercise a neighbour's privilege and pay another visit to the great work. You won't mind, dear?'

I shook my head. I knew my mistress was remembering the earlier occasion when Arthur Rawdon had arranged our inspection and the supercilious consulting engineer escorted and lectured us. How naïve and innocent I'd been then, doting on every word which confirmed the prowess of structural designers. How horrified I would have been to know what would come to pass. How little I'd known of life and pain, of myself. I'd resembled an outline drawn on a page, before I gained three-dimensional reality.

*****

Mr Leather had long since moved on to supervise the designs for other reservoirs and he now came to Dale Dyke infrequently. Mrs Ibbotson and I were received, on our second visit to the dam, by the resident engineer, Mr Gunson, who had overseen the construction work. He was earnest, affable and entirely straightforward in his description of both the progress made and the problems the project had encountered.

'We closed the outlet pipes this June, ma'am, to let the reservoir fill. Even so we open the valves now and then to regulate the level of the water and let the pressure on the dam build up slowly. That's the valve house down there, do you see? With the weir and the spillway for the overflow beside it. The overflow provides a permanent escape channel if ever the pressure should grow too great.'

He shook his head wearily. 'It hasn't been an easy job. I'll be glad when it's complete and water being pumped to people's houses in the town. After the first realignment, we had numerous difficulties in acquiring the land we needed and that put things back by several months. Then we kept finding underground springs which threatened to compromise the stability of the embankments. I had to insist upon foundations sixty feet deep instead of ten, as specified in the original plans.'

'Better to be sure than sorry.'

'Indeed, yes, ma'am. It's an onerous responsibility. I call to mind each day the tragedy at Holmfirth twelve years back.'

I looked enquiringly. 'I've never heard of that.'

'Dreadful business, miss. Ninety-five killed when the dam there collapsed. Fearful destruction.'

'You weren't employed there, Mr Gunson?'

'No, ma'am, but it was the same firm of consulting engineers. Mr Leather's uncle headed it then. They were roundly criticised at the inquiry after the accident, as were the construction engineers. Negligence, ma'am.' His voice was sonorous with distress.

'It speaks well of you, Mr Gunson, that you're so alert to the lessons of that earlier disaster. It gives me confidence there will be no repetition.'

Mr Gunson thanked the old lady for her kind words and helped her up into her carriage, for a more comfortable return to the Hall than the previous ascent by donkey cart three years earlier.

'He's an honest, well-meaning man, I think,' Mrs Ibbotson observed. 'I hope his skill matches his intentions'

I did not, this time, urge the reliability of trained engineers but, for no good reason, I shivered.

*****

I smoothed my dark silk skirt over the hoop of my small crinoline and anchored the fancy lace over my coiled hair. Mrs Ibbotson had insisted I wear my best dress, made for me in Scarborough, on the occasion of the first, unavoidable visit by Mr and Mrs Arthur Rawdon following our return to the Hall. I was dissatisfied with my appearance but my mistress smiled approvingly as she entered the drawing room and that gave me confidence. Shortly afterwards a brougham drew up in front of the house and a barrage of high-pitched instructions was delivered.

'Oh dear!' Mrs Ibbotson looked mischievous. 'Mrs Rawdon seems very much in control.'

355

I bit my lip to repress a giggle. It was wonderful how my mistress knew when to deflate tension. Then, in a moment, I was being greeted, with effusive condescension by the erstwhile parlour-maid and a polite bow from my own rejected suitor. I welcomed Lizzie's unstoppable stream of inconsequential gossip, even though it was tinged with annoying overtones of superiority, for it absolved everyone else from making conversation. Mrs Rawdon's speech retained strong elements of the Sheffield dialect but she was trying, with exaggerated care, to speak as her husband did. I needed only to nod and murmur agreement. I didn't look at Arthur.

'We met your brother and his wife the other day.'

I regarded Lizzie with more interest.

'Poor Tom. Good enough grinder, I'm sure, but not likely to better himself. I was surprised he married Chrissie Mallon.'

'He always admired her,' I felt it necessary to interject.

'Oh, indeed, but if one is wise one grows out of childish infatuations, is it not so, my love?'

Arthur was deeply uncomfortable. I could sense it without seeing his face. I glanced across to Mrs Ibbotson as the lady rose, her lips compressed with a trace of irritation.

'Mrs Rawdon, I wonder if you would care to accompany me upstairs. There are some small garments made long ago for a child I lost, which may be of use to you. I don't know why I kept them so many years but it seems fitting they should pass to my husband's sister's son, for his progeny.'

Lizzie arose in a flutter of excitement and I started to move as well but I saw Mrs Ibbotson's frown and recognised it was my mistress's wish I should remain. I stared into my lap, interlacing my fingers firmly.

As soon as his wife had left the room, Arthur Rawdon spoke. 'Sarah, last time we met...'

'Please don't refer to it, Mr Rawdon. It's all in the past.'

'I was angry and discourteous. I should apologise.'

I stood up, facing him for the first time. There was tiredness in his eyes and he looked older. 'There's no need. It's all over and done with.'

'Not quite, Sarah. I think of you often and now I see you, so elegant and refined...I was impetuous, reckless, and I'm living to regret my recklessness.'

'This is improper, Mr Rawdon!'

'You were hard towards me, Sarah. It seems you're hard still.'

'Hard as stone. It's my nature.'

'Even stone may be fractured. When that happens, a torrent of passion may break through the breach.'

'It isn't right for you to say such a thing!' Not for a moment did I believe he knew the truth of his assertion, how I'd been swept away by tumultuous sinful emotions, but it was a disquieting metaphor. 'Please say no more.'

He looked abashed. 'Forgive me, Sarah, but there's much I don't understand.'

His diffidence brought back the recollection of our early meetings, when I'd waited for him in the kitchen garden joyful to have won his affection. For an instant I was sorry for him.

'I hear your wife returning, Mr Rawdon. We will hold no more such conversations.'

Sadly he nodded and opened the door for Lizzie to sweep in triumphantly, bearing a large pile of fancy baby linen edged with finest Nottingham lace.

'These will do very well for the infant's everyday wear, my love,' she carolled.

I knew I must call upon my brother and his bride but I put it off from week to week, finding various excuses for delay. In the last days of October, as the skies became greyer and swirls of valley mist obscured the view from the Hall, I realised I could prevaricate no longer. I mentioned the matter one afternoon after my mistress finished writing a letter to Mrs Ashington, with whom she'd corresponded since their return from Scarborough.

'I wondered when you would choose to go,' Mrs Ibbotson said quietly. 'Will you also visit Malin Bridge? You may take the carriage.'

'That's very kind, ma'am, but I will not go to see my father.'

'Still so resolute?'

'I don't wish to see him.'

'I think you fear that if you saw him, immobile and helpless, you might forgive him.'

I must have looked startled but the old lady continued implacably. 'I think moreover you fear that if you forgave him, you would come near to forgiving yourself.'

'I can never do that.'

'Oh, dear! The stubbornness of youth! As you grow older you will learn there is little immutable in this life and it isn't wise to apply simplistic judgements.' No doubt seeing my flush, she moderated her reproof. 'I didn't mean to sound so tart, my dear. Go to see your brother on Saturday afternoon. I have some business to attend to then. My lawyer and the rector of Bradfield are both to call on me so you may take your time.'

I sent a message in advance and received a note back from Tom, welcoming my visit and confirming he would be able to take Saturday afternoon off work. I left the carriage, with its driver, on the north side of the river and crossed the footbridge beside the mill, to approach the house standing beneath the cliff. My brother was looking out for me and he ran from the door to swing me into the air with jubilation.

'Sal! You've come at last.' He set me down and stepped back, appraising me. 'My word, you've become a fine lady, lass. Not sure us humble home's good enough to entertain you.'

I gave him a gentle cuff. 'Idiot! How's Chrissie?'

'She's resting. Gets tired these days. Come and see her.'

I restrained him, gripping his arm. 'Tom, are you happy?'

I detected a flicker of pity in his eyes that I should ask such a question. 'More than you could understand, Sal.'

Sheepishly, I let myself be led into the neatly furnished parlour where I gained the rapid impression of a well-ordered, decently kept home. Chrissie was sitting by the fireside with her feet up on a cushioned stool.

'Sarah!'

'Chrissie! Don't move.'

'It's me ankles. They're right swollen.'

Remembering Mrs Strines' pregnancy, I was surprised to see Chrissie grown so large but my mistress was petite and there was scant room for growth in her small frame, whereas Tom's wife was tall and curvaceous.

We sat chatting contentedly and I was reassured to see the easy unaffected way my brother and Chrissie related to each other. Doing arithmetic in my head, I suspected they'd anticipated their nuptials but this was common and now they were lawfully wed so no harm was done. It certainly did not behove me to assume a moralistic stance and delicacy prevented me enquiring exactly when they met each other again. Perhaps I'd been wrong to imagine there were several months after the death of Chrissie's fiancé when her whereabouts could not be explained. Perhaps, following that bereavement, she'd turned quite soon to Tom, in grief and desolation, seeking to be consoled and find security. Of course she would not have moved to Malin Bridge until they decided to marry but she was probably already intimate with Tom. At all events, it was clear a deep fondness had developed between them and I rejoiced for them both.

As we shared recollections, Chrissie reminded me how we'd met, when she was with Annie, outside Norfolk Market Hall.

'Her and her husband came to see us back in September. She told me how she'd written to you when I went away for a bit. She hadn't got your answer when I saw her but she sent me a letter the other week saying you'd replied afterwards, from Scarborough.'

'Her letter was delayed at Ranmoor before it was sent on to me. Dr and Mrs Strines were most apologetic it had been misplaced.'

I noticed Chrissie bite her lip and wondered if she was in pain but it was only a momentary reflex. In an instant Tom's wife was asking eagerly about Scarborough and I was pleased to launch forth on a vivid description of the spa, the assemblies, the concerts, the fashions, the fishing fleet, the harbour and the rescue I'd witnessed. Tom guffawed.

'You lived the life of a lady there, Sal. That's what's given you these airs and graces.'

'I've got no airs and graces!'

'Oh, I think you have, love. Tom's right. But it comes natural to you. Way above our station.'

'Don't tease, Chrissie.'

It was beginning to grow dark when I said goodbye. Tom walked across the bridge with me to re-join the carriage. He admired the gleaming paintwork and polished leather of the upholstery and he exchanged cordial words with the old coachman. He handed me into the vehicle.

360

'Come again, me lady, if tha condescends to.'

I thumped him playfully. 'I'm glad to have seen you so happy, Tom. Take care of Chrissie. She's looking tired.'

'She's fearful of the birth and so am I, Sal. There's many don't pull through'

'You mustn't think so, Tom.'

'I couldn't bear to lose her.' I pressed his hand and his stricken expression changed. 'Our Da would like to see you, Sal. He says so often.'

'I'll think about it.'

I signalled for the carriage to drive off and waved at my brother without saying more. I knew there was nothing for me to think about for my resolution held: I would not visit Malin Bridge.

*****

On my return to the Hall, I found Mrs Ibbotson weary from receiving her visitors but she rallied herself to ask after Tom and his wife.

'I think they're truly happy together. It's rather remarkable to me but it does seem so.'

'You've revised your opinion of young Mrs Webster?'

'She seems completely respectable now, much less flippant than I remember, although of course she may be subdued because of her condition.'

Mrs Ibbotson laughed. 'What a strict judge you would make, my dear. It's your Methodist upbringing no doubt – of the New Connection, as I recall.' She motioned me to sit. 'There's a little business I must tell you of, Sarah, now it's concluded. We must be serious for a moment.' I looked at her anxiously. 'Don't worry, I trust I shan't imminently expire but I have put things in order against the time I do. You may not realise, my dear, but I have a life's interest only in the Hall and when I pass on it will go to Mr Ibbotson's nephew, as his heir.'

'To Mr Rawdon?' My voice came in a whisper.

'No, no. Thank heaven! Oh, the thought of Lizzie Rawdon queening it here! No, Mr Ibbotson had a brother as well as a sister and this brother, who died before my husband, has a son. He will inherit. He lives in the south of England and may choose to sell the Hall, or live here only occasionally. That's for him to decide.'

I was puzzled why Mrs Ibbotson was so insistent on telling me this.

'I'm concerned about your future, Sarah, when I'm gone. You would easily find another position but I'd like to see you with a measure of independence. No! Don't say anything. I had wondered whether to bequeath you the old housekeeper's cottage, up on the hill – it's within my gift – but I've decided it's too remote for a young woman who needs company and some culture in order to flourish. I've therefore made provision in my will for you to receive a modest allowance, sufficient for life: an annuity, they call it. It won't render you wealthy but it will enable you to make your own choices and if, in time, you should choose to wed, you won't be penniless.'

I ignored my mistress's last words but rose in protest. 'Mrs Ibbotson, it isn't right that you should do...'

'It's done, my dear. My lawyer has the document. The rector has witnessed it. We shall say no more about it.'

I bowed my head, fighting back tears. That night I prayed, with complete sincerity, for Mrs Ibbotson's continued health into considerable old age.

Chapter 35: December 1863 - February 1864

On a bitterly cold morning two weeks before Christmas, Chrissie Webster's waters broke and she went into labour. Her husband, greatly alarmed that it was happening sooner than he expected, ran to fetch a neighbour from the cottages across the river, a woman of homely appearance and comfy disposition. This experienced and tactful matron explained to the trembling father-to-be that seven or eight-month babies were entirely normal and often as well developed and hardy as those that took their full time in the womb. She encouraged him to depart to the alehouse but he would not go. Instead, old Mr Woodhouse, the landlord, wisely cajoled the young man to join him upstairs where he produced a bottle of something stronger than beer.

It was a long and painful birth but half an hour before midnight Tom, somewhat befuddled, heard two sounds which differed from the terrifying moaning that had preceded them: a low gasping roar of triumph, in something like his wife's voice, and a harsh penetrating cry, which seemed to throb with annoyance that its owner's pleasant sojourn had been so rudely disturbed. He hurtled down the stairs into their bedroom.

'You've got a daughter, Mr Webster. Right bonny, she is. See.'

He glanced briefly at the wrinkled face, which made him think for a moment of a shrivelled bilberry, and turned quickly to his wife.

'Chrissie, Chrissie, how are you?'

'How d'you think, daft 'un? Right glad it's over and fair worn out.'

Her sallow face was drawn and still damp with sweat but her eyes were luminous. Tom kissed her gently and she reached up to ruffle his hair. 'I'm right tired, Tom.'

'What shall us call her, love? Have you decided?'

She nodded. 'If you're happy, we'll call her Grace. She is a grace to me.'

'And to me, love.'

He kissed her again and she closed her eyes. By half an hour, Grace had arrived a year to the day from when Will died and Chrissie believed fate had recompensed her for her misery twelve months earlier.

Their neighbour bustled over with the baby, now cleanly wrapped but bareheaded. She did not hold with the presence of fathers so soon after a delivery but she was courteous. 'Here's your daughter, Tom Webster. Proper red-head she is too.'

He regarded the disagreeable looking infant with interest and then burst into wholly incongruous laughter. Chrissie, who had seemed dreamily abstracted, looked up at her husband in surprise.

'She's ginger, love, right carroty! Not your lovely colour.'

'Her hair'll darken,' Chrissie answered severely. 'Expect I looked like that at birth. Now go back upstairs, love, and let me rest.'

Apologetic, sincerely caring and still laughing merrily, the new father did his wife's bidding while she cast a regretful eye on her daughter's gaudy head.

*****

A week later Sarah paid a brief visit to see her niece. She was accompanying Mrs Ibbotson on their way to Penistone, where they were to spend Christmas with Dr Stephen Strines' family. As before, the carriage stopped beyond the footbridge and Grace's aunt slipped across the river to greet mother and child and bring a small stylish gift.

Chrissie had been nervous that her sister-in-law would see little resemblance to Tom in the infant's features.

364

He had made no comment on the matter, delighting to tell everyone their daughter had a miniature version of his wife's chin and her beautifully shaped eyes, but he still chuckled at Grace's crudely flamboyant hair. His wife, naturally, was uncomfortably aware that the baby also possessed, in addition to this colouring, a small approximation of Nathaniel Copley's pointed nose. As yet, of course, there were no spiky teeth. Fortunately Sarah would not recognise the originator of the infant's features.

The drawer from an old cabinet had been pressed into service as a crib and Mr Woodhouse fashioned a pair of curved rockers to go beneath it and give gentle movement when it was pushed from side to side. Sarah bent low over the cradle to peer at the child whose abundant hair was now mostly covered by a woollen bonnet. She smiled at her brother.

'It's not only Chrissie she favours, Tom. Her dear little nose is just like our mother's.'

'Why, I never thought of that!'

'Men are so unobservant. Do you remember our mother, Chrissie? She had a rather sharp-cut nose. Grace will have the same.'

Overjoyed, Chrissie embraced her husband and his sister and smothered her daughter's much scrutinised face with kisses. Sarah then needed to re-join her mistress for their journey but she promised to visit again in a few weeks, after their return to the Hall, and she left on the crib a pretty ivory teething ring with a tinkling, silver-plated bell.

Chrissie remained fearful that when Annie came to visit she would inevitably recognise Grace's likeness to Mr Copley. She'd written to Acorn Street announcing the birth and hoping Mrs Crookes would soon meet the infant, but privately she hoped for snow to delay a visitation. In the New Year, however, the weather was unseasonably mild, although extremely wet. The new mother grew increasingly anxious, from day to day, that her friend would arrive unannounced so, when a letter in Annie's handwriting was delivered, she opened it in trepidation.

Her relief and pleasure on reading the note were deep and sincere. Annie's congratulations and delight were balanced by the happy news that she herself had only recently become aware that she was again with child; and she was already smitten with the debilitating sickness which afflicted her during the early months of her previous pregnancy. Sadly, she would be unable to travel to the Loxley Valley until this miserable phase of expectant motherhood was past. Reading of her friend's condition, Chrissie smiled broadly. Babies could change markedly in a short time and initial resemblances might prove fleeting. Meanwhile she gladly disseminated the information, vouched for by Sarah, that Grace bore the legacy of the late Nellie Webster's nose.

*****

By early February the weather had deteriorated. Day after day precipitation fell: sleet and hail followed rain, turning to snow. For forty-eight hours the valley was blanketed by a covering several inches deep, even at levels well below the usual snow line, before torrential downpours washed most of it away, to begin the cycle anew. With the rivers in spate there was extensive flooding in the riverside fields and walking on muddy ground became hazardous.

On a day when a break in the clouds promised a short respite, Chrissie set out for Malin Bridge to visit her father-in-law and his wife. She carried Grace tied across her chest, swaddled in her thickest shawl, and she picked her way with care along the treacherous path. She observed the rushing Loxley, swirling its usual debris of twigs and leaf mould amid the discoloured effluent from a dozen forges upstream. She smiled at a dipper perched on a rust-encrusted rock protruding from the stream, while the waters buffeted its sanctuary only an inch or two below its feet. She too had found her resting place now, she thought contentedly, no longer like the driftwood she had watched in the Porter Brook. She and her daughter were anchored by Tom's love and protection.

She remembered how she'd resisted the idea of becoming a grinder's wife, leading a life of repetitious drudgery, even with Will. Well, she'd tried something more adventurous, more cosseted. She'd adopted a pretence of gentility and it proved not just empty but pernicious, masking heinous evil. Now she welcomed the calm tedium of domesticity, blessed with the gift of Grace, and she was learning to respond to the gentle rhythms of the valley. Yet she couldn't be sure this serenity would last. She didn't know if she could trust herself to remain forever satisfied with her undemanding refuge. She feared her old restlessness might return and, sometimes, discomfort at the deception she'd practised on Tom made her afraid she would reveal her secret and risk everything she'd gained.

She reached Malin Bridge and turned to the row of terraced houses stretching up the hill, sideways to the river, at the bottom of which the older Mr and Mrs Webster lived. Sam's fading strength had diminished further in recent weeks. He could no longer haul himself up and down the stairs as he had done, using arm muscles alone, and he'd become a prisoner in the upper bedroom. Visits from his daughter-in-law and grand-daughter brought him a solace he'd not expected to find through fallible human agency. He smiled upon the wayward, occasionally irreverent, young woman as if she were a blessed being from paradise – although he rebuked himself for such a blasphemous thought. He rejoiced wholeheartedly at the sight of his grandchild, glowing with health, utterly innocent of the world's wickedness.

While his wife sat awkwardly with Chrissie drinking tea, he clucked at the infant's smiles and gave her his knobbly finger to grip. When she was lifted into his arms, he let her dribble onto his collar, in a way he would never have tolerated from his own infants, and he made cooing noises, which in years gone by he would have thought unbecoming for a lay preacher.

'If only Sarah were more like Tom's wife,' he mourned to Hephzibah after Chrissie and Grace had left. 'If only she would come and humble herself. But I'll not write to ask her. I will not grovel to my own daughter.'

Mrs Webster snorted. 'Hard, unfeeling girl, she always was. Disrespectful and sinful. She's shown no honour to her father. You should forget her, Samuel.' Disconcerted by her husband's lenience towards Tom's wife, Hephzibah felt at liberty to traduce her step-daughter.

After leaving her father-in-law, Chrissie stopped outside the Stag Inn to speak to Mrs Armitage, the landlord's mother, and she proudly drew back the shawl to display her daughter's face so it could be duly admired. She saw Aunt Ada, crossing the road at some distance from them, and waved politely but she was relieved that her relative merely inclined her head and did not turn to join them. Their uneasy truce was best sustained by the minimum of contact. Then, as the light was starting to fade, she set out to return home by the riverside. There were several mills lining the bank for the first part of the journey, casting their shadows across the path, but when she emerged onto clearer ground beside the meadows she began to sing softly to herself. She hadn't advanced far, however, before she heard her name called resonantly behind her.

'Chrissie Webster'

She recognised John Bettison's voice and turned, expecting to see him in company with his winsome son, but he was alone. He bounded with long-legged strides along the track to catch up with her.

'Glad to see thee recovered from thi childbed. Is baby doing well?'

'She's very well, thank you. And your son?'

'Left him at my sister's because of the weather. He's not as strong as I'd like. I'm on the way to fetch him now.'

She resigned herself warily to the necessity of walking beside the farmer for the rest of the way to the footbridge at Little Matlock and she was grateful for his hand to steady her on a few patches of ground where the ice was already forming as the sun went down. Their conversation was sporadic and unexceptional so Chrissie relaxed. She hoped he recognised that his provocative behaviour towards her previously had been unwelcome and, whatever he'd discovered about her indecorous past, he appreciated she'd become a respectable wife and mother.

A little before the footbridge, the track turned a corner on the edge of a thicket and, although she hadn't realised it, they were screened from view in all directions. Off her guard, crooning to Grace as she ran her finger over the child's gurgling mouth, Chrissie found herself twirled round and John Bettison's lips hard on her own while the baby, trapped between them, began to whimper. Furious, she struggled free, trying to soothe her daughter with her hand while tongue-lashing her assailant.

'How dare you! You bastard! What d'you think I am? I'm wed to a decent husband. I don't want no filthy goat sniffing round me. Get away from me!'

'What do I think tha art, love? Dost really want to know?' He cupped her face in one hand, fending off her scratching nails with the other. 'Why the tastiest little whore in t'Loxley Valley, I'd say. And I mean to have thee, lass. Like all them others. Dost know who thi baby's Da is?'

She slapped his face and screamed but he laughed, seizing her wrist.

'Too far for them in houses by the mill to hear thee, love, and thi man won't be home for an hour yet. I'll come back with 'ee and take his place in thi bed. How would tha like that?

'Me landlord'll smash your skull in.'

He let her go, smirking. 'I can wait, lass. I can tell tha'rt not ready. Next time I'll treat thee proper. I'll bring the money to pay 'ee. What dost charge?'

Expecting no answer, he strode off along the path to Loxley village.

*****

When Tom came home later that evening, he seemed not to notice she'd been crying and she was glad of it. He bent, beaming, over Grace as she slept in her cradle and then ate his supper with gusto. After a while it occurred to him that Chrissie was unusually quiet and he looked across at her blotched face and swollen eyelids.

'Is summat wrong, love?'

'Just feeling a bit low,' she said with an attempt at a self-mocking grin. Her voice cracked and she tried to disguise it as a cough.

'Something's happened. You're not ill? There's nowt wrong with Grace?'

'No. Nowt wrong. I told you...'

The tears welled up as she spoke and she wanted to run away, to hide her wretchedness from him, but she could not. In a moment he was holding her to his chest while she wept freely, waiting until her sobbing subsided.

'Did that John Bettison pester you?'

She looked up in surprise and alarm. 'How d'you know?' She wiped her nose.

'Man's got a name as a damned nuisance. Should have told you about him. Didn't know you'd met him. I went down to Malin Bridge after work, to have a drink with some of the lads. Saw Aunt Ada as I came along road. She said she thought he were following you. He has eyes for all the pretty girls.' Tom paused, appalled at the extent of her distress. 'He didn't hurt you, did he?'

'No, he didn't hurt me.'

'I'd break his bloody neck if he'd laid a finger on you.'

'It were what he said,' she whispered, amazed at her own weakness, wondering how far her admission would lead her.

Tom cuddled her tenderly. 'Motherhood's made you all soft and gentle. Thought you'd deal with the likes of Farmer Bettison with a flick of your fingers. You've had to do with worse'n him, I'm sure.'

She twisted away from him. 'What d'you mean by that?'

'Nowt. Don't be touchy. I weren't thinking, love. What did he say to upset you so?'

She drew herself up to face her husband squarely. 'He said I were a whore. Any man's.'

'By Christ, I'll see to him!' Tom looked as if he would rush out into the night instantly but Chrissie put her hand on his arm. She was composed now, composed and resolute. Her moment of decision had come.

'Tom, there were truth in what he said. There are things I should tell you.'

'There's no need, love. I know about that Eb Pyle.'

'Tom! How d'you know? When'd you hear?'

'Love, I were a grinder in Sheffield, remember? He were big in the union. I knew of him but I didn't hear you'd been mixed up with him 'til it were over atween you. By then

371

you were with Will and like to wed. Sarah told me that. Eb Pyle were old history. It meant nowt. It means nowt.'

She looked up into his open, sincere face and she could bear her pretence no longer – whatever the consequences. 'Tom there's more.'

He laid a finger firmly over her lips. 'I don't want to hear. You'll say nowt.'

'Tom…'

He held her at arms' length. His face had a new maturity and he spoke sternly. 'Didn't you promise to honour and obey me?'

'I did but…'

'Then I order you'll say no more. D'you hear, Chrissie? You came to me and I love you more than my life. Now we've got Grace and I love her too. That's all that matters. There's no more for you to say.'

She started to tremble, overwhelmed by wonder.

'D'you hear me?'

He reached out to rock the cradle where Grace had begun to sniffle. 'Quiet now, little lass. Eeh! She's smiling at me. Pretty as a picture you are, you imp.'

He turned back to his wife and took her in his arms. 'And a couple of lads and me'll teach that bleeding farmer to mend his manners, so don't you fret no more, Mrs Webster. You're safe. I promise.'

Freely, he had given her release into a new life unencumbered by deceit. His gift was indescribably precious.

Chapter 36: January - March 1864

After the snow thawed it was the wettest winter anyone could remember; even on good days there was fine drizzle. At the Hall, as in the villages, we deplored the sodden ground, the mud-choked paths and the depressing dampness which infiltrated the house and caused mould to grow in the larder. We reminisced about the previous year's deep-lying snow and how isolated communities had been cut off for days: whatever inconveniences had been suffered then, we said, it was unequivocally better to have ice and frost under clear skies than this perpetual downpour. I was certainly of that mind when I arrived back at the Hall with Mrs Ibbotson after our stay at Penistone over Christmas.

Once I'd stowed our wet clothes and unpacked our travelling bags, I joined my mistress in the drawing room. Mrs Ibbotson was reading a letter and, smiling broadly, she looked across at me.

'Another letter from Mrs Ashington in Newcastle. I'm always glad to hear from her. She's a good correspondent and she writes to tell me something I was greatly hoping to hear.'

'Her health has improved, I trust.'

'A little but it isn't that. I have a confession to make to you, Sarah. Sit down while I tell you.'

Mystified, I did as I was told. I was pleased to see the mischievous twinkle in the old lady's eyes but could not imagine what it presaged.

'Two months back I learned from the rector at Bradfield that the parish of Christ Church, Stannington, was in need of a curate to assist the elderly vicar. It came into my head to mention Mr Charles Ashington to our rector and he passed on the details. It was all rather complicated but Charles's mother now tells me he's been offered the position and has accepted. He will be arriving there shortly.'

I pursed my lips. Stannington village sat high on the ridge between the Loxley and the Rivelin, some two miles up the hill from Malin Bridge. The parish contained several collections of houses and scattered farms as well as some of the workshops and mills in the valleys.

'I'm surprised, ma'am. I'd understood Mr Ashington hoped to work in Newcastle, in a poor city district.'

'His mother mentions that. It seems curacies in such areas are not readily available. Poor parishes cannot afford the extra stipend, small though it would be. So Mr Ashington has decided to accept a post in a more rural location, to gain experience. When he's able to have a parish of his own I expect he'll return to the city.' The old lady grinned wickedly. 'Do you suppose the presence of a certain serious young woman, a few miles up the valley from Stannington, could possibly have influenced his decision?'

I rose to my feet quickly. 'Please don't jest, ma'am. Mr Ashington has no interest in me, nor I in him.'

'Quite so, my dear, but I shall be bound to invite him to the Hall from time to time.'

'Of course; but it's a matter of polite indifference to me.'

'Quite so.' The enigmatic grin reappeared.

*****

Charles Ashington duly visited the Hall soon afterwards and, as before, I felt at ease in his company. He paid me no inappropriate compliments but talked enthusiastically about his new charges in the parish – the families of agricultural labourers, millers, grinders and miners who worked the seam of ganister used in new methods for steel-making in Sheffield. He admitted he had much to learn but declared he was already delighted by the countryside round about. He was interested in everything:

the lives of his parishioners; the mechanisation being introduced into some industrial processes and the hostility towards it; the music of the local bands; the church's fractious relationships with the vigorous Methodist chapels in the area; and the flora and fauna of the valleys and moors. He was eager to foster schooling throughout the parish and he talked of forming a tug-of-war team. I was happy to admire and enjoy the breadth of his rapidly acquired knowledge and detected no challenge to my emotional equilibrium in his pleasant, open cordiality.

Mrs Ibbotson evidently had a particular liking for the young man and he spent some time later in the day speaking privately to her. A week later he called at the Hall again and thereafter he was a regular visitor. Each occasion was equally agreeable and my appreciation of Mr Ashington's straightforward nature began to grow. He seemed eminently fitted for his calling, so sincere, so vigorous, so dedicated. I found it puzzling that he seemed content to talk to me at length about his preoccupations but it required no effort on my part to show interest in the varied subjects he raised, to ask thoughtful questions and even, occasionally, to express timid opinions of my own. When I did so Mr Ashington would fix his widely spaced grey eyes on my face and murmur, 'that's shrewd', or, 'that's a good point' or, once, 'why didn't I think of that!' It was very gratifying.

His visits became small beacons illuminating my otherwise uneventful life but it still worried me that I was not fit company for so estimable a clergyman. His friendship for me was ill-advised; any greater interest was out of the question.

*****

As the days drew out a little during February, Mrs Ibbotson's health began to decline, not dramatically but

375

insidiously, and she seemed to lose energy. The dreary weather, the rain pouring down the windowpanes every day and the sight of the washed-out, sodden landscape did nothing to lift spirits or encourage excursions. She became preoccupied with the dam, fearing it would be tested by such extreme conditions – and she was not alone in this concern. From the housekeeper, Mrs Staniforth, she gleaned much of the gossip in the neighbourhood, especially that deriving from various other Ibbotsons who lived at Low Bradfield (thought to be distant, if irregular, descendants of her husband's family). For the last four years these local worthies and their fellow villagers had argued about the dam, the probable benefits it offered, its cost and stability. Most deferred to Arthur Rawdon, who lived among them and insisted the engineering designs were scrupulous, the construction unquestionably able to withstand the worst tempest. Yet there were still murmurs of anxiety.

When the rain slackened, I walked down the hill to see for myself the wild water, stirred up by the wind, beating on the wall some two feet below the level of the overflow weir. I spoke to Mr Gunson, who was inspecting the site at the time, and was reassured by the care he was paying to the final stages of the project, before the dam and reservoir became operational. I did my best to satisfy my mistress that the works were in reliable hands and, as I'd been told, robust enough to withstand a hurricane.

Returning uphill from another walk one day, I saw the distant figure of a horseman approaching the Hall along the track from Bradfield. I stared, not wanting to believe my eyes, but there was no doubt – the caller was Robert Strines. He hadn't visited Mrs Ibbotson since her illness twelve months earlier and I felt very uncomfortable at the prospect of encountering him again. When I reached the house, he was explaining debonairly to Mrs Staniforth that he'd needed to attend to some business in Hillsborough and took it into his head to call at the Hall and then ride home to Ranmoor over the hills: it would salve his conscience which told him he was too infrequent a visitor to his aunt. 'What does Robert Strines know of a conscience?' I thought.

I regarded him coolly while he regaled my weary mistress with the antics of young Robin – the most precocious child for miles around, it seemed – and described the prosperity he and Mrs Strines were enjoying. He was tediously self-obsessed and I wondered how I could ever have found him attractive but he was oblivious to this, clearly flattering himself that I was still captivated. He sought to draw me into the conversation with smooth provocation.

'Does your charming companion have any new admirer, aunt? Is she allowed to think of such things?'

'Sarah makes her own decisions but I believe she has attracted the fancy of an excellent young clergyman hereabouts. I'll say no more.'

Dr Strines looked enquiringly at me but I sat unmoving, my face expressionless. It was fortunate he could not detect the turmoil I felt at Mrs Ibbotson's ridiculous assertion. After a while the old lady announced she would go to her room to rest but she insisted I need not attend her and her nephew was welcome to stay longer if he wished. I was not pleased to be left alone with the doctor and he immediately began to ask about the admirer his aunt had so roguishly mentioned. While I parried his questions, I racked my brains how to change the subject. He'd already spoken at length about the household at Ranmoor and there seemed nothing further I could ask about his family, so remembering an incident which still troubled me, I clutched at a topic which might divert him from my supposed romantic interest in another.

'Did you ever find out more about the strange letter you received, the one with quaint spelling regarding some poor child?'

He regarded me oddly. 'As I suspected, when the police visited the house at Nether Edge, they found no child and nothing amiss, simply some mature ladies dependent on the charity of benefactors. What was distasteful, Sarah, was that I was actually visited by the writer of the letter; or rather she came in search of you after you'd gone to Scarborough. She had some cock and bull story about looking for your brother.'

My jaw dropped and I couldn't stifle an audible gasp. 'When did this happen, sir?'

'Oh, only a week or two after you left. I can't imagine you ever knew the vulgar young woman. I suppose she must have had some contact with your brother, while he was in town – young men do make unfortunate acquaintances, you know.'

'What was she like?' I hoped my enquiry sounded inconsequential.

'An ostentatious beauty, I must allow. Extraordinary vivid eyes and thick auburn curls. Enough to turn any young man's head; but she was not respectable. Not at all. It was clear she plied her trade at the house she wrote about – a common harlot, I'm afraid. I trust she never found your brother.'

'My brother is a married man and devoted to his wife,' I said sternly.

'Good, good, so no harm was done.' He lay back in his chair and extended his arms. 'Now, little kitten, enough of this. Will you give me a kiss for old times' sake?'

The withering look I gave took him aback. 'No, sir. That is past. I must go to my mistress.'

He reached out to detain me but I evaded him and marched from the room with an attempt at dignity. Shortly afterwards I heard Mrs Staniforth showing him out from the front door. My ordeal was over.

Later, while helping Mrs Ibbotson undress, I caught the old lady's eye and frowned.

'Do I detect a frisson of displeasure, my dear? I hope my nephew was not obstreperous? I judged you would be well able to deal with him now.'

'No, ma'am. It's not him I have a bone to pick with on this occasion.'

My mistress was all innocence. 'Surely you don't mean it is I who have offended?'

'You know very well, ma'am, you told a naughty untruth. To imply that Mr Ashington and I had any interest in each other was reprehensible.'

'But excusable in the circumstances, Sarah, to put my nephew in his place.'

'I suppose that's true,' I conceded grudgingly.

'I meant no more than that. Have I inadvertently put my finger on a tender spot?'

'No, ma'am. Of course not. Please let us leave the subject.'

Sitting alone in my own room, I quickly dismissed the badinage concerning Charles Ashington from my mind for I knew it had no basis whatsoever. My thoughts were entirely occupied with the appalling revelation concerning Chrissie – and Tom. All my discarded suspicions crowded back into my mind with renewed intensity. If the woman, who had become my sister-in-law, called at Ranmoor during late May in the previous year, looking for Tom, when he had already been in Malin Bridge for months, and if she had come from a whore-house at Nether Edge where, horrifyingly, she'd 'plied her trade', then it was assuredly impossible that Grace was Tom's child. I felt bile rise in my throat. My brother had been tricked, atrociously gulled, by a calculating, evil trollop. Chrissie had practised on Tom, dear

379

guileless, loving Tom, the same callous deception Robert Strines had wanted me to use, should the need arise, towards Arthur Rawdon.

Profound disgust seized me: outrage on behalf of my brother; searing uncertainty about what I should do now I knew the incontrovertible truth; revulsion from all that was involved in the vile, double-dealing relationships between men and women.

Chapter 37: 1-11 March 1864

In the early days of March Mrs Ibbotson took to her bed. There'd been no sudden collapse but a moment of giddiness left her weaker and somehow her stiffened leg refused any longer to take her weight. She sent a message to her elder nephew in Penistone to visit when he had leisure and, in the meantime, allowed the local physician to examine her. He was noncommittal about her condition. Her mind was still alert and I tried hard to keep her entertained, while each of us hid her anxiety from the other.

Around midday on the sixth of March Mrs Staniforth brought up a note which had just been delivered to the house from Arthur Rawdon. Mrs Ibbotson asked me to read it, not liking to admit that her own sight had become hazy. I smiled as I opened the paper. 'Mrs Rawdon has been safely delivered of a son, to be called after his father. It seems she is very weak, after a considerable ordeal, and the baby is small but neither is a cause for concern. That's good news.'

Mrs Ibbotson grunted. 'Poor child,' she said inscrutably.

Two days later the old lady seemed rather vague and dreamy, murmuring to herself when she was not dozing, but by evening she'd rallied and eaten a few spoonfuls of apple jelly. She lay back with her eyes closed until, as the clock was striking nine, she pulled herself up in her chair and asked me to lay aside the book I was reading. 'My dear, there's something I must say to you. You will be angry with me but it must be done.'

'Angry with you?' I affected shock at the notion but feared my mistress was becoming confused. The lady's next words were genuinely shocking.

'When I've mentioned Mr Charles Ashington as having more than a passing interest in you, Sarah, you've dismissed the idea without compunction and treated it as a silly fancy on my part. I cannot continue to let you think this, my dear, because I know the truth of the matter and I urge you to consider it carefully. Do you not like him?'

I took a deep breath, 'I like and esteem him greatly as a friend, ma'am. There can be no more between us.'

'He hopes for more, my dear and he has much to offer you. His family have raised themselves from humble origins and he will make a dedicated clergyman.'

My agitation could not be disguised. 'Please, ma'am, I beg you not to go on. I find it difficult to credit what you're suggesting but, if you have any reason to think it likely, it's the more important for me to reject absolutely the least possibility that I might entertain his advances.'

'That's strongly put.'

'Please, ma'am, it's embarrassing for me to remind you that I can never think of marriage. Not to any respectable man, least of all a clergyman. I allowed myself to be irreparably soiled and now I accept the consequences. As I have sown, so shall I reap. I've turned my heart to stone.'

'Stuff and nonsense! A sincere cleric, above all, should be prepared to forgive and love you as you are, if you told him your misfortune.'

I stared at her, appalled. 'I will never tell another person of my disgrace nor will I practise deceit.'

Mrs Ibbotson sighed wearily. 'I know, my dear, I know. That's why I told Mr Ashington everything, for you.'

'What!' I staggered back from the bedside, frozen with horror. Had she taken leave of her senses, of all comprehension of what was decent? 'You told him Robert Strines had been my lover?'

Mrs Ibbotson's wrinkled face assumed an expression of abject contrition. 'I'm afraid so. When he first came to the Hall. It hasn't deterred him from subsequent visits, has it?'

I put my hands over my eyes. 'I can never bring myself to meet him again. You must excuse me in future if he calls. I'm so ashamed.'

'I knew you'd be upset and feared you might overreact. But I don't have the luxury of waiting for things to take their natural course and risk seeing them go wrong through your virtuous obstinacy. I've needed to do what I could while I'm still able. I have little time left and none to indulge conventional inhibitions. Do you understand?'

Mortified, I took my mistress's hand. 'I know you meant well, ma'am. Let's forget the matter. You mustn't tire yourself and squander your strength. Please rest now.'

The old lady shut her eyes gratefully and I sat in silence staring into the darkness through the window, struggling to discipline my emotions and drive away any dangerous delusion that happiness could ever be mine. Outside, the rain continued to lash down with unremitting force and the wind began to pick up, buffeting the eaves and cornices of the venerable building.

*****

The intimations of mortality which I experienced on the dismal morning of the 11th March concerned my mistress, no one else. Dr Stephen Strines had called, drenched from his ride to the Hall over sodden moors and flooded watercourses, and he spoke gloomily to me.

'She's sinking, Sarah. I can't tell how long her decline will last but I judge her time is coming. I think she knows it too. She's composed herself as if she had no more to do on earth and her mind is centred elsewhere. I'll stop at High Bradfield on my return journey and ask the rector to call.'

Numbed by sadness and incredulity that the old lady's vigorous spirit would not surmount this latest setback to her health, I tended her with devotion. Mrs Ibbotson pressed my hand now and then and spoke a few words so I knew that, behind those shaded eyes, intelligence still functioned and love responded. It seemed unlikely any crisis was imminent.

The rector spent some time in the sickroom and then spoke in kindly manner to me. Mrs Staniforth brought us tea and we sat in the drawing room listening to the raging wind and the rain flagellating the windows. We could see small trees in the garden bent to the ground before they sprang upright again and we heard the vicious crack as a branch of the old elm crashed onto an outhouse, dislodging slates to clatter into the cobbled yard. The whistling and howling round chimney stacks and gables had an eeriness which complemented the blinding sheets of hail.

'It's a fearsome day, sir.'

'Never seen it so rough, Miss Webster, in all my days. I met Mr Gunson as I was riding here. He was bound for the dam to check it was withstanding the onslaught. He seemed confident it's soundly built but these conditions are outwith all normal expectations. I trust those engineers added a good margin to their calculations.'

I saw the rector to the door as he braved the tempest anew. He had told me how weakly Lizzie Rawdon was, after giving birth, and in other circumstances I would have walked to Low Bradfield to visit the new mother and admire her child, but there was no question of leaving Mrs Ibbotson to venture out so far. In any case I doubted I would have been able to stay upright against the ferocity of the blasts sweeping in, over the reservoir, from the high mass of Bleaklow.

As the afternoon drew on and my mistress slept, I watched men moving backwards and forwards far below, by the dam. I could distinguish Mr Gunson's gig, standing stationary in the lee of a wall, and horses tethered beside it. Men were huddled in conversation, mufflers tied over their caps to keep them anchored, and one or two superior officials grasped their high hats while their capes billowed out behind them. There was evidently much need for discussion but nothing to suggest urgent action was required.

In the late afternoon as darkness was beginning to fall, there was a brief lull in the storm and the wind subsided. Down in the valley, I made out a figure climbing into the gig and some of the workmen starting to trudge away from the embankment. I summoned Susan to sit with our mistress and threw on my travelling cloak and pattens. Then I squelched down the waterlogged slope as quickly as I could, to reach the track from the dam just as Mr Gunson's gig appeared. I called to him and he drew the vehicle to a halt.

'Miss Webster, this is no weather for you to walk out in.'

'I've been watching the comings and goings at the dam. Is there any cause for concern, sir? The water level in the reservoir looks dreadfully high.'

'Don't distress yourself. It's designed and built to hold back a greater capacity than is collected yet. There's fully eighteen inches of leeway below the embankment wall.'

'But the wind has been driving great waves along the reservoir.'

'It would look worse from your viewpoint on high at the Hall. Believe me, everything has been provided for, Miss Webster. If necessary we can open the overflow pipes to take off some of the water. They were installed for just such an eventuality. I've been giving reassurance to some farmers from the dale who came up to see if all was well. They've returned home with confidence after I explained everything. I'd never give false comfort, believe me. With luck the force of the wind is abating now. I'm returning home to Sheffield but I'll come again in the morning.'

I thanked Mr Gunson, with apologies for delaying him. His calm demeanour was reassuring and I thought him much more trustworthy than the dismissive and patronising Mr Leather, whose professional aplomb had troubled both mistress and maid on our first visit to the construction works.

Unfortunately, however, Mr Gunson's optimistic view of the weather proved misplaced. After I regained the shelter of the Hall and removed my dripping bonnet and cloak, I heard the wind pick up once more. Then, while I sat with Mrs Ibbotson during the evening, the rafters two floors above us began to creak, with windows shaking alarmingly in their frames. There were more crashes in the yard, where heavy stone slabs on the roof of the stables broke from their fastenings and skittered down to smash in fragments. Later, a sharp snap, followed by a grinding slither and thump, told me another brittle branch had fallen on top of the outhouse. More damage requiring repair. When would it end?

During the storm I tried to read but from time to time I walked round the room hoping to calm myself, to quieten my fears for my mistress and drive away other irrational terrors. Twice I lifted the corner of the curtains to peer out, down the hill, seeing only unbroken darkness and the beating rain but, at around eight o'clock, I went to the window again and gave a little cry at what I saw.

'What is it, Sarah?' The invalid's voice was distant and strained.

'There are lights, ma'am. Lanterns, they must be, down by the dam.' For my mistress's sake I fought down my own panic, trying to sound unconcerned, to find a harmless explanation which could allay my misgivings. 'I suppose they're inspecting the embankment to make sure all is well. They probably do so regularly.'

'I hope nothing is wrong.'

'No, no, ma'am. I'm sure all is well.'

386

I went to the old lady and told her of Mr Gunson's assurances. Mrs Ibbotson nodded and shut her eyes, seeming to drift in and out of sleep for some while, sometimes murmuring words I could not catch. When next she came to herself, she raised a frail hand towards the window and I resumed my position there, with the curtain pulled back, giving a commentary on what I could see and interpret.

'There are more lanterns now. I can see little figures in their light and a gig has arrived. I glimpsed it just now by the wall where Mr Gunson's was standing this afternoon. He's very diligent. He must have decided to return from town to check for himself that the wall is withstanding the tempest: just as a precaution. It doesn't look as if anything worrying has happened. When the lanterns move, I can see a glimmer of water beyond the embankment, billowing but safely confined. I think they're simply making sure everything is all right. The weather is so awful.'

I described the movement of the lanterns, as they snaked and flickered along what must be the top of the embankment, noting that one or two appeared to descend some way below the stone parapet, presumably to the valve house. I reminded my mistress about the purpose of the overflow pipes.

'They're taking care that nothing goes amiss. Mr Gunson is a good meticulous man.'

Mrs Ibbotson shut her eyes again and I banked up the fire before returning to my seat to take up my book. There was nothing to be heard but the lashing rain and the moan of the wind. In a little while we were both dozing.

Chapter 38: 11 March 1864

Down by the dam the purposeful activity Sarah detected was in reality more frenetic than she imagined. It was as well for her peace of mind, for the next three hours or so, that she was not privy to the anxiety gripping those who sought to avert an impending disaster.

The crack in the outer slope of the embankment had been spotted as the light was fading, just after Mr Gunson went home for the day. It was about halfway along the barrier, parallel with the top of the dam, running for about fifty yards and, when found, it was wide enough to insert the blade of a pen-knife. Some of the overlookers and contractors, who stayed in huts near the construction site, had been summoned at once but there was a divergence of opinion between them.

'It's only a frost crack, if you ask me.'

'Can't take a risk, mate.'

'Wind's whipping up the water in the reservoir something awful. Embankment's taking a terrible battering.'

'The dam's designed to cope with it.'

'Never known a storm like it. Pissing rain from Lancashire and wind from the devil's arse.' One navvy had a poetic turn of phrase but his colleagues were unimpressed.

'Stands to reason. Ground's sodden. Might give way.'

'Nah! Crack's only on the surface. Can't possibly go through to the puddle clay. Absolutely no danger, I tell you.'

'My sister lives by Bradfield Bridge. I'm going to tell her to get family out. They can sleep the night with her in-laws up the hill.'

After many similar conversations men drifted away in the early evening, reassured by the overlookers or resolved to safeguard their own folk in case the worst happened. Nevertheless, one of the more cautious contractors sent his son on horseback to ask Mr Gunson to return from his home in the centre of Sheffield.

When the resident engineer arrived back at Dale Dyke, he was concerned to see the crack had widened to take two broad fingers. Conscious of the anxious faces surrounding him in the gloom, he resolved not to reveal his misgivings and declared the damage almost certainly superficial, but it was clear to him that precautions must be taken. He found they had already lifted the sluices to let the water through the outlet pipes and he endorsed this action as entirely sensible. The prudent contractor, who had sent for him, urged him to inspect the valve-house, explaining the difficulty they'd experienced in opening the valves, jammed tight by the pressure of water in the reservoir.

'Took half an hour to turn the screw, sir. Five men pushing. Got them open at last. Should take some pressure off.'

Mr Gunson regretted the delay in opening the valves but his inspection showed they were now operating satisfactorily, so he grunted and hurried back to the top of the embankment, slipping now and then on the loose gravel. He clutched his tall silk hat with one hand, thinking how much more serviceable the workmen's headgear was in such weather – but it was important to maintain one's professional dignity. A gust caught the waterproof cape which protected his overcoat, clipping his cheek with a stinging blow, but he brushed it aside nonchalantly.

Then he bent down over the crack again and caught his breath. It had not diminished. Indeed, as he lifted his lantern to peer into its dark recess, it seemed to widen and a few fragments of soil tumbled down the outer slope in a miniature avalanche. The earth at his feet shivered and he realised, with horror, he could put his whole hand in the gap. He straightened, hesitating as he considered the enormity of what he must do. The responsibility was his. The alternatives which faced him were dire.

'Get the gunpowder. We must blow up the weir.'

The screech of wind and buffeting rain distorted his words and the tallow candle in his lantern was guttering. The workmen, straining to hear him, stared at the darkness in incomprehension. What was he saying? Were they really to smash the weir? Five years it had taken them to construct Dale Dyke reservoir and dam. Were they to ruin the entire scheme? The occupants of Sheffield's squalid courtyards would lose the chance of clean water and dozens of mills and forges along the Loxley Valley would be deprived of an assured supply to turn their wheels. Thousands of pounds would have been squandered.

'Christ, sir, do you mean...?' one man began nervously.

'For God's sake, step to it! If the water pressure isn't reduced the whole thing'll blow. There's hundreds live in the valley, by the riverside. They'll be drowned in their beds if the embankment goes.'

Jolted by Mr Gunson's urgency, the men scrambled to fetch the gunpowder, to gouge a hole in the stone blocks of the weir and pack the explosive inside. It was a laborious task: streams of water ran down onto picks and chisels from saturated cuffs and mufflers while damp-softened fingers struggled to grip slippery handles. They worked intently, concentrating to carry out this unimaginable requirement – to destroy their own handiwork. The overlookers shook their heads in despair but they were relieved that there was someone else in charge, to make decisions and, if necessary, carry the blame.

While the men struggled to execute his orders, Mr Gunson spoke to the senior contractor, tramping backwards and forwards as he waited to hear that everything was ready to detonate the gunpowder. His impatience was aggravated by fraying nerves and he was still uncertain whether his drastic decision was justified. Why had nothing happened yet? Surely the gunpowder was in place? What were they doing? He strode towards the place where men were crouching, shielded by a buttress from the wall of the overflow, and they signalled to him to bend down beside them.

'Just lit the fuse again, sir.'

'Again?'

'Didn't go off first time. Rain must have put it out.'

The man peered round the corner of the buttress. 'Still alight this time. Any minute now. Duck everyone.'

They waited, braced for the detonation, willing the gunpowder to explode, the weir to collapse, but they heard only the ferocious billows beating in the reservoir above their heads and the gusts pummelling the stonework.

'Dear God, the powder must be too wet.'

'Shall us try again, sir?'

'Wait.' Mr Gunson stood up, wondering if he had been panicked into precipitate action. 'I'll take another look. Maybe the opening of the outlet pipes is having more effect by now.'

He started to make his way back along the embankment, trying to calm his palpitations, to think logically. He had every confidence in the designers' competence and he'd personally supervised the contractors during the main construction. He told himself there could be nothing seriously wrong, the extreme weather of recent days was certainly testing the dam, but not to destruction – that was a ridiculous idea. He knew the safety margins and they were ample. Besides, the reservoir was not filled to capacity. It was not yet operational. He had been reassuring local people all day there was no danger. That must be true.

He bent down holding his lantern aloft and allowed himself a small thankful smile. The crack had not widened since he last examined it and that should mean the pressure had stabilized. The overflow pipes were doing their job. Good. The split was merely superficial after all and it would not give way. His first judgement had been correct and they could leave the weir intact. He drew himself up to look along the length of the fissure. There was no sign it had extended.

'Look out!'

At the shout from one of the contractors he glanced up and was momentarily paralysed in disbelief. Above him a sheet of water was poised on the brim of the embankment. A brief gap in the clouds allowed moonlight to illuminate the impending surge, picking out the silver-capped bubbles which flecked the line of foam, before it swept down the slope. He gasped and staggered out of reach of the impact, believing he might be carried away by the cascade, but it was quickly gone, swallowed up in the crack, and the embankment was unimpaired. Needless panic again, he told himself, beating the spray from his face. It was only a freak wave driven over the wall by the wind from the high moors beyond the reservoir. Nothing to worry about. 'Control yourself, man,' he thought severely.

He wondered if anything else could be done in the valve-house to drain off more water and decided to go and see but, as he turned, the force of the gale drove him forward down the slope, almost causing his knees to buckle. Dear God, what a night! The phrase 'elemental barbarity' came into his head from somewhere. He straightened the skirts of his long coat fastidiously. He must not be blown over in the sight of the workmen. He envied the grip of their hob-nailed boots and held out his lantern to find where the ground was firmest, picking his way carefully through the mud.

Another cry from the far end of the embankment made him look back and this time he had no opportunity to rationalise his arguments or consider his professional dignity. He gaped at the top of the dam in terror. In the centre of the wall a segment thirty feet wide was loosening, teetering, ready to subside down into the valley. Before his eyes the barrier disintegrated and the destructive torrent scoured through stone and clay, tearing open the rift with its uncontrollable momentum, releasing a towering wave nearly one hundred feet high. While the earth shuddered beneath him and the rumble of destruction deafened him, John Gunson ran.

'It's all up. The embankment's going.' He heard himself stammer this unnecessary warning as he stumbled towards his companions. They were ranged beyond the dam, their eyes riveted on the spectacle as the wall of water crashed down on the hapless valley at a speed of eighteen miles an hour. The dull thud of an explosion, almost obscured by the noise of the flood, told them the gunpowder had at last ignited and blown a now useless hole in the weir. The irony was lost on them for the frustrations and dilemmas of the night had turned to tragedy.

The bowl of the hills, where the infant River Loxley burbled its way down from the moors, was a tranquil spot before the navvies arrived with their barrows, trucks and donkey carts to build Dale Dyke dam and reservoir. Thereafter, for five years, it had resounded to the creak of their pulleys and the pounding of their hammers, man-made disturbances which carried to the scattered habitations on the higher slopes. Those sounds were puny compared with the reverberation which now filled the valley: the furious bombardment of nature released from artificial constraints, as five hundred million gallons of water obeyed the dictates of gravity and crashed downhill, sweeping aside whatever petty obstacles stood in the way.

The resident engineer sank to his knees on the squelching ground, his mind devastated by the catastrophe. He mourned the demolition of his proudest achievement as he would the loss of a fully grown child. He despaired of his career which until that instant had promised recognition and advancement, but now would be held up to scrutiny and found wanting. He tried to concentrate his sorrow on these personal disasters, not because he was an unfeeling man but because he could not bear to imagine the havoc about to be wreaked on the sleeping residents of the Loxley Valley.

'God Almighty have mercy on them,' he sobbed impotently.

*****

I had tucked Mrs Ibbotson into bed but she was restless and I stayed with her while she tossed and turned.

'Go to your bed, my dear. My sleep will come when it comes. You need rest.'

'I'm not sure I could settle, ma'am.'

Around midnight I went to the window again, as I'd done a dozen times, and I saw the lanterns still moving about. The continuing activity worried me but there was no way of knowing what it meant so I nestled back in my chair by the bed. Not long afterwards a dull rumble roused me and I sat up as the sound intensified into a thunderous roar. Mrs Ibbotson also heard it and raised her head, levering herself up on her elbows. I ran to the window and pulled back the curtain.

'Oh, merciful heaven!'

I stood transfixed, one hand extended towards the window, the other clamped over my mouth.

'What is it?'

'Oh, ma'am. It's going. The wall is collapsing. All the lights are shining on it. Oh, dear heaven! Do you hear?'

Mrs Ibbotson threw back the blankets but she lacked the strength to get out of bed without help. I staggered towards her and the old lady raised her arms to draw me down beside her. We hugged each other in our helplessness and despair, understanding that a cataclysm of destruction had been loosed on the valley.

'The stones have fractured,' my mistress said desolately. 'There are farms, villages, forges in the path of the tidal wave. Oh, my dear, your family...'

'I must go, ma'am,' I whispered. 'I must go to see.'

'At first light, my dear. May God shield them.'

Chapter 39: 11-12 March 1864

In the house at Little Matlock Chrissie and Tom were awake at midnight. Grace had disturbed them with her crying and her mother, sitting in bed half-awake, put her to the breast.

'She'll maybe sleep for rest of night after this.'

Tom yawned. 'Let's hope so. She's got a mighty yell for a little 'un. Knows what she wants too.'

He lay back, regarding mother and child through bleary eyes, cherishing the sight. He moved closer and caressed Chrissie's shoulder. 'How soon d'you think it'll be before us has another?'

Elbowing her husband sharply, Chrissie moved Grace to the other side. 'What d'you think I am, Tom Webster? One of rabbits in the field, breeding two or three times a year?'

He stroked his wife's head and exclaimed delightedly as he lifted a long loose hair. 'Need a new keepsake for my watch chain. Old one's right grubby now. It broke in two.'

She snuggled against him, as he put his arm round her, grinning at his sentimentality. Then she looked up suddenly.

'What's that noise?'

'Just wind getting up again.' He hesitated, jerking himself more awake. 'No, there is summat else. Ground's shaking. What the hell?'

He hauled himself out of bed and into the parlour to open the outer door. 'Christ Almighty!' He slammed it shut. 'Quick, upstairs. There's a great surge of water coming down river. Dam must have burst.'

She scrambled from the bed, grabbing an extra shawl from the cradle to throw around Grace and they rushed to the stairs, shouting for Mr Woodhouse to wake. They'd only just reached the landing when the leading edge of the deluge gained new ferocity as it was driven against the cliff face below Acorn Hill and crashed into the house, ripping open a hole in the side wall. They stared for a second, dumbstruck, as water swirled into their downstairs rooms with such force that the wooden settle was smashed to pieces instantly and the flimsy partition between their kitchen and parlour crumpled.

Tom pulled Chrissie into Mr Woodhouse's bedroom at the back of the house. The elderly man, his face as colourless as his nightshirt, was standing on his bed. He had lit the candle in a lantern. 'They said the dam would hold.' He sounded stupefied. 'Me mates walked up there in afternoon – saw chief there. He said it were sound.'

'Afraid he were wrong, Mr Woodhouse.' Tom opened the window and peered out. 'Thing is, will the water reach us, up here?'

'What can you see, love?'

'House is in middle of flood. Coming down valley something fearful. Made a channel between house and cliff. Reckon it'll only get worse.'

At that moment the deafening sound of the water was accompanied by the creak and scream of tortured wood below them. The floor under their feet began to sway and Tom pulled the bedstead under the window. Then the crunch of breaking timber was smothered by a shuddering boom, as the wind whipped up the torrent to such violence that the gable end of the house shattered. The shock hurled them all against the bed and as they pulled themselves upright, bruised but not seriously hurt, they saw they were now on an unstable platform overhanging a seething whirlpool. The ceiling joists over most of the ground floor had collapsed and two thirds of the outer walls had completely vanished.

'Could us break through into loft?' Mr Woodhouse asked doubtfully.

'Can't trust to rest of house staying put. Only one chance, I can see.' Tom threw up the sash window and heaved himself onto the ledge. The steep, uneven rock face was several feet away, across the roaring conduit which now flowed around the back of the building. 'If I can manage to jump over, I could fetch ladder we keeps on ledge up there, what we used to mend roof. You could crawl across it. No time to waste. I'll have to try.'

'Oh, Tom.' Chrissie reached up to touch his face and he quickly kissed her fingers. After that he turned, stood on the ledge and vaulted into the darkness. They could hear nothing but the ferocious tumult and she thought her heart had ceased to beat. She imagined his body, with vainly thrashing limbs, somersaulting down, down...

'Good lad! He's made it.' Mr Woodhouse had his head out of the window and was holding up his lantern. At his words, Chrissie drew breath again and a tear trickled down her cheek onto Grace's forehead as she tied her daughter to her chest. She heard her husband's shout as he lowered the ladder towards the window and they hooked its last rung over the bedpost, while Tom threw all his weight on the other end to anchor it.

'Off you goes, Mrs Webster. Take it careful, on hands and knees. Don't look down.'

Mr Woodhouse helped her through the window and onto the ladder laid flat across the gulf. She crouched on it, gripping the sides, to get her balance before moving forward. Grace was squeaking with alarm as she hung in the folds of the shawl, secured at her mother's neck and waist. The wind hissed over Chrissie's back, whipping up her night shift, and all the time the juddering ladder was jolted from side to side by the strengthening gusts. Desperately she clung on until the squall abated. With horrifying clarity she caught sight of the gleaming fury which raged beneath her and she gritted her teeth. Then, gingerly, she began to edge forward.

398

Midway across she felt the vibration as the chimneybreast, which had so far withstood the assault on the house, teetered and folded itself into the waters, throwing up spray all round her. Doggedly, scarcely knowing how she did so, she held on and continued her traverse, until Tom was reaching out, steadying her and lifting her safely, onto the shelf of rock above the precipice. They both held the ladder while Mr Woodhouse, with unexpected agility, scrambled across to join them.

They stood hugging each other with relief until Chrissie began to shiver uncontrollably. Their nightclothes were drenched and the biting wind cut through them. Grace, encased in sodden shawls, had begun to scream.

'Need to get you somewhere dry and warm,' Tom said.

'How can us, love? We'll have to stay here till water goes down.' Her teeth were chattering.

High above them they heard shouts and saw the gleam of lanterns. Some of their nearest neighbours downstream, had also escaped, with ingenuity and good fortune, and were calling to them to climb the rocky path up the cliff to where the landlord of the Rock Inn on Acorn Hill had brought out blankets and something warming to drink. Tom bit his lip.

'It'll be difficult to see the way and ground'll be right slippy.'

Mr Woodhouse was more confident. 'I know where path goes, Mr Webster. I been up and down it all me life, could do it blindfold. I'll lead way. Keep close behind me and take care not to lose thi footing.'

Tom turned to Chrissie. 'Think you can manage, love? You're shaking summat awful.'

'Will you take Grace? You'll be more sure-footed. It'd help if I have both hands free.'

Tom took the infant and embraced his wife, who insisted he should go first so she could pick her way carefully without holding up his progress. So they started up the track, zigzagging between windblown trees and scrubby bushes, avoiding slippery outcrops of rock, until near the top, the gradient became steeper and the path was a mud chute, threaded with gnarled surface roots and broken branches.

Chrissie paused momentarily, looking up, and she rejoiced to see Tom already near the crest of the ridge where lanterns were clustered to greet him and light her own route. She had not far to go now. She started out again, slithering a little on the slime, using her hands to feel her way and grasp tree trunks or tufts of vegetation to give her leverage. And then, off balance, on an unexpected patch of rough gravelly soil loosened by the rain, she trod awkwardly and her weak ankle turned, throwing her forward. She screamed and scrabbled desperately to gain a purchase on the treacherous ground, digging bare toes and fingernails into the mud, frantically seeking to halt her glissade. It was to no avail. The waterlogged mire beneath her gave way, leaving unanchored roots waving in the air, and she slid helplessly. She tried to clutch a clump of shrivelled bracken but it was not stout enough to bear her. As it broke free it dislodged the protruding stone on which she sought a foothold, and she was flung hurtling towards the abyss.

Tom, watching her steady ascent with joy, heard her scream and saw her fall. He rushed to the cliff edge, thrusting Grace into Mr Woodhouse's arms, ready to thunder down the path in a useless attempt to save her but his neighbours held him back.

He saw the splatter of foam where she hit the churning water in the channel behind the house, before she was obscured. Frenziedly he clung to the hope that she might find refuge on a tree trunk or grip some shattered masonry but, after a little, he saw the swirl of white being carried out into the centre of the torrent. He never knew if he imagined or heard her call, as the waters drew her under, never knew what name it was she cried out as she was taken from him.

Chrissie had hit her head as she was propelled down the cliff but the icy water roused her and she struggled to seize hold of a hefty-looking log bouncing along beside her. For a moment it gave her buoyancy and she looked up at the cliff top where Tom and Grace were visible. Men were holding Tom. She called his name. Then the rotten wood of the tree trunk crumbled in her hands and she knew she was lost.

Sucked down into the vortex, she was still conscious as the water filled her mouth and nose. She shut her eyes and, in her mind, she whispered, 'Will', as the flood embraced her. When she was hurled against the inundated debris of her home the impact broke her arm but she did not know it. Her now insensible body was spewed out of the ruins of Little Matlock and, captured by the current, whirled downstream along the valley of the Loxley, past the devastated village of Malin Bridge, and on into the River Don.

Chapter 40: 12 March 1864

Where the surge was funnelled between high banks and cliffs it deepened and its speed intensified; reports said afterwards it would have outpaced the fastest racehorse. Grinding wheels, paper mills and wire works were reduced in seconds to single gable-walls. Cottages, barns and privies crumpled into the spume, while heavy iron machinery and craftsmen's hand tools were churned together indiscriminately with several tons of coal from a shattered wagon and twenty sacks of potatoes stacked in an outhouse. The death toll was increasing. Men, women and children were swept out of upper rooms torn open by the onslaught: some were still lying in the beds which became their waterborne biers. Men working at night in a wire mill, used to the noisy rhythm of the waterwheel and the sizzle of the metal rods they were heating, failed to notice the tumult outside. They were whisked from the jagged ruins of their workplace into the maelstrom of hissing steel and steaming water.

The worst was yet to come. On the curve of the Loxley, where the River Rivelin joined it, the small village of Malin Bridge bore the brunt of the midnight flood. Dozens of its occupants were wakened by the thunderous din of crashing brickwork but were helpless to withstand their fate. Whole families were carried away. Around one hundred villagers were drowned.

The insistent wave of devastation rushed onwards, through Hillsborough and Owlerton, to where the Loxley flowed into the River Don. There the inundation gained renewed force, pent up again by narrow banks. An eight-foot wall of filthy water, with its gruesome cargo of detritus, was channelled down the larger river between close-packed factories, tanneries, breweries and neat terraced houses, still sweeping with it whatever was moveable. At Neeps End gas works tons of coke were borne into the torrent and vile smelling smoke filled the nostrils of unfortunates trying to flee. On the east bank of the river, smallholders kept horses, pigs and rabbits and for a short time ghastly animal screams filled the air before their carcases joined the macabre freight whirling downstream.

In the centre of Sheffield fetid water swirled under doors and into shops, smashing windows and woodwork, releasing a variety of merchandise into the aquatic dance of death. Wooden toys, new-fangled photographic apparatus and a lending library of three thousand books floated away towards the distant sea. Most bizarrely, drapers' dummies, wearing elegant flounced dresses or smart frock-coats, joined the tumbling cortège of the once-living who were clad only in their now tattered nightwear.

Next morning, while the bereft mourned, stories were recounted of lucky or resourceful escapes. Some survivors had leapt from windows into trees or smashed their way into adjoining houses on higher ground. Others had been trapped neck-deep, awaiting their doom, when the flood began to subside. Nevertheless, the destruction of property was visible for more than ten miles downstream of Dale Dyke: homes and workplaces, forges and mills smashed, submerged in slime, denuded of their contents. In all, some two hundred and fifty people lost their lives, their bodies stranded on toppled masonry as the water receded or carried far away from their villages, hurled against bridges and embankments by the current. Disfigured corpses straddled tree trunks jammed against congested debris in the heart of the town; others were borne miles beyond its boundaries. A few were never found.

*****

From before daybreak the centre of Sheffield was abuzz with news of the catastrophe. Eb Pyle, on his way to work, caught snatches of conversation as he reached the throng gathered on Lady's Bridge. He found it difficult to believe that the rumoured collapse of a dam, in some remote valley nearly ten miles away, could be causing havoc in the town. He cursed the gabbling, gawping bystanders blocking his way.

He was not feeling at his best after a rowdy and bibulous meeting of the union committee the previous evening. He was conscious of his ragged cuffs and dirty neckerchief. Since Edie died two months ago, he had nobody to darn and wash for him, unless he paid good money for help. He'd left the house in Tenter Croft and taken the spare room Joe and his wife rented out; but he didn't care for the woman's cooking.

Bloody cow, he thought savagely of his deceased spouse. She'd just curled up and expired without warning one day. Maybe he'd kicked her in the belly the night before but he'd done that often enough without her dying on him. He supposed he'd have to find some other floozy to wed, in order to re-establish a bit of domestic order in his life. He was standing for higher office in the union and needed someone to skivvy and keep house, as would befit his new status. Whoever she was she'd learn her place soon enough. He cradled his fist in anticipation.

Working his way through the crowd, he glanced into the river and was astounded to see the accumulation of debris cluttering the banks and driven against the arches of the bridge. The water had subsided now, exposing some of its grim booty which had become a source of fascination to the audience. Men were clambering over tree trunks and cupboards, beer barrels and twisted machinery, to retrieve human remains. Eb wrinkled his nose with distaste as he observed them lift the distorted corpse of a child from the

404

thick mud, after digging round the little hand which had poked out from the sediment, seemingly disembodied. He stared in disbelief at other limbs projecting from the slime.

And all of a sudden he saw her.

She was lying in the centre of the river, up against the middle buttress of the bridge, spread-eagled across a massive boulder, her head turned to the side, her face in profile. One arm hung limply in the water. Her hair, full of mottled leaves and twigs, had fanned out around her shoulders. Her thin nightshift, ripped and sodden, clung revealingly to her torso, her legs were slightly parted.

He lunged forward, elbowing onlookers aside to lean over the parapet.

'Chrissie!'

'Dost know her? Poor lass, she were a beauty.'

He ignored those around him. His eyes travelled obscenely over her body and he lusted for her in death, as he had in life. He put his hand to his crotch.

Then he saw the wedding band on her finger and spat with disgust onto the shoe of the woman next to him. Offended, his neighbour turned her head to offer a rebuke but, seeing his manic look, she kept silent.

The men in the river had reached her now. They eased away some of the debris entangled in her hair and round one leg, pulling down her ragged skirt to preserve her decency. Eb seethed with jealousy as they touched her thighs and he would gladly have throttled those who handled her so respectfully.

Very gently, they rolled her on her side, in order to lift her in a decorous manner, and as her head lolled over there was an audible intake of breath from the spectators, a susurration of horror and outrage. The left side of her face, previously hidden, had been ripped apart, buffeted against the many obstacles it struck on its journey into the heart of Sheffield. Its flesh had been torn away, leaving only a battered cheekbone and empty eye socket, spattered with filth.

Unable to fight his way through the mass of people pressing behind him, Eb Pyle grasped the parapet of the bridge and shut his eyes. His stomach somersaulted and his mouth filled with bile until, with overpowering force, he vomited into the death-freighted waters from Dale Dyke reservoir.

Chapter 41: 12 March 1864

The coachman had been summoned to harness the horses and be ready to leave the Hall at dawn but even earlier than that the old man received an account, from the neighbouring farmer in the valley, describing the immense destruction below the dam. For the first mile the flood raged across open land and its earliest casualties were uprooted trees and enormous rocks torn from their agelong resting places and tossed about like marbles. No doubt tiny voles and water rats, unable to swim in the swirling ferment as their burrows were inundated, were battered into those rocks and tree trunks. They were soon joined, the farmer said, by the larger carcases of his cattle and pigs, bloating as they travelled with the tidal wave, jostled in the water with five tons of turnips which he had piled in the corner of a field to feed his animals. The knobbly vegetables must have bobbed incongruously alongside the cadavers.

Duly warned by the farmer's description, I steeled myself to see horrors but I struggled to conceive what might have happened downstream. The breach in the embankment itself was fearful enough. Only part of the wall, which had crowned the high bank, was still in place, sagging towards a wide rupture where the water had cascaded over the shattered lip of the dam. In front of it, the gentle grassy slope, previously threaded by the small stream of Dale Dyke, was unrecognisable. A broad swathe of rock-strewn silt obliterated familiar features and the chasm, carved through it, hinted at the weight and force of the cataract which had poured across the terrain. Yet by daybreak only modest rivulets bubbled through the scattered remains and, above the scene of desolation, within the natural cradle of the hills, the shrunken reservoir gleamed in the early sunshine of a calm spring morning. It was as if the ferment of the previous night had been a savage dream.

407

Before we'd travelled far, we saw the first carcases of animals protruding from the mud and huge trees snapped like twigs. The nearest house and bridge had been swept away and, as we entered the settlement of Low Bradfield, the scale of the devastation began to be apparent. Two more stone bridges, the mill and the newly built school had been utterly demolished, along with many cottages. Several houses were left with ragged holes in their sides and, stranded in the mud around the ruins, were kettles and dolls, cabbages and panniers, embroidery samplers and Bibles swept from their homes. I stared in amazement and signalled the driver to stop so I could descend.

The dwelling where Arthur Rawdon had lodged previously and the nearby house, where he and Lizzie had lived since their marriage, were both ripped open. The interiors were exposed, almost denuded of furniture, for the flood had carried with it every moveable it could embrace. Wedged among broken floorboards, pinned by a fallen roof beam, a bedstead hung precariously over the footpath beneath. It sheltered no occupants. Bricks and tiles littered the slimy ground at my feet, in which shards of window glass and fragments of twisted metal were embedded. I turned away from the sight, dazed by the magnitude of what I must confront.

Seeing a knot of people along the road leading uphill, I joined them to ask for news of those who had lived by the riverside. My heart leapt as I recognised Arthur's former landlady and I heard with relief how the inhabitants of the village had received warning when the boy, sent to summon Mr Gunson back to the dam, called out to them that there might be danger. Many prudent souls had evacuated low-lying property during the evening and remained alert for the first sound of impending disaster. Just a few, I was told, confident in the expertise of the engineers, stayed stubbornly at home, fleeing at the last minute. There had been only one fatality.

'Sad to say, miss, it were Mr and Mrs Rawdon's new-born son, swept from her arms as she hurried from the house when the water came. They should have left before, when they were warned.'

I didn't wait to hear more. 'Where are they?'

The woman indicated an unscathed house on higher ground and I ran in agitation to hammer on the door. I was shown into a little parlour and in a moment Arthur Rawdon joined me. His face was haggard and his clothes unkempt.

'Oh, Arthur, I'm so dreadfully sorry. How is poor Lizzie?'

To my consternation he flung himself into my arms, sobbing in heartrending misery, nestling his head against my shoulder. Because there seemed nothing else to do, I stroked his mud-streaked hair until he was more composed and then sat with him on the small couch, holding his hand. Between gulps and renewed tears, he insisted to me that he was responsible for his son's death and his wife's inconsolable delirium.

'During the day yesterday there were rumours. Men went to the dam to see the resident engineer. When I got home from Agden they told me Mr Gunson had said there was no cause for concern. That satisfied me fully. I thought there couldn't possibly be cause for concern. Even when the watchmen sent for Mr Gunson to return, I dismissed it as over-caution by men who didn't understand professional work. The calculation of stresses and volumes were most carefully made. We'd allowed ample margins. I was sure of it. But if the ground were not stable... if greater allowances should have been made... Oh, Sarah! Such was my conceit. My hubris!'

'Arthur, you must not blame yourself.'

'But I must! Because I worked on the design, because I believed nothing could go wrong. I rejected the advice of wiser folk. My pride persuaded me they were foolish, ignorant men who allowed themselves to panic. Oh, my wretched pride! It was my duty to protect them... my family... Lizzie's been very weak since the boy was born... and the little lad...' He faltered and I held him again until he grew calmer and sat upright.

'Lizzie kept to her bed in the evening and I told her she was safe to remain there, with the baby in his crib. I read by lamplight until late and was preparing to retire when I heard the roaring up the valley and the shouts of neighbours. I knew then how negligent I'd been. We rushed to leave the house, Lizzie in her nightgown clutching our son. I had an armful of whatever I could seize. The first bombardment caught us as we were going up the garden steps, outside the door. We had to cling to the railing to avoid being carried with the wave and to drag ourselves beyond its reach. I dropped all the useless paraphernalia I was holding and in the tumult the child was swept out of Lizzie's arms.'

He paused, his body heaving silently. 'I shall never forgive myself for my foolhardiness and I think Lizzie never will. If she recovers...'

'If she recovers?'

'She's so distraught, I fear for her mind. The birth was a difficult one. She may not survive another. She was so happy to have little Arthur and I have murdered him.'

'No! Don't say such a terrible thing. Many people may be dead. There will be other dreadful stories. You're not to blame.

'But I had a part in the design! I would not listen to reasonable worries. I put my family at risk. It is my punishment.'

410

He seized my shoulders, wild-eyed. 'I should not have married a woman I did not love. I've set myself to be a loyal, diligent husband and, when my son was born, I thought I was rewarded with an heir to cherish with my life. Instead... instead... it was his life that was taken and I must bear the guilt forever. It is my punishment. Oh, Sarah!'

I held him away from me. 'This is not right, Arthur. You've had a terrible loss and are deeply shocked but you must not speak like this. You are not to blame for what has happened but your duty is to Lizzie. You must pull yourself together.'

I rose but he snatched at my dress. 'Don't leave me, Sarah. Stay.'

His appeal stunned me but I forced compassion aside. 'I have others to see to. I must go to Little Matlock – and to Malin Bridge. I fear I also may have been terribly bereaved.'

I pulled away from him as he reached out imploringly. 'Sarah, I beg you.'

'I cannot.'

Fending off my own distress, refusing to acknowledge his neediness, I turned on my heel and left the room.

*****

As we drove on down the valley the appalling consequences of the flood were evident all around us and I dismissed from my mind the agonising episode I had just endured. Much of the hamlet of Dam Flask was gone: the inn shattered, the wire mills torn to pieces, heavy machinery flung aside by the tide. Small groups of the dispossessed stood forlornly looking at the wreckage of their homes and workplaces, peering at the miscellaneous flotsam and detritus which decorated the muddy banks where the water

411

had receded. Personal belongings, domestic utensils and cherished heirlooms were ripped and shattered. At Rowell Bridge the grinding mill, where Tom worked, had been reduced to a tumble of bricks and timber, with only the tops of the great waterwheels visible, choked by the accumulated mire.

Past the village of Loxley, which stood mostly unscathed on higher ground, we turned back towards the river, to where it narrowed beneath the cliff at Little Matlock. It was obvious the flood had gained in fury here, when its progress was checked by the defile, and great trees had been torn up by their roots, some still partly immersed in the channel. The mill had gone, its millrace now part of the single watercourse, and cottages beside the track were badly damaged. Across the river a small protuberance, like a broken tooth, marked the remains of the shattered house and I reached out a hand to stop the carriage, tears filling my eyes at the thought of my brother.

Then I saw, in the distance, the figures standing below the cliff- face, on the other side of the Loxley, and I could distinguish Tom, bareheaded, holding a baby to his chest. My heart danced with relief. There were several women in the group, their shawls drawn over their hair, and I never doubted Chrissie was among them. I didn't wish to think about Chrissie; it was not the moment. Tom's home was destroyed but he and his family were safe. That anxiety, at least, could be set aside.

'Shall us stop for a bit, miss?' the coachman asked as I wiped away a tear.

'No, thank you. We'll visit my brother on our return. It'll be difficult to get across the swollen river here, with the footbridge gone. Go on to Malin Bridge.'

We passed other ruined forges and waterwheels submerged up to their axles in fallen bricks and slime. Astonishingly, men were already out with spades and shovels clearing the rubble, lifting the broken remnants of homes and workplaces with bare hands, beginning the enormous task of re-establishing the life of the valley. Elsewhere small gatherings of people stood silently around a shrouded bundle on the ground and I realised each was a body, newly recovered from the scene of havoc.

I became aware of other figures along the track ahead: two carriages, with well-dressed passengers, stopped by the roadside – spectators who had hurried so quickly to the valley, to gawp at the tragedy which had befallen its inhabitants. I glared as we passed them, scorning their intrusive curiosity, hoping they did not think I was one of them, come to indulge in ghoulish voyeurism. Within the numbness of my mind, anger was stirring.

As we drove further downstream the sunlight beamed on a fragment of wrought metal protruding from the morass. Its gleam seemed unsuitable, mocking and callous, but I no longer looked for hidden messages in the landscape. Omens which once appeared encouraging had too often proved misleading, false harbingers of optimism. I'd learned to be wary in giving my trust, recognising that disappointment was the usual outcome, and I reminded myself that my role must be to serve and to endure, nothing else. It had always been so, despite doomed attempts to thwart my destiny. No chink of light glimmered through the closed door of my earlier existence and it was impossible that anything admirable could emerge from this cruel world of desolation.

When Mrs Ibbotson's carriage followed the curve of the river into Malin Bridge, I saw clearly the unspeakable calamity visited on my birthplace. Poised on the tip of land where the Loxley and the Rivelin met, the substantial buildings of Tricket's farm had been reduced to a single fractured wall with steps leading into a gaping hole which had been the cellar. Dead animals had been carried into its

413

flooded recesses and their heads and legs stuck up through the silt as if displayed on some demonic butcher's slab. The bastion of the Stag Inn, renowned for Mrs Armitage's home brewed beer, was toppled and at the next building the floorboards of an upper room tilted over the cavity below

Of human occupants from the farm and inn there was no sign. Bridges across both rivers had disappeared, rows of cottages and filecutters' workshops were reduced to piles of bricks and huge rocks had been deposited in the quagmire covering the waterside street. The little schoolhouse where I spent happy hours had dwindled into a pile of rubble. The terrace of houses, where my father and his wife lived, climbed uphill and was still standing although battered, but their home was at the bottom of the slope and I could see the tidemark just below its drooping eaves.

The end of the world might look like this, I thought: every familiar feature shrouded by mud and beneath that mud, or carried away in the remorseless torrent, the bodies of people I'd known all my life. I shuddered and drew my cape tighter across my shoulders. It was a nightmare past imagining. Surely an event so catastrophic must bring with it finality for survivors as well as victims, all touched by violent loss? I felt disorientated, misplaced, raging, uncertain of my own identity. I bit my lower lip to stop the tears. Now was not the time to weep. There was much to be done, much yet to be discovered. The time for weeping would come later.

I left the carriage and looked around desperately for someone I knew. Two men were approaching, carrying the body of a small child. I turned towards them but they scowled.

'Enjoying your sightseeing, are you, miss?'

'This were my grandson, see. Good spectacle, ain't it?'

414

I recoiled but a woman, following the men, hastened forward splashing through the mud. 'No, no! She's not a sightseer. It's Sarah Webster. Sarah, it is you? Oh, you poor love.'

Chrissie's Aunt Ada embraced me, tears streaming down her gaunt cheeks. I looked at her steadily. 'My father...?'

'Come and sit down, love. He's gone, I'm afraid, him and Mrs Webster, dear friend of mine, she were.' She led me to an upturned horse-trough, ripped from its plinth several hundred yards upstream and now lodged by the trunk of a fallen tree.

'They've been taken to the Yew Tree Inn, above the waterline. All them as are found here are taken to the Yew Tree. But there's many more missing, swept down river. Fellow from Owlerton says he see'd bodies hurtling by his window, with odd arms and legs too, can you believe? They're still getting some poor souls out of houses where they drowned in their beds. Whole families. Mrs Armitage and all her kin at the Stag Inn – another friend of mine, she were. May God have mercy on them. Blessed are the dead who die in the Lord – the Book of Revelation, chapter 14, verse 13.'

Despite her mournful manner and her tears, Aunt Ada had not forgotten her texts and she seemed to derive some satisfaction from her catalogue of misfortune. I listened distractedly.

'I must go to see them. My father...' Despite my attempt at self-discipline, I had begun to cry.

'Sit a bit first, love. You'll need your strength for the ordeal before you. The Good Lord comfort you. He sendeth rain on the just and the unjust...'

Further along the river, a ladder had been put across broken masonry to reach a large tree toppled on its side. A man in his shirtsleeves was perched dangerously on it, stretching up to retrieve a tiny white object caught in the branches. He made a gesture over the small corpse and handed it down reverently to a lad who was helping him. I had seen the man, similarly jacketless, engaged in practical action once before. Then he'd helped to save two lives in the sea at Scarborough; now he could only seek out the deceased, bless them and ensure they were treated with dignity. He was coming towards us.

Aunt Ada had risen. 'This is the gentleman found your folk, Sarah. Right godly man of the cloth he is, though he's an Anglican. Come down the hill from Stannington to help, he has. I'll leave him to speak to you.'

Even in my distress, the irony of my dead father being tended by a Church of England clergyman did not escape me; but I'd forgotten that I should be abashed to encounter the man who knew of my shame. I blew my nose and wiped my eyes.

Charles Ashington sat beside me. His face was smeared with grime and his trousers caked with mud. 'Miss Webster, I'm so sorry. I learned they were your father and his wife, in the first house over there. It was humbling to find them.'

'Humbling?' That was an unexpected word.

'Folk from most of the lower houses in the row managed to escape by knocking holes through the walls of their bedrooms to climb into their neighbours', up the slope, above the waterline. The fellow next door to your people broke through the wall to help them do the same but your father...'

'My father had no use in his legs. He was injured in an accident.'

'Mrs Webster had pulled him across the room but the water was rising and poured through the shattered window. The man next door needed to save himself and she could not drag her husband through the opening.'

416

'But she could have escaped herself?' I was filled with incredulity. Charles Ashington took my hands.

'She chose to stay with him. They were enfolded in each other's arms. They drowned together on the floor.'

For a moment I clung to him, unable to speak. Then I withdrew my fingers. 'I hated my father's wife. She stole him while my mother still lived.' There was desperation and distrust in my voice.

'She must have loved him dearly nonetheless.'

That spurred my indignation. 'How could someone so despicable be capable of loving self-sacrifice?'

'Human hearts are complicated things. We're not equipped to pass moral judgement on the weaknesses of others. We're even liable to misunderstand our own.'

I ignored his pious toleration. 'We quarrelled and I wouldn't go to see them afterwards. I wouldn't go when my father was injured. I never went and now it's too late.'

I turned away, choking on my words, remembering all Charles Ashington knew of my own transgressions. Was he subtly reminding me of my sinfulness? I struggled to sound self-possessed. 'Please don't let me keep you from your task. Others need your comfort more greatly. I will go to see my dead father and my stepmother. Then I must find my brother and tell him of our loss.'

He looked pained. 'Forgive me, Miss Webster, but you mustn't tear yourself apart with reproaches. We are all faulty creatures. Faced with such overwhelming tragedy, we're rightly chastened but you mustn't embrace extra burdens of guilt for what cannot be remedied.'

I trembled but tried to speak crisply. 'Please don't pity me, Mr Ashington. I'm grateful for all you've done.'

The tears trickling anew down my cheeks gave the lie to my composure and I dabbed them fiercely with my sodden little handkerchief. Charles Ashington drew a larger cloth from his pocket.

417

'Here,' he said, 'I've wiped my own sweaty brow with it so it's hardly clean but it is fairly dry.' He smiled and I welcomed this reminder of his down-to-earth practicality and humour. It calmed me and I smiled back, murmuring thanks. I expected him to leave me then but he did not. He took my hand again.

'Miss Webster, on this dreadful day we're all anguished by the disaster which surrounds us. We must let our pain at such loss teach us to see other matters in perspective. Now is no time for me to say all I'd wish to, but will you allow me to call on you in a few days to speak of what is in my heart? You must know what I long to ask.'

I gasped in confusion. The implication was absurd. 'But, Mr Ashington, how...? You must not... I cannot...' I withdrew my hand as if his touch was scalding my flesh.

'I may come to retrieve my handkerchief, may I not?'

I stared at him, missing any renewed hint of merriment in his eyes, and did not answer.

He touched my cheek lightly. 'God keep you until then, Miss Webster, and show you that you're not called on to punish yourself for the rest of your life. I beg you to consider how we may best fashion our lives as worthy memorials to those who've perished here in the valley. I pray you will be by my side as I try to do so and that I may cherish and support you through all adversities.'

Then he moved away from me, wading with deliberate steps through the turbid water to join his companions in their nightmarish task of salvage.

*****

I visited the temporary mortuary at the Yew Tree Inn and returned to the carriage crushed by what I'd seen. I felt adrift in a world I didn't recognise and clung rigidly to my one certainty – that I must accept the sacrifice required of

418

me in order to expiate my guilt. I dismissed Charles Ashington's benevolent words and deluded aspirations. They must not distract me from my self-evident duty. First, I must fulfil my remaining obligation to visit the survivors at Little Matlock and give Tom news of our father's death. Later I would confront and subdue the tumult of my feelings, banishing forever any futile flicker of hope that the sentence I had passed on myself could be mitigated.

Chapter 42: 12 March 1864

Because of the broken bridges, we were forced to make a circuitous journey to cross the swollen rivers and it was late afternoon before we reached the Rock Inn on Acorn Hill. I'd surmised that those made homeless below the cliff might have taken refuge in the hostelry on higher ground and, if so, it would save me the difficult descent down the path to the riverside where I'd glimpsed a group of people that morning. I was a little puzzled that Tom hadn't sent to make enquiries at Malin Bridge as to our father's safety, for I thought he could have walked there easily enough, but there must, of course, be much to detain him at Little Matlock. He and his family must have lost everything.

At the door of the inn when I enquired for Mr and Mrs Webster, the woman looked at me doubtfully.

'Are 'ee kin, miss?'

'Tom's sister.'

The woman sighed and pointed to a door. 'He's in there, miss.'

He was sitting on a bench in the small cluttered storeroom, among barrels and firkins, with Grace on his knees, rocking her to and fro awkwardly. He looked up with vacant eyes as I entered but, when he saw me, a thin, painful smile of relief twitched the corners of his mouth.

'Sal, thank 'ee for coming.' His tone was flat.

I thought I'd come to Little Matlock to share the grief of our father's loss with my sibling and to find some small respite from the unalloyed horror of the day with those who had survived. Looking at my brother's face, I knew how profoundly mistaken I'd been.

'Tom, what's happened?'

He shook his head, unable to speak. He lifted the baby, clasping her to his chest as I'd seen him holding her from across the Loxley. He gulped and silent tears ran down

420

his cheeks. I found it unnerving to see him weep. I waited and, after a little while, he sniffed and wiped his eyes on his sleeve. Then he spoke tartly, matter-of-fact in his account.

'Chrissie were drowned. Us all managed to climb across to the cliff but then she slipped and the flood took her. I saw her go. She surfaced and looked up at me. I thought she'd got hold of a branch and might be saved. But then she were swept away in a great swirl of water and I saw her carried off downstream in the surge, amid all the other shattered flotsam.'

'Oh, Tom! I didn't know. I thought you were safe. I saw you with Grace, across the river this morning.'

'You've been to Malin Bridge?'

'Yes, Tom. They're both gone, I'm afraid.'

He nodded and bowed his head, as if he expected no other outcome. 'Heard the village were hard hit.'

I didn't choose to pass on the details Charles Ashington had given me. I didn't trust myself to speak of Hephzibah Webster's devotion, nor did I think Tom needed to know of it – certainly not at that moment. I was alarmed by the rawness of the suffering he already experienced, the blankness in his expression.

He looked up suddenly. 'Did you see anyone you knew there? Some on higher ground must have escaped?'

'Chrissie's Aunt Ada is unharmed.' To my surprise he heaved a deep sigh of relief.

'She was your landlady, of course. You're fond of her?'

'I hopes she'll take us in, Grace and me, and that she'll have a care for Grace while I find work again. We've lost everything from the house and we needs to find a wet-nurse. It's a mercy there's a woman here has milk enough to feed Grace for a while. Don't know how quick I'll get work. I hear Rowell Mill's gone.'

'If you need help, Tom, to tide you over, I have a little money.'

'That's good of you, Sal.' The acidity crept back into his voice. 'Don't doubt in time there'll be talk of compensation from the Water Company. Be an enquiry, perhaps. But they'll not pin blame on anyone. They'll shrug off the loss of a few grinders' families: but maybe pay out for forges destroyed and loss of business.'

'Surely they won't be so callous! Don't let your grief make you bitter, Tom.'

'Bitter! You sits there and tells me not to be bitter!' His anger erupted. 'You knows I've loved Chrissie since I were a lad. Never another for me. Never thought she'd wed me. Just when the miracle happened and we was so happy, with Grace and all – to have her took from me! To see her whirled away and I were helpless to save her. You expects me not to be bitter!'

I felt profoundly uncomfortable. It was obviously inappropriate to tell my brother at such a time what I had pieced together of his wife's recent past, before she joined him at Malin Bridge, but his unshakeable faith in Chrissie was irritating, had always been irritating.

'You've put her on a pedestal.'

'What's that meant to mean?' he snapped and the baby began to whimper. At once his voice changed as he sought, inexpertly, to quieten Grace.

'There, there, love. I know you wants your Ma bad as I do. Us've got to manage with each other, me lass.' He smoothed back fronds of the infant's vivid coloured hair and ran his finger along her prominent little nose.

I bit my lip. I tried to sound conciliatory. 'I didn't mean to upset you. I know how much you loved her.'

'Do you?' He flared at me again. 'How could you know a thing like that? She were more full of life and

422

excitement and loving than you'd ever understand. You're become a dried up, unfeeling old maid: what can you know?'

I stood up, furious that in his ignorance he still judged me incapable of passion. 'You're beside yourself, Tom. Perhaps I should leave.'

'Beside myself! Christ, you sounds grand, Sarah Webster! Living with gentry has made you too fine for your humble kinsfolk. That's what our Da thought too! You stuck-up, prissy bitch, you never went to see him. When he were near dying, paralysed, you never went. Only when he's safely put in his coffin, did you deign to go!'

I could feel my own suppressed rage rising and choking me. If I let it explode, I wouldn't be able to check what I said. I made one last attempt to deflect Tom's anger. 'I know I was in the wrong.'

'Oh, that's good then! You knows it now. How convenient that you knows it when 'tis too late to do anything to set it right. D'you think Chrissie enjoyed Da's preachifying and his wife's snide remarks? But she went to see 'em, charmed 'em, and before long Da loved her like his own – better'n his own...'

'Chrissie visited them?' I heard my voice shaking with guilt and jealousy and disgust.

'Regular. Da didn't miss you so much lately.'

That broke the façade of my self-control and I would not be answerable for the consequences. 'How dare she impose herself on father! It's bad enough she bewitched my brother. She tricked you all, you gullible fools!'

Tenderly, Tom put Grace down in the wooden box he'd borrowed to act as a cradle and tucked a ragged blanket round her, but when he turned towards me his expression was venomous. 'I hope you'll take that back. I knows we're both fraught but I warn you, Sal, I'll not let you bad-mouth my wife.'

'I'll take nothing back, you blind idiot. She was a good-for-nothing hussy who attracted men like flies round a turd. She was a whore!'

Tom struck me hard across the face, with the flat of his hand, and I tasted the blood on my lip. Neither of us moved. I looked at him spitefully. There were no constraints now. I would blast to smithereens the bogus moral high ground he'd assumed.

'Grace is not your daughter!'

My declaration hung in the air and there was moment of silence but then my brother reeled away from me, laughing. 'Oh, Sal, is it that you've discovered?'

I gasped, astonished. 'Chrissie told you?'

He sat down heavily. 'She had no need. D'you think she'd have come to me if she hadn't been in trouble? I always knew that was when she'd come – the only way she'd come. Have you any idea what she'd been through? The man she loved and was to have wed died in her arms and a sadistic lout threatened her and her friends.'

Tom's humility was as infuriating as his constancy. I would spare him nothing. 'The child is not Will Turner's.'

He ran his fingers through his hair. 'I may not have your brains, Sal, but I can count the months.' His quiet sarcasm gave way to renewed virulence and he jumped up again. 'Who asked you to stick your nose into our business, sniffing and prying after scandal, bursting with disapproval? You hypocritical shrew!'

I stood my ground. I'd gone too far now to yield. 'Tom, you can call me whatever foul names you like and you can hit me again but it won't alter facts. Chrissie came to you from a whorehouse. That child is some lecher's by-blow.'

'She is my daughter!' Tom's cry thundered in the small room and, as he thumped his fist on a barrel, tankards on a shelf above rattled. 'It's my name recorded in the register of births and my name she'll carry till she weds: my

424

name freely given. She's all of Chrissie I have left and I will cherish her. In your prudish, blinkered world, can you that even imagine that, Sarah? You're become narrower than our father with your pious sneering and you sound just like him.'

My brother's contemptuous use of my full Christian name, for the second time, stung me as cruelly as his insults. I sank onto the bench. 'I don't understand how you can be so forgiving.'

He dropped down to sit beside me, looking exhausted. His wrath had dissipated. 'Don't think your brother's a saint, Sal, but I've learned what's important to me. And don't think Chrissie were the opposite, neither. When she left Will Turner's family, after he died, she sent them money to make it easier to cope. She sent it secret but they guessed it came from her.'

'She told you that?'

He put his hand gently over my mouth. 'No, she did not. Nor never would. They guessed. Annie's husband told me, quiet like, when they visited. Why do you always want to find the bad in people? Does it make you feel superior, moralising about their weaknesses?'

His words echoed those Charles Ashington spoke to me only a few hours earlier and I shivered. 'I'm not superior. I know that too well. I judge myself harshly because I have no excuse. But there's so much I can't fathom. My head's reeling.'

My brother's red-rimmed eyes held pity and wisdom in their depths. 'Learn to forgive, Sal. You'll not lose by it. Start with yourself.'

I rose and dabbed the cut on my lip. He could not know how pertinent and lacerating I found his advice. 'There's so much happened today. I lost my temper. I said what I shouldn't have done, Tom.'

He nodded. 'So did I, Sal, but maybe it were good for both of us to let off steam like.' He paused. 'I shouldn't have hit you.'

'Perhaps I deserved it.' I bent down to look at Grace who gurgled at me. 'May I visit you when you're settled with Chrissie's aunt?'

'If you can stand Ada's chattering! Best look up some Bible texts first.'

I gave him an affectionate slap and then hugged him. 'God bless you, Tom, and keep you strong. Look after – my niece. I'll come soon.'

Scarcely conscious of my surroundings, I slipped away from the Rock Inn and returned to the carriage. Then we trundled our way back up the valley of desolation to the Hall where, I was well aware, my beloved mistress lay dying.

*****

Mrs Ibbotson had weakened in body and mind during the day, as ever more lurid details of the catastrophe were brought to her house. Dr Stephen Strines, who had been sent for, told me there was little anyone could do except to keep her comfortable. I sat by her bedside all evening, sometimes speaking quietly in the hope that she could hear but mostly lost in bewilderment while she slept.

My mind was in turmoil. A jumble of images crowded into my head: frightening, inchoate, fragmented, challenging, yet meaningless. How could I come to terms with all that had happened, all I'd learned? So much I'd regarded as immutable had been demolished, just as the place of my birth and childhood home had been shattered. The combination of human error and nature's force had demonstrated how suddenly the valley and its inhabitants could be devastated. How puny and frail the foundations of my world had been. It was a terrifying thought. Yet, I was as greatly troubled by the unexpected revelations I'd received, of human behaviour, of unpredictable human goodness. Old certainties had fractured like water-riven stone.

I'd been profoundly mistaken in much I'd assumed, misguided in my simplistic judgements. The unpleasant step-mother, whose earlier conduct I justly execrated, had chosen to stay to the end with the helpless man she loved. The severe father I spurned so self-righteously, so vindictively, had gained comfort from the visits of a worthless daughter-in-law who took the trouble to charm him. Chrissie! Dazzling, wayward Chrissie, whom I'd been ready to decry even after her horrific death: deceiving, lying, self-serving Chrissie could be generous in friendship and inspire lifelong passion. She'd been loved by my brother with unblinkered devotion. Tom himself, whom I'd deemed a bemused simpleton, had shown he was mature and wise beyond my understanding. He comprehended everything and was prepared to forgive everything. He was awe-inspiring.

In humility I accepted that I could learn from these people I'd misjudged. I'd been foolish to believe I was capable of discerning the truth about others. Truth was layered and complicated. I should not pass judgement simplistically. Perhaps not even on myself. I'd condemned my transgression and shame, with the fervour of an Old Testament prophet about whom my father preached with such power and hypocrisy. I'd refused to allow myself the possibility of reprieve, rejecting all compromise with imperfection. Was I merely running away from the reality of a flawed world?

In defiance of my just deserts, I was being offered absolution by one who was clear-eyed and not deluded, who wanted me for my own sake to complement and support him in his life's work, honourable work which could enable me to redeem my earlier faults. What justification had I to snub him? Lucid in my thinking now, I admitted to myself that he was a man for whom I felt sincere affection, in whose company I was mysteriously at ease – with whom it would be possible to find abiding love, to share a loving partnership. I should allow myself to rejoice in that revelation.

I bowed my head, thinking of Chrissie's tragedy and my good fortune. It was not a question of deserts. Neither of us deserved what happened, what awaited us. Fate was arbitrary, capricious. What mattered was how generously we responded to the chances we were given, the choices we allowed ourselves to make. Chrissie had come to know that, I felt sure, and I was humbled.

I drew Charles Ashington's grimy handkerchief from my sleeve, pressed it to my cheek and reverently kissed it.

I resolved to honour those who'd been lost by the toleration I showed to others in future and I would cherish the loving husband I did not deserve. My stony self-containment had broken apart and a great surge of joy and hope flooded into my heart.

Looking up, I realised Mrs Ibbotson's eyes were open, although I doubted if the old lady could see through the milky film which clouded them. I didn't know if she had any sense of hearing but I spoke out loud all the same.

'I saw Mr Ashington at Malin Bridge, ma'am,' I said, surprised at the firmness of my voice. 'He wishes to call to ask me a particular question. I've reflected on so much today and know how stubborn and perverse I've been. I shall not refuse him. I think you would give us your blessing, dear mistress.'

I did not imagine it. On the right-side of Mrs Ibbotson's taut mouth there came the merest flicker of movement, a tiny twitch which was enough to serve for a smile.

So I smiled too – a radiant smile, I think.

428

Historical Note

Most characters in Driftwood and Stone are fictitious but their stories are set against well-recorded historical events. The Sheffield 'Outrages' of the 1850's and early 1860's were the subject of a Royal Commission of Inquiry in 1867 and its findings influenced the Trade Union Act of 1871 which legalised trades unions and put them into a legally regulated framework. The account of the Acorn Street explosion, described in the book, is based on contemporary records. The event in the book involving Mr Paterson is also based on a recorded event although, in this case, the details of chronology, location and victim have been changed.

The information given about the prevention and treatment of grinders' disease is based on the published research (1857) of J.C. Hall, MD, physician to the Sheffield Public Dispensary.

The disastrous Sheffield flood of 1864 is the subject of many publications, to which the author of this book is indebted. Of particular inspiration have been the Hillsborough Community Development Trust's publication, *The Great Sheffield Flood*, and Peter Machan's *The Dramatic Story of the Sheffield Flood*. The Coroner's Inquest, held soon after the flood, was followed by a three man commission which sat for six months in Sheffield Town Hall considering claims for damages. The Act of Parliament, within which the commission operated, severely limited the payments allowable for loss of life.

The author

Pamela Gordon Hoad read history at Oxford University, and the subject has remained of abiding interest to her. Her main career was spent in local government and, after working for the Greater London Council, she held the positions of Chief Executive of the London Borough of Hackney and then, for seven and a half years, Chief Executive of Sheffield City Council. Later she held public appointments, including that of Electoral Commissioner when the Electoral Commission was established. Subsequently she became involved with several voluntary sector organisations and for three years chaired the national board of Relationships Scotland.

She had always hoped to write historical novels but was not able to pursue this ambition until after she 'retired'. She undertook the research which forms the basis of *Driftwood and Stone* while still living in Sheffield and produced the first draft of the story after moving to live in the Scottish Borders. She then set it aside while working on the series of books set in the Fifteenth Century about the young physician and investigator, Harry Somers. Now all six of those books are published she has turned back to *Driftwood and Stone*, to refine and re-edit the text and bring it, at long last, to publication.

Pamela has also published short stories with historical backgrounds in anthologies published by the Borders Writers Forum (which she chaired for three years). On behalf of the Dorothy Dunnett Society, she acted as a judge in the annual historical short story competition which the Society runs in conjunction with the Historical Writers Association.

Books in the Harry Somers series of mystery-thrillers by Pamela Gordon Hoad

The Devil's Stain: From humble beginnings, Harry Somers becomes a physician but he is led into rash entanglements and troubling affairs of state including a treasonable plot. '*A tense fifteenth century English murder mystery, full of twists and turns*'.
ISBN 978-1-909411-46-3

The Angel's Wing: Harry seeks refuge in the northern Italian states. He studies at the University of Padua but his investigative skills are called on and they involve him in dangerous intrigue. '*The action and drama of the first book continue in this compelling sequel as Harry gains a reputation for his medical skills whilst becoming embroiled in the politics of fifteenth century Italy...*'
ISBN 978-1-909411-49-4

The Cherub's Smile: Harry returns from exile and takes service with the Duke of Suffolk who is negotiating a truce between England and France. He soon finds he must juggle his own allegiances. '*I felt I was there, caught up in the turmoil of fifteenth century England, and the characters were totally "real" – as well as intrigue, there is friendship, passion and disappointment... and pathos.*'
ISBN 978-1-909411-52-4

The Martyr's Scorn: Harry faces personal distress and is menaced by old enemies as rivalries between nobles at the English court intensify. '*A thrilling read. I could not put the book down. With so many strong characters, a real sense of the period and twists and turns that almost take your breath away, the writer has truly excelled herself with this* *latest addition to the Harry Somers series. Outstandingly good.'* ISBN 978-1-912513-61-1

The Prophet's Grief: Harry becomes involved in Jack Cade's uprising against corruption and injustice but his conflicting loyalties are difficult to reconcile as violence erupts. *'It plunges the reader into a medieval world of rivalry and conflict, remarkably brought to life by a truly gifted writer and packed with giddying twists and turns...'* ISBN 978-1-912513–62-8

The Seraph's Coal: in 1453 Harry acts as physician with the English army sent to recover Aquitaine for the English King, Henry VI. He uncovers a treasonable plot, makes dangerous enemies and experiences the horrors of the battlefield. Yet the greatest challenge of his professional life is still to come and the animosity of opponents, old and new, awaits him in England. As violence escalates in his homeland Harry is caught between loyalties but the trials in his personal life may present him with the hardest choice of all. *'Ongoing intrigue, conflict and personal heartbreak test the good doctor to the limit and keep the reader in suspense to the very end. Another "must read" from Pamela Gordon Hoad!'* ISBN 978 1 912513 63 5

Silver Quill is an exciting new publishing group producing fabulous books for children, teens, young adults – and not so young adults. Take a look at our website, meet our authorsand browse through the titles we have to offer. Every book is a thrill with Silver Quill.

www.silverquillpublishing.com

Lightning Source UK Ltd.
Milton Keynes UK
UKHW011304171221
395649UK00002B/43